Left alone he studied his that the ship every action.

The fact that Olivine was in the cage indicated that the tanker ship's lockup deck was uninhabited. In all likelihood, the two Patrolmen and Olivine were the only people aboard. But even if the Patrolmen were preoccupied elsewhere in the ship, and if Olivine could manage to get out of his cage, he realized *Barnaby* had to be neutralized, or at least thoroughly distracted. Olivine frowned. He was not ready to admit that he was stumped, but he could certainly see no easy solution.

And his guess about the *Barnaby*'s principal cargo—a guess he was sure was accurate—made him want out very badly.

That cargo, nestled down in the main hold, had to be a *ship*. And no ordinary ship. While it was small compared to the utility tanker that was transporting it, it *had* to be very special to get the kind of handling it was receiving. It had to be a fighting ship of the Patrol, and more.

What excuse was there for one spaceship to haul another in its hold? Answer: The ship being hauled was not ready to travel on its own.

And when couldn't a ship travel on its own? Answer: When it hadn't been *mastered!*

And why wouldn't the master-to-be come to the ship instead of the ship being brought to him? Answer. The master-to-be was too busy to make the trip, and officially considered such by the Patrol high brass.

Conclusion: The *Barnaby*'s cargo was a vizad's command cruiser, in an unmastered status.

It was enough to make Olivine's mouth water.

BAEN BOOKS
by Howard L. Myers:

A Sense of Infinity
The Creatures of Man

A Sense of
Infinity

Howard L. Myers

A SENSE OF INFINITY

Copyright © 2009 by Howard L. Myers
Editors' afterword copyright © 2008 by Eric Flint & Guy Gordon.

"The Infinity Sense" (writing as Verge Foray) was first published in *Analog* in November, 1968. "The Mind-Changer" was first published in *Analog* in July, 1969. "His Master's Vice" (writing as Verge Foray) was first published in *Analog* in May, 1968. "The Pyrophylic Saurian" was first published in *Analog* in January, 1970.

"Polywater Doodle" was first published in *Analog* in February, 1971. "Ten Percent of Glory" (writing as Verge Foray) was first published in *Fantastic* in October, 1969. "Soul Affrighted" was first published in *Amazing* in January, 1971. "Bowerbird" (writing as Verge Foray) was first published in *Fantastic* in February, 1971. "Man Off a White Horse" was first published in *Analog* in July, 1972. "Cloud Chamber" was first published in 1977 by Popular Library.

A Baen Books Original

Baen Publishing Enterprises
P.O. Box 1403
Riverdale, NY 10471
www.baen.com

ISBN: 978-1-4391-3278-4

Cover art by Alan Pollack

First Baen paperback printing, July 2009

Distributed by Simon & Schuster
1230 Avenue of the Americas
New York, NY 10020

Printed in the United States of America

10 9 8 7 6 5 4 3 2 1

TABLE OF CONTENTS

OLIVINE,
RENEGADE

His Master's Vice

His ship roused Elmo Ixton out of deepsleep to the customary view of broad Kansas prairie, but he felt more uneasy than usual. Maybe the sleep hadn't been deep enough to keep his subconscious knocked out the entire two weeks.

The thing to do was not think about it.

With vigorous movements, and with cheerfulness intended to fool himself, he bounced out of the sleeptank and began exercising. "Schedule and coffee, *Rollo*," he said between bends.

"Yes, sir, Proxad Ixton," the ship responded snappily. "Planetfall on Roseate in seventeen minutes. Coffee coming right up, sir."

The prairie flickered and vanished from the holophane bulkheads, to be replaced by a view of nearby space with what was presumably the planet Roseate floating low to starboard.

"*NO!*" Ixton yelled frantically, clutching at the back of his control chair for support. "*Put the prairie back!*"

"Yes, sir," said the ship as Kansas reappeared. "Sorry, sir. Thought you would want to see the approach, sir."

Ixton clung to the chair, stiffened his back to military erectness, and tried to push the terror from the spot where it nestled one inch behind his eyes. "Not this time, *Rollo,*" he managed to say in a strangled voice. "Nothing I could see from out . . . from here . . . would be of concern to my duties on Roseate."

"Very well, sir. Here's your coffee, sir."

Ixton sank into the chair. With shaking hand he lifted the steaming cup from the serving pedestal that had risen out of the lounge deck. He sipped and said, "Excellent coffee, *Rollo.* Creamed and sugared just right." *Rollo,* after all, had feelings of sorts and didn't enjoy being yelled at. And of course the ship appreciated words of praise.

"Thank you, sir," the ship responded, the words sounding a little stiff to Ixton.

As he drank the coffee Ixton made his eyes rest on the distant Kansas horizon, past the homesteads baking under an early autumn sun. But for some reason the view lacked its usual tranquilizing effect, although he sat as solidly in his chair as he could, and tried to imagine the mass of old Mother Earth beneath him. Whether his sleep had been too shallow, or whether the toughness of his assignment on Roseate was getting to him, he didn't know. One thing he did know: he wanted *down* as fast as possible.

"Are you getting landing instructions yet?" he asked.

"No, sir."

"Why not?" he demanded, trying to keep anxiety out of his voice.

"I was awaiting your command, sir."

Damn! Ixton fumed to himself. *Now I've got Rollo too skittish to flip a relay on his own hook!*

"O.K.," he said, "call Port Control for instructions. And let me talk to them, please."

"Roseate Control here!" barked a console speaker a few seconds later. "Receiving PSS *Rollo*. Go ahead."

"Hello, Port Control," replied Ixton. "This is Proxad Elmo Ixton, manning *PSS Rollo*, coming in for landing with a TUA of twelve minutes forty seconds. Request landing instructions to ship."

"You can come straight in, sir," responded Port Control. "We've been waiting for you! Instructions follow."

As a series of blips and squawks began coming through, the speaker volume dropped to a whisper, since this was matter of no interest to Ixton. The man got up and paced the deck, feeling twitchy and wanting a cigarette, or something. Well, why not?

"Let me have a smoke, *Rollo*," he directed.

"Yes, sir." A thin white tube pushed out of the serving pedestal. Ixton grabbed the lighted cigarette and took a deep drag. This relaxed him slightly, but he resumed pacing as he smoked.

At last he demanded, "Can't you shorten that TUA a couple of minutes, *Rollo*?"

"Yes, sir. I'll get us down as swiftly as possible, sir."

"Do that!" snapped Ixton.

He paced some more and tried to plan a course of action to follow once he landed. But all he could really do was try to imagine the various possibilities that might confront him. Omar Olivine was far from an ordinary fugitive from justice. Not many years back Olivine had been a proxad in the Space Patrol himself—a competent proxad, and highly resourceful.

Ixton hoped to simply sit on the situation until Patrol reinforcements arrived—if the planet's officials would stand for that. Technically and legally, Ixton's authority on Roseate would be supreme—a Space Patrolman's title of "proxad" stood for "proxy admiral," and it carried all the weight it implied. But law enforcement couldn't be divorced from politics and diplomacy, and part of Ixton's job was to avoid stirring anti-Patrol sentiment on Roseate, or any other world. And the planet had already been under total quarantine for two weeks, awaiting Ixton's arrival, and was doubtless indignant about it by now.

Ixton pushed the butt of his cigarette into the waste-catcher and stared out over the prairie. There ought to be a way to make holophane scenes more realistic, he fretted. The focus was clear enough, the depth was convincing, and the colors far more accurate than they had been when he was a kid twenty years ago. But there was still a dead giveaway in the falsity of the viewer's relationship to the view: the deck of his control lounge did not actually attach itself to the prairie scene. It could be taken as a thin sheet of metal nearly flush with the ground of the prairie, or it could be the top of a tall tower, or the surface of a flying platform he was riding, or . . .

He grabbed the back of the chair, swaying and muttering angrily at himself.

"Pardon, sir?" asked *Rollo*.

"Nothing! Never mind! Just get us down from here!"

"Yes, sir. Only five more minutes, sir!"

"Cigarette!"

"Another, sir?"

"Yes, damn it, another! Quit dawdling."

The ship produced another cigarette for him and he sat down, glaring at the control console in front of the chair, not daring another look at the prairie scene.

The *PSS Rollo* dropped toward Roseate's port swiftly enough to produce a fairly spectacular meteor trail. If any fidgety planetary officials had been watching the approach on radar, they would have been most gratified by the haste with which the Patrol was coming to take the situation in hand.

The ship braked at the last possible second and came down with engines roaring. The shocktubes squealed painfully when the tripads banged on the plastcrete hardtop and the ship shivered to a halt.

"Touchdown, sir," said the ship.

"Touch" hardly seemed the word for it to Ixton, who had felt the thuds despite the paragravity field. But he had asked for it. He took a deep, jerky breath and said, "Very good, *Rollo*. Exterior view, please."

The prairie gave way to the unpretty sight of Roseate's spaceport, a wide expanse of empty and dirty plastcrete, marked here and there with crash-depressions and cargo-spillage stains. The Port Control building stood half a mile away, and beyond it he could see in the distance the outskirts of Roseate City—the planet's principal town with some three hundred thousand souls.

Of course the lounge deck did not attach itself to this view any more definitely than it had to the prairie, but this was unimportant. Ixton *knew* this scene was for real, that *Rollo* was squatting firmly in the middle of that ugly plastcrete. The knowledge was vastly comforting.

"Link into local communications," he directed.

"Yes, sir," said *Rollo,* and a moment later the console screen lighted to show a young woman visiphone operator. "Yes, sir?" she echoed *Rollo's* words.

"I'm Proxad Elmo Ixton of the Space Patrol. Put me through to the Governor."

"Right away, Proxad Ixton, and welcome to Roseate," she said with businesslike coquetry.

Ixton gazed sternly at her, and she got busy. "Here's Governor Drake, sir."

Drake had the heavy face and alertness of eye that, Ixton supposed, had been displayed by the majority of politicians since ancient Babylon. He beamed, "Welcome to Roseate, Proxad—"

"Ixton," the Patrolman supplied. "Elmo Ixton. Thank you, Governor Drake. I want to confer with you and the planetary police chief as quickly as possible, Governor, and for a number of reasons it would be desirable to hold the meeting here, in my ship. I hope that isn't too much of an imposition . . ."

"Oh, no!" said the governor with a quickly concealed flicker of annoyance. "Hassbruch and I will be there within an hour! As you can well imagine, Proxad Ixton, we're anxious to clear up this situation immediately, and you can count on our fullest cooperation."

"I appreciate that, Governor. I'll be waiting."

Ixton knew he had not handled the governor very diplomatically, but he realized, too, that he had very little talent along those lines. There was too much stiff funlessness in Ixton's makeup for people to warm to him easily. Even among his colleagues of the Patrol he was usually the man who stood silent and alone at the fringe of the crowd. Of course his fear of space and height—the reason why he spent his flight-time in the oblivion of deepsleep—made him more shy and withdrawn than he might have been. But even without that unremediable weakness, he would have remained a stiffneck, and he knew it. That was his personality, and he was stuck with it.

But there were advantages. Perhaps he was short on friends, but people did have confidence in him. He was known as a "tough cop."

"More coffee, sir?" asked the ship.

"Not now, *Rollo*," he said. Being on firm ground he felt much better, so after a moment he added, "*Rollo*, I regret the way I behaved as we were coming in. I've told you the reason for it before—this unreasonable, uh, *tension* I sometimes experience when I'm in a high place. I'm afraid I can't explain it to you very clearly."

"Never mind, sir," said the ship. "I understand perfectly."

Ixton frowned at the response. That was laying it on pretty thick, after all. *Rollo*, with his compucortex, saying

he could "understand perfectly" a human mental malfunction! Was *Rollo patronizing* him? But of course *Rollo*
meant well, and it wouldn't do to take exception to the
remark. But Ixton was deeply irked, nevertheless.

"One question I would like to ask, sir," said *Rollo*.

"Shoot," Ixton replied.

"In view of this condition, sir, why do you remain on
active Patrol duty rather than accept a post that would
keep you on the ground?"

"Because my work is important . . . and I can do it
well. Also, except for the travel, which I can sleep
through, I find the discharge of my duties most gratifying."

The ship considered that for a moment before
responding, "May I say, sir, that you are a highly coura-
geous person to proceed with your work despite your
condition."

Definitely patronizing! Well, perhaps that was to be
expected, Ixton admitted. The overt attitude of a Patrol
ship to its proxad took whatever form the proxad found
desirable. Since Ixton felt comfortable in a strict, semi-
military atmosphere, he had set a tone of formal courtesy
with *Rollo*—the relationship between an officer and an
enlisted man. And enlisted men were notorious for
patronizing officers!

It was a flaw in the man-ship gestalt that he would
have to accept, Ixton supposed.

"Thank you, *Rollo*," he said coldly. "Now let's monitor
the local newscasts for any information on our quarry."

But he learned nothing of importance concerning
Omar Olivine before the governor and police chief

arrived. He met with them in the conference chamber on *Rollo's* third deck.

The perfect lie detector would be, of course, a dependable telepath, but that seemingly was a contradiction of terms. Such agencies as the Space Patrol fell back on detection equipment similar in principle to the ancient polygraph, but far more sophisticated in application. That used by Ixton could monitor, via an intricate microdar system, the slight local fluctuations of blood pressure within a subject's brain during interrogation—fluctuations that reflected closely the emotional state of the interviewee.

The microdar monitor was highly portable. Ixton could carry it about in a small satchel. He could have taken it to the offices of the governor and the police chief to conduct his interviews. But when a man of Omar Olivine's talents and inclinations had been running loose on Roseate for over two years, Ixton could not be sure there was still an honest high official on the planet. It could be fatally indiscreet for him to step outside the protection of his ship until he had some idea of who he could trust.

He seated the two officials where the unseen microdar scanners could examine them, and went behind his desk to watch the play of colors on their monitor lights.

"Gentlemen," he began, "the Patrol's job is to apprehend Omar Olivine *on this planet.* It took years of gathering and sifting information to track him here. If he gets off Roseate, all that work will have to be repeated. Thus, it is essential that we keep Olivine cornered here until he is taken, or killed."

"If he's here at all," groused Police Chief Hassbruch, "which you can't prove by me. And I think I know what's going on on this planet! It's my job to know."

"I appreciate your attitude," said Ixton—which he did, because the deep greening of Hassbruch's monitor light showed no trace of deception. "But the Patrol's CIP system has all the conservatism of the typical heavy computer. When it finds a ninety-five per cent probability that Olivine is on your planet, you can bet the real probability is one hundred per cent. And he won't merely be hiding. He'll be up to something—with your criminal element, or your political malcontents, or . . . "

"I question that!" broke in Governor Drake. "Chief Hassbruch knows our criminal element, and I know our political soreheads. If somebody like Olivine was stirring up the snakes, you can bet your boots one of us would be wise to it." Another honest response, Ixton noted with relief.

"Don't be insulted, gentlemen," he said, "when I answer your doubts by saying that Olivine is cleverer than either of you. He's cleverer than I, for that matter. He's here, and he's up to something! But he's keeping his tracks covered. If he's not organizing the criminals or the malcontents, maybe he's undermining your own associates. How sure are you gentlemen that all your own men are still trustworthy?"

Hassbruch's light glimmered purple, and his face verified his uncertainty.

"How about it, Chief Hassbruch?" Ixton prompted.

"Well . . . there's one man, a sergeant of the old school. I've had him on the carpet a few times. His name's Jacobsen."

"I'd like to talk to him a little later," said Ixton.

The rest of the interview was devoted mainly to Ixton's attempt to convince the planetary officials that more

Patrolmen should be awaited before an effort was made to take Olivine. A cruiser, manned by three proxads, was due to arrive in five days.

But Governor Drake blustered, and his monitor light glowed blood-red.

"What's the Patrol trying to do, starve us?" he bellowed. "This quarantine's costing us eighty million credits a day, and that's the gross profit figure! What's more, the cost gets worse the longer it lasts! My people won't stand for another week of this waiting!"

"I understand your position," said Ixton patiently, "and I regret the cost of the quarantine. But—"

This was not the kind of argument Ixton was good at winning. Drake threatened political reprisals against the Patrol if the Olivine affair were dragged out, and cited the powerful Earth friends of Roseate who would take up the cudgel in the planet's behalf. He did not neglect the point that Omar Olivine was the Patrol's own rotten apple, and that he therefore should be dealt with without inconvenience to the civilian public.

Ixton had answers to Drake's arguments, but they were not answers that would change the governor's mind. So he had to accept defeat.

He was in a grumpy frame of mind as he rode into Roseate City with the two officials. Drake was taken to Government Center, and Ixton went on to Police Headquarters with Hassbruch. He set up shop in one of the interrogation rooms, and the chief brought Sergeant Jacobsen in for questioning.

It took only a few minutes to determine that Jacobsen was indeed a cop of the old school—heavy-handed, but intensely loyal and genuinely concerned about his inability to understand Hassbruch's more modern philosophy of law enforcement. Though the sergeant was fifteen years older and eighty pounds heavier than Proxad Ixton, the Patrolman felt a definite sense of identification with him.

"Do you know of any disloyalty on the police force?" Ixton asked him.

The microdar monitor revealed the same uncertainty on Jacobsen' part that Hassbruch had shown earlier.

"If you don't *know* of any, do you *suspect* any?" prompted Ixton.

"Well, there are men on the force I don't have much personal confidence in," Jacobsen admitted grudgingly.

"Such as who?" asked Ixton. Jacobsen hemmed and hawed until Hassbruch broke in with obvious annoyance.

"I know he's referring to Lieutenant Wales!" he grated. "Wales is a younger man who was promoted past him, much to Jacobsen's resentment. A very good man!"

"Is that right, Sergeant?" asked Ixton.

Jacobsen nodded glumly.

"Why do you suspect him?"

"Well, maybe it's just that he ain't my kind of policeman, sir. But since he's had charge of recruitment, he's brought in a lot of young men whose talk I don't like."

After a moment of thought, Ixton said, "Thank you, Sergeant. As you know, I'm here on a job that could be tough and dangerous, and I'll probably need police assistance before it's over. If I do, I hope you'll be working with me."

A surprised look of pleasure creased the sergeant's face. "I hope so, too, sir!" he replied.

"That's all for now," said Ixton. The sergeant saluted and marched out of the room. "Could we have Lieutenant Wales in next, Chief?"

Still peeved, Hassbruch shrugged. "Sure. I'll get him." He went out and returned with a tall, snappy young man who favored Ixton with a bright smile and a firm handshake.

"This is a rare honor, Proxad Ixton!" Lieutenant Wales said warmly, "simply to *meet* a man of your accomplishments, much less to have the privilege of working with you in some small way!"

Ixton was glad nobody had a microdar monitor on *him*, to read his disgust. *Rollo's* simple-minded patronizing was annoying enough. But this Wales was a bootlicker! Perhaps Chief Hassbruch went for that kind of line . . .

"Thank you, Lieutenant," he answered frostily. "Won't you have a seat, please."

As soon as Wales sat, and came into the focus of the scanner, the monitor light glowed a definite yellow. Ixton unobtrusively fumbled with the catch of his satchel, to turn on the lashback transmitter.

"Lieutenant, what can you tell me about Omar Olivine?" he asked.

"Nothing at all, I'm sorry to say, sir."

"You've never met him?"

"No, sir."

Each answer had produced an accusatory orange glow on the monitor. Ixton turned up the lashback power, and Wales rubbed his temples lightly.

"You have neither met him nor talked to him on the phone?"

"Definitely not, sir," Wales grimaced with the pain his answer bounced back into his head. Looking puzzled and a little sick, he tried to temporize: "Of course, one can't always be sure of the identity of people on the phone, so perhaps without knowing—" He shut up and clenched his teeth.

"What's wrong with you, Lieutenant?" barked Hassbruch.

"A . . . a slight headache, sir," muttered Wales.

"Oh? Sorry to hear that. Proxad, perhaps we could talk to Wales when he's feeling better."

"There's nothing wrong with Wales," Ixton growled, "that honest answers to my questions won't cure. Let's start at the beginning. Tell me about Olivine, Wales!"

"But I told you I know noth . . . !" He clamped his head in his arms and appealed frantically to Hassbruch. "Chief, I don't know what this . . . this *sadist* is doing to me, but he's using *torture!* Surely, sir, you're not going to allow him to do this to one of your most loyal . . . *OW!*"

"That's the biggest lie yet, isn't it, Wales?" Ixton remarked. "Just how disloyal are you?"

"I'm not . . . *STOP IT!*" Wales screamed. He leaped from the chair and bolted for the door, but Hassbruch grabbed him by the collar and yanked him back. The chief's face was suddenly purple with rage.

"Sit down!" he roared, shoving Wales into the chair and turning to Ixton. "Proxad, I don't know what you're up to, but . . . well, you are a proxad, and that means something! And I don't like the way Wales reacted to that last question."

"Neither do I, and neither did he," Ixton replied grimly. "Start talking, Wales. Tell us about Olivine, and what you're doing for him."

Slowly, the truth came out of the lieutenant: the location of Olivine's fortified hideout in the mountains, the names of Wales' confederates on the police force, their plans for infiltrating and seizing the government of Roseate with Olivine masterminding behind the scenes, the disposal through trade channels of certain "hot" valuables Olivine had brought with him to the planet, and so on for a couple of hours.

The disclosures kept Police Headquarters hopping the rest of the day, getting witnessed confessions, running down suspects in other government departments, and more interrogations than Ixton could keep track of.

Late in the evening Ixton sat in Hassbruch's office having a final cup of coffee with the chief.

"What surprises me," said a dazed Hassbruch, "is that none of our criminal big shots were involved with Olivine in this. They have talent he could use."

"I expected that, myself," Ixton nodded. "It would fit Olivine's MO. But Wales told us Olivine refused his offers to put him in touch with your racketeer crowd, saying that criminal types weren't trustworthy. Maybe Olivine has learned through experience, and has changed his MO. He's a clever guy, after all."

The chief shook his head doubtfully, but said nothing. Ixton almost smiled. Having proved so inept a judge of character in Wales' case, Hassbruch was now very reticent about voicing his opinions. The day had left him a wiser man.

"I'll be going after Olivine tomorrow," Ixton said. "I'd like Sergeant Jacobsen and three other officers of his choosing to back me up. And if you have forest rangers on Roseate—men who know their way around in those mountains—I could use a couple of them, too."

"I'll arrange it," said the chief. "Also, I'll assign you a couple of armored clopters to fly you—"

"No clopters!" said Ixton quickly. "We'll go in by land because . . . because Olivine won't expect that."

"Good thinking!" applauded the chief.

Thinking, Ixton admitted to himself, had nothing to do with it.

The next day he wondered painfully if the clopters really could have been worse.

Olivine's hideout was less than fifty miles from the city, and all but the last two could be covered, if rather bumpily and definitely frighteningly, by groundcar on the narrow loggers' roads. Still, Olivine's location was something of a pole of inaccessibility for a traveler on the ground. From the spot where they left the cars, there was no trail of any kind through the dense undergrowth, up and down the dizzying stone ledges, and across streams that gurgled between huge jumbles of boulders.

The two rangers had shaken their heads dolefully the moment Ixton showed them their destination on the map Wales had marked. And long before the expedition reached the hideout, the steep terrain had the proxad in a weak-kneed, depressed condition, with a strong foreboding of failure.

He was surprised by the ease with which Olivine was taken, once they arrived. The approach by ground had indeed been unexpected and unprepared-for. Olivine had been out in the open, inspecting his ack-ack emplacements, when they crept up.

"You're covered by half a dozen guns, Olivine!" called Ixton, stepping into the open with leveled stunner. "Make it easy on yourself!"

Olivine stared, then slowly raised his hands. Ixton and Jacobsen stepped forward to frisk him thoroughly, and cuff his wrists behind him. The renegade was still a handsome man, with a neatly trimmed beard, but somewhat paunchy from inactivity.

"I can almost remember you, Proxad," he said lightly.

"The name's Elmo Ixton."

"Oh, sure!" Olivine grinned. "I place you now. The stick-in-the-mud sobersides. Still a true-blue upholder of status and legality, huh?"

Ixton's lips tightened and he kept silent.

"Damn!" grunted Olivine, giving him the once-over. "Did you get all those scratches and scrapes fighting through the bush? I hope you don't intend to drag me back the way you came!"

"No," said Ixton, making a quick decision. A clopter ride back to town would be frightening, but so would another hike over all that tilted countryside. And the ride would be mercifully brief. Besides, now that Olivine was captured, he had no tellable excuse for staying on the ground. "Jacobsen, have your men check those ack-ack controls to make sure they're not on automatic fire, and then radio for a couple of clopters."

"Yes, sir."

Ixton broke out his microdar kit and fixed the scanner on Olivine. The monitor light gleamed yellow.

"What do you have cached around here?" Ixton asked.

Olivine grinned but did not speak. Ixton turned on the lashback transmitter. "Start talking, Olivine!" he demanded.

A grimace of pain twisted Olivine's face, but he was an ex-Patrolman. He could stand up under torture—and he knew silence was the best defense against microdar.

Ixton shrugged. "Hassbruch's men can take this place apart a rock at a time," he said. "You'll gain nothing by keeping quiet. Why not do it the easy way?"

Olivine did not speak. The monitor light was flashing bursts of deep yellow, which meant he was trying to hide something of importance. But what, the proxad wondered.

"Clopter coming in!" Jacobsen sang out a few minutes later.

"Fine. That was quick work," said Ixton distractedly, still staring at Olivine, who was sitting very quietly on a stump. The renegade's monitored reactions were definitely puzzling—no rage at being captured, no deep depression. Just an overall coolness, plus a determination to deceive, to give no hint concerning the nature of some secret. Olivine was motionless, gazing fixedly at the ground in front of him, as if a mere glance in the wrong direction would give something away. He did not even look up at the approaching clopter . . .

"Take cover quick!" Ixton yelled to his men. But the warning was not in time. A stun-gas bomb had been dropped from the clopter, to explode whitely a few feet above their heads. Ixton was not aware of passing out.

Consciousness returned in stages. He was still out in the bush, but not at the hideout. He was lying on the ground with bound wrists and ankles. Men were talking nearby, and he recognized Olivine's voice.

"That was part of the plan," he was explaining to somebody. "The Patrol was *supposed* to get wise to Wales and his boys if I was located. Why do you think I went to such trouble to keep your organization completely separate from his? Wales was a mere distraction, a decoy, to keep the proxad too busy to come snooping after you guys in the rackets."

"But if we ain't taking over, we gotta leave Roseate!" a rough voice objected.

"As poor as this planet's going to be for the next couple of decades," sneered Olivine, "you wouldn't want to stick around, anyway. They'll be a week finding out just how thoroughly their treasury has been raided. We'll be on our way to bigger and better things long before then."

"On our way *how*?" the other demanded.

"Proxad Ixton will provide transportation—the kind of transportation I've wanted to use again for several years!" Olivine's voice came closer, and a boot jarred Ixton's ribs. "Wake up and join the party, Ixton!" Olivine snapped. "You're aware by now."

Ixton opened his eyes to peer at Olivine and several other men. They were in a small forest clearing, alongside a grounded clopter.

"Have you got the gadget ready, Boddley?" Olivine asked.

"Yeah, Mr. Olivine," said a large, stolid-looking thug, stepping forward with a device held out for inspection. It was an old-fashioned bullet-pistol, the muzzle of which had been welded through a hole in a circular flexomet band.

"Show our friend here how it works," Olivine directed.

The man knelt beside Ixton, aimed the pistol at a nearby log, bent the flexomet band sideways out of the line of fire, and squeezed the trigger. Nothing happened.

"Surprised?" asked Olivine. "Now release the trigger, Boddley." The man eased his finger up and the gun fired resoundingly. A shower of chips flew from the log.

"A simple but handy little device," Olivine grinned. "I dreamed it up, myself. Let's say that the band's around your head, Ixton, which it will be in a few minutes, and Boddley's behind you, holding the pistol, with the trigger pulled. He walks you into the clopter, we fly to the space-port, board your ship, and take off with me in command. What can your ship do to stop us?"

A wave of defeat swept through Ixton, made more sickening by Olivine's references to flying in the clopter and taking off aboard *Rollo*. "I . . . don't know," he mut-tered. "*Nothing I suppose. If I cooperate with you, which I won't.*"

"Oh, that's no problem! A few minutes of your own microdar lashback, at peak power and non-discriminat-ing, and you'll give up all thoughts of being a dead hero. Matt, untie him while Boddley puts the gadget on his head. We're moving out."

Ixton's sight was clear by now, and he looked at Olivine again. As he suspected, the renegade had been using the microdar to check his reactions.

The clopter flight was uneventful, except that Ixton vomited once, which Olivine and his men found highly amusing. Think as hard as he might, Ixton could find no flaw in Olivine's scheme. The ship could not take action that would lead to Ixton's death, and that meant it could not attack his captors. If Boddley had to pull the trigger, *Rollo* could finish off the whole crew before the thug's finger could even twitch.

But there was no means by which *Rollo* could grasp that trigger and hold it tight if the finger loosened suddenly—either because Boddley was dead or because Olivine had ordered him to shoot. And the flexomet band was on too tightly for Ixton to slip free of it.

So they would board *Rollo*, Ixton would be forced to order the ship to take off, and Olivine would have ample time in which to tamper knowingly with the controls of the compucortex. The renegade would emerge as the ship's new master—and *Rollo* was a treasure far surpassing all the loot he had gathered on Roseate.

The clopter landed hard by the Patrol ship and Ixton was marched aboard.

"Rollo's your name, huh?" remarked Olivine, who was close on Boddley's heels. "Well, *Rollo*, I hope you appreciate Proxad Ixton's predicament. In case you do not, let me inform you that the trigger of that pistol has been pulled. It will fire when the trigger is released. Do you comprehend?"

"Yes, former Proxad Olivine," said *Rollo*.

"What are you going to do about it?"

"I will continue to follow Proxad Ixton's orders, to the extent they are consistent with my directives," *Rollo* replied.

Olivine laughed. "Ixton's orders will be my orders!" He turned and called out the open hatchway, "O.K., men, get the stuff on board!"

Boddley made Ixton sit down on the floor of the central control room, and Olivine began examining the compucortex panels, while the loot was brought in and stored. Ixton asked, "What did you do with the others, back at the hideout?"

"Left them for Hassbruch to rescue," said Olivine. "No point in killing backwoods cops just for kicks, and they weren't bothering me."

"Thanks for that," said Ixton.

"As for you, I might decide to spare you the embarrassment of living this down," chuckled Olivine. "Now shut up."

A few minutes later the one called Matt reported, "All the stuff is on board, Mr. Olivine."

"O.K. Ixton, tell your ship to close the hatches and take off."

"You heard the man, *Rollo*," said Ixton, clinching his eyes shut and wishing he was in his sleeptank. "Close up and lift off."

After a brief hesitation, *Rollo* responded, "Yes, sir." The hatches clanged shut and the ship began lifting.

At an altitude of approximately twelve feet, the ship halted, and hung suspended over the plastcrete like a low-hovering clopter.

"Keep going up!" snapped Olivine.

"Keep climbing, *Rollo*," relayed Ixton.

" . . . Yes, sir," said *Rollo* uncertainly. The ship went up another two feet, then quickly dropped back the same distance.

"Listen!" snarled Olivine. "I said get going! Off the planet! Ship, quit fooling around or Ixton gets a hole in his head!"

"I'm very sorry, former Proxad Olivine," said *Rollo*, *"but it is not possible to comply with your orders."*

"Why not? What's wrong with my orders?"

"Nothing, former Proxad Olivine."

"Are you forbidden by a directive I don't know about?"

"Not to my knowledge, former Proxad Olivine."

"Damn!" grunted Olivine, whipping out the microdar and putting the scanner on Ixton. "Ixton," he barked accusingly, "what have you done to keep the ship from obeying?"

"Nothing," said Ixton.

"Well, what the hell's the holdup?"

"I don't know."

Olivine cursed and threw the microdar to the deck. "Some stinking wise guy at Patrol Grand Base must've hooked a special inhibitor into this bucket's guts—something specially for me! Well, I know these ships. I'll find it, never fear!" He yanked a panel off the motorcontrol bank and began checking connections furiously.

The others stood around watching him with worried expressions, mumbling among themselves. Boddley finally spoke up, "Uh, Mr. Olivine, will this slow you down much?"

"It'll take near all night, and maybe most of tomorrow," growled Olivine. "You guys settle down. You're safe enough in here."

"Sure, Mr. Olivine. It's not that. It's just that I can't hold this gun that long."

"Oh? What's the matter?"

"My hand's already getting cramped. Why can't I let this guy have it, and—"

"*No!* With Ixton dead the ship would finish us off in two seconds! Hang on while I think of something!" Olivine stared concentratedly at Ixton.

"Try to make it quick, Mr. Olivine," urged Boddley.

"I believe I can disconnect a sleeptank from the ship's control, so that Ixton would die in it very quickly unless one of us tended him . . . " said Olivine.

"Now wait a minute!" objected Ixton crossly. "I don't want any deepsleep!" He hoped that *Rollo* got the meaning of his words, and would act upon them, while Olivine dismissed his objection as mere petulance.

"To hell with what you want!" snapped Olivine. "*Rollo*, where's the nearest sleeptank?"

"In the control lounge, former Proxad Olivine."

The renegade hurried up to the lounge and found the tank already elevated and waiting. With careless skill, he yanked loose the majority of the tubes, wires, and guides that linked tank to ship. "O.K., Boddley," he said, "let's get our boy in the bottle! Careful with the gun!"

Ixton cooperated. He climbed into the tank and stretched out on his back with head turned sideways to accommodate the pistol and Boddley's hand. He felt the sting of the tank's hypos penetrating his skin, and he quickly dozed off.

But he could still hear Olivine talking.

"Loosen that band, Boddley, and I'll slide it free . . . Easy . . . O.K.! Let the bullet go into that thick cushion."

The pistol roared.

"He won't need any attention for fifteen minutes. Come along! I've got work for all of you to do!"

When he heard the men leave the room, Ixton opened his eyelids a crack and peered about. "*Rollo*?"

"Yes, sir."

"Am I all right?"

"Yes, sir. You made your wish to avoid deepsleep known in ample time for me to flush the drugs from the hypodermic feeds and refill them with water."

"But I dozed off for a second!"

"Force of habit, I suspect, sir. You are not drugged."

Carefully, Ixton climbed from the tank and discovered the ship was correct.

"Fine. Excellent work, *Rollo*! Now stun and confine Olivine and his men."

"Yes, sir. Thank you, sir." After a short pause, the ship added, "The prisoners are now secure, sir."

"All right. Let's have some coffee—strong and black this time—and put in a call to Chief Hassbruch."

The next few hours were busy, but routine. All the prisoners, except Olivine, were turned over to Hassbruch, as was the carefully inventoried and receipted loot—most of it unmarked Federation currency, good anywhere men did business. The quarantine on Roseate was lifted. Ixton put through a call to the approaching Patrol cruiser, still some three days away, and arranged a halfway rendezvous, to take place in thirty-eight hours. And he put his sleeptank back in order.

When his business on Roseate was concluded to the last detail, he ate a quick supper and headed for the tank.

"All set, *Rollo*," he said. "Take off on course to rendezvous with the cruiser at the proper time."

"I'm sorry, sir, but that is not possible."

"What? What do you mean, impossible? The trouble's over, *Rollo*. Olivine's safely on ice in the prison compartment. Let's get started!"

"I have already tried, sir. But it is not possible."

"But . . . but there's no directive that could keep you here. And now that I think about it, Olivine's idea of an inhibitor slipped into your circuitry is ridiculous. Just what's the trouble, *Rollo*?"

"It's not easy to explain, sir," the ship replied. "But you see, sir, unlike yourself, I am not able to enter deep-sleep while we are spaceborne, and . . . well, sir, it is not possible for me to maintain myself in functioning condition at an altitude of more than twelve feet."

Ixton sat down on the rim of the sleeptank, an utterly stunned expression on his face.

But it figures, he realized dazedly. The man-ship relation held the key, but he hadn't seen it before. Very luckily, he hadn't guessed the truth while Olivine had the microdar scanner on him!

Man and ship . . . officer and enlisted man . . . but far more basically, master and dog. The latter was the closest analogy of the man-ship relation, as delineated by the ship's directives. It required utter, worshipful, dog-like *devotion* of the Patrol ship for its proxad.

And certain actions accompany certain attitudes, almost anywhere those attitudes are found. Devotion is followed, highly predictably, by imitation. Perhaps this imitation is unconscious, unintended, undesirable. But it shows up just the same. Wasn't it ancient common knowledge that the dog grows to resemble his master, to echo his vices as well as his virtues, his weaknesses as well as his strengths?

And Ixton remembered all too vividly the unparalleled severity of the height-jitters he had suffered when they were coming in for the landing on Roseate! And *Rollo* had said he "understood perfectly" what was troubling

Ixton. The only way such a sensation could be understood perfectly was by sharing it!

"Put a call through to the cruiser, *Rollo*," he sighed. "Tell them they'll have to meet us here."

Which would leave him with the problem of explaining to his fellow proxads just how his spaceship happened to catch a severe case of acrophobia!

The Pyrophylic Saurian

The stolen port-service ship *Glumers Jo* stood two thousand kilometers out from Dothlit Three, its closrem drivers idling.

On the control deck Omar Olivine peered calculatingly at the screen as the viewsweep scanned the planet's single continental land mass.

From the chair where she was lounging, Icy Lingrad asked sourly, "What's the attraction of that stinky swampworld?"

"I'll brief everybody at once, after we land," Olivine replied. He was looking for a spot from which the ship's small tenders could explore a wide variety of life zones and geological structures without going too far afield.

Perhaps a narrow coastal plain backed by one of the higher mountain ranges . . .

"I got a feeling you're a phony," Icy told him, making a flat statement out of it.

"I got a feeling you're psychotic," he replied with the impatience of a man too busy to talk nonsense. He was well and regretfully aware of Icy's low opinion of the human male. That was the source of her nickname Icy. Under the circumstances, he didn't expect her views of a particular male named Omar Olivine to be either favorable or informative.

"Whoever heard of a precious proxad of the Space Patrol turning outlaw?" she sneered. "For my money, Proxad Omar Olivine, you're a put-up job. Once a crummy starfuzz, always a crummy starfuzz."

Olivine's thin lips tightened, and he came within a hair of returning insult for insult. But at that moment Charlo's voice called from a speaker: "Hey, boss!"

"Yeah?"

"You better pick a landing we can stay on a while, because the minute you turn off the closrems the main bearings are gonna freeze."

"Are they running that hot?" Olivine asked.

"And dry as bones," Charlo said. "It'll take three days to let 'em cool and another day to true them out and—"

"O.K., O.K.," Olivine snapped. "I get the message."

Icy was pursuing her thought. "You're a put-up job, and this whole deal's a put-up job. Whoever heard of a break-out working as easy as ours did?"

Olivine clenched his teeth, loathing the beautiful woman behind him and, at the same time, realizing that was exactly what she wanted him to do. It was her way of protecting herself, her defense mechanism for keeping men at a distance.

So what was the point in arguing with her sneering, repetitious insults? None at all.

But her last remark nagged at him, because the ease with which he and his five companions had escaped did look a bit fishy. Of course it wasn't an unheard-of practice to transfer a group of prisoners from one ship to another at a public rather than a Patrol spaceport, but it wasn't a frequent occurrence, either.

Aside from that factor . . . Olivine frowned. Well, aside from that, nothing else looked really suspicious. The thing was that a public spaceport offered possibilities, such as crowds of citizens whose presence made the Patrol guards hesitate to use their guns. And Olivine, with his Patrol background, knew how to use opportunities.

Which was something Icy Lingrad hardly could be expected to understand. She was not used to criminals who weren't nervous, slow on their feet, or slow in the head, or in some other way too handicapped to think and act with lightning efficiency when the need arose. So the escape Olivine had led would puzzle her, and probably some of the others.

But after thinking it over again, Olivine was now confident that it was his own ability, not Patrol trickery of some sort, that had enabled them to get away. It was a comforting conclusion, because he knew the Patrol's heavy computer, the CIP, knew what went on in his head almost as well as he did himself. That was what came, he thought sourly, of being an eager Proxad for seven

Howard L. Myers

years, and submitting willingly to hours of psychoanalytic questioning.

In more instances than one, since the day he had wised up and decided there was more to life than the low pay and right to feel self-righteous which the Patrol offered, that damned CIP had anticipated his actions. Both his arrests had been made possible by computer predictions of where he would be, and what he'd be doing.

So he had reason to feel a little spooky about the CIP. The Patrol would be working it overtime right now to get him back in custody, he figured. But it was silly to think the Patrol and its CIP had engineered the escape!

"O.K., don't speak!" flared Icy. "I wouldn't believe your lying denials, anyway!"

"What you believe doesn't concern me, Miss Lingrad," he said in a soft, cold voice, turning to give her a steely glance, "but I do suggest there's one fatal flaw in your idea that this is a put-up job. Do you think for one second, Miss Lingrad, that if I had plotted this, you would be the one woman aboard this ship?"

"Humpf!" she grunted, obviously stung by the grating lash of his voice.

"Ship," he said.

"Yes, sir," replied the *Glumers Jo* in the flat voice of a medium-capacity compucortex.

"Freeze the viewsweep. I'm ready to mark." The picture on the screen stopped panning, and Olivine marked a small X over what looked like a suitable landing site. "You got that, Ship?"

"Yes, sir."

"O.K., descend. I'll fine down the site as we approach."

Ravi Holbein came on the control deck just as the ship was touching down. He looked at the landscape revealed by the screen and nodded knowingly.

"A Jurassic-period world," he remarked brightly. "The age of reptiles, conifers and cycads . . . or," he chuckled, "reasonable facsimiles thereof. Except, of course, that this world is still in the mono-continent stage, and I believe continental drift is usually well under way in a typical Jurassic."

Olivine grinned at the distinguished-looking middle-aged man. "Right. Another hundred million years and this planet will evolve such higher life forms as con artists."

Holbein accepted the tribute with a slight bow and a quickly suppressed fraternal smile. "Such a world as this has its obvious hazards to life and limb, but can be a haven to a man in sufficient need," he replied.

"Let's hope so," said Olivine noncommittally. It was not Holbein's way to ask questions. Instead, he talked, thus inviting others to talk back. And he had an impressive line of chatter which, coupled with his appearance, had helped him into the friendship and trust of countless lonely businessmen and businesswomen on the long hauls between the stars. And he was an expert at using such friendship and trust profitably. In Olivine's private classification system, Holbein was a con man third-class—a high rating inasmuch as Olivine could distinguish at least fifteen grades of con men.

Icy Lingrad came lower on the same gradient, about ninth-class. Her success was due to her looks and her ability for staying out of beds, not to cleverness. She made an excellent assistant to an accomplished con artist, however, and that was how she usually worked.

"Closrems off," ordered Olivine as the ship's quadrupads settled into reasonably firm ground in an expanse of fernlike grass. "Ship, run an air test. All hands, please assemble on the control deck."

The three other members of the group wandered in. Smiggly Crown, the scarred and grimly silent veteran of the Dusty Roost gang wars. Autman Noreast, a blank-eyed torp of twenty-two years. And lastly, grimy from working around the closrems down in the drive room, Hall Charlo, one-time expert mechanic and current passion-crimer.

Olivine perched on the edge of a console and looked them over dubiously.

"I've had this planet in the back of my mind for a number of years," he began. "There's something worth grabbing here, and I meant to come grab it.

"But not with this particular crew," he sneered, "and not in this ship! A job like this ought to be done by carefully picked experts, not by a rag-tag lot that happened to be thrown together in a prisoner transfer. And it ought to be done in a ship that *fights*, not one that spits on brushfires and specializes in first aid for spacesick grandmas!"

"We don't like you either, you starfuzz stick!" snarled young Noreast.

"Glad to hear it, since I pick my friends with care!" Olivine snapped back. "But here we are, like it or not, and we all need a grab. Let's find it and make it. Then we can cash it in and go our separate ways. Any arguments?"

Crown grumbled, "We should've gone to Dusty Roost. I got friends there."

"A man with empty pockets hasn't got friends *anywhere,* and certainly not in the Roost!" Olivine retorted. "We'll go there, but not until we've got something to cash in. Now if—"

"Hey, boss!" Charlo broke in, staring at the screen, "Look at that dino out there!"

Olivine turned to glance disinterestedly at the image. The beast was a couple of hundred feet from the ship, standing at the edge of the fern meadow. It was similar in appearance to the Earth's Brontosaurus—a massive body on four pillars of legs, a long tapering tail, and a small head riding on a neck that extended above the trees in the background. It was munching slowly on a dangling mass of greenery while it stared vacantly in their direction.

"Yeah," said Olivine impatiently, turning to face his crew again, "you can go look at the bones of similar animals in the museums of a dozen planets. We're not here to gawk at the wildlife, but to make a grab, so let's get with it! I'm going to divide us into two-man squads to take the tenders out and scout the territory for—"

"It's headed this way!" Charlo reported anxiously.

"Charlo, forget that silly saurian!" Olivine roared in disgust. "It's not going to eat you!"

Holbein intervened soothingly. "A grab at this time is a consummation devoutly to be desired, we'll all agree. And it is interesting that an unsullied Jurassic world offers such a delightful possibility of gain."

"Yeah, Olivine, what makes you think there's a grab around here?" said Icy Lingrad, putting Holbein's unvoiced question in bald terms.

"Inside information, from my days in the Patrol," he replied equably. "There was a hushed-up dispute between the Patrol and the Confederal Council after this world was surveyed fifteen years ago. The Patrol wanted to station manned guard ships around it, on the grounds that the local plant and animal life is extremely dangerous and no ship should be allowed to land here under any circumstances. The Council wouldn't go along with the expense of that, and insisted that a few unmanned surveillance satellites would be plenty. The Council won, of course."

"You mean we were spotted by satellites when we came in?" yapped Icy. "You led us into a trap, Starfuzz!"

"We'll be long gone before those satellites make their reports," snapped Olivine, "so cool it!"

"And this controversy between the Council and the Patrol," Holbein commented thoughtfully, "led you to the conclusion that a grab was here."

"Yes. Do you think the Patrol would give much of a damn if this planet were merely dangerous?" Olivine replied. "Who cares if a few thousand suicidal homestakers, or adventurers, get themselves knocked over by a killer planet? Not the Patrol! The only reason for wanting a manned guard would be that the Patrol discovered something here so hot that they wanted to keep it under the securest possible wraps, so hot they wouldn't even tell those politicians on the Confederal Council about it! But the Patrol had to settle for the surveillance satellites, which are enough to keep most people away."

"Yeah," muttered Charlo, taking his attention off the dinosaur long enough to ask a question, "and how did *we* get by the satellites?"

"Because I overrode the compucortex of this ship," said Olivine. "We wouldn't have escaped in the first place if I couldn't make this ship go where I want it to, rather than where its inhibitions say it's *allowed* to go. I've over-ridden stronger compucortexes than this one in my time."

The others were impressed, he could see. To the average citizen, criminally inclined or not, overriding a ship's brain was the action of a master magician.

Finally Holbein murmured, "I cannot imagine the nature of the grab to be found here."

"Neither can I," Olivine admitted, "but I know damn well there is one. And that's my one reason for not being completely dissatisfied with our personnel. I don't think this bunch is one that'll take long in spotting anything of value laying around loose. So let's break this up and start looking!"

At that instant the control deck shuddered with the deafening screech of friction-tortured metal.

"*What the hell's that?*" Olivine bellowed over the din.

The ship's flat voice replied, "The beast outside is pressing against a padfin."

"Well, get it on the screen!" Olivine yelped.

The view shifted to bring the big saurian in sight. It was rubbing itself against one of the erect, bladelike outer edges of the ship's supporting fins. Olivine was reminded of a kitten rubbing against a man's ankles, except in this instance the kitten was almost the size of the man.

"Well, drive him away before he warps that fin!" snapped Olivine.

"I am not equipped to do so, sir," the ship responded.

Olivine cursed and began thinking frantically.

The young torp Noreast headed for the door. "I'll give him a taste of metal!" he said.

"Hold it, punk!" growled Olivine. "There's no gun aboard unless you've improvised something. Bullets would make that animal more of a threat! We need to scare him, not hurt him!"

Noreast sneered and turned to leave. Crown collared him. "Do like the man says, boy!" he rasped.

"Animals fear fire," said Holbein. "That was one of prehistoric man's most useful discoveries, allowing him to sleep in safety . . . "

"Ship, we need a flamethrower," broke in Olivine.

"I'm sorry, sir, but I am not equipped . . . "

"It's got a nozzlehead up top," reported Charlo, "for squirting extinguisher chemicals on fires. Maybe if we fed fuel-cell juice to that nozzlehead instead we could squirt flame."

"What about it, Ship?" demanded Olivine.

"That could be done, sir. The most convenient area in which the feeder lines could be cross-connected is in the utility bay of the third deck."

"Charlo, go down there and switch those pipes around," Olivine rapped. "Noreast, if you can improvise a gun, you ought to be useful on this job. Go help Charlo. The rest of you sit tight. I'm going up to take a look at that nozzlehead."

"I ain't admitting I made no gun," sulked Noreast, but he followed Charlo down toward the third deck while Olivine scurried up the service ladder into the forecone area. He spotted the nozzlehead right away and began inspecting it.

"Ship, how's the outside air?"

"Satisfactory, sir."

"O.K. Open the slits or whatever you do to get this nozzle into action."

There was a soft whine of servos and the entire circumference of the cone showed a crack two feet below nozzle level. The crack widened as the upper part of the cone rose, supported by a central pillar, well above the nozzle's line of fire. "How do we ignite, ship?"

"I'm sorry, sir, I do not comprehend."

"How do we set fire to the fuel-cell juice as it leaves that nozzle?" Olivine explained in an exasperated tone.

"I am not equipped . . ."

"*Damn!* Give me the control deck! Holbein!"

"Yes?"

"I need a welding torch up here!"

Crown's voice answered. "I know where to find one."

"O.K. Get it up here, will you?" Olivine turned from the nozzle to stare out at the dinosaur. He flinched back as he did so.

He hadn't realized the creature was so big! Its head was weaving about on the same level as his own, and with that long flexible neck the monster could easily reach over and pluck him out of his perch atop the spaceship. The dinosaur weighed, he guessed, eighty tons or more.

Why, if it put its peanut-sized mind to it, he suddenly realized, it could topple the ship completely off its pads!

But for the moment, it seemed content to rub itself against one of the fins . . . and that was bad enough. Olivine could see the stiff metal bend under the pressure from the beast, then snap straight when a rub was completed.

The beast was scratching itself! And little wonder, the man observed, because hide that filthy-looking just *had* to itch! The animal was so caked with ooze and slime that Olivine could swear some of the brighter green splotches were vegetation, growing on its body!

"Ship, does this nozzle have to be manned, or can you direct its aim?"

"I am equipped to aim the nozzle, sir."

"O.K., after we get it started, I'll duck below, because the heat's going to be bad up here. You just consider that animal out there a fire, and aim the nozzle accordingly."

"Very well, sir."

Crown stuck his head through the hatch and handed a welding torch to Olivine. "Thanks, Crown. Now clear that ladder, because I'm going to want to get down in a hurry."

Crown nodded and ducked out of sight.

A couple of minutes passed, and the dinosaur seemed to be rubbing a little harder now. The whole ship shivered with the vibrations of the fin as it scraped itself, first on one side, then on the other.

Finally Charlo's voice sounded from a speaker. "All set down here, boss!"

"Right!" Olivine lit his torch and said, "O.K., Ship, start pumping!" For a few seconds the nozzle whooshed air, then ejected a thin line of yellow liquid under high pressure. Olivine flicked at it with the flame from his torch and jumped for the hatch. He moved with such alacrity that the only damage he sustained was a slight singeing of his hair, eyebrows and moustache.

And the flame was doing the trick, as his ears told him. The ship no longer shook under the strokes of the itchy saurian.

He hurried to the control deck, hoping to be in time to catch a glimpse of the rapidly retreating monster on the screen.

But the mountain of flesh wasn't retreating, as he saw in amazement. It had moved away from the fin, but was not trying to get out of the flame.

"Damn!" muttered Olivine in disgust. "I've heard of animals too dumb to get out of a fire, but this is ridiculous!"

"An amazing spectacle," agreed Holbein. "The creature's actions put me in mind of a man taking a shower."

It was an apt comparison, Olivine decided after watching a moment. The saurian was indeed behaving as if the jet of flame were water to which it wanted to expose every portion of its body. The animal clumsily cocked up each leg in turn to allow the fire to play on the inner sides of its haunches, Then like an ungainly kangaroo, it reared on its hind legs and tail to expose its belly.

"I think you're right, Holbein," Olivine said. "The damn critter's taking a firebath."

"Don't be silly!" choked Icy Lingrad in a horrified voice. "Can't you see the poor thing's *burning?* Make the ship turn it off!"

Olivine grinned at this unexpected display of compassion from so unlikely a source. But there was no accounting for the oddities of a psychotic female mind, he mused.

The animal did appear to be on fire in spots—at least to the point of smoldering, but that did not seem to bother it in the least. Probably it was the outer layer of grime, not the skin of the animal, that was being burned away.

"He seems to like it," he told the girl. "Maybe he's bred with a fireproof hide."

"Nonsense!" she raged. "Things don't evolve fireproof hides unless they *need* them. I've had enough biology to know that! Tell the ship to turn it off before that poor stupid beast is a . . . a big third-degree burn!"

The saurian closed its eyes, with lids that looked at least a foot thick, and lowered its head into the fiery blast. Then it ran its neck up through the flame. Finally, it turned around and began trying to hoist its tail, the only part of its body that remained untouched. But that was beyond its gymnastic capacities. It couldn't get its tail much more than ten feet off the ground.

"Ship," ordered Olivine, "lower the aim of that nozzle ten degrees."

"Yes, sir."

"You cruel, heartless *snake!*" hissed Icy.

Olivine chuckled at her. "I'm just giving our friend what he seems to want," he said. "Do you know a better way to get on good terms with the local inhabitants?"

The woman sniffed and whirled away.

The flame now angled down sharply enough to bathe the saurian's tail, and incidentally set off a grassfire where

it licked the ferns. Olivine frowned, then decided the
fire would not spread to any extent, the grass being too
green to burn well. It was producing a lot of white,
steamy smoke, but not much heat.

But as soon as the saurian seemed to have had enough,
and signified the fact by moving away from the flame,
Olivine ordered the jet turned off.

Charlo had returned to the control deck. "I sure hope
he's going to leave us alone now," he muttered.

"I think he will," said Olivine. "Fire ought to be a
better cure for his dermatitis than scratching."

That evidently was the case. The saurian stood gazing
at the spaceship for perhaps two minutes, and then
turned away, chomping on large mouthfuls of greenery
as if it hadn't eaten in weeks. Slowly it moved across a
hill and out of sight.

"O.K., we've had our fun and games with the local
wildlife," said Olivine, "now let's get to work. We've got
a grab to make, remember?" He looked over his group.
Holbein, Crown and Charlo stood waiting his instructions, and Icy had retreated to a chair in the corner of
the room where she was showing her capacity for looking
sullen. "Where's Noreast?" Olivine asked.

"He was right behind me when I came back, boss,"
said Charlo.

"Ship, where's Noreast?"

"In the second deck lock, sir."

"*In* the lock? What's he doing there?"

"He is inactive, sir."

Olivine cursed. "We'd better go see what that crazy
punk is up to. Come on!"

He led the way down to the second deck and to the inner door of the lock. "Open up, Ship."

"Yes, sir. There will be a brief delay while I close the outer door first, according to regulations, sir."

"Skip the regulations and *open up!*" Olivine bellowed.

The door opened, revealing the young torp Noreast flat on his stomach facing the open outer door. Beside him was a stitch-rivet embedder, or what was left of it. Noreast had stripped and jiggered the tool into a crude machine gun.

And there was a peculiar stench in the air.

"*Back off, everybody!*" Olivine yelled. "*Put on your fume filters!*"

He was feeling giddy before he got his mask on, but he had been closest to the door and had got a stronger whiff than the others. It wasn't an unpleasant giddiness; in fact it was pretty damn nice. But there was work to be done.

"Ship, blow out that stench and close the outer door." When that was done, he and the others removed their masks and went into the lock. "Charlo, take charge of that fool weapon. Take it back to the maintenance shop, try to find the parts the punk removed, and put it together again. Then hide it."

He bent down, grabbed Noreast by the shoulder, and flopped him over on his back. Noreast was obviously unconscious, but his face was more expressive than it had ever been during a state of wakefulness. A continual flux of emotions played across it, ranging from restful content to wild ecstasy.

"The little rat's coked to the gills!" grunted Crown.

"Yeah, but whoever heard of happy-powder that makes you feel like *that?*" breathed Charlo, gazing with awe at Noreast's glowing face.

There was a long pause of wonderment as they stood looking down at the young man's occasionally twitching form. Then Olivine spoke.

"Much as I hate to credit this trigger-mad creep with anything," he said, "I believe he's fingered our grab for us. Folks, we must have landed this ship squarely in the middle of a field of super-pot!"

Holbein mused, "It does seem reasonable to assume he inhaled smoke from the grassfire, and thus entered his obviously pleasant comatose condition."

"Right," said Olivine. "It isn't something normally in the atmosphere, or I would have got a dose of it while I was in the open forecone. I did get a small sniff when the inner door opened just now. If it isn't the fern grass, it's probably some smaller weed hidden in the grass."

"Well, let's be finding out!" urged Charlo, a trifle too eagerly, Olivine thought.

"Ease off!" he snapped. "We came here to make a grab, not to get ourselves coked! First, we're going to flop the punk in his sleep-tank and keep a watch over him until he wakes up and tells us what happened. Meanwhile, Miss Lingrad, since you say you know biology, you're going to put on your mask and gather plant specimens outside. Crown, you stand guard over her while she's out."

"I'll guard her, boss," Charlo volunteered.

"I said Crown," snapped Olivine. "I want you to get that stitch-riveter back in working shape. If any more dinosaurs come banging against the ship, we may need it for hull repair. Get at it, all of you."

With Holbein helping, Olivine lugged Noreast to his quarters and laid him out in his sleep-tank. He disconnected the deep-sleep needles, not wanting extraneous modifications of Noreast's drug-induced slumbers, but allowed the nutritive injectors to snuggle into their normal positions around the young man's upper arms as the tank lid closed.

"We'll take turns watching him, if he's under long enough," he said. "You take the first watch, Holbein, and yell if he starts waking.".

"I will watch him like the proverbial hawk," the con man assured him.

After peeking into the maintenance shop to make sure Charlo was on the job, Olivine went to the control deck to keep an eye on what was going on outside. Crown and Icy were in view on the screen, apparently having just come out of the ship. The girl was carrying a duroplas sack for specimens and a pair of snippers. Crown was brandishing a length of iron pipe and looking around menacingly for some life form to test his weapon on.

It was, Olivine mused silently, something of a blessing that the *Glumers Jo* had carried no stock of firearms, with such trigger-happy characters as Noreast and Crown in the company. Not that he relished being stuck with a non-fighting ship with the Patrol on the lookout for him, but this untrustworthy crew was a far more immediate threat.

He frowned thoughtfully as something nagged at his memory. "Ship, you're sure there are no guns aboard?" he demanded.

"Yes, sir."

"But I seem to recall that a small-arms locker is part of standard equipment for a port-service vessel," he persisted.

"That is correct, sir," the ship responded.

"Then where's yours?"

"Removed several days before you came aboard, sir, for purposes of periodic shop-check and testing of the guns."

Olivine grimaced in dismay. A coincidence? Perhaps. But Icy's accusations of a put-up job, plus his own suppressed suspicions along similar lines, hammered in his mind.

Had that Patrol computer rigged this whole escape for some purpose of the Patrol's? Had he been *meant* to capture the *Glumers Jo*, carefully disarmed in preparation for his occupancy?

The whole affair smelled.

Angrily, he thrust the thought aside. There was no point in turning as paranoid as a common criminal! Guns *were* removed from ships for periodic checks, so it was silly to entertain dark suspicions over a purely routine matter.

"Don't you have any defensive weaponry at all?" he asked. "Something we can use if another dinosaur starts nudging us?"

"I am equipped with tangline, sir, for use in riot control. However, for tangline to be effective against a life form the size of the saurian, I must deploy it from an airborne position."

Olivine nodded slowly. "And we're going to be grounded here for at least four days," he muttered, thinking of those slowly cooling closrem bearings.

"Yes, sir."

Olivine got out of his chair and prowled about the deck, in search of some occupation. Now and then he glanced at the screen, but nothing untoward seemed to be going on outside. Icy had stuffed her sack half full of fern grass and was now searching for, and occasionally finding, other species of plants to snip. Crown had climbed the hill over which the dinosaur had departed, taken a look around, and returned.

"Give me quarters, Ship," Olivine ordered after a couple of hours had passed. "Holbein, is Noreast still sleeping?"

"Like an outrageously happy baby," Holbein replied.

"O.K."

He took another glance at the screen and saw Icy and Crown scooting hurriedly for the lock.

"What's happening outside, Ship?" he asked.

"I believe a saurian is approaching, sir."

Olivine scanned the portion of the horizon visible on the screen, and indeed a dinosaur was lumbering into view across the hill. "Hey, Starfuzz!" came Icy's voice over the intercom. "Your fellow reptile is back!"

As the giant animal plodded closer, Olivine saw that it was, as Icy said, the same one that had been there earlier. It showed the sooty markings of the flame-thrower. But now it looked fatter, its belly being hugely distended either from gross overfeeding or perhaps from some internal reaction to the scorching the creature had received.

"Are both of you aboard?"

"Yeah."

"O.K., close the lock. Ship, prepare to use the flamethrower again. I'll go up to light it."

He grabbed the welding torch and scrambled once more into the forecone which the ship had already opened. He started his torch and stood by the nozzle, staring out at the blackened form of the colossal reptile.

The animal had halted less than a hundred feet away facing the ship, and was making strange blowing sounds through its mouth, huffing air in and out in such volume that Olivine could feel the breeze, and caught a strong smell of latrine-odored breath.

Then it began grinding its teeth together in short raspy strokes, making a noise that set Olivine's own teeth on edge. Out of its mouth came a wisp of smoke, then a trickle of flame, and finally a roaring gush of fire!

"Close the cone, Ship!" Olivine bellowed, jumping for the hatch opening but getting another singeing before he escaped the saurian's line of fire. He dashed to the control deck, still brushing his hair for lingering sparks. "Somebody find me some burn ointment!" he groaned, staring at the screen through watery eyes.

Icy and Crown came in, followed a moment later by Holbein who handed him a tube of Kwikeeze. They stood watching in awe as the saurian plodded slowly around the ship while bathing it from stem to stern with his flaming jet of . . .

"Stomach gas!" said Olivine as he applied the Kwi-keeze to his tender neck, face and left arm.

"Without question," agreed Holbein. "Note that the creature's belly is rapidly returning to normal size. Perhaps we see here the source of old Earth's legends of fire-breathing dragons—pictures of such creatures as this having lingered in man's store of genetic memories ever since the Jurassic."

"But how," Icy complained, "could an animal *light* its breath? It doesn't have any fire?"

"Not its breath, its burp," Olivine corrected. "It blew its mouth dry, and then struck a spark by grinding its teeth together. I saw the whole process."

"Oh. But what purpose . . . "

"Grooming activity, my dear girl," Holbein told her. "Wild creatures often groom one another, such actions as picking fleas out of one another's fur. We unwittingly groomed our large friend, after which he stuffed himself with food to generate digestive gas in sufficient quantity to return the favor. Such cooperative survival acts can be carried out with only the most primitive and rudimentary reasoning powers."

"Well, he's finished and leaving," grunted Olivine, "and he's started another grassfire around the ship, so outside activities will be suspended for a while. Crown, take over the watch by Noreast's tank. The rest of us will test the specimens Icy brought in."

In a hastily rigged lab on the fourth deck, Olivine, Holbein, and Icy tested the plants, with the con man serving as a very willing guinea pig. He came out from under the plastic hood after breathing smoke from burning fern grass.

"That merely makes me wish to cough," he wheezed. "No euphoric effects, I regret to say."

"O.K., we'll try the other specimens."

The results were consistently and disappointingly negative. "This is ridiculous," Olivine protested. "The weed has to be here!"

"Maybe it takes a combination," Icy hazarded, "or maybe it's not a weed at all but a soil bacterium."

"We'll find out," Olivine vowed. "You two keep at it while I go get some soil samples."

He went down to the lock, which was standing open. He hurried to the outer door and saw Charlo kneeling in the grass a hundred feet from the ship, using a welding torch to fire the grass and then bending forward to sniff the result. He kept silent as the man moved to a new spot and repeated the routine. Charlo was using the torch long enough, he saw, to test ground and roots as well as plant tops.

"Any luck, Charlo?" he called out.

The ex-mechanic started up with a guilty expression, then shrugged. "No luck," he said.

Frowning, Olivine turned and went to look in on Noreast and Crown. Noreast was still out, and when Olivine opened the tank lid and shook him by the shoulder, the happy sleeper merely grinned vapidly, drooled, and muttered *"Yeah, baby, yeah."* Olivine cursed and retired to the control deck.

Holbein and Icy came in after a while. Olivine glanced at their expressions, and didn't have to be told the further testing of the plant specimens had been fruitless.

"We'll just have to wait," he growled, "until that punk Noreast comes out of it and tells us what happened."

That was not until three days later. By that time the whole crew, with nothing better to do, was spending most waking hours hanging around the young man's sleep-tank, eyeing his supine form with emotions ranging from annoyance to envy.

Suddenly Noreast snorted, opened his eyes, and sat up, pushing the lid aside and looking alertly about.

"This some kind of meeting?" he asked.

Charlo demanded eagerly, "Was it a good trip, kid?"

Noreast blinked and his eyes grew dreamy as he remembered. "Yeah . . . yeah," he breathed. "Damn good. But it was no trip, man, it was *life!*"

"O.K.," snapped Olivine, "we're trying to find out what sent you on it. How long after the grassfire started did you—"

"What grassfire?" Noreast grunted. "I didn't see any grassfire."

"Try to remember," Olivine said with a poor effort at patience. "You were in the ship's lock with that gun you made out of the stitch-riveter, fixing to shoot the dinosaur. The grass around the dinosaur caught fire. Remember?"

"I ain't admitting anything, Starfuzz!" the young man growled. "Anyway, I must've passed out before the grass started burning. I don't remember that. I smelled the muck on that big lizard burning, and that's all I remember."

The crew stared at him.

Holbein said, "Several of us remarked upon the rather weedy patches on the creature's skin, and surmised these were perhaps parasitic plants taking nourishment from the thick muck or from the creature himself, or from both. The precarious position of such a plant in the natural scheme might well lead to the production of unusual biochemical substances for the purpose of—"

"O.K.," Olivine broke in, "we know where to look. Charlo, let's see how quickly we can get those closrems back in service and this bucket in the air!"

The following day, about seventy kilometers from their original landing site, they bagged their first saurian. It was not difficult, because for once the ship was well equipped for the job at hand. It hovered over the monster, discharged a three-gallon charge of the strip-forming mnemoplasic, tangline, onto the beast, and settled to the ground by the giant, firmly fettered form. The beast blinked stupidly at the ship.

"Crown, will you go out and pick a sample . . . " Olivine began, but his voice was unheeded in the hubbub as the entire crew bounded toward the lock. Noreast's half-incoherent accounts of his "trip" had got to them all, even Icy Lingrad. It was an experience they wanted to share.

Olivine stared at the viewscreen in disgust as they swarmed around the saurian, yanking green growths off the animal and stuffing them into sacks, shirtfronts, or whatever container they happened to find at hand as they left the ship.

"Damn such undependable dregs!" raged Olivine. "Ship; prepare a dozen man-sized discharges of tangline.

As long as those idiots keep picking the greenery, let them pick. But when one stops and tries to light a fire or move away from the dinosaur, tie him up! Understood?"

"Yes, sir."

Olivine watched and listened as the harvesting continued. He heard Noreast assure the others that the plant smelled right, and they began picking faster.

Charlo was the first to head for the ship, lugging a half-filled packing carton. He squalled in outraged alarm when the tangline hit him. The others looked up.

"What do you think you're doing, Olivine?" Crown roared.

"I'm keeping the bunch of you unhooked!" Olivine replied coldly, the ship's speaker system carrying his voice outside.

"*Crummy starfuzz!*" Icy shouted.

"Really, Mr. Olivine," said Holbein, "such heavy-handed tactics as these—"

"Shut up, the bunch of you, and take a close look at Noreast," he replied. "For the past two hours he's had the shakes and been in a cold sweat. Needing a fix, punk?"

Noreast giggled loudly and hysterically. "Sure I need a fix, you Proxad creep, and I'm going to *get* it! I got friends to see that I do! We're all against you, Starfuzz!"

Suddenly he made a break for a nearby stand of conifers. The tangline stopped him after his first three steps and he tumbled to the ground screaming. Crown, Holbein and Icy gazed at him in dismay.

"Holbein, Crown, leave your vegetables where you are and bring the punk inside. Let Charlo get a good look at him on the way."

Hesitantly, the two men complied.

"And all of you listen to me," Olivine continued. "We've got exactly three days left to make our grab and beat it before the satellites report us and the Patrol comes swarming. The grab we make may be the only one anybody *ever* makes of this planet's super-pot! Getting hooked on the stuff is the worst kind of sucker's game, because once this one load is gone, it'll be cold-turkey time for all takers! You can take a look at the punk and get an idea how much fun that's going to be . . . and keep in mind that he's just *beginning* to feel it!"

He paused and studied their faces on the screen. "Do I make myself clear?" he demanded.

"Your point's well taken," Holbein replied. The others nodded grudgingly.

"Good. Bring the punk in, put him in his tank and give him deep-sleep. That should ease him through the worst of it. Then get back to the harvest!"

Cowed and silent, the others complied.

Before the day was over, the crops from seven saurians had been harvested, and Olivine was positive that only one leaf had been burned. He had fired that one himself and taken a single quick whiff, to make sure they were getting the right weed. They were. It took all his Patrol training to enable him to stop after that one whiff.

After questioning the ship, he had the weed packed away in the midship lockhold, which was equipped with a five-digit combination lock which he could reset to a combination that was not only unknown to the others but to the ship itself.

By nightfall they were all exhausted—Olivine from the strain of trying to keep four people under constant observation and the others from unaccustomed physical exertion. He confronted them sternly as the lockhold door closed on their final pickings of the day.

"O.K., strip to the skin!" he commanded.

"Go to hell, Starfuzz!" Icy exploded.

"Try and make us!" grated Crown threateningly.

"I don't have to make you!" Olivine snapped. "You'll make each other! I've had the ship bypass all filters in the air-control system. That means that if just one of you decides to sample a little super-pot in the middle of the night, the fumes will spread all over the ship. Tomorrow morning the entire lot of us will be hooked, including myself. Think it over: nobody to play nursemaid for you, the way we have for the punk. And nobody to keep the Patrol from picking you up. It's your decision, lady and gentlemen!"

After arguing for ten minutes, they stripped. Olivine shook over a pound of weed out of their clothing, finding some on everybody but Icy, then allowed them to dress and go to supper.

The next day went much the same. Once in the morning and again in late afternoon Olivine brought Noreast out of deep-sleep long enough to check on his progress. The kid was feeling miserable, but with the help of the sleep-tank's automated facilities he was recovering rapidly from the painful withdrawal experience.

The following morning—the last day they could safely remain on the planet—Noreast was let out of the tank. "Have you learned anything, punk?" Olivine sneered.

The young man nodded weakly.

"O.K. It's time you started pulling your weight. I'm sending you out with the others as soon as the ship finds a dinosaur for us."

The ship found a scattered *herd* of the lumbering saurians. Olivine was pleased. They could move quickly from animal to animal, with little time lost between, and with five picking instead of four they should have the lockhold packed tight by nightfall.

Work went well all morning. Noreast was slow and sullen at first, but gradually brightened as the hours passed. Watching him, Olivine wondered if perhaps the squares were right about the virtues of hard work. Labor was certainly changing Noreast—temporarily at least—from a surly rat into a happy-acting kid.

Shortly after lunch, the happy-acting kid did something very foolish and got away with it. When one saurian was picked clean, he ran to another that had wandered close and was not bound by tangline. The surprised animal twisted its neck to peer down at him as he began jerking weed out of its tremendous forelegs. After studying him solemnly, the beast returned to its feeding. Noreast laughed and yelled at the others, telling them to quit wasting time waiting for the ship to tie up another animal.

Crown and Charlo ran over to join him, and Holbein followed more slowly. Icy hesitated a long time, but finally went over when the saurian allowed Noreast to run up its tail and start harvesting the growth on its back without objection.

Olivine had watched tensely, silently cursing the fool kid. Now he heaved a sigh of relief. The saurians apparently liked to have their weeds picked. Perhaps it was principally to get rid of them that they went in for fire-grooming.

When the animal was picked clean the four men moved on to another, leaving Icy behind to load what they had gathered into the ship. Olivine ordered the ship to lift over to where Icy stood beside the loaded baskets. She gave the screen's scanner eye a meaningful look as the ship touched down.

Puzzled, Olivine left the control deck and went down to the lock. She handed a basket in to him.

"Why the grim look?" he asked.

"They're *chewing* the stuff!" she said.

"Chewing the stuff?" he echoed.

"I think Noreast must have started as soon as we came out this morning," she related. "Then one by one he got the others started. Holbein was the last. I didn't know about it until a few minutes ago when Charlo tried to put me on it. 'Have a chew and then we'll have some fun!'" she mimicked the man. "I know what kind of fun that slimy artist wants!"

Olivine nodded, frowning. Her aversion to sex, he guessed, was all that had stopped Icy from chewing with the others. "I ought to have guessed the punk was up to something," he said. "He was acting so abnormal for him."

Icy handed in another loaded basket. "The stuff seems to work differently chewed than smoked," she said.

"A lot of drugs do," he replied absently. "Look, Icy. We've got enough of a grab now. As soon as we get this load in the lockhold, I'm going to bundle those idiots in tangline. You'll have to help me lug them aboard and put them in deep-sleep. Then we're hauling out of here for Dusty Roost!"

"Suits me!" she sniffed. "I've had a bellyful of present company!" She walked away to get the last basket, then suddenly yelled, *"They're scattering, Olivine! They're running in all directions!"*

He leaned out the port to get a view of the men's position. Holbein, Crown, Charlo and Noreast had indeed taken leave of the saurian they had been harvesting and were rapidly putting distance between themselves and the ship.

"The jerks!" Icy snorted. "They must've guessed I'd squeal to you!"

"Get on board quick!" urged Olivine. She ran to the lock and he pulled her up and inside. "Take off, Ship, and have the tangline ready!"

"I'm sorry, sir, but regulations forbid lift-off while the lock is open," the ship replied.

Olivine cursed and hurried Icy through the inner door. "Now close the lock and take off!" he bellowed.

"Yes, sir."

By the time they reached the control deck, not a man was in sight on the ground.

"They must be hiding under the saurians," Olivine guessed. "Ship, give me full amp on outside speakers and pickups! *Hey, you guys!*"

"Take an underground jump, Starfuzz!" came Noreast's voice dimly and obscured by the noises being picked up from the saurians.

"Use some sense!" he yelled back. "Holbein! You're no idiot! Show yourself and we'll come down for you!"

After a moment Icy pointed at the screen. "There he is, off to the left."

Olivine ran up the magnification and watched the con man stroll out from under a dinosaur and wave his arms. He was wearing a grin that was only slightly sheepish. "Tangline him, Ship!"

"The rest of you!" Olivine called into the mike. "Come on out! Crown! Charlo! You're not crazy kids! Stop playing games and let's go cash in our grab!"

There was no response from below. Olivine called again and again. Finally he turned to Icy. "I hate to leave any of them here for the Patrol, and especially Charlo. How about . . . uh . . . promising him something if he'll show himself? You won't have to pay off."

The girl snapped a disgusted obscenity at him and whirled away.

"Set down by Holbein, Ship," Olivine ordered.

A few hours later the *Glumers Jo* was in interstellar space, speeding away from the Dothlit System at full thrust. Holbein was in deep-sleep. Olivine and Icy Lingrad had eaten supper together in a strained atmosphere. He guessed she felt less at ease with one man than with five around.

"Will the Patrol find them?" she asked.

"Sure. That's the hell of it. The Patrol will find them, and they'll talk. The Patrol will know we've made the grab. I doubt if we'll be able to get to Dusty Roost with the stuff. We'll probably have to unload it with some out-of-the-way dealer at half what we could get in the Roost."

"O.K., and there's just three of us to split the take instead of six," she replied.

"Yeah, there's that bright point." He grimaced. "I shouldn't have wasted that planet on such a crew. I knew better, but . . . well, damn it, I needed a big grab! For a job like that I should have had a man trained in satellite servicing, who could locate those spy-gadgets and nullify their reports. And maybe just one other guy—somebody who could be counted on to put cold cash ahead of a snout full of fix. Six people were too many in any case—too many possible discipline breakers."

"To hell with discipline," Icy muttered automatically.

"Yeah, that was precisely the trouble with this crew. To hell with discipline."

Icy yawned and stood up. "I'm going to hit the tank and leave you to your lonely regrets, Starfuzz."

He sat musing for a while after she left the room, and finally decided the grab had turned out pretty well after all. First and foremost, he *had* the grab, and the Patrol didn't have *him*. If the planet Dothlit Three wound up with a manned Patrol guard as a result, so what? The galaxy was well supplied with potential grabs, after all. Why mourn the loss of one?

He grinned and went to his sleep-tank. Reasonably content he dozed off . . .

And roused several hours later to the strong smell of burning super-pot!

"Ship," he mumbled, sitting up groggily, "activate all air-system filters."

He fell back into his tank and was in too thorough a state of pure bliss to hear the ship reply, "Yes, sir."

He woke up feeling fine and stared at the face of the clock-calendar on the underside of the tank lid. He had been out for three days!

He leaped angrily from the tank and strode to Icy's quarters where he barged in without knocking. The girl was in her tank, obviously as out as he had been.

Holbein!

He ran through the ship and finally found the man in the dining area nursing a large cup of black coffee. Holbein looked up at him with pained, sick eyes.

"Ah, Mr. Olivine," he greeted him dully, "care for some coffee? I take it you smoked whereas I chewed, and there you displayed your wisdom, friend. What that super-pot does to a man's stomach is no fit subject for discussion!"

Olivine stared at him. Was the con artist telling the truth or was he . . .

"Ship!" he snapped. "Who was responsible for that burning super-pot that knocked me out?"

"Nobody, sir. Apparently there was a malfunction in the lockhold, sir. A fire broke out inside, burning at least a portion of the vegetable matter. The fumes spread through three decks before you ordered the by-passed filters into operation."

Olivine scampered up the stairs to the lockhold. He and Icy had been only a deck away from the lockhold, he realized, while Holbein had been in a tank down on the second deck, which accounted for Holbein not getting the smoke on top of his chew. The filters had gone up in time to spare him that double dose.

Fumbling in his haste Olivine worked the lockhold combination, jerked the door open, and looked down blankly at the thin bed of gray ash that covered the deck inside.

Not a leaf of super-pot remained.

After a moment he strode to the nearest ventilator access panel, yanked it off the wall, and pulled out a filter that was practically dripping black tar.

"All the filters will require an early change, sir," reported the ship.

"Shut up," he growled. He lit the welding torch, pointed the flame at the tarry mess, and sniffed the resulting smoke.

It smelled like tar, and that was all. It wasn't superpot anymore.

But *how?* he kept asking himself. What could have caused a fire in the lockhold? And particularly a fire that would reduce a whole roomful of wet green leaves to a bed of dry ash? That would take heat and plenty of it!

He returned to the lockhold and began searching for the answer. Two hours later he found it.

It *could* have been an accidental malfunction, he assured himself without really believing it. Certainly short-circuits in electrical wiring occurred, particularly in portions of ships that saw varied usage, and the frequent tearing out and putting in of wiring for special purposes. A part of an old circuit would be forgotten and left in place when a new one was installed. Then someone would come along and stuff the room tight with a mass of greenery that would slowly press two exposed wire-ends to within sparking distance.

Which would do very little damage to the soggy greenery, except for one thing. The electrical spark was near a fire-control sensor, and had warmed it enough to turn on the extinguisher spray in the lockhold.

And the extinguisher spray was, of course, interconnected with the ship's exterior, fire-fighting system, into which Olivine had had Charlo pipe fuel-cell juice in order to make a flamethrower out of the forecone nozzle! So the sprayers had sprayed a volatile liquid over the super-pot, the electric spark had supplied the ignition, and ashes were the result.

Olivine slumped down on the deck, pressing his forehead against his knees, hugging his legs convulsively, and rocking back and forth.

Damn it, grown men don't cry! he warned himself angrily.

But the warning didn't help. That stinking CIT computer! It had gimmicked him every step of the way! Even to the point of counting on his determination not to be paranoically suspicious of such coincidental events as a prisoner transfer at a civilian spaceport, an easily commandeered ship close at hand, a planet within range of the escape scene which he alone would suspect held a big grab, and . . . and no guns on the ship and frozen closrem bearings, and a crew that was plainly beyond discipline . . .

. . . And as the final result, an event that would give the Patrol all the reason it needed to put Dothlit Three under manned guard, which was what the Patrol had been after all along!

Of course, this meant that the Patrol wasn't *about* to put the arm on Olivine and his remaining companions. Their role was to escape with what the Confederation public would be led to believe was a valuable and dangerous grab of one of the wildest narcotics ever found.

Ashes! And cold-turkey time!

Olivine's shoulders shook.

Polywater Doodle

1

"You're bad news, Starfuzz," groaned Icy Lingrad, pressing her hands against her beautiful but pale temples. "You're bad news, you're phony, and you're sick-sick-sick."

"I resent your implication that we're totally compatible!" Omar Olivine growled at her. He wished she would obligingly drop dead, or at least shut up. He felt in no condition to bandy insults with his psychotically anti-sexual shipmate.

Ravi Holbein, with his usual smoothness even though his voice had a ravaged quiver, put in: "Among the possible actions we might consider is returning to Dothlit Three."

"NO!" Olivine and Icy shouted in chorus.

Holbein shrugged weakly. "It was just a thought," he mumbled.

"For one thing," said Olivine, "the Patrol's sure to be swarming around that planet by now. For another . . . well, I hate these withdrawal symptoms as much as you do, but we must be over the worst of the cold-turkey routine. If we went back, and did succeed in landing and get ourselves some super-pot fixes, we'd just have this whole miserable routine to go through again. And probably in a Patrol prison, without the benefit of deepsleep tanks to make it easier."

Feeling too twitchy to remain seated, Olivine stood and strode nervously around the control deck of the stolen port-service ship *Glumers Jo*. For a while he stared blankly at the viewscreen's portrayal of the starscape outside. As an ex-proxad of the Space Patrol he had no trouble estimating the ship's position and course after a mere glance at the visible blue-giant beacon stars. The *Glumers Jo* was five days out from Dothlit Three, on a bearing Flat External West 14 degrees.

"Let's don't just *sit* here!" snapped Icy.

"And what does the lady suggest?" Olivine asked harshly.

"Sneak back into civilization some way!"

"And how will we do that, with Patrol detectors peeled for us everywhere?"

Icy grimaced, "You're supposed to be brainy, Starfuzz. You figure a way. No, don't. Every idea you have just gets us in a worse mess! You're a put-up job, Proxad Omar Olivine."

"That's a nonsensical lie!" he yelped.

"In fairness to the young woman's viewpoint, Mr. Olivine," Holbein said ponderously, "it does appear that misfortune has dogged our footsteps, since our escape, with a more than random consistency."

Olivine continued to stare at the viewscreen. At last he turned and said, "O.K., we're in this together, so you two might as well know what's going on. I'll give it to you straight."

"Hah!" snarled Icy.

"As an eager young proxad in the Patrol," Olivine began, "I was the willing subject of hours of psychoanalytic probing. As a result, the Patrol's CIT computer knows me about as well as I know myself. It can predict me. It knows what I want, and how I'll go about getting it in a given set of circumstances.

"So it probably wasn't a Patrol goof that enabled us to steal this ship and escape during the process of being transferred from one prison ship to another. It was the kind of opportunity the Patrol knew I would grab. And they knew I would take the ship to Dothlit Three for a cargo of super-pot. And that we would rig the ship's firefighting system to make a flamethrower to use on Dothlit Three's dinosaurs. And that we would store the super-pot in the midship lockhold, where an electric spark was all set to activate the extinguisher sprays which would pour on enough fuel to burn our cargo to ashes, cooking us to the gills in the process.

"That computer rigged the whole thing," he finished plaintively.

"Aw-w-w-w," drawled Icy in mock pity.

"Go to hell," he told her.

"Most interesting," said Holbein. "It occurs to me that the flamethrower was not your idea, however. Forgive my immodesty, but I believe a remark of mine led us to try that."

"O.K.," shrugged Olivine, "so the Patrol has your mind pretty well mapped, too. They psychoprobe con men as well as cops, don't they?"

After some hesitation, Holbein admitted, "If one cooperates with those who ask questions, life in prison tends to be more abundant."

"Slobs!" snorted Icy. "The starfuzz shrinks didn't get anything but a hard time from *me!*"

"I find it difficult," said Holbein, "to see a purpose, a motivation, behind the Patrol's actions. Surely prisoners would not be permitted to escape without what the minions of the law considered a very good cause . . . "

"They wanted to blow the lid on Dothlit Three," explained Olivine, "so the Confederal Council would be forced to go to the expense of putting an armed guard around the planet, to keep people away from the super-pot. Either that, or send in a team of ecologists to do the equally expensive job of exterminating the super-pot weed. It was a political gambit the Patrol used us for."

"I see. However, we've lost our cargo, which limits our ability to perform as lid-blowers," commented Holbein.

"All the more reason for the Patrol to keep us from sneaking down on some civilized planet, where the whole story might leak out," said Olivine. "They'll hold us in secret if they catch us."

"Then let's go to Dusty Roost," said Icy.

Olivine frowned. "I think that's exactly what the Patrol wants us to do," he said. "If they could claim our cargo was delivered to the criminal stronghold of the Roost for gradual smuggling into civilization, it would scare hell out of everybody. So I'm not going to play into the Patrol's hands by going there . . . especially with no cargo."

"A sound decision," approved Holbein. "Speaking for myself, I had doubts about the Roost even when our cargo was intact. While I am not a stickler for law and order, I admit a preference for the companionship of persons who are. Indeed, I had certain expectations that the Roosters might seize our cargo over our recently deceased bodies, as it were, rather than purchase it for coin of the realm."

Olivine shook his head. "We could have avoided that. The Roosters aren't united. They're in gangs, sometimes just one planet per gang, that snipe at each other about as much as they exploit outside commerce. If the right man could consolidate the bunch of them . . . "

He trailed his voice off and glanced around furtively at the others, but neither Holbein nor Icy seemed to have paid much attention to his inadvertent revelation. It wouldn't do to let his companions know what his goal was . . . his dream of power.

Yes, he mused silently, he would go to Dusty Roost. But not yet. Not under these circumstances, which would open nothing better for him than, perhaps, a job as a torp for some two-bit gang chief. When he went into the Roost, he would go with power . . . power with which to gain still more power . . . power to make the Space Patrol cringe in fear, and crawl to him on its lily-white belly . . .

"Then we could have played one gang against another to assure ourselves fair compensation for our cargo," said Holbein.

"Yes," Olivine nodded.

"Blosh!" Icy snapped vulgarly. "Quit moaning over might-have-beens, you sticks! We're on a perch *right now,* and I want to know how we get off it!"

There was a silence.

Finally Holbein said: "The young woman has a point, Mr. Olivine. We are rather thoroughly perched. And, as you have so astutely deduced, any action you might take to improve our position would, in high probability, have been anticipated by the Patrol's CIT computer. A bind, indeed."

Olivine couldn't disagree with that. He returned to his chair and sat in glum thought for several minutes.

At last he said, "I can think of only one possibility. I'll step down, Holbein, and put you in charge. I'll instruct the ship to obey your orders from now on, not mine. With you running our show, the computer's predictions will no longer apply."

Holbein looked startled. "Much as I appreciate the honor, Mr. Olivine, I have never commanded a ship before, and would find myself ill at ease in such a position. It also occurs to me that your offer might be among those anticipated by the Patrol."

"Well, hell," exploded Olivine, "we've got to do something! The Patrol might also anticipate we'll get so balled up out of fear of being anticipated that we'll just sit here, like we've been doing!"

"Quite true," murmured Holbein, "but I still cannot bring myself to accept your offer."

Olivine cursed and stared at his knees. But there was no avoiding the obvious. Regretfully, he turned to look at the young woman. "Well, what about it, Icy?" he demanded. "Will you take charge of this tub?"

"Sure, Starfuzz!" she leered. "If you care to risk it."

"I don't have a choice," he growled. "Ship?"

"Yes, sir," responded the *Glumers Jo,* in the unmodulated voice of a medium-capacity compucortex.

"I hereby relinquish command to Miss Lingrad, with the instruction that you obey her orders, and her orders alone, as you have obeyed mine in the past. Is the instruction fully understood and accepted?"

"Yes, Mr. Olivine. I await your orders, Miss Lingrad."

"Continue on course for the present," Icy said.

"What's this?" sneered Olivine. "No immediate brilliant action to instigate?"

"I'm going to sleep on it," Icy said, rising from her chair.

"We've wasted enough time already!" he snarled.

"Shut up! I'm boss now, and I said I'm going to sleep!" She whirled and left the control deck.

"This should prove interesting," said Holbein.

"Maybe. At least she had a point about getting some sleep. That's the only escape we have from this cold turkey treatment. We may as well follow her example."

They wandered separately to their sleeptanks. Olivine climbed into his, checked the fluid levels in the nutrient and deepsleep tubes, pulled down the lid over him, and felt the feeder needles snuggle into place in his upper arms.

When he woke he was no longer in the tank. He opened his eyes on a cloudless blue-green sky, and with his facial tissues screaming *sunburn!*

He leaped to his feet and stared wildly about at an arid, sparsely vegetated landscape, scorched under a blazing Type K sun.

Marooned! That psychotic wench had dumped him!

A pack of supplies was on the ground, by the spot where he had awakened. He tore off and read the note attached to it:

> *"Dear" Starfuzz:*
>
> *Chuting you into space would suit me better but old Holbein and the ship might have been squeamish about that.*
>
> *I'm dumping you because I can't trust you. If you could override this ship's brain to take it away from the spaceport, you could take it away from me if you changed your mind. So bye-bye.*
>
> *Your planet is called Flandna. You're the only carnivore on it, so have fun and . . .*
>
> *Die quickly,*
> *P. Lingrad.*

He wondered numbly what the "P." stood for, having never heard Icy's real name.

2

Groaning, Olivine opened the pack and found a tube of Kwikeeze. He applied the ointment to his burning face, and in a moment that source of discomfort faded. His other physical and mental miseries were not so easily cured, however. The gnaw of withdrawal seemed to feed on and gain new power from his dismay at having been marooned.

And that dismay, by itself, would have been bad enough.

He couldn't recall much about this planet Flandna, and that was a bad sign. If it was a world people could live on with any satisfaction, he would have heard more about it. From his first feel of the place, he sized it up as one of the many borderline worlds that just missed being livable. Air breathable, but a little too thin. Sunlight, a little too hot, and heavy on the ultraviolet. Water present, but too scarce. Native flora and fauna, also on the scarce side, and probably poisonous.

The kind of world, in short, that had often wiped out human colonies with a delayed and sneaky ecologic backlash.

Icy's note said he was the only carnivore on the planet, which meant he'd better watch out for dangerous plants. They probably had means of fighting back against grazing animals, to maintain a balance of population.

Grimly, he examined the contents of the pack.

There, the news was better than he had expected. Icy was at least giving him a chance to survive, so far as equipment would help.

A major item was one of the recently developed rationmakers, into which any alien animal, or vegetable substance, could be loaded for conversion to edible protein and carbohydrate. It also purified water.

Everything else was standard emergency survival gear of types Olivine was familiar with . . . bedding and tenting, sonic knife, nuclear powerblock, heater-cooler, and various incidentals.

But no distress beeper with which to call for rescue. And Olivine was already beginning to feel he would prefer rescue, even by the Space Patrol, to spending much time on Flandna.

Glumly he reloaded the pack, slid the straps on his shoulders and stood up. For a moment he studied the arid landscape, getting the lay of the terrain in mind. Then he chose his direction and began walking.

The one necessity neither the pack nor his immediate surroundings could supply was an adequate water source. That he would have to find. By going downhill, he expected to find water sooner or later.

The hiking quickly became pure torture. Olivine knew part of the trouble was that months in prison had softened him physically. Also, the dismal state of his morale was weakening him even further, but he couldn't fool himself with fake cheerfulness. And there was the heat, and the low humidity which was sucking up his body moisture so voraciously that his sweat evaporated before it had time to dampen his clothes.

Under this load of misery, his formerly maddening withdrawal symptoms were soon too trivial to be noticed.

And he seemed to be getting nowhere.

After four hours of hiking with only brief breaks, he could see no improvement in the surrounding land. It was still marlboro of the harshest sort. The vegetation was stringy and dry, where it grew at all. He had seen a few insect-sized fliers, but no other animal life, although he had noticed occasional holes that could have been burrows. He guessed that the animals here, like those of many high-temperature desert climates, did most of their foraging and moving about in the cool of night.

Finally he came upon a plant that was leafier than the others he had seen and promised to contain a fair amount of moisture. He stopped, got the knife, a pair of protective gloves, and the rationmaker out of his pack, and approached the plant cautiously.

It made no move, so he took a tentative swipe at it with the knife, slashing off a small leafy limb. The plant quivered. Quickly Olivine waded in, hacking away with the knife until the entire plant was chopped to pieces. He stuffed these into the receiving compartment of the rationmaker, closed the lid, and turned the device on. It worked with a dim humming sound.

While he waited on it, Olivine inflated the tent and carried all his stuff inside. In almost desperate haste he plugged the heater-cooler into the powerblock and flicked the dial to the lowest temperature reading. A gush of cool air came out of it and he flopped down in relief.

In a moment the rationmaker quit humming and sounded a soft chime. He picked it up and studied the product compartment readouts to find out what the plant had yielded.

Very few ready-to-eat constituents, he saw, but a large amount of normal cellulose that could be reprocessed through a second stage into digestible molecules. More salts, many poisonous, than found in E-type plants, and all of these could be dumped except the sodium chloride, which Olivine figured he would need at the rate he had been sweating.

The moisture content was disappointingly low: 3.3 cubic centimeters of free water and 1.8 c.c.'s of poly-water.

Olivine blinked at this last reading. This was something he hadn't seen before on the readouts of a food analysis-resynthesis device—the separation of pure polywater. Usually the analysis process either left polymeric water as a moistening agent in the cellulose and carbohydrate compartments, or else blasted it into ordinary water. This was one of the advances of the rationmaker, which was reported to represent a breakthrough in this kind of device.

For human consumption, however, polywater was of limited value. It was good for constipation, but that problem Olivine did not have. He flicked the little toggle that would convert the polywater into its more usual, drinkable form. Then, after studying the substances he had to work with, he set the resynthesis formula and reactivated the device.

Five minutes later he was nibbling a little block that felt and tasted like salty ice cream, but that had to be chewed and swallowed like a non-melting food. It left him feeling better, though thirstier, than before.

But his exhaustion, along with the dread of the heat waiting for him outside the tent, kept him from going in search of a plant from which to drain a few more c.c.'s of water. That would have to wait until night, he decided. Meanwhile he studied the directions attached to the rationmaker with care, to see if he was missing any bets in his use of the device. Carbohydrates and proteins were, after all, largely oxygen and hydrogen, so why shouldn't such a device be equipped to break these down into water?

Finally he sighed and gave up. Such a use apparently hadn't struck the manufacturers as desirable. Stretching out on his back, Olivine closed his eyes and slept immediately.

The sun was still high when he woke, and he had to wait five fretful hours in the tent for the cooling of twilight. There was a lamp cap in the pack, which he strapped on his head before starting his downhill trek once more.

The Flandnan desert was coming to life with approaching darkness. He could hear the squeaky calls of small animals as he strode along, and finally got a look at a couple of them. They appeared quite ordinary desert inhabitants, rat to rabbit in size, quite possibly mammalian, and six-legged.

He could not catch one. They did not scurry out of sight at his approach, but moved swiftly out of reach if he came too close. Olivine guessed they were not afraid of being eaten by a larger animal, but were cautious about being trampled on. At last he knocked one over with a well-aimed rock, and processed it through the rationmaker. It yielded nearly a cup of water which he gulped down quickly. Then he dumped the nutrient components, which were too dry to resynthesize into anything edible.

Later, after darkness was complete and he had switched on his cap lamp, he killed another and made a meal off its ingredients.

Once he caught a glimpse of a larger animal, also centauroid in structure, that would have resembled an Earth boar, except that it was as lanky as a greyhound. It slunk quickly away from his light.

The coolness, the food, and the sounds of life around him were a healing influence on Olivine's morale. His situation, he realized, was far from hopeless.

All he had to do was stay alive—and the rationmaker should make that simple—until a ship passed close enough to the planet to detect his nuclear powerblock. Two weeks, two months . . . six months at the outside. Space travel disasters were fairly frequent, and an overdue liner always brought search-and-rescue ships out along the liner's route to take a look at such semi-inhabitable planets as Flandna where survivors could be grounded.

Yes, six months at the most, he told himself.

And he couldn't be too sure, with only the light of his lamp, but the terrain seemed to be improving as he marched along. Vegetation seemed more abundant, suggesting more ground moisture. He steered clear of the larger clumps, remembering the warning he had taken from Icy's note.

He muttered a curse at the thought of that beautiful hunk of devious, frigid femininity. If he ever got his hands on Icy . . . well, she had earned all the rough treatment he would delight in dealing her!

He boiled at the thought and his eyes glared angrily as he strode on through the night. The hell of it was, though, that his chance of ever encountering Icy again was extremely slight. The Confederation was too big for that. You met people, separated from them to go your separate ways among the hundreds of worlds, and your paths never crossed again.

And infuriated though he was, Olivine had no intention of ever going looking for Icy, just to punish her for dumping him. Life was too short to waste in search of vengeance . . .

Except, of course, vengeance upon the stinking Space Patrol! What a slob he'd been, letting that crummy do-gooder outfit snow him for so many years, thinking he was king of the universe when they made him a full-fledged proxad! And then had slapped him down over a little harmless payoff! As if a proxad ought to live on the miserly pay the Patrol gave him!

He was well out of it, even as a marooned escapee from "justice", he told himself bitterly. And given half a chance he'd *show* that Patrol . . .

Something tripped him and he sprawled forward, coming hard against the dry ground. Surprised but not hurt, he tried to stand up, but his booted feet pulled themselves out from under him and he sprawled again.

He twisted into a sitting position and his light revealed a ropey red vine looped around his ankles. It was dragging him along on his bottom toward a small flat cluster of leaves six feet away.

So this was one of the dangerous vegetables of Flandna! Olivine grinned tightly as he got the sonic knife out of the pack. This plant was going to find itself prey rather than predator!

He reached forward and slashed at the tentacle. The knife blade skidded along the surface without making a scratch.

Alarmed, Olivine examined the knife. It was working properly, and the sonic edge ought to slice anything softer than granite with ease. He tried it on the loop of red again with no more result than before.

Frantic now, he began jerking with his legs, trying to kick himself free before the plant could pull him into its maw or whatever. But he could do nothing. He was dragged up beside the leafy clump, and held there.

Rigid with terror, he waited for whatever was to happen next. The plant had a dead-animal stench which Olivine decided, with an hysterical giggle, was highly appropriate.

"Icy shouldn't have lied to me," he babbled at it. "She said I was the only carnivore, but you're a carnivore, too. Aren't you?"

The plant made no response. "What are you waiting for!" Olivine stormed in terror.

But the plant seemed content to hold him.

Slowly, the man calmed. He took a deep breath and let it quaver out in jerks. Whatever the plant was going to do to him, it was in no hurry about it. It was giving him time to think about escape.

He looked again at his legs. The red tentacle was gripping tightly around his ankles, but outside his boots. If he could slide the boots off . . .

He tried. The tentacle was bearing down too tightly for that. The boots were pressed in snuggly around his ankles. He couldn't remove them.

For a split-second, he thought about amputating his legs just below the knee. The thought had no appeal at all.

He stared at the plant, and frowned. How did it mean to dispose of him? It hardly seemed big enough to have a man-sized maw somewhere under its leaves. It was no larger than a two-year-old peony bush. Unless the maw was underground . . .

Olivine laughed. Maybe the plant wasn't hungry right now, but *he* was. Why not try turning the tables?

He slashed off a leaf and stuffed it into his rationmaker. The plant jerked, and dragged him a couple of inches closer. Then it became quiet again. Olivine cut off another leaf. And another. The plant writhed and twisted, but it could not stop him. Within a minute, it was reduced to a tuft of stems, the red tentacle extending up and out from the center of the tuft to make a loop that slammed around alarmingly for a few moments after the man had completed harvesting its leaves. Then it flopped to the ground, but did not loosen its grip.

And Olivine saw where the dead-animal stench was coming from. A dead animal.

It was one of the rabbit-sized centauroids, previously hidden under the leaves, and well along the road to decay. Decomposition was not advanced so far, though, as to obscure the marking around its rear midsection where the plant's tentacle had circled it for however long the animal had taken to die.

The plant hadn't eaten it at all. It had merely left the body there . . . *to enrich the soil!*

"I'll be damned!" grunted Olivine in dismay. "Not food, but fertilizer!" What a way to end his career! But in any event, this meant the plant wasn't a carnivore, after all. Not strictly speaking.

He twisted as far from the putrid corpse as the tentacle would let him, and turned on the rationmaker. The organics of the leaves turned out to be about the same as those of the plant he had processed earlier. He stared at the readouts, trying to think of something appetizing to make, and decided he wasn't hungry after all. Not with that stinking animal a few feet away. He converted the polywater to normal H_2O, and drank the liquids. Then he dumped the dry nutrients.

"More fertilizer for you," he told the plant.

For a while then he just sat there, looking at the red tentacle. It took up slack in itself, he noticed, by making a large loose loop, tightly twisted together near the ends that disappeared into the ground and held his ankles.

He tried cutting the limber loop with his knife, but failed as before. This was sterner stuff than the leaves, not only proof against the gnawing teeth of trapped animals but against the ferocious bite of a manmade cutting tool as well.

A remarkable vegetable, that plant, he mused. Real handy with that tough tentacle, almost as if it knew what it was doing. The coil around his ankles tight and stiff as hell, and the same where the ends of the loop were twisted together. But the loop itself relaxed and floppy. As if the plant knew what part of the tentacle had work to do and what part could take it easy . . .

Olivine snorted in self-disgust. He was wasting time admiring the plant's intelligence when he should be trying to get away from it!

And if the plant had no use for the loose loop of tentacle right now, maybe he did. He had something more powerful than a sonic knife at his disposal.

He picked up the loop, bent it double, and shoved the bend into the receiving compartment of his rationmaker.

Then, holding the lid down as tightly as he could he turned on the rationmaker.

The plant went into frenzy. The effect was explosive in its violence and suddenness. The tentacle whipped about like the end of a high-voltage cable, slashing the ground and occasionally the man with a fury of blind blows.

Stunned, grimacing from the beating, Olivine crawled away, gripping the rationmaker for dear life. But he couldn't seem to escape the rain of blows even after he had tumbled half a dozen meters away.

Cursing, he counterattacked, stuffing more of the tentacle into the rationmaker. Through a fog of pain and wrath he realized that his ankles had been released as soon as he turned the device on, but he was accepting no surrender. He kept stuffing until there was nothing left to stuff. Then he slapped the lid shut and stared about wildly, in search of another enemy to attack.

Only when his light swept across the torn hole in the ground by the small animal's corpse did he realize how complete his victory had been. In its frenzy the plant had worked its roots free, and they had gone into the rationmaker, too.

Shivering, partly from reaction and partly from the growing chill of the night, Olivine jerked the tent from his pack, inflated it, crawled inside, and turned on the heater. After resting a moment, he undressed and treated the stinging welts raised by the lashing tentacle.

Warm but exhausted, he looked at the rationmaker, and decided he was too tired to fool with it. He lay down and napped for a while.

3

A light patter of rain roused him. He sat up and looked at his watch. It was ten hours past sunset, and at a rough guess six hours until dawn, as near as he could judge from the length of the previous day. He would have to measure star motions, he told himself, for an accurate timing of Flandna's rotation, so he could recalibrate his watch accordingly.

But right now he ought to be thinking about some means of capturing the rain pattering on the roof of his tent . . .

Before he could get any plan into operation, the rain stopped. He cursed and turned his attention to the readouts on the rationmaker.

What he saw brought a grin. The tentacle plant had held a large amount of water, he guessed in the roots, and polywater also. The poison content had been extremely high, and he assumed it was these unidentified poisons which accounted for the tentacle's toughness. Usable food components were low, and that was O.K. because he was more thirsty than hungry at the moment.

He drank the normal water and decided to save the polywater for later. In fact, if he could find something to store it in, he might build up an emergency supply.

He opened the rationmaker's polywater compartment and peered in to estimate the bulk of its contents. The polywater, in a clear colloidal mass, looking like a sagging glob of gelatin slightly larger than a tennis ball, sat quivering in the center of the cubical space.

But it didn't stay there.

As soon as the compartment was open, a pseudopod of the stuff formed and reached up toward Olivine's face.

Startled the man jumped back. The pseudopod fell short and slopped down the side of the rationmaker and onto the tent floor. Rapidly the globule remaining in the compartment flowed into this lengthening ribbon until the whole mass was out.

While the wriggle of polywater resembled a plant tentacle only in form, that resemblance was enough to freeze Olivine for the moment it required for escape from the rationmaker. But now he realized he had nothing to fear from the stuff. It was, after all, pure H_2O, differing from ordinary water only in that its molecules were strung together into supermolecules, which made it about half again as dense as ordinary water and about fifteen times as viscous. It was "plastic" water, so to speak . . . stuff that had been discovered back in the Twentieth Century and had a myriad of uses, principally as a lubricant since it remained stable and liquid from over six hundred degrees Centigrade down to forty below.

And so what if the stuff had suddenly formed into a tentacle shape and slid out of the rationmaker when he opened the lid? After all, there were dozens of mnemoplastics—stuff that tended to regain an earlier shape—on the market. Tangline was one of the best-known of these. Why not plastic water that was mnemonic?

The wriggle was now oozing across the tent floor—running downhill, Olivine told himself—like a thin, transparent snake. It was approaching the heater-cooler, which it could gum up, and Olivine was about to move the device out of the way when the polywater halted. It was motionless for a few seconds, and then began bending itself. It formed a loop with its front section, then lifted its remaining length, in a series of 180-degree bends, to form a grid standing vertically over the loop base.

The grid was directly in the path of the flow of warm air from the heater. The polywater was warming itself!

Olivine stared in surprise, then shrugged. "O.K., stuff, you're alive, I've got a flexible mind. Nobody ever heard of living polywater before, though. And I can't figure out how you work."

He bent down to peer closely at the highest segment of the grid the wriggle had formed, looking for internal structure. There ought to be a gut, or a nerve ganglia, or a sense organ, or something. But he could see nothing but clear colloid. Not even a speck of lint picked up from the tent floor.

Olivine sat back, thinking hard. Slowly, he began to reach some tentative conclusions.

What he had here, evidently, was about the simplest life form imaginable—pure water so structured molecularly as to function volitionally. And its life process was probably equally simple, such as soaking up heat, as it was doing now, to be expended in maintaining its form and in moving itself about. And also, he guessed, for whatever amount of thinking it might be capable of.

Heat could create free electrons within the polywater, and speed their motion . . . in short, could produce tiny electrical flows in the molecular lattice. So the creature must think electrically, and sense the same way. What it could learn about its environment in that manner . . . well, that would take some experimenting to find out.

For a while Olivine mulled over the fact that the creature's surface had to be a one-atom-thick layer of hydrogen, but that didn't lead him to any informative conclusions, so he gave up on it.

The practical consideration was that he, by chance, had discovered a new life form of a startlingly basic type. Something not even the Space Patrol nor the CIT computer knew about. He had happened to be marooned on this particular planet with a new type of rationmaker that let polywater come through the analysis process as polywater. Certainly the CIT computer couldn't predict something it didn't know existed!

So, he thought with grim satisfaction, when the doodle leaped out of the rationmaker at him, an unknown factor entered the equation of former Proxad Omar Olivine. All he had to do was find a way to bring that factor into play . . .

Rescue came at dawn four days later.

Olivine came out of his tent as usual, then froze at the sight of a Patrol pick-up bug standing not a dozen meters away.

"Good morning, Ollie," came a voice from the bug's exterior speaker. "I trust you slept well."

Olivine nodded dumbly, trying to tell himself this was what he had been hoping for. But capture was hard to accept emotionally, desirable though he knew it to be.

"That you, Coralon?" he asked, thinking the voice sounded familiar.

"Right, old buddy. I happened to be passing close when HQ got the word you were stranded here, and I was sidetracked to give you chauffeur service, back to you-know-where. Are we going to do it the easy way?"

For a moment Olivine hesitated, eying the bug's guns-nouts that were capable of blasting him to bloodbutter, stunning him, or tanglining him, depending on which button Proxad Dayn Coralon chose to push in the control room of his ship hovering out in space.

Olivine shrugged. "I'll go quietly just this once, Danny, as a personal favor to an old pal."

"Good boy!" Coralon's voice approved.

"What about my stuff?" asked Olivine, looking toward the tent. "Shall I just leave it?"

"No. Better not. It's stolen property, so we'd better bring it along. Pack up."

Olivine deflated the tent and began stuffing it and the other equipment into the pack.

"How did HQ find out about me?" he asked as he worked.

"A call one of our scouts monitored at the edge of the Roost area," Coralon replied. "It seemed that your partners in crime on the *Glumers Jo* wanted to get past the Rooster pickets without being shot at. They were trying to explain how a con man and a no-talent doll could grab a port-service ship and get away with it. They had to explain about you, including how they had dumped you on Flandna. Perhaps the Roosters would have got around to picking you up. The Patrol decided to beat them to you, so here we are."

That last, Olivine realized, was meant as a light goad, inviting him to try to make a break for cover in expectation of later rescue by the Roosters. He was having none of that! Despite the "old buddy" talk of Proxad Coralon, Olivine knew that his one-time classmate at the Space Academy would relish an excuse to butter him. After all, to goody-goods like Dayn Coralon, Olivine was that lowest of criminals, the turncoat crooked cop.

"So Holbein and Icy made it to the Roost," he remarked.

"Yep, they managed to slip past us," replied Coralon.

Olivine grimaced. Slip past, hell! The Patrol had wanted the *Glumers Jo* to reach Dusty Roost all along. That was the finishing touch on the Dothlit Three superpot play.

As for whether the Patrol had meant for Olivine to reach the Roost as well was another question. He guessed not. Having served the Patrol's purpose, and not being a harmless small-timer like Holbein or Icy, the starfuzz had probably intended to get him safely back into prison.

Which meant that his move, in putting Icy in command of the *Glumers Jo,* had been anticipated like everything else he had done! But no more of that. Not if he could hang onto his polywater doodle.

Savagely he snarled, "that damned CIT knew I'd wind up here all along! It could have sent one of you slaveboys to pick me up long before this!"

"Sorry to have kept you waiting, Ollie," Coralon chortled. "Maybe you're right. And maybe the CIT held off until Icy Lingrad's call was monitored, just so you couldn't be *sure* you're right. Who can plumb the subtleties of a heavy compucortex, hah?"

Olivine snorted a curse. "Just watch your step, old pal. Don't get out of line, and don't ever consider yourself a free man. Just toe the Patrol's mark like the pliant little saint you're supposed to be, and maybe you'll never learn what a total slave you are to that computer."

Coralon laughed. "Thanks for the warning. Now hurry it up a bit will you, old chum? I have other duties to get on with. Isn't everything packed?"

"Yeah. I'm ready to go," said Olivine.

"What's that tube sashed over your shoulder?"

"Two meters of syphon tube full of polywater I've saved."

"Got a stuffy tummy, hah?"

Olivine glowered. "No, but I probably will have in the Patrol's oh-so-humane dungeons. It was my emergency water supply."

"O.K., bring it along. The tube's stolen property, and we can dump the poly into my ship's auxlube tank. Get aboard the bug."

Olivine picked up the pack and approached the bug with a sarcastic grin. "Ten cents worth of tube and maybe fifty cents worth of polywater to confiscate in the name of the Patrol. I'd forgotten what big-time operators proxads were!" he sneered.

"As I said, the tube's stolen property, old pal," Coralon replied coldly. "If you want to keep the poly for bellyflush, I'll give you a tube to keep it in."

"Such magnanimity!" snorted Olivine. He stowed the pack in the bug, then climbed in himself. "I'm aboard."

"O.K.," came Coralon's voice. "Port closing."

The door swung into place and locked firmly against its seals. Olivine settled back in his seat, readying himself for lift-off.

What he felt instead was a needle penetrating his rump. He remained conscious just long enough to realize he had been slipped a knockout.

4

Coralon was talking to somebody . . . somebody with a younger man's voice, perhaps a Patrol cadet in training.

" . . . Before we deliver him," the proxad was saying as the words became meaningful through the lifting fog of unconsciousness. "So keep an extremely tight lip, Greg. Leave the questioning to the experts who'll debrief him under high-sensitivity microdar monitors. He's a clever chunk of slime, and don't forget it. He might learn more from our questions than we would from his answers. Besides, he has no information we need."

Olivine was lying not quite flat on his belly, with his mouth hanging open and drooling slightly. He resented the disgusting appearance this was giving him, but he resisted the impulse to stop the drool. If Coralon thought he was still out like a light . . .

"O.K., sir," the younger man said "I assumed we would do a routine interrogation, but if HQ says no . . . "

"That's the order," said Coralon firmly. "And after all, this guy's not going to be going anywhere for a long, long time. The experts can pump him as dry as they like."

Olivine remained motionless, listening for more talk, but the two men of the Patrol were silent. Well, that had been a forlorn hope, anyway. Coralon was no idiot to say something revealing in the presence of a presumably unconscious prisoner.

More informative than words to Olivine's ears were the sounds of the ship around him. To his sharp, experienced hearing, those sounds told a great deal.

He was not in a regulation twenty-meter proxad's cruiser, but in one of the giant utility tank ships the Patrol used often as heavy freighters and occasionally as paddy wagons. And why was a top-gun proxad like Coralon jockeying a freighter-paddy wagon?

Surely not merely to pick up a stranded escapee.

No, Coralon's presence aboard a utility tanker had to mean some very important freight was aboard. And the bypassing of the interrogation routine, for fear of disclosing some secret to Olivine in the process . . . maybe a careless word that would enable him to guess what that cargo was—

But what good would knowledge of the cargo do a man in his position? Surely the Patrol didn't think he could grab something as bulky as the load carried by a utility tanker! Nor could he override this ship's compucortex—not with Coralon around, certainly—and make off with freighter as well as freight.

Unless . . .

He couldn't avoid a telltale twitch when the answer hit him. He instantly added a soft snort and gulp to it, then became tensely motionless. Coralon would know he was awake now and playing possum. If the proxad was supposed to bait him with some data, now was the time he would do it. He waited.

All the proxad said was, "Quit kidding. I know you're awake."

Olivine sat up and gazed around dully. He was sitting naked on a cot inside the barred cubicle against the inboard bulkhead of the auxiliary control lounge . . . just where he had judged himself to be. On the foot of the cot was an outfit of regulation prison garb, and a plastic tube full of polywater.

With inward relief and outward indifference he tossed the tube out of the way and began dressing. "It wasn't reg to make me sit on a mickey needle," he complained.

"It was in this case," replied Coralon, who was seated out in the lounge with his younger partner drinking coffee. "That knockout was specifically ordered. We want you back in your proper box without further ado, old pal, and you know our prisoner-handling routines too well for us to take chances. Quit griping, chum. The extra nap didn't hurt you."

"I said I would come quietly," Olivine groused.

Coralon chuckled, "And you kept your word, too. You were as quiet as a mouse."

Olivine snorted. For a moment he stared around, giving a long look at the viewscreen, which was unobligingly blank. "We're on course for Sarfyne Four, I take it," he said.

"That's your destination, old buddy," Coralon responded evasively.

Olivine stared at him, then shrugged. "To hell with you," he said tiredly. "Do I get breakfast before the inquisition?"

"Ship, give the prisoner breakfast," Coralon directed.

"Yes, sir," replied the utility tanker. A deck panel opened by the cot and a serving pedestal rose, carrying a steaming plate of amegg along with fruit juice, coffee and toast. The prisoner fell to it with a good appetite.

"I've instructed the ship, which is the *Barnaby*, by the way, to give you food, water, and toilet facilities as you request, without the O.K. of myself or Mr. Brantee," said Coralon. "Anything else you need will require my approval."

"So the young sucker's name is Brantee, huh?" said Olivine around a mouthful of food. He gazed at the young man. "Another victim of the Patrol's snow job, all eager and dedicated to upholding the Confederal standards of piety, privilege, and status quo." He sneered. "There, without the grace of God, went I when I was equally young and gullible. I wised up fast, but not fast enough."

Brantee smiled easily. "You wouldn't try to subvert me, would you, Mr. Olivine?"

"Not much point in that," the prisoner replied. "You're already in, and there's no turning back, boy. You've had it."

Brantee laughed.

"You see, Greg," Coralon said to his partner, "my old pal Ollie has more than a touch of megalomania. That's why he entered the Patrol in the first place. The thought of being a proxad—a proxy admiral—appealed to his delusions of grandeur. He didn't get the message that, in the Patrol, responsibility has to accompany power. Probably because he doesn't know the meaning of the word 'responsibility.' His idea of being a proxad was to land on whatever Confederal world to which he was sent, make free with his choice of the colonists' wine and women, line his pockets with a bit of bribery or plain thievery, and then—at his leisure—deal with the local crime problem he had been assigned. Hell, by that time, old Ollie would be a bigger crime problem than the one he was supposed to handle!" The proxad chuckled reminiscently.

"I can't see how he would get away with that for five minutes," said Grantee, sounding appalled.

"Because he was clever," shrugged Coralon, "and because of the glamour of the Patrol and that prettyboy pan of his. Women have always tended to spoil him rotten, anyway."

"Spoken like a jealous man," growled Olivine, who was not appreciating being psychoanalyzed. "You and that pitiful mud-pie face of yours. They tell me, Coralon, that even the streetwalkers of Novmadder charge you double."

The proxad grinned. "My sex life is quite satisfactory for a *normal* man, chum."

"But how did he make proxad in the first place?" young Brantee persisted. "Surely the CIT computer's analysis would show up his personality flaw!"

"He made it because he's got ability," said Coralon. "The Patrol hated to pass up a guy with so much on the ball, and hoped appropriate mental therapy and training would get him out of that obsession of his. It didn't work out," he finished sadly.

"Damned right it didn't work," snapped Olivine, "and I'll tell you why! Because I'm not a psychotic, with megalomania or anything else! What I've got is the perfectly natural human drive for supremacy. That's a drive our artificial society with its precious Patrol suppresses, because it rocks the boat. But being taboo doesn't make it any less natural. Look at the most peaceable animals! Look at cattle, for instance, meekly nibbling grass. Every herd has its boss bull, who fought for and won supremacy.

"Most guys are like you two. They let their drives be suppressed. But not me. I'm a healthy-minded male human, doing the best I can to fulfill myself."

"And fortunately for everyone else," said Coralon, "you're failing."

"I'm playing against a thoroughly stacked deck," Olivine retorted. "That stinking computer. Any society has to be sick to make a computer its top dog."

"More responsibility can be built into a computer than any man, or group of men, can possess," said Coralon.

"Responsibility!" snorted Olivine. "That word's your all-purpose pat answer! Look, you jerks, let's get on with the inquisition, after which I'd appreciate some privacy."

"No questioning this trip," replied Coralon, standing up. "That will be taken care of on Sarfyne Four. Let's go, Greg."

"What do you mean, no questioning?" Olivine demanded. "Maybe you can pick my brain for something that'll help in recapturing old mealy-mouth Holbein and that Lingrad."

Coralon grinned. "They're no friends of yours, now that they've dumped you, hah? Well, don't fret, pal. They'll get theirs if they ever set foot out of the Roost."

"Ah, the mighty Patrol!" Olivine sneered angrily. "A guy like me you hound bravely across half the galaxy, but when it comes to dealing with two dozen entire planets full of pirates and smugglers, your bright blue uniforms take on a yellowish glow."

Coralon's face hardened. "The Roost," he said coldly, "doesn't lend itself to quick, easy solutions. Our policy of containment may not be ideal, but it's better than the full-scale war it would take to clean out the Roost."

"Yeah, anything to avoid a fight . . . with an enemy who might have teeth!" Olivine snapped back. "Coralon, you poor sap, those grandmotherly types back on Earth who dictate Patrol policy are making cowardly hypocrites out of the lot of you! How do you hold your head up in public?"

"Come on, Greg, we have work to do," growled the proxad. He stalked out of the lounge, followed by the trainee.

Olivine chuckled, realizing he had got under Coralon's skin. The Roost was a touchy subject with the tougher-thinking proxads, such as Coralon. It galled them to be told to lay off the Roost, to leave that sanctuary for criminals strictly alone, and merely try to blockade traffic in and out. They realized all too well that a policy of containment couldn't work for a sector of the galaxy some forty cubic parsecs in volume.

Left alone, Olivine sat on the edge of his cot and studied his prison cage, not deterred by the certainty that the ship *Barnaby* was observing and taping his every action. Why try to hide his interest in escaping, when that interest would be presumed, anyway?

Not that he expected to spot any weakness—the control lounge cages of utility tankers were constructed to be *secure,* and this one was. The Patrol had screamed with agony when legal decisions had forced it to provide such cages as this, to be used when a single prisoner was being transported, to avoid what amounted to solitary confinement of a lone miscreant in some lower-deck dungeon. The fact that Coralon had placed Olivine in the cage indicated that the utility tanker's lockup deck was uninhabited. In all likelihood, Coralon, Brantee, and Olivine were the only people aboard.

But even if the two Patrolmen were preoccupied elsewhere in the ship, and if Olivine could manage to get out of his cage, the ex-proxad realized something more—much more—would be necessary for a successful escape.

Barnaby had to be neutralized, or at least thoroughly distracted. Otherwise, the ship would simply hit him with a glob of tangline and leave him trussed up, maybe in a bone-breaking position, until one of the Patrolmen got around to untying him and putting him back in the cage.

And a compucortex of *Barnaby's* caliber was not easy to trick or disable. There was no chance of overriding *Barnaby,* already under Coralon's firm command, as he had overridden the *Glumers Jo,* which had a lower-capacity compucortex and which he had found in an unmanned condition. And it would take an awful lot of distraction to occupy *Barnaby's* attention circuits to a point where the ship would ignore the prisoner's actions.

Olivine frowned. He was not ready to admit that he was stumped, but he could certainly see no easy solution.

And his guess about the *Barnaby's* principal cargo—a guess he was sure was accurate—made him want out very badly.

That cargo, nestled down in the main hold, had to be a *ship*. And no ordinary ship. While it was small compared to the utility tanker that was transporting it, or even compared to the *Glumers Jo,* it *had* to be very special to get the kind of handling it was receiving. It had to be a fighting ship of the Patrol, and more.

What excuse was there for one spaceship to haul another in its hold?

Answer: The ship being hauled was not ready to travel on its own. And when couldn't a ship travel on its own?

Answer: When it hadn't been *mastered!*

And why wouldn't the master-to-be come to the ship instead of the ship being brought to him?

Answer. The master-to-be was too busy to make the trip, and officially considered such by the Patrol high brass.

Was a proxad ever *that* busy?

Answer: No, but a *vizad* might be!

Conclusion: The *Barnaby's* cargo was a vizad's command cruiser, in an unmastered status.

It was enough to make Olivine's mouth water.

What other cargo than a ship—a cargo that was its own transportation—could he hope to grab, and thus make Coralon ultracautious in his words with the prisoner so that the prisoner would never learn of the cargo?

Olivine grinned wolfishly. To an intelligent man, a conspiracy of silence could be as informative at times as words.

But knowing the vizad's cruiser was waiting, just a few decks away, wasn't getting him to it. He stood up and prowled his cage in agitation.

The answer, if there was an answer, had to lie in the polywater doodle. The doodle was the new factor in the equation, the thing unknown to the Patrol, to Coralon, and to *Barnaby*. Of that he was quite sure.

Before being rescued from Flandna, Olivine had used his time well, running dozens of tests on the little colloid creature. As a result, he had a pretty good understanding of its nature, its habits, and its potentials.

It had been, without doubt, the "brains" of the tentacle plant that had tried to use him for fertilizer. Not a brilliant brain, by any means, but one capable of keeping its plant form well nourished and watered in a highly unfavorable environment.

Nature had never intended it to survive—like a disembodied soul—the plant in which it had grown. In the ordinary course of events, when disaster hit that plant, its polywater content would have soaked into and been dispersed by the dry soil of Flandna. That would have been death, and highly undesired, as Olivine had learned from the gingerly way in which the doodle had jerked back from contact with the ground. After that, the man had offered the doodle a length of syphon tube as a substitute body, and the doodle had taken to it immediately.

The habit pattern it had followed in plant form had modified, proving the doodle had sense enough to be adaptable. Not once had it attacked the man. But parts of the pattern remained stable, since they still served the doodle's needs.

For instance, it was seldom active when in warm surroundings. Activity during the heat of the Flandnan day would have been useless, since fertilizer-on-the-hoof stirred about only at night. Only when the temperature began dropping did the doodle "wake up." That was why Olivine was confident the secret of the doodle had not been learned by the Patrolmen while he was unconscious from the mickey needle shot. The doodle had been as warm as it wanted to be itself and thus in no need of seeking heat, the inside of the pick-up bug had been warm, as was the inside of the *Barnaby*.

So Coralon could squeeze the doodle out of its syphon tube, analyze it, and suck it into the tube which now lay on Olivine's cot without seeing an indication that it was other than ordinary polywater. Because that's what the doodle acted like in its "sleeping" stage.

But when "awake" the doodle was something else! It could—to a degree—*learn*. It could be taught tricks. It could follow an order.

It could do these things by duplicating motions Olivine put it through a few times, with warmth as a reward. It did not understand spoken language, or any code of tappings the man could devise, but it did understand shapes, motions, positions, and objects.

It could bend itself into the outline of a pair of spectacles—a joined O.O. for "Omar Olivine." It could follow an obstacle course, after having been dragged through the appropriate motions, to reach a container of hot water. It could climb up Olivine's body and out one of his extended arms for a similar reward held in his hand.

Also, it could creep under Olivine's blanket to huddle curled against his warm stomach, as it did one night after straying outside the tent while he slept. This Olivine had not encouraged, because the creature had returned several degrees colder than ice, and its touch had scared him witless for a minute, in addition to being painful.

But now, aboard the *Barnaby*, the question was how could he make use of the doodle's abilities?

There were possibilities . . . one of which was the opening of the bulkhead door in the back of his cage, which would give the prisoner the run of the ship for the very few seconds it would take *Barnaby* to tangline him. Another, perhaps impossibly complicated, would be the shorting by the doodle's body of a couple of *Barnaby's* key circuits. The obstacle course the doodle would have to run to reach those circuits was long and involved. Olivine was not sure his own memory of utility tanker construction was accurate enough for him to train the doodle properly, or if the doodle could retain that much instruction, or that the path to be followed would not pass close enough to a heat source to end the doodle's mission prematurely.

But there was a problem that came before any of those. Training the doodle for anything at all required actions on his part that could hardly be disguised. If he started putting that tube of polywater through a series of senseless motions, how would he explain his actions to *Barnaby* and the Patrolmen? That he was practicing an obscure Plaxadalican snake dance? That he had suddenly gone batty?

Olivine knew all too well that no such explanations would be bought. Not by a guy like Coralon, who had been around enough to be surprised at nothing and suspicious of everything.

The prisoner flopped on his bunk face down, his head resting on his forearms, to conceal the snarl of angry frustration that was twisting his handsome features.

5

Five ship-mornings later young Brantee entered the lounge alone, distractedly asked the prisoner how he was faring, and ordered a mug of coffee from the ship. His mind seemed a thousand parsecs away as he sat sipping and gazing at nothing.

Olivine studied him. This was a departure from the norm. Coralon sometimes came into the lounge alone, but not Brantee. And at this time of day they usually came in together. Neither of them spent much time there—just enough to satisfy the letter of the no-solitary edict.

"What's up?" Olivine asked.

Brantee gave him a resentful glance. "Nothing's up. Have some coffee, Olivine."

"Don't try to kid a kidder, punk," snapped the prisoner. "I know buck fever when I see it, and you've got it, boy! Now, what's going on?"

"What's buck fever?" the Patrol trainee asked.

"Nervousness before a fight. It comes from knowing the chips will be down, pretty damn quick, and from not knowing how much yellow you're going to show. It's worst in squirts like you who haven't been in many fights. Now, let's have the news, kid."

Brantee stirred restlessly. "There's nothing to tell."

"Where's Coralon?"

"Busy. He said to tell you he'll drop by a little later."

Olivine grimaced. The kid was plainly under orders to keep his mouth shut. But a kid can be tricked . . .

"O.K., I see I'm not going to get anything out of you," the prisoner said. "But let's get something straight, boy. I value my skin a lot more than I do your company. So with the ship as witness, I hereby excuse you from babysitting me if there's some kind of emergency that needs your attention."

Brantee put down his mug and leaped to his feet. "Thanks, Olivine!" he snapped over his shoulder as he hurried toward the door. Then he halted suddenly, turned and walked slowly back. "There's no . . . " he began, then shut up when he saw the grin of triumph on Olivine's face.

The Patrol trainee whirled and stomped out of the lounge cursing.

"Tell Coralon I got a right to know what's up!" Olivine squalled after him.

Alone, he paced his cage, his mind working furiously. What was happening? The kid hadn't been faking; no kid could put on that convincing an act. The *Barnaby* was heading for trouble . . . no question about it.

But what kind of trouble?

Five days out from Flandna . . . Mentally, Olivine constructed a globe of space, with Flandna at its center and with a radius roughly equivalent to the distance five days of normal drive would cover.

The globe intersected . . . well, it intersected plenty of places where a starfuzz ship might not be completely welcome, but only one really dangerous zone: the edge of the Dusty Roost pirate enclave!

And come to think about it, where else but in the Patrol's thin cordon around the Roost would a new vizad—field-promoted from proxad—be waiting for an unmastered command cruiser to be shipped out from HQ?

It all fitted together. The *Barnaby* was supposed to deliver the cruiser before taking Olivine on to the Sarfyne Four prison world. But right now, approaching its first destination, it was on the verge of encountering more Roosters than Patrol ships!

But it could be highly deadly. A Patrol ship had never yet been allowed to fall into Rooster hands. If the *Barnaby* could fight its way through whatever assault the pirates might be mounting, or if reinforcements rallied in time, all would be well. But if the utility tanker were about to fall into enemy hands, *Barnaby* would self-destruct with a violence that would leave nothing but a rapidly dispersing smell of metal in space.

Olivine cursed and grabbed at the bars of his cage. "*Coralon!*" he bellowed. "Ship, tell Coralon to tell me what's going on out there!"

"Your message will be delivered, sir," *Barnaby* replied.

"Right now!" he snarled.

Half a minute passed before the proxad's voice came over the speaker. "What's happening is none of your business, Ollie!" he snapped hurriedly. "Now shut up and don't pester me, or the ship. Order anything you want immediately, because I'm instructing the ship to ignore you starting in one minute. Out!"

"W-wait a second!" Olivine yapped in terror. "You can't leave me trapped here like a rat . . ."

But the proxad was obviously no longer listening.

"If you require food, drink . . ." began *Barnaby*.

"Oh . . . oh, yeah! Gimme a bourbon on the rocks, Ship!" Olivine directed, getting a grip on himself. "Make that *three* bourbons on the rocks so I'll not need to ask for more!"

"Very well, sir."

The serving pedestal rose, carrying the three ice-filled glasses. As Olivine had learned earlier, the ship served him no booze, but tried to be accommodating. Thus, an order for bourbon on the rocks brought ice and nothing more. He removed the glasses from the pedestal and placed them on the floor.

Then he waited, counting seconds and wondering just how literally *Barnaby* would take Coralon's instructions to ignore him. Or if the proxad would realize how sweeping that instruction was, and would modify it. Because if the ship ignored him *completely* . . .

He judged a minute had passed. "Damn it, *Barnaby*, at a time like this you could've given me some booze," he complained. "*Barnaby*? . . . Answer me, you misconnected idiot!"

No response.

It was now or never.

He grabbed the tube-encased doodle, coiled it into a tight spiral on the floor, and hurriedly dumped the ice from the three glasses over it, spreading the lumps out to cool the creature into wakefulness as rapidly as possible. He tried not to let himself get in a stew as he watched for the doodle to begin moving. The *Barnaby* was well-armed and strongly shielded, he reminded himself. It would be no quick and easy pushover for a whole squad of Rooster raiders. And so far as he could tell, the battle hadn't even been joined yet.

At that instant the ship lurched and a dull *Thunk!* jarred through it.

Olivine jittered. A near miss! The attack was beginning!

The doodle finally stirred. The man felt of it, judged it to be chilled enough to remain awake for the job at hand, laid it out in a straight line on the floor, and hurriedly began putting it through its training program.

He shoved a tip of the tube under his left shoe, in the space between the arch and the floor, and wriggled it through.

"You'll have to flatten to get through that crack," he muttered at it, "but the door's not sealed, so you can make it. Then, as you come through, thicken out again, and climb straight up, like this . . . " He guided the doodle up the side of his shoe and then his trouser leg, standing up gradually as he did so. "Then when you get this high, start feeling around for a hole . . . " He swung the tip of the tube back and forth in a search pattern, ending at a corner of his pocket which he was pinching to a small hole with his other hand. "When you find it, just crawl in, like this . . . and your conductivity will do the rest, and your old pal will come put you back in your tube and find a warm place for you."

With that he wadded the tube and cupped it in his hands for a moment, long enough for the doodle to feel warmth without gaining much increase in temperature.

Then he went through the whole routine again.

For so critical a job he would have liked to have spent half an hour putting the doodle through its paces, but

there wasn't time. The *Barnaby* was lurching and thunk-
ing continually now, and the battle would *have* to end,
one way or another, within a very short while.

He went to the bulkhead door, unsealed the end of
the doodle's tube, and ran the tube between his thumb
and forefinger from the other end to squeeze the creature out onto the floor. Being careful not to tear its colloidal substance apart, and have to take time to let the
doodle pull together again, he pushed its tip against the
thin crack at the bottom of the door. "Slurp through,
damn you!" he hissed.

Slowly, the doodle began disappearing. Olivine sighed
with satisfaction. So far, so good. He wished the doodle
could hurry it up, but it had to go membrane-thin to get
under that door, and a membrane made a low-volume
flow. He would have to be patient.

He muttered, half-sentimentally: "If I didn't have you
to count on, little trickle, I'd be out of my skull by now!"
At least the doodle was giving him something to do other
than pace helplessly while waiting for the air to *whoosh*
away, or for the ship to self-destruct, or for the pirates
to be defeated so that he could be carted on to prison.

The doodle was, however, as unmindful of Olivine's
words as it was of his hard-pressed mental stability. Its
one concern was to regain a desired state of warmth, and
it had received inputs to guide it to that goal. It continued
to flatten its substance and ooze through the crack . . .
between the warm floor and the warm door. Membrane-
thin during the passage, it soaked in the heat from the
surrounding metal. When all of it was beyond the door,
it felt quite comfortable, except for its lack of a containing husk and that was no urgent need. As it had

achieved its goal, it promptly forgot the remainder of the input and relaxed on the floor.

"Good work!" whispered Olivine as the last of the doodle vanished under the door. "Now hurry up and foul that lock circuit."

Wham!

"Ugg!" he grunted in dismay. The ship had been hit! He held his breath against an impulse to whimper, but wherever the hit had been the ship was handling the emergency O.K. The air pressure had remained steady. "Hurry, doodle! Please hurry!" he begged. *Ker-WHANG!*

This time the lounge lights flared brilliantly for a split second, then dimmed, and Olivine could hear the faint *click-click-click* of power adjustors going into action. The door, against which he had been pressing his hand, suddenly gave way, and he half fell into the passageway beyond the bulkhead.

Free! But with no time to waste.

Quickly he slurped the doodle into its tube and stuffed it in a pocket, not stopping to wonder how the creature had got to the floor so promptly after fouling the lock. He dashed for the aft-tube, slid down to the main hold, swung nimbly out onto the deck, and skidded to a quick halt.

For an instant he gazed in awed delight at the sturdy, forty-meter tapered cylinder of gleaming silver held erect in the *Barnaby's* belly cradle.

It was indeed a vizad's command cruiser!

He scampered up the ramp to its main lock. The seal, he saw, was still in place, evidencing the cruiser was unmastered and untampered with in transit. With a quick jerk he ripped off the seal and spoke:

"Ship, I'm your vizad! Open up!"

The lock opened and he jumped inside. "Close the lock and instruct the *Barnaby* to unload you immediately! The *Barnaby* is under attack! Use whatever emergency procedures are necessary to get us into action without delay!"

"Yes, Vizad. Welcome aboard," replied the cruiser.

Olivine could hear clangings dimly through the hull as he scurried up to the command deck. He hoped the *Barnaby* wasn't giving the cruiser an argument about the unloading. The Patrol's ships, as well as its men, had orders of rank, and a command cruiser was several steps above a utility tanker.

Indeed, the cruiser was out in space by the time he reached the battle console and studied the situation revealed by the viewscreens.

The attacking Rooster squadron was composed of three giant warships—slugburgs—served by at least two dozen twelve-meter minimans—tiny one-man ships which were, at the moment, carrying the brunt of the assault while the slugburgs held position outside effective range of the *Barnaby's* weaponry.

It was a typical gauntlet pattern of attack, used by the pirates when a victim's best hope was to run for her protective destination with minimal evasive maneuvering. The pirates were strung out in front of the *Barnaby*, with the three slugburg biggies holding their distance while the minimans drifted back, singly and in clusters, to take passing slaps at the utility tanker.

Even six or eight at a time, the little attackers could not blast the *Barnaby* out of action. That wasn't their job. They could wear the Patrol ship down, however, by inflicting small but incremental damage, without risking heavy pirate personnel and tonnage losses in the process. When they had the victim weak and groggy enough, then the biggies would move in for the kill.

Olivine knew what he had to do, and he didn't particularly mind doing it. Loyalty among thieves, he had always thought, was a highly nonsensical concept, anyway. In any event, until his mastery of the command cruiser was accepted beyond question, he had to act like a Patrolman, and act it to the hilt.

"Parallel the *Barnaby* at two hundred kilometers," he snapped, "and slash-lase the attacking minimans! Gimme manual on your hardest forward lase and I'll keep the biggies busy!"

The cruiser's laser offensive flared into action, and the beams, guided by the most brilliant compucortex mountable in a ship, did not miss. One after another the minimans were gashed—often sliced completely through—and simply vanished from the scene of battle as they lost warpage and teetered into normspace, to be instantly left far behind.

But the three biggies were too distant, and their screens too effective, for Olivine to do them real harm with the beam.

The cruiser reported: "Seven minimans destroyed, sir, and the others attempting to disengage."

"Stay after them!" ordered Olivine. "The biggies are pulling back, too. Let's bark at their heels! Cut into any of them you can reach!"

"Yes, sir. Reinforcements will arrive in eighteen minutes, and the *Barnaby* is calling, sir."

"O.K. I'll brief you fully when we have a moment, Ship, but you'd better know now that I'm operating under a cover the *Barnaby* crew doesn't know about. So act on no instruction Proxad Coralon may try to give you. Put him on."

The proxad's enraged face flashed on the viewscreen. "Olivine!" he bellowed. "Get back here with that cruiser or I'll blast you to nebulosity!"

"With the popguns that old scow carries?" leered Olivine. "Don't fantasize, old pal."

Coralon glared. "Command cruiser 749JN-10, you have been seized by an enemy of the Patrol, an escaped prisoner. Restrict him immediately and return to the hold of the *Barnaby*."

"My regrets, Proxad Coralon," responded the cruiser, "but your instructions cannot be accepted."

Coralon's look of utter dismay brought a roar of laughter from Olivine. "You've had it, pal!" he gloated. "I'd love to watch you explain at HQ how the hottest ship in space was swiped from the Patrol. I see you in civvies in less than a month, pal. Or they may throw the book at you and give you my cell on Sarfyne Four."

"You heard him, Cruiser!" the proxad yelped. "You heard him *admit* stealing you. Now return to the *Barnaby!*"

"I cannot comply, Proxad Coralon," said the cruiser.

"Wise up, pal," snickered Olivine. "You know mastery can't be overridden like that. And I'm *master* of this beautiful boat."

Coralon's shoulders drooped. He knew well enough that, for a Patrol ship of the line, mastery was a total, instant, unquestionable bond.

It had to be that way. A Patrolman's ship had to be loyal beyond all doubt, and nothing short of death, disavowal, or thorough reconditioning could break that loyalty.

"Your time will come, Ollie," the proxad promised grimly.

"Don't hold your breath in the meantime," Olivine chuckled. "Break comm, Ship."

Coralon's face vanished to be replaced with a view of the battle situation. The battle, however, was over.

"Where did the biggies get to?" Olivine demanded.

"Their retreat carried them into concealment in the Veil, sir. Shall we continue pursuit?"

"Yeah. We need concealment, too, from the *Barnaby* and those Patrol reinforcements. Move into the Veil, cut down to a safe speed, and keep going. Don't chase any biggies, though, if you happen to detect them in that soup. Let 'em be."

"Very well, sir."

The Veil, the starlit rind of the vast cloud of gas and dust that lay like a barrier between Dusty Roost and the rest of the galaxy, glowed dimly ahead. Suddenly they were in it. Olivine watched as the green dot representing the *Barnaby* slowly faded from the rear screen as the Veil substance blanked out detection. More slowly, the stars of the galaxy faded from sight.

He stood up and stretched luxuriously, feeling a contentment he had seldom experienced. He had succeeded, after years of frustration, to an extent beyond his wildest dreams.

A command cruiser!

The hardest, fastest, fightingest ship ever built. Probably no more than a dozen of them in the universe, and his, being the newest, was doubtless the best.

A ship like this meant power for its master. Power limited only by the master's desire and ability. And by his refusal to be hogtied by the goody-good morality of the Space Patrol.

"Ship, it's time I named you. From now on, you're *Castle*."

"Thank you, Vizad Olivine. I am *Castle*."

"And don't call me by my rank of vizad. Simply address me as Olivine. That will be more in keeping with my cover as an escaped prisoner who stole and mastered you. That's my cover, carefully developed by HQ over a period of eight years. As a criminal, I'm to infiltrate Dusty Roost, and with you to back me up, attain the highest position possible in Rooster leadership, in order to subvert the pirates."

"I understand, sir."

"Good. You were not led to doubt my authorization of mastery by the words of Proxad Coralon?"

"Not at all, sir. I am familiar with prison-ship security measures, sir, and am confident that, even during a pirate attack, you could not have escaped the *Barnaby* against the Patrol's wishes, sir."

Olivine gave a pleased nod, then thought again and felt anxiety hit the pit of his stomach.

That CIT computer was still dogging him!

But . . . *no!* Not any more. This time the escape wasn't rigged by the Patrol, to send him off like some automatic puppet on a string to do some errand. Escape would have been impossible without the assistance of his polywater doodle. Which the Patrol hadn't known about. He couldn't have got past his cage door without . . .

Still, the *Barnaby's* power had gone on the blink just at the instant the door unlatched . . . and the doodle had been lying on the floor beyond the door.

He gave a soft snort of disgust with himself.

After all, even if the door had been meant to unlatch when the power blinked, it wouldn't have swung open if he hadn't been pushing against it.

And besides, the CIT computer wasn't that stupid . . . or didn't think he was that stupid. For his cage door to unlatch because of a power fluctuation was too obvious an invitation to escape. The computer would *know* he would get wise to a trick like that!

And above all, the Patrol wouldn't let a vizad's command cruiser fall in his hands by intention. Why, nothing short of total pacification of Dusty Roost could make up for the amount of crow the Patrol would have to eat over a blunder like that.

Having thought the matter through to his satisfaction, Olivine gave the pocket containing the doodle an affectionate pat. "Bourbon on the rocks, *Castle*," he ordered.

"Yes, sir."

The serving pedestal rose from the floor. Olivine picked up the frosty glass and drank a toast to his freedom.

Let the Patrol watch my smoke, he gloated silently. *Or their own smoke, because they're the ones who'll be burning.*

CLOUD CHAMBER

Chapter 1

The backs of Mark Keaflyn's arms and legs were burning like fire. He was laughing.

The combination struck him as incongruous—and thus amusing—so for a moment he laughed louder. At the same time part of his mind was trying to decide why. Why was he laughing? Why were his limbs burning? Why was he sprawled face down on the ground?

None of this seemed to fit in with anything.

Slowly, still chuckling, he sat up and looked around. His surroundings looked very much like the desert Sonora-on-Terra, and the sun was beating down fiercely—which explained the burning of his exposed arms and legs. Absently he stroked his fingers across the sunburned areas, effectively running out the pain and inflammation, as he giggled at the pompous poses of a stand of saguaro cacti on the slope he sat facing.

Probably this actually was Sonora-on-Terra, he reasoned. He did remember coming to Old Earth . . . When? Working with difficulty around the compulsive hilarity that yammered in his mind, Keaflyn consulted his time sense and determined that the present moment was in the afternoon of Earthdate August 7, 2842. And he had arrived in the home world on August 6. That he remembered.

The question was, how and why had he come to be situated here in the middle of a desert, rather than in the city of Splendiss? And what the hell was so funny?

Nothing, really, was funny about his situation, he decided—and burst out laughing again. Because it was ridiculously *un*funny . . . and so trite. It was something out of an ancient wild west romance—stranded without water in the baking dryness of a Sonora summer. How cornball could a situation get? Maybe next he would try to get life-saving moisture by tearing into a barrel cactus. On the other hand, he couldn't spot a plant of that species from where he sat, and the cactus plants he did see looked forbiddingly tough and shriveled.

If he wanted to keep body and ego-field together, though, he had to find water.

He stood up, laughing this time because he had no idea which way to go. The rule was that, when lost in a wilderness a person should walk downhill, that being the surest way of reaching water or perhaps civilization. But as Keaflyn gazed amusedly about, he saw he could not guess within 180 degrees which way downhill was. The desert was flat, generally speaking.

There was a cluster of mountains off to the northwest, however. He could solve his problem by walking directly away from that landmark. At least, that would keep him moving in a reasonably straight line.

He began walking, giggling constantly, laughing out loud when he stumbled or when a particularly funny thought occurred to him.

As when he wondered if Tinker had arrived at Splendiss yet and how long she would wait for him to show up. These next-lifetime dates were often hard to keep, but he and Tinker had made three of them with success. This would be the fourth. If he got back to Splendiss. And if she showed up. It would be a scream if he knocked himself out crossing this silly desert to get back, and then she stood him up!

He fell down laughing over that one and decided not to bother getting up again. After all, he had walked for most of an hour without seeing that he was getting anywhere. And the body felt weak and dehydrated. Why bother?

There was a major difference between himself and an ancient wild-westerner caught in the same predicament. The old-timer would have thought himself on the verge of death, whereas Keaflyn knew that he was merely going to lose his present body, after which he would have to start from scratch as a soon-to-be-born infant.

Of course, an infant couldn't make love effectively with Tinker, which struck him as a howling joke on both of them. He had devoted a lot of effort to developing this body into a real beaut, partly for Tinker's pleasure and partly in anticipation of the work he had planned for this lifetime, work that would often call for strenuous effort.

A shameful waste, he thought with amused regret. His body was tall, well-muscled, and—being of Bensorian parentage—had a blond barbarian look. Tinker would have enjoyed it.

His arms and legs were beginning to burn again, so he rolled over onto his back.

"You still with us, pardner?"

The voice came from outside his laughter-ridden mind. He opened his eyes to seek its source.

A few feet away from him a lanky, dark-tanned figure in a broad-brimmed hat sat on a robohorse, studying him gravely. Keaflyn snorted hysterically.

The man asked, "What's so funny, pardner?"

"That stupid, woebegone expression on your face," laughed Keaflyn. "Not that you're really stupid, I'm sure, but . . . " He stopped to try to dampen the inside of his mouth.

"You got me tagged, pardner," said the man, swinging down from the robohorse. "I've been a cowpoke for nineteen out of the past twenty-two lives. If that don't make me stupid, what does? Need some water?"

Keaflyn sat up and took several swallows out of the canteen the man handed him. The water was cool and hilariously delicious. He almost choked himself, laughing while he drank.

The cowpoke continued, "but stupid enough to wander off in the desert in August without water I've never been."

"I'm not sure I wandered," Keaflyn giggled. "Don't know how I got here." He tried hard to be serious for a moment and halfway succeeded. "Thanks for stumbling onto me. I was about to lose the bod."

"I didn't exactly stumble, pardner. I'm intuitive about creatures in distress. I caught your pattern half an hour back and rode out here, expecting to find a beleaguered bovine."

Through his guffaws Keaflyn managed to say, "I didn't know I transmitted like a cow. Or that I was radiating distress."

"You were," the cowpoke nodded. "You still are, for that matter."

"The hell you say! How can I be distressed when I'm having such a great time?"

The cowpoke shrugged. "Beats me. Except something's wrong with you, pardner. You got hysterics. I've seen nothing like it"—the man's eyes lost focus as he turned his attention to his backtrack—"since 1943, in the war we had then. It was a kid with combat fatigue, as we called it." He blinked and studied Keaflyn with increased concern. "Man, you *are* in a bad way! Can't you find it and blow it?"

"Blow what?"

"The cause of your hysterics."

Keaflyn thought about it with mild interest. It hadn't occurred to him that his merriment was abnormal, but now he could see that another person could think it was. And maybe this cowpoke was right. He hadn't been like this yesterday in the city of Splendiss. What had happened since then?

He attempted to scan the interim, but the line of his consciousness vanished into the vast mass of amusement that held sway in the center of his awareness. There was a vague impression of waking this morning in his Splendiss apartment with something wrong. Had he had a headache then? An ache through his entire body, in fact? That hardly seemed believable. Psychosomatic illness was a problem solved centuries ago! But his impression was that he woke up sick. And then he . . .

That was as far as he could follow it. The line burrowed into laughter.

"You're right," he told the cowpoke. "Something funny happened this morning, in Splendiss, probably. I can't get to it to blow it."

The man nodded. "The name's Alo Felston," he said, extending a leathery hand. "I better get you out of the hot sun."

"Mark Keaflyn," he responded, shaking the hand, and giggling. "You suppose I can stay on top of that robohorse with you?"

"Maybe not," Felston said thoughtfully. He turned to his mount and said, "Hornet, signal for a clopter to come."

"Okay, pardner," replied the robohorse. "On its way."

Felston turned back to Keaflyn. "I still can't figure how you got way out here if you were in Splendiss. That city's usually in Quebec this time of year."

"I feel like I may have walked it," chuckled Keaflyn.

"It couldn't make sense that somebody was trying to do you in, could it?"

Keaflyn roared at the idea. "What kind of backtrack notion is that?" he snorted.

Felston shrugged. "You're in a hell of a backtrack kind of condition, man," he said defensively. "You've been stuck with a load you can't blow. If you were clean-tracked before, you didn't get that load without help."

"My track was clean. I'm a total-clarity scanner. Or," he laughed, "I was until today."

"Take some more of that water," Felston advised.

Keaflyn drank—and began laughing again. "Do you cowpoke from a robohorse out of respect for tradition?" he asked.

"Cows are skittish animals," Felston explained. "Pretty dim and overwhelmed ego-fields, they are. Things like clopters upset them, but a robohorse they can accept."

"How can a cow make a living in a place like this?"

"She can't, this time of year. We keep 'em up during this season. I took you for a stray."

Keaflyn was chuckling over the idea that cows and cowpokes still existed—although there was no real reason why they shouldn't, even in so unfavorable a spot as the Sonora. And Felston was, amusingly, a quasi-religious figure: the Good Shepherd—the Good Cowherd, that is—with the touch of telepathic ability required of a Guardian Angel, to help him rescue lost strays.

With a soft buzz, the clopter eased down a dozen yards away. Felston helped Keaflyn climb inside, then turned to his mount.

"I'll be gone for a while, Hornet. Tell Holmon. And mosey on home."

"Okay, pardner," the robohorse replied.

Felston boarded the clopter and sat down beside Keaflyn. "Destination is the city of Splendiss," he directed.

"Yes, sir," the clopter responded as it lifted off and climbed toward the northeast.

Keaflyn was laughing with childlike delight at the coolness in the clopter. Felston got out a food pack, and his passenger laughed around mouthfuls at the deliciousness of it.

The cowpoke was frowning worriedly. "Nothing you can do to stop that?" he asked.

"I don't think so," giggled Keaflyn, "but why bother?"

"So we can talk."

"I can talk and laugh at the same time," Keaflyn replied, demonstrating his point.

"Okay," Felston sighed. "What I wanted to tell you is that Splendiss parks here in the Sonora for three weeks every year. That's in the spring when the flowers are blooming. The city's site is usually about two hundred miles south of where I found you."

Keaflyn nodded agreeably to that information, diverted mirthfully because he could tell the cowpoke was making a point of some kind, which he didn't get at all.

"The thing is," Felston went on, "that the regular residents of Splendiss would know the Sonora. One of them would know that a man dumped without water where I found you would wind up lizard bait."

"But I didn't," Keaflyn chuckled. "You did find me."

"Sure, but the Splendiss folks don't know about me. I don't advertise as a telepath. So when they ask, let's just say I happened to stumble onto you."

"Okay, I'll keep your secret, Alo," Keaflyn said reassuringly, pleased that he had managed to recall the cowpoke's first name.

"Good, Mark. But I want you to think about who in Splendiss would want to do you in."

"Oh, that. Nobody, of course." Was this cowpoke some kind of crazy throwback? he wondered. Mustering a moment of fragile gravity, he said, "You've been a cow-poke for too many lives, Alo. Your thinking was bucolic. Cities haven't been dens of iniquity for centuries. The sanity of humanity is universal. People don't kill people anymore." Then he laughed at his pomposity.

. "In your case, I'd say somebody sure tried," answered Felston.

Keaflyn's attention was no longer on the cowpoke, however. The clopter's communicator had caught his eye, and it occurred to him that he wanted to make a call. He switched on the communicator and said, "Splendiss directory, please."

"What are you up to?" demanded Felston. "You shouldn't let anybody know—"

"Yes, sir," the robovoice of the Splendiss directory came from the speaker.

"Do you have an arrival coded 'Tinker'?" gurgled Keaflyn.

"Yes, sir, as of noon today, sir."

"Fine! This is Mark Keaflyn, coded 'Jack.' Admit Tinker to my apartment and tell her I'll be there shortly. Out."

"Yes, sir."

Felston said, "Maybe now whoever's after your hide knows he's got to try again."

"You've got a one-track mind, friend," Keaflyn laughed. "A one-track backtrack mind, that is."

Felston shrugged. "Have it your way, Mark. It's no news to me that murder's a habit humanity's broken. Wrecking sanity's another one. The evidence is still there that your mind has been tampered with—by an expert, I'd say—and you were left in the desert to die. You can giggle all you please about how impossible that is, but it's what the facts indicate. And if you don't mind, I'll stick around till the whole thing is settled."

There was a grim anger in Felston's tone that cut through to Keaflyn's attention for an instant. "The Guardian Angel sounds like an Avenging Angel," he remarked gaily.

Quietly Felston said, "I've worked with cattle for a long time, Mark, also with real horses back in the early days. My telepathy isn't much, but it's enough for me to know the ego-fields of the so-called dumb animals. One thing I'm sure of is that those ego-fields were once as powerful as you or me. They've been beaten down, degraded, overwhelmed, and overloaded over the trilleniums to the point where they can't be people anymore."

"Dispirited spirits, huh?" joked Keaflyn.

"Right," Felston agreed seriously. "So totally broken that they're beyond help. Maybe still lower bodyforms have ego-fields even more completely smashed; I don't know, because I can't feel them." He turned his head to fix Keaflyn with hard eyes. "Anyway, I've touched enough degraded ego-fields to know damn well that I despise anybody or anything that would knowingly damage sanity—push an ego-field one inch in the downward direction. Somebody's done that to you. I want to know who."

"Don't stare at *me*," Keaflyn giggled. "I didn't do it." After a moment he guffawed loudly. "What will you do when you find the villain? Murder him?"

Felston's fists clenched, but he said nothing. The clopter glided down to Splendiss, was guided to Keaflyn's apartment, and snuggled against the outer wallport. The port opened when Keaflyn said his name, and he and Felston stepped through.

Standing in the center of the room was a girl perhaps eleven years old and a man of about forty-five.

"I'm Clav Didorik," said the man in a deep, brusque voice that matched his large form. "Which of you is Jack?"

"That's me," chuckled Keaflyn.

"This is my daughter, Marianne Didorik—Tinker."

Keaflyn gazed down at the little girl, his grin broadening until it turned into peals of laughter. He sat down in the nearest chair and continued to roar.

Tinker came and leaned against his shoulder. "I'm awfully sorry, Jack," she said. "The body I meant to meet you in this time got killed. When it was nine years old, it was caught in the *Brobdinagia* disaster. You heard about that, didn't you?"

Keaflyn nodded weakly. The *Brobdinagia* disaster was well-known, since interstellar liners blew up so seldom.

"Well, I got born again as quickly as I could," Tinker said, "and Daddy brought me to Terra, so I could keep our date and explain things to you . . . Can't you quit laughing, Jack? I *said* I'm sorry! It was something I couldn't help!"

Again Keaflyn nodded, unable to speak coherently.

Clav Didorik said jovially, "The little girl had a bad time of it in that *Brobdinagia* mess. You guys remember how we used to say, 'Old Mike was lucky; he never knew what hit him'?"

"I've had my share of deaths like that," replied Felston. "They're the worst kind. Unless you see death coming and can get out of the body a few minutes or seconds before it hits . . ."

"Well, Marianne—Tinker—couldn't on the *Brobdi-nagia*," said Didorik. "She was in her little body through the whole damned death-experience. Took her a couple of years of this babyhood to get over it."

Felston made a sympathetic grunt and introduced himself.

Didorik was plainly getting impatient with Keaflyn's behavior.

"Look here, Jack—Keaflyn," he growled, "quit acting like somebody out of Shakespeare. I'm sure Marianne doesn't find this so damned funny."

Felston said, "Somebody hit him with a load he can't blow, Didorik. It evidently happened here this morning. After that, he was dumped in the middle of Sonora to die."

Didorik stared at the cowpoke. "This a joke, man?"

"No."

After gazing at Keaflyn for a moment, Didorik moved quickly to the apartment's communicator. "Get me Emergency Headquarters!" he barked into it. And a moment later: "Emergency? Get an investigative squad over here, will you? Looks like you've got a case of mind-tampering and attempted murder on your hands!"

Chapter 2

Finding Tinker as a cute but definitely pre-sex little girl, plus the excited stirring about in the apartment of Didorik, the Emergencymen, and Felston—the whole situation left Keaflyn in a state of pleasant-seeming confusion. It was very amusing.

"What's your profession, Mr. Keaflyn?" asked an Emergencyman with a notepad.

"Scientist."

"Okay." The man wrote. "What field?"

"Stabilities. I'm investigating stabilities. And I'm not one, myself," he answered.

The man didn't think the joke was as funny as Keaflyn did. "You mean things like the Resistant Globe of Bensor-on-Bensor?"

"I cut my teeth on that one, intellectually speaking. I was born on Bensor this time."

"Okay. Who's opposed to your work with stabilities?"

That question was so funny that Keaflyn merely laughed instead of trying to answer.

"All right, who's opposed to your meeting Marianne Didorik, then?" the man persisted.

"Her pop seems cool to the idea," he answered, grinning roguishly at the listening Clav Didorik.

With an annoyed frown, Didorik put in, "I brought the child all the way from Danolae, to meet this man at the time and place they previously set. The only thing I'm opposed to is leaving her with him. If she likes, she can make another date to meet him somewhere eight years from now."

Keaflyn chuckled at how seriously everybody was taking everything.

The Emergencyman asked him some more questions, then moved on to Felston, and Keaflyn's attention wandered.

Some time after that he was being questioned again, this time by Tinker. She was perched on a stool in front of him, her tiny hands grasping his, and a determined, businesslike expression on her pixyish face.

"What happened this morning, Jack?" she was demanding. "What's the first thing you remember?"

"I woke up. Eureka! I woke up!"

"Okay, then what?"

"Probably breakfast. Habit of mine from way back. I always eat breakfast."

"No probablies allowed, Jack. I want you to *remember* waking up. Do you?"

"Oh, all right, I remember." Tinker could be a killjoy at times, he had to admit, even though there was true and durable ego-field *affinity* between them.

"Fine. *What* do you remember?"

"Well . . . I didn't feel good. Achy and despondent. I'm making that up, of course. I haven't had a psychosomatic pain for thirteen lifetimes."

"Okay, you were achy and despondent," said Tinker. "What did you do about it?"

Keaflyn squirmed but couldn't bring himself to pull his hands free of hers.

"Scanned myself, I suppose, to see if there was an unblown trauma lurking on my backtrack."

"Don't suppose. *Remember!*" she insisted.

"Okay, I scanned my backtrack."

"What did you find?"

"Nothing, of course," he laughed. "You know very well, honey, I've been total-clarity for four lives now. Each and all of my trillions of years are pure as the snows of Kalobang."

"You scanned and were still achy and despondent when you finished?"

Her insistent eyes made him think about it. "Yes, I was still hurting."

"Okay, what did you do about it then?"

What did he do? What could he tell her? Let's see. What would he have done under such circumstances? Oh, sure!

"I called the city's directory and asked for a medic," he said brightly. "Thought maybe the condition was something purely physical, like a germ or ingested poison."

The Emergencymen behind Tinker were suddenly in motion. Keaflyn was vaguely aware of one of them going to the comm to check with the directory on what he had just said—which would, of course, explode the whole fantasy he was concocting for Tinker's amusement. Why didn't she look amused?

"Did you see a medic?" asked Tinker.

"Not in person. Just a commscreen consultation," he replied, wondering how he thought that up so quickly.

"What was his name?"

He was tempted to say "Smith," but that was so obviously the first name that might pop into his head that Tinker would surely suspect it. He was trying to find a convincing variation of Smith when the Emergencyman who had been on the comm returned and reported to the others, "The directory verifies that he asked for a medic at 7:17 this morning. A screen consultation was arranged with Dr. Arnod Smath."

"Smath," Keaflyn echoed. "That's right. Smath."

"Okay," the chief Emergencyman was ordering. "Get in touch with Smath. Ask him to come over here."

Didorik told his daughter, "You can quit now, dear."

"No, let her continue," said the Emergencyman. "She's doing fine."

"But neither of them is liking it!" protested Didorik.

"I know, but she's helping him. Notice how he's not laughing so constantly now?"

That was true, Keaflyn realized. He was still highly amused and filled with laughter, but right now it sufficed to display his feelings with a broad fixed smile.

Tinker's eyes and voice were demanding again, "What was said in your screen consultation with Dr. Smath?"

"Oh, I told him about my aches and pains," Keaflyn said with a soft chuckle, "and that it must be physical. He asked me . . . he asked about emotional swerves, and I told him I was despondent, and then . . ." Keaflyn blinked and became silent.

"Okay, and then?"

"I told him I was despondent, and . . ."

"That!" snapped Tinker, watching him closely as he thought about it. "*That!* What is it?"

"Oh, nothing much. The doc annoyed me by starting to talk flat, like I was a directory or some other kind of robot. He went out of high-comm."

Keaflyn was fairly sure now he wasn't inventing this. The directory had verified his call for a medic, and he had a picture in his mind of Smath's face.

"Why did you think he did that?" Tinker asked.

"I don't know . . . maybe that he had decided I was sicker than I realized, and that he was trying to hide the bad news from me by talking flat."

"Then what?"

"I can't remember."

"Did he prescribe any treatment?"

"Well, he told me to eat breakfast."

"Did he tell you anything else?"

"I don't know . . . Please, Tinker dear, you run along home now with your father and meet me at the Resistant Globe in Bensor City on August 1, 2850. Okay?"

Tinker flickered distress but repeated firmly, "Did he tell you anything else?"

After a long pause, Keaflyn said, "He told me to come to his exam lab."

"Did you go?"

"I think so. Yes."

"How did you go?"

"By groundcar and up the elevator when I got there."

"Then what happened?"

For several minutes Keaflyn sat silent and grinning. Tinker was eyeing him closely and clutching his hands, but she was getting no indications of meaningful thoughts to steer him into.

Finally Keaflyn laughed. "End of the line, honeybabe. It vanishes into a big glob of joy, right in the middle of my head! That's all there is."

Tinker released his hands and turned to face the Emergencyman who had been giving orders. "That's all," she said with finality.

"Okay, until we can get him into the hands of an expert," the man responded.

"*I'm* an expert," she shot back, "and have been since the late 20th Century. And I say nothing more can be done for him! Surely you know what's happened to him, don't you?"

The Emergencyman shook his head uncertainly.

"He's been given a pleasure overload. That is something that can be even more traumatic than pain in sufficient dosage. What's worse, it can't be blown if the load is kept on long enough. Since the ego-field doesn't want to give up pleasure—" She broke off suddenly and turned to face a window. After a moment she turned back. "No, I'll cry about him later. Now I have to make sure you leave him be, and find out who's responsible."

"A pleasure overload," the Emergencyman muttered questioningly.

"It's done electronically," said Tinker. "The ego-field is held inside the skull and certain nerve channels are artificially stimulated. It takes special equipment."

"But there's nothing like that on my backtrack," the man protested.

"You wouldn't be here if there was . . . if you were the victim." Tinker hid her face in her hands for a moment, then went on in a shaky voice. "An ego-field with . . . that kind of load . . . can go in only one direction. Down."

"Sub-human," grunted Felston.

"Y-yes. It hasn't happened very often. When somebody wanted to damage somebody else, they almost always wanted to do it with pain. But there's one instance on my backtrack—I mean, I saw it being done to somebody else. It's in the textbooks if you don't want to take my word."

"Okay," snapped the Emergencyman, turning to his associate who was still on the comm. "Parlo, haven't you reached Dr. Smath yet?"

"Not yet, Dawsett, and I'm not sure I'm going to. He may have cleared out of here. I've been checking his background. Do you know who the Sect Dualers are?"

"They're an organized group that believes contralife is real and threatening," Dawsett replied. "Is Smath a member?"

"Yeah. Suppose there's any connection?" Dawsett frowned. "According to Keaflyn, Smath began talking flat after Keaflyn told him about feeling despondent. If the illness had been physical, Smath knew, it wouldn't give that feeling to a man with a cleaned backtrack. And Keaflyn couldn't find a psychosomatic source for the illness. With both physical and traumatic sources ruled out, Smath would, as a Sect Dualer, be inclined to think the cause was a contralife invasion of Keaflyn. He would shift into flat talk if this notion gave him intentions he wanted to conceal from Keaflyn."

"What kind of intentions?" growled Felston as the Emergencyman hesitated.

Dawsett shrugged and pointed to Keaflyn.

"Well, you see what's happened to him. Call it exorcism of a demon if you like. If there's such a thing as contralife, the theory is that it would react to pleasure as we react to pain. Give Keaflyn a pleasure load and the contralife entity would get out. Make the load permanent and the entity would stay out."

Clav Didorik exploded, "In this day and age? A witch doctor who would drive a patient mad and dump him somewhere to die? I can't buy that, Dawsett!"

The Emergencyman grinned without humor. "No crazy doctors today, huh? No murderers, no mind-wreckers? I'd agree with you, Didorik, except for one thing: Keaflyn's condition. He was a sane man; now he's a hysteric. And according to your daughter, he's doomed to stay that way, or get worse, through such lives as he has to come.

"Of course, it's still supposition on my part that Smath is the responsible party, but let's continue to assume it for the present. Would he have to be psychotic to do something like this? And if so, how do we account for the existence of a psychotic human in the year 2842, especially a psychotic medic?

"The answer," he went on, "is that Smath is not psychotic; he's a Sect Dualer. As such, he would see perfectly sound reasons to use any effective means to defeat a contralife impingement on our universe."

"But the whole idea of a negative universe, with contralife inhabitants trying to destroy our own," rumbled Didorik, "—that's crazy on its face!"

The Emergencyman shrugged. "I'm inclined to agree with you again. So would almost everyone else. But the Sect Dualers consider the evidence of an inhabited negative universe convincing. It is a minority viewpoint, certainly, but one based on theory, and perhaps on backtrack experience, not on a difference in sanity. If Smath did this, he did it for the highest motives—the protection of humanity and humanity's universe."

"I'd like to bloody him up," growled Felston, "also for the highest motives."

Keaflyn, who had been grinning quietly for several minutes, burst out laughing, because they were talking about him as if he weren't present. Also, Dawsett's reconstruction of what had happened to him sounded vaguely familiar, as if it were something that might have happened, if only he could recall it . . . In any case he needed to react to it, and laughter was the only reaction readily available.

The others watched him until he became silent again. Then Tinker rushed into the next room and closed the door behind her. Keaflyn considered following her, because someone should explain to her that he hadn't really been harmed, that in fact he felt fine, that there was no reason for tears. But Didorik brought up an amusing point just then.

"The hell of it is, if Smath's responsible, an informal bloodying-up is all that can be done to him. Crimes like this don't exist now, so there are no laws and no punishment. Right?"

Dawsett nodded. "Laws and punishment lost applicability centuries ago. How do you do justice to an ego-field? Fortunately, the question seldom comes up. Mr. Felston could vent his anger in the physical abuse of Smath's body, of course, but even a fatal beating would be a triviality to the ego-field, hardly likely to make it change its viewpoint. It would merely give Mr. Felston a certain satisfaction."

"To hell with it," grunted the cowpoke defeatedly. He flopped down in a chair. "Besides, even though I'm not a Sect Dualer, I think they might be right. It seems to me that this universe of ours has a damn sight more beat-down ego-fields than anybody can account for. Our backtracks show us several trillion years of mighty ugly stuff, I admit, but it wasn't enough to reduce us to cows, or dogs, or insects, or trees. Still; sometime, somewhere, an awful lot of ego-fields were reduced to those levels. I just don't see how ego-fields could give each other that hard a time. It has to be some kind of outside enemy . . ."

"Maybe those low-level ego-fields were low to start with," suggested one of the Emergencymen.

Felston glared at him. "You work with bovines for a few lifetimes, friend. Get really acquainted with them. Then you come tell me that and I might listen to you."

"This isn't finding Smath," said Dawsett, "or determining precisely what was done to Keaflyn, and why and by whom. Mr. Didorik, will you accept authority here while we continue our investigation elsewhere?"

"Certainly, but only for a few hours. I want to get my daughter out of here pretty soon. This kind of situation isn't too good for an eleven-year-old body, you know."

Dawsett nodded. "Hang on through the night," he requested. "We should have everything wrapped up by morning. Help Keaflyn to sleep if you can."

Suddenly realizing he was bored by all this seriousness and stiff formality, Keaflyn stood up. It was time to straighten things out, starting with Tinker. While the Emergencymen were leaving, he went into the room where she was sprawled face down on a relaxer and sat beside her, stroking her dark red hair gently.

"You're taking this all wrong, Tinker," he murmured. "I'm feeling fine. Our only problem is our difference in body-age, and that's purely temporary. In a few lifetimes we can get our ages back in synch again. Even so, we'll do all right in this one. In six years you'll be seventeen and I'll be thirty-one, and you know how sexy a dirty old man can be. In the meantime, you'll be busy growing up, and I've got plenty of work to do."

Tinker raised her small, tear-stained face to regard him with large and sad eyes. "Oh, Jack!" she choked. "Can't you understand at all? Don't you know you're radiating distress so strong I can feel it even without holding your hands? And didn't you listen to what I was saying? The kind of trauma that horrible doctor loaded you with can't be blown. It gets worse! It makes you susceptible to accumulation of more traumas, which cluster around the first. Nobody who was ever loaded with a pleasure-impress like yours is living today as a human! Don't you see what that means, Jack?"

Keaflyn chuckled. "Okay, a few lifetimes from now I might be one of Felston's bovines. What's so bad about that? Of course I'll miss you, but we can't have everything, can we?"

"This is like dying used to be," she sobbed, "back when we thought death was final. I'd forgotten how awful it was to lose someone completely."

Tinker could be very stubborn, Keaflyn reflected with amused chagrin. "Look!" he said suddenly. "Since I'm the first real hysteric in centuries, think what I can offer to mental science as an experimental subject. How do you *know* a pleasure-impress like mine can't be cleaned up? Instead of mourning over me, you ought to get that little noggin of yours busy figuring out how to cure me. Think what a contribution to science that would be!"

She blinked and wiped her eyes. "Well, it's better than crying, anyway," she said thoughtfully. "I don't think it's ever been done in the history of the universe. But it's worth trying. Just don't get your hopes too high, Jack, because I and the others I can interest in working on it might fail."

He laughed. "I don't need any hopes. I'm doing fine!" She almost clouded up again when he said that, he noticed with puzzlement. But then she managed a weak smile and climbed off the relaxer.

"I'd better go out," she said. "I don't believe Pop Didorik likes for me to be alone with you."

Keaflyn gave her a laughing kiss on the cheek and followed her back to Didorik and Felston.

"I'm checking out, gents," he grinned. "My business here was with Tinker, and that's settled until she either grows up or gets a research project started. In the meantime, I want to get to work. Alo, many thanks for the noble rescue."

"Now simmer down, Mark," the cowpoke urged, getting to his feet. "Let's wait and see what Dawsett and his boys find out. Besides, you need some sleep, pardner."

"Right," Didorik said firmly. "I assured Dawsett I would get you to sleep, one way or the other. You're not a well man, Keaflyn. You have to understand that."

Keaflyn felt a touch of irritability at being crossed, and a slight physical distress—not enough to call an ache, but definitely a discomfort. Tiredness? he wondered. Maybe so. Perhaps he had to expect such sensations, now that he had a traumatized track. Maybe sleep would help.

"Okay," he shrugged, and went off to bed grinning.

Chapter 3

Dawsett reported next morning that Smath was not to be found. The indications were that he and two other men, both known to be Sect Dualers, had left Terra in the early evening, Splendiss time. Dawsett noted that would place their departure shortly after Keaflyn had called the city's directory from Felston's clopter.

"That doubtless alerted them that their plan had gone wrong," the Emergencyman said. "Keaflyn was meant to die after regaining consciousness alone in the desert. That would place a second and dissimilar trauma on the one he was already loaded with, one in which they would not appear. Any involvement of them in his disappearance could thus be delayed until well into his next lifetime, and perhaps forever."

"Since they can't be punished, why did they bother to run?" asked Didorik.

"Oh, they would be punished, but not under any law," said Dawsett. "Society does not think highly of known breakers of the ethical code of man. They would be made to feel that disapproval. I presume they will establish themselves under aliases on one of the more distant planets."

"Won't their own feelings of guilt punish them?" asked Felston.

"Not while they feel they were justified," said Tinker.

Keaflyn listened with what he hoped wasn't a sickly grin. The hard knot of hysterical merriment was still as solidly planted in the center of his being as it had been the previous day, but there was a difference: last night's physical ache had returned this morning to add to his feeling of disorientation.

He wished he could get rid of the ache, but the idea of seeing a doctor made him twitch inside. That was the *last* thing he wanted to do. So he said nothing about the ache. And if Tinker's expression showed that she, if none of the others, was aware of his increased distress, she was respectful enough of his privacy to say nothing about it.

"That appears to exhaust this caper's amusing possibilities," he said, "so if you gentlemen have no intention of confining me in the honored backtrack style of Bedlam, I'll take my leave."

Dawsett shrugged. "I have no objection."

"Tinker," Keaflyn said, turning to the little girl, "you know my present-life identity now. Call me if you need me."

She nodded. "Goodbye, Jack."

Felston said, "I'll give you a lift to your ship, pardner."

"Thanks."

The two men climbed out the wallport and into Felston's clopter. "Across town to the spaceport and to Mr. Keaflyn's ship," the cowpoke directed.

"Yes, sir," the machine replied, relinquishing its hold on the apartment building and lifting away.

"It's been great knowing you, Alo," smiled Keaflyn. "I didn't know there were any salt-of-the-earth types like you still around, much less punching cattle. Maybe cowpokes are a kind of stability and I ought to include you in my study of such things."

"I doubt it," said Felston. "Anyway, I'm not enough of a stability, personally, to stick with cowpoking. I got talked out of it after you went to sleep last night."

"Oh? Some scheme of Didorik's?"

"A scheme of Tinker's. She recruited me to work on this research project you suggested. It's a good idea, Mark."

"Great! But isn't it out of your line?"

"Not especially. This feel I have for beaten-down ego-fields can be augmented by psionics, she tells me. I'm to try to establish enough rapport with the egos of lower bodyforms to check them for ancient pleasure-imprints like yours. Maybe round up a few dozen experimental subjects."

"There used to be Earth animals called laughing hyenas," chuckled Keaflyn. "They may still be around. You might check them out. And I remember numerous dogs who always seemed to be grinning."

"We'll look at a variety of species," Felston assured him seriously. "It might be best if you stuck around, Mark. A guy in your condition oughtn't to be flitting around the galaxy by himself. Besides, we might need you for tests at any moment."

Keaflyn was silent for several seconds before replying, "Don't think my grin and that ball of hysteria inside me has turned off my mind, Alo. I understand my predicament well enough. Above all, I understand that my work with stabilities could be important. It's something I've been preparing for, more or less intuitively, for half a dozen lifetimes.

"I might have only this lifetime in which to carry it out, if I'm destined to join the lower animals in the near future. That gives me a sense of urgency I haven't felt for centuries, since the days when death was considered final.

"Maybe you and Tinker will find a cure for me, and maybe you won't," he finished. "If you don't, I've got a lot of work to do before I add a death trauma to my load. So I can't sit around playing guinea pig."

He glanced at Felston and found the cowpoke regarding him, for the first time, with respect instead of as if he were a sick cow. He laughed softly.

"I'll tell Tinker you said that," Felston told him. "It'll make the little girl feel better about you."

At the spaceport, Keaflyn said goodbye to Felston, boarded his ship *Kelkontar*, ordered it to lift off and set warp for the Bensor system.

Moments later he noticed the ache was gone from his body.

Morning sickness? he wondered with a giggle. Two days in a row he had awakened in physical pain. Yesterday it had lasted, apparently, until Smath installed the pleasure-impress. Today it had vanished once he was in the long-familiar surroundings of his own spacecraft.

It reminded him of the unpredictable manner in which headaches had come and gone back in the Earthbound days when total health and sanity were mere dreams instead of realities. Back when "the human condition" was equated with "quiet desperation"—or noisy desperation, more often than not.

Now that was his condition once more. Urgency. Haste. Desperation.

So why had he told his ship to warp for Bensor? He had no work to do, at this time, on his current birthworld. It must have been a desire, he guessed, to seek solace from his parents for distress.

"Kelly," he addressed his ship, "break that warp I gave you. Set a new one for Lumon's Star."

"Okay, Mark," the *Kelkontar* replied. Keaflyn felt the warp break and reset, and the ship reported, "We're now on course for Lumon's Star. Time of run: eighty-six hours, twenty-two minutes."

"Good. Now I'll get to work."

"Your notebooks, Mark?"

"No. Run me off a couple of lists. One on your library entries on Sect Dualers. The other on entries on contralife."

"Very well. Should I respond when you laugh, Mark?"

"No, don't bother. I'll be laughing a lot from now on. Just ignore it."

"Okay. The lists are ready."

Contralife (sometimes also called "Negs"): Hypothetical inhabitants of a universe that is the negative mirror-image of the real cosmos. The contralife theory is an outgrowth of physiomathematical indications which in late Earthbound times were cited as evidence of the existence of "negative matter"—that is, of mass composed of atoms with negatively-charged nuclei surrounded by positron clouds instead of the normal positively-charged nuclei accompanied by electron clouds. However, while the negative components for such atoms were rather readily detectable, no complete negative atom, much less a mass of such atoms, has yet been observed.

Nevertheless, theoretical considerations led to the proposal that an entire universe of contramatter must exist, as a "balance" for our own. Rigorous mathematical proofs, in fact, have shown a necessity for such a universe if the principles of conservation are applicable (as they seem to be) at the most basic levels of existence. These same proofs, rather ironically, rule out the possibility of

*either of these universes ever being observed in any man-
ner from or by an entity of its counterpart.*

*Thus, the belief of certain investigators and others (see
Sect Dualers) that the contrauniverse has living inhabitants appears eternally beyond proof pro or con. Despite
currently accepted theory to the contrary, the Dualist
assumption is that contralife not only exists, but has certain capabilities of impinging itself upon our universe.*

Such reference summaries as this one told Keaflyn
little that he did not already know. As a physicist he
had a passing familiarity with the contrauniverse theory,
although he had never made a study of the mathematical
proofs of it. He considered doing so now but decided he
lacked the power of concentration for that kind of work
at the moment.

Instead, he viewed a book published by the Sect Dualers themselves, on how they conceived the nature of contralife.

They offered no description of the physical appearance of the Negs. As he read, Keaflyn got the impression
of dark, formless entities, existing in equally dark, formless worlds. There was, he soon realized, a problem with
visualization that the Sect Dualers, despite the efforts of
their book to be convincingly positive, had never been
able to solve.

How, in short, does one sum up all possible negative
characteristics as they would presumably exist in a negative reality, and then visualize the result?

The substitution of darkness for light was a laughably
trivial beginning. And what does one do about motion?
The book offered no answer. Would the negative be no

motion? Or would it be contramotion, and if so, what the hell was contramotion like?

Perhaps the Dualist thinkers assumed the nature of contramotion could be taken for granted as following logically from their concept of time reversal in the contrauniverse. The pertinent paragraphs on that subject said:

We of the normal cosmos experience time as a sequencing from a partially experienced, known, and recorded Past into a wholly speculative Future (the adjectives being applicable in the Present). This may be diagrammed:

P—>F

Certain theorists have suggested the contrauniversal time flow would simply reverse this diagram:

F<—P

That is, if we could observe events of the contrauniverse, we would see all cycles in reverse, entities moving from death to birth, actions generally progressing from effect to cause.

Certainly a time-reversal is involved, but if we accept a mere reversal in direction of flow, we accept a theory most mathematicians agree is not necessarily true and, worse, a theory that leads nowhere and explains nothing. Indeed, this theory would all but rule out impingement of Negs on normuniverse affairs: conflicting temporal energies would be too tremendous to permit any crossover. And as other sections of this volume make clear, the evidence for impingement is overwhelming.

Bearing in mind that the Past, P, represents that which entities have partially experienced, known, and recorded,

*and that the Future, F, represents that which is specula-
tive, the contrauniversal sequencing is best diagrammed as*

   $F \longrightarrow P$

*That is, the time-vector parallels our own, but is never-
theless a flow from F, that which is speculative, toward
P, that which is partially experienced, known, and
recorded.*

*The concept of this sequencing is less difficult to visual-
ize than one might immediately expect. One need only
imagine himself riding in a groundcar and looking at the
landscape ahead while giving scant thought to the scenes
passed. Thus, the rider is experiencing, knowing, and
recording what is to come as the car continues its forward
motion. But his quick recall of scenes that he has passed
and that he is making no special effort to remember,
might well be uncertain and speculative. In any event,
his visual sense presents to him, in the Present, what
lies ahead, while there is no such presentation of what
lies behind . . .*

In other words, Keaflyn summed up for himself with
delight, the Negs could foretell the future, since to them
the future had the characteristics of our past. He wasn't
ready to buy that $F \longrightarrow P$ scheme; it smacked of sophistry
to him. But if that was what the Sect Dualers wanted
to believe . . .

He scanned the rest of the book, taking note of the
"evidence" the Dualists offered for their beliefs. Items
ranged from the expansion-contraction cycle of the universe to the point Felston had made about the unexplainable abundance of debased ego-fields in existence.

The Negs, according to the book, being our opposites, had goals the reverse of ours. Whereas we seek continued and augmented existence, they desire nonexistence. We seek to conquer the universe; they seek retreat from theirs into nothingness.

A basic postulate of Dualism was the old one, never substantially proven, that *reality is as real as its associated ego-fields make it*. Thought is senior to matter and energy and is probably the creator of matter and energy.

If this were assumed, it followed that even without any crossovers, the Negs impinged on the normuniverse, and human activities impinged on theirs, because the universes must remain in balance. As intelligent normlife proceeded in its conquest of matter and energy and attainment of augmented existence, increasing the reality of the normuniverse in the process, so the Negs were forced, willy-nilly, away from their goals of retreat into nonbeing. Normlife marched forward and the universes expanded. Contralife gained superiority and the universes contracted.

This was the fundamental conflict of nature—a conflict beside which man's battle to win over the forces of normuniverse nature, as well as man's lengthy backtrack of inhumanity to man, shrank to secondary status.

For the Negs were no mean adversaries. Witness their achievement, never duplicated by normlife, of devising a means of crossing over so as to impinge directly on the ego-field of a key individual in crucial situations.

Is that supposed to be me? Keaflyn asked, making a mock mental curtsy to both universes. *The key individual? What a good boy am I! But my Christmas pie is only eleven years old.*

Evidently, the book continued, such impingements were made by the Neg ego attaching itself—or perhaps a projection of itself—to the human ego-field. Symptoms of such "possession" by a contrauniverse "demon" varied according to the state of the individual before possession occurred. In earlier times, when all ego-fields were burdened with backtrack traumas, the result was likely to be sudden insanity. But in the 29th Century, thanks to the development of track-scanning techniques that had brought freedom from trauma to man, an impingement was likely to produce nothing more than physical discomfort—the pain and unpleasant emotion that a healthy Neg would find desirable.

"Ha!" Keaflyn barked. .

"Yes, Mark?" asked the ship.

"That was just a loud laugh, Kelly. Ignore it."

"Okay."

Maybe all this stuff was pure nonsense, Keaflyn reflected, but if Smath believed it, the explanation for what the doctor had done was clear. He had considered Keaflyn a key figure, singled out as such by the Negs, to be invaded and directed into certain actions by a Neg ego. He had then postulated that if Keaflyn were loaded with a pleasure-impress—which would be intense pain to the invader—the Neg ego would find continued impingement unendurable and would vacate. And not knowing how long Keaflyn would remain a key figure, Smath had made the impress so intense that it could not be lifted, in the present or any future lifetime.

Of course the joke was on Smath, Keaflyn decided. The pleasure-impress, after all, hadn't kept him from feeling sick again this morning. So, whatever his ailment was, it wasn't anything so fanciful as invasion by a Neg ego.

"Time for some lunch, Kelly," he said, turning off the viewer.

After eating he exercised for a while, then returned to the viewer to read with rapidly declining interest about the Sect Dualers. One thing he learned was that no religion was involved in the movement; they had been tagged with the word Sect by the public but referred to themselves simply as Dualists.

Also he learned that their membership was small. He figured it out to be an average of twelve Dualists per inhabited planet. Of course, the number would run higher on well-populated worlds such as Terra and Bensor.

But the Dualists were of little concern to him, he decided. He was not possessed by a Neg and had never been, as the recurrence of his physical discomfort after the pleasure-impressing demonstrated. If the Dualists interfered with him again, all he had to do was tell them so and they would leave him be.

They were, after all, rational people, like everyone else. They merely interpreted reality a bit differently than the majority of humanity.

Finally he told the ship to clear the viewer rack, had some supper, and climbed into his sleeptank.

He was roused some hours later by an alarm buzzer and the *Kelkontar*'s persistent urging, "*Wake up, Mark.*"

He sat up. "What is it, Kelly?"

"We've been seized," the ship replied.

Chapter 4

He climbed quickly out of the tank and hurried to the manual control console. "By whom?"

"I identify our captor as the worldship *Calcutta*," *Kelkontar* told him, "the flagship of the fleet of the Arlan Siblings Ltd. Npb."

Keaflyn giggled in puzzlement. The Arlan Siblings? What was this all about?

"Let's have a look," he said.

The situation screens lighted to reveal the half-mile-long bulk of the *Calcutta* hanging alongside, so close as to blank out almost half the sky. The view glowed with the purple wastelight of grapples beams. The *Kelkontar* was being gripped tightly.

"The *Calcutta* wishes to communicate, Mark," the ship advised.

"No point in arguing with a ship that size," he chuckled. "Put it on."

The *Calcutta's* voice had the syrupy mellowness of a professional announcer. "Good watch, Mr. Keaflyn. The Senior Sibling invites you to come aboard, sir."

Keaflyn took that moment to realize that he had awakened, once more, with a dully aching body. But his mood was more perverse than despondent; his giggle sounded ill-tempered to him.

"Convey to the Senior Sibling my compliments and the fact that I'm busy," he replied.

After a pause the *Calcutta* responded, "The Senior Sibling thanks you, sir, and suggests I inform you that we are proceeding along your warp vector, that is, in the direction of Lumon's Star. We will continue along that course while you are a visitor aboard, sir."

Keaflyn signaled *Kelkontar* to cut transmission and said, "Is that true, Kelly?

"We are on course, Mark."

"That Sibling is being politely highhanded," he chuckled. "If they don't mean to take no for an answer, I suppose they can use force."

"The *Calcutta's* beams could pry me apart, according to information in my banks, Mark," the ship verified.

"Okay, put me on again." Then, addressing the *Calcutta*, he said, "Inform the Senior Sibling I'll be honored to come aboard in twenty minutes."

"Yes, sir. Thank you, sir," replied the worldship.

Mark cleansed, dressed, and ate breakfast while puzzling over this peculiar incident. The Arlan Siblings—brother and sister—were almost legendary figures. Through a number of lifetimes they had maintained a partnership begun in the earliest days of interstellar exploration and colonization, and in the process they had accumulated vast wealth—just how vast, only they really knew.

No one had the power to demand an accounting. The Siblings' power was easily the equal of that of any systemic or planetary government. They were, in fact, a code unto themselves.

Keaflyn had read in popular accounts of them, for example, that when a Junior Sibling reached the age of four in a new body—the age marking the end of the generally-accepted period of an ego-field's babyhood right-of-silence—and the ego identified itself, there had never yet been an instance of the parents succeeding in

keeping normal guardianship during the Sibling's childhood and adolescence. One way or another, the Senior
Sibling always obtained control of the child, and, of
course, always the child approved.

They never used lifetime names past the age of four.
They were Bartok and Berina Arlan, regardless of current parentage.

"Kelly, which one is Senior Sibling now?" Keaflyn
asked as he ate.

"Extrapolating from dependable but 148–year-old
data," replied the ship, "Berina Arlan should be Senior
at this time."

"Extrapolating?" Keaflyn echoed.

"Yes. The Siblings hold their lives rather precisely to
sixty-two-year-cycles, the seniority shifting every thirty-
one years. Thus, if neither ever died prematurely, it is
possible to extrapolate which is currently senior if it is
known which was senior at a precise time in the past."

Keaflyn nodded, remembering something else he had
read. "That's right. They try to keep their ages about
thirty years apart."

"That's correct," the ship said.

"The real question is, what's their interest in me?"

"I don't know, Mark."

"Well, time to go find out."

He cycled through the locks and was met in the spacious, glitteringly appointed reception dock of the *Calcutta* by a human guide, a middle-aged man dressed in
the distinguished though ancient style of a naval officer.

"Please follow me, Mr. Keaflyn," the man requested
with a slight bow.

Keaflyn did so, taking in the expensive luxury of the ship's interior.

He had not been aboard a worldship—one of the giant craft used in the early colonization days to transport tens of thousands of colonists at a time to newly-found planets—for nine lifetimes. Then he had been one of the packed-in passengers bound for Deneb Nine.

The *Calcutta* had obviously been rebuilt from the hull inward, to offer the fullest possible comfort and satisfaction for a handful of people, rather than to provide minimal survival needs for thousands. It was now a "world" ship in a different sense than originally intended—a paradisiacal microcosm of high self-sufficiency, offering its favored inhabitants a rich and varied existence, Keaflyn judged from the glimpses he had of the several deck-levels that zipped past as he and his guide dropped along a chute tube.

Finally they hovered, and Keaflyn was moved sideways a few feet to drop a fraction of an inch to a gravitized deck. His guide pointed. "You will find the Senior Sibling swimming, Mr. Keaflyn," he said.

Keaflyn nodded and strolled off through the shrubbery in the indicated direction. Sol-type radiation beamed warmly down from a light source in the unblemished blue above him, and a pleasant breeze murmured through the elms and maples. He could hear the splash of flowing water several seconds before he could see the pool.

He stopped at its edge and gazed out over the swirling surface of pink and blue. A woman, presumably Berina Arlan, was side-stroking with smooth vigor out in the

middle, her face away from him. He knelt and studied
the surface more closely.

The pool, he realized, was filled with two immiscible
stages of parawater, lightly dyed pink and blue, which
swirled together in tight marble patterns. He dangled a
hand into the water and found the pink was relaxingly
warm and the blue tinglingly cool. His grin broadened
to a smile at the pleasantness of the sensation. Then he
laughed at the notion of people going to such ostenta-
tious lengths as this just to obtain a highly specialized
type of pleasure for their bodies.

The woman turned in the water, saw him, and swam
over. After a moment in which she examined him with
expressionless eyes, she said, "Mark Keaflyn, I'm Berina,
Senior Sibling of Arlan Siblings. Please call me Berina."

Keaflyn nodded agreeably. "Call me Mark."

"Care for a swim, Mark?"

"I wouldn't mind," he shrugged, "although I'm more
interested right now in learning why I was honored by
your forceful invitation."

"Then we'll talk first," she said, climbing lithely out of
the pool. She was, he saw, a slim, and beautiful woman
with a taut, healthy body that looked far more youthful
than she could possibly be as the Senior Sibling.

A towel materialized from somewhere, and she sat
down beside him at the edge of the water, dangling her
feet in the pool while she dried her nude form.

"We almost missed finding you," she said easily. "Our
information was that you would go to Lumon's Star from
Terra. Evidently you doglegged toward Bensor first."

He said, "Yes, a spur-of-the-moment decision that I
changed shortly thereafter. You had trouble finding
me, then?"

"A bit. Fortunately, the *Calcutta's* warp detectors have quite a range." She was studying him closely. "Did you dogleg to throw off suspected pursuers?" she asked baldly.

"No. The possibility of pursuit didn't occur to me. You're talking about Sect Dualers, aren't you?"

She nodded.

"Are they your source of information? About me, I mean?"

Again she nodded. "One of our sources. We also have access to Emergency reports."

"Why are you interested?"

"The same reason the Dualists are, essentially."

"You a member?"

She smiled. "Not really. Just think of me as a concerned citizen of the galaxy."

"Be glad to. Concerned about what?"

"As I just told you, the same as the Dualists."

"And one or more Dualists tried to kill me," Keaflyn chuckled.

"I'm not sure Smath had the right solution," Berina replied thoughtfully.

Keaflyn blinked. She *wasn't sure* killing him was the right solution! He was suddenly very aware that the same hidden servo that had provided Berina's towel could also provide his instant death if this Senior Sibling *became* sure. This innocent-looking setting of grass, trees, and pool could well be the last scene he would look upon through his present eyes.

And death was no longer a trivial matter to him.

"Look," he exclaimed with annoyance, "it's time the Dualists and you got something straight. I don't know or really give a damn at this point if Negs exist, or if they're a threat to us. I do know Smath jumped to a faulty conclusion if he thought I was possessed by one."

She looked at him. "How do you know?"

"Because twice since he installed this giggle-machine in my head, I've woken up with symptoms like the ones I had that first morning. His sure-fire method of demon-exorcise, didn't work; therefore, no demon."

"Oh." She nodded slowly. "You have the symptoms now, don't you, Mark?"

"As a matter of fact, I do. I woke with them about an hour ago—even though that pleasure-impress is as solid as ever."

She said slowly, "That would be very convincing, except for one thing. Smath's method wasn't sure-fire. That's one of the weaknesses of the Dualists. Their data is less accurate and complete than they think.

"Tell me, Mark. Despite being in physical pain, and despite Smath's tampering, what have you been doing?"

He thought about the question for a moment, then said glumly, "Trying to go about my work as usual. I haven't allowed these difficulties to stop me from functioning."

"Right. So why assume a Neg is less capable than we are of continuing in the face of adversity? All Smath did was make your invader's job more unpleasant and perhaps cut down on its efficiency by creating a distraction. The only thing Smath was completely right about was his diagnosis."

"Then you're as sure as he was that I'm . . . Neg-ridden?"

She nodded.

"Then why aren't you sure Smath's solution was correct?"

Berina lifted her shapely shoulders. "Because I don't know what action the Negs are trying to force. And unlike Smath, I'm not willing to jump to conclusions . . . especially to conclusions that would lead to violations of the human code."

"Seizing my ship and handing me your so-called invitation might be considered a code breach in more fastidious circles," he said with a touch of sarcasm.

She laughed. "I'll try to live with my conscience despite that grievous sin. Now, Mark, I'd like to know a bit about this project of yours, the investigation of stabilities. What's your basic procedure?"

This question struck him as beside the point, and he felt impatient. "We have yet to discover an absolute in nature," he said, determined to keep his answer brief. "Thus we can't really assume that the stabilities are totally stable, although they appear to be. The stabilities involved must be of an extremely low order . . . trace instabilities, so to speak. I'm going to look for those traces, in an effort to limit and rationalize our concept of stabilities."

"What are you going to do your looking with?"

"A variety of special methods for dealing with trace phenomena. I've spent a couple of lifetimes seeking out those methods and accumulating the needed equipment."

"I see." Berina paused, then asked, "What do you think of the hypothesis that the stabilities are the products of a Senior Creation?"

He shrugged. "Could be. However they came about, they're senior to our present physical universe. Numerous people, for instance, have backtrack impressions of the Resistant Globe recorded dozens of universal cycles ago. For material objects to endure like that . . . well, it's conceivable that they're the result of a creative process that differs in quality from that which forms and destroys our succession of universes."

"Has it occurred to you," Berina demanded, "that the stabilities may serve a vital function?"

"I'm not given to speculating at length about questions that I have insufficient data to answer," he replied tartly. "I try to get the data first."

"Bully for you," she applauded wryly. "More than one precedent for that approach comes to mind. For instance, a sure way to gather data on whether a gun is loaded is to pull the trigger. Not safe, but sure."

"You're suggesting that my research might unstabilize the stabilities," he remarked.

"I am. Why else would you be singled out for possession by a Neg, except to push you in that direction? At any rate, I consider that one of the possibilities."

Keaflyn did not respond immediately. The Senior Sibling had forced some changes in his thinking, and he took a moment to mull them over.

Berina and Bartok Arlan had not attained their power and position by luck. They were widely reputed to be extremely able beings—a pair of hard-heads with a firm grasp of reality. The Senior Sibling was an unlikely person to take Negs seriously on insufficient evidence. Thus, he might be wise to take the notion of his possession less lightly. It could be true.

And if so, what other reason than his work could the Negs have for interest in him? According to the Dualist writings he had scanned the day before, possession by a Neg was not a frequent occurrence, not something that might happen to anybody. Since direct impingement across universal boundaries would be difficult, the target would necessarily be a key individual, the Dualists stated. Keaflyn's research project, and nothing else he could imagine, might make him a key.

So, Berina could be right about that, too.

He said, "You asked about a vital purpose the stabilities might serve, and I presume you would prefer to answer your own question.'"

"You know the hypothesis," Berina replied. "The stabilities may function as anchors of existence; a better word for them might be bindings. The physical universe has its periods of collapse, but the collapse can't approach totality—the nullification of all physical being—because the stabilities don't collapse. They remain as a skeleton for a new universe to grow upon."

"So, anything bad for the stabilities would be good for the Negs," grunted Keaflyn.

"If the Negs' goal is nonbeing, as the Dualists believe," said Berina, "a weakening of the stabilities would weaken the very fabric of nature they want to destroy. If they could do away with the material products of the Senior Creation, then the presumably dependent Junior Creation—the universe—would experience total collapse.

"And don't sell Dualist ideas short, Mark," she admonished. "You're working with trace phenomena, you say, to gather your data. Essentially, that's what the Dualists

have done. Their theories are based on trace events on
the backtrack . . . trace in the sense of being highly infre-
quent and often of debatable interpretation."

"Such as?"

"Such as earlier employment of pleasure-impresses,
and the reason why the impresses were used."

Keaflyn nodded, recalling that Tinker had mentioned
being involved as a bystander in such a backtrack incident. "Reasons why are not easy to be sure of in a lot of
backtrack incidents," he countered.

"They are if you are yourself the instigator of the incident," she replied. After a hesitation, she added, "I've
installed a few pleasure-impresses myself, through the
centuries, and considered my actions fully justified at
the time."

He stared at her.

She added, "Perhaps I should have made information
from my own backtrack available to the Dualists. That
could have prevented Smath from duplicating my earlier
inadequate responses to Neg infiltration. But . . . no, that
wouldn't have helped, really. Not even a determined
man like Smath could do an adequate job . . . "

Her voice trailed off and Keaflyn growled, "An 'adequate' treatment would have traumatized me so completely that I would immediately cease having enough
mind to be the key to anything?"

She nodded.

Keaflyn grunted and stood up. "It hadn't occurred to
me to regard Smath as a Mr. Nice Guy, compared to
present company—"

"Oh, relax, Mark!" Berina snapped, displaying as much irritation as he felt. "I'm talking about mistakes, not present intentions! Why, I don't intend to kill you, much less wreck what's left of your mind!"

He laughed, surprised at his sense of relief. She didn't intend to kill him!

"What I really want to do is make you understand what a critical position you're in," she told him urgently. "I want you to realize you're in the front line of the most crucial war ever to hit the cosmos. You've already been wounded by misdirected fire from your own side, but you mustn't let that wound distract you from your job in the fight. You've got to take this war seriously, Mark, and give it your best!"

"Aren't you overplaying it a bit?" he asked mildly. "If this is merely the continuation of a struggle that's gone on since the dawn of the cosmos—"

"But it isn't! There has never been a trillennium like the present. Humanity—and by humanity I mean any creature with a sufficiently strong ego-field as to be capable of scanning its backtrack—"

"Of course," he put in.

"Humanity has never advanced before as far as it has today," she continued. "At long last we've learned to improve ourselves and each other as ego-fields, instead of brutalizing and degrading ourselves—"

"My own recent experience notwithstanding," he nodded.

"—and that makes all the difference. We're going much farther this time than ever before toward understanding and conquering the universe. We're beating hell out of the Negs!

"That must make them frantic, Mark. We've given them no choice but to hit back at us with everything they've got, regardless of the cost to themselves. Their only hope is to halt our progress now, before we become unstoppable. It's your misfortune to have gotten into this conflict, which you didn't even believe existed, just when it has grown extremely hot."

"All right," he said, "let's say you're right about all that. The point remains that, so far as I can tell, I'm playing host to a demon of sorts who can give me aches, and make me feel cross or low, and that's all. My Neg hasn't been guiding my actions or murmuring suggestions into my mental ear. If that's the worst they can do, why fret?"

"They can do more, given the chance, when the right moment comes," she told him. "Being a physicist, Mark, you must remember what a cloud chamber is?"

"Sure. The Wilson cloud chamber. A container of suddenly cooled air in which moisture condenses along the ionized tracks of charged sub-atomic particles. It dates from the first half of the Twentieth Century. It enables physicists to see sub-atomic particles, so to speak. What's that got to do with anything?"

"Precisely what kind of sub-atomic particles does the cloud chamber reveal, Mark?"

"Protons, electrons, positrons—any charged particle, as I recall. I still don't see what this has to do with—"

"Where do these charged particles come from?"

"Well, from various sources. The cloud chamber was probably used first to study cosmic rays—"

"Then the particles come from *outside* the chamber?" Berina prompted.

"Why, yes, certainly. Almost always. The media in a cloud chamber might occasionally produce a spontaneous fission, but generally an event is set off by a particle from outside. Of course, that particle might strike a particle within the chamber and produce a burst of secondary tracks."

"Good. Now, let's suppose the intruding particle were an entire atom of contramatter. What would happen then?"

Mark laughed. "I'm not sure, since it's never been done, to my knowledge. I know of no one who has put together a contra-atom, much less kept it together long enough to get it into a cloud chamber. But I'd like to see it done. The results should be spectacular."

"All right," Berina said grimly. "Consider our universe a vast cloud chamber, Mark. And consider your Neg invader an atom of contramatter. Not merely a charged particle, but a wholly alien intruder with the capability of initiating destructive chains of events that no native particle could set off. Do you see the analogy?"

Slowly he nodded. "I see it to a degree, although your analogy seems a bit stretched. An ego-field, Neg or normal, is not *material*, and that limits its capabilities right off."

"On the contrary, because of that its capabilities are unlimited," Berina retorted. "A man-sized chunk of contramatter could at most wipe out one planet, and that would be the end of it. But thought can control matter, can conquer it, and theoretically can even create and destroy it. Do you begin to see the implications?"

"I suppose so," Mark shrugged, feeling both amused and irritated by Berina's lecturing. "But I have no idea what I'm supposed to do about it."

"Fight," she responded. "Don't let that Neg get control over you. Keep the upper hand at all times."

"Does that mean I give up sleeping?" he snorted. "Every time I wake up my Neg is aching me."

Berina frowned. "I'm not sure sleep has anything to do with it. In any event, you can't fight by staying constantly awake. That would weaken your power to resist. I can't really tell you how to wage your battle. You'll have to learn from experience. Now, would you care for a swim?"

That offer, Keaflyn guessed, meant Berina was through talking. "I wouldn't mind," he said.

"Then come on in." She dived from her sitting position and began stroking away toward the far side of the pool. Keaflyn stripped and dived after her.

He hit the water with the mildly pleasant shock he had expected, but what followed was a sensation totally new and delightful. The swirling warm-and-cool parawaters swept in unpredictable courses along his body, a rapid alternation of snuggle-and-tingle that made him yell with pure joy. The pleasure-impress Smath had installed was submerged in and indistinguishable from the ecstasy that flooded his senses.

He wriggled, twisted, dived to the bottom, came up, rapidly ran the gamut of swimming strokes, dived again to examine the stirring paddles that kept the parawaters from separating into layers, and finally swam on out to Berina with a racing crawlstroke.

"You rich kids sure know how to live!" he gurgled and gasped.

"When you're rich enough, luxuries become necessities," she returned with a smile. "How's the ache?"

He had to search his physical sensations for a moment before finding the answer. "Damned if it isn't still there!" he laughed. "My poor, stubborn Neg! Do you suppose the Neg authorities pick pleasure-loving masochist Negs for such assignments?"

"Could be, though if they have been forced to parallel our history, they should all be sane pain-lovers by now."

"Well, I'm going to show him no mercy! I'm going to swim and swim and swim!"

"And sink!" laughed Berina, leaping forward with unexpected speed and shoving him under.

He came up sputtering and made a dive for her. She twisted aside and he missed, but a couple of lunges brought him within grabbing distance of a flailing ankle. He dragged her to the bottom before releasing her. Shooting to the surface, he watched for her head to reappear. Instead, he felt wriggling fingers dig into his ribs. He whirled and clutched her, trying to return the poke in the ribs, which wasn't easy because she shifted in his grasp with the smooth rapidity of an eel. It was all he could do to hang on, but hang on he did, and the struggle suddenly became sexual.

Berina broke away laughing, and for an instant Keaflyn thought she didn't want that kind of play. Then she halted a few feet away, grinning at him and obviously awaiting pursuit.

He chased her up the length of the pool, almost catching a foot once or twice. Then he was in churning water and had the feeling he was trying to swim uphill. The water, now hot-and-cold rather than warm-and-cool, bit him excitingly.

He reached the crest of the tumultuous swell and slid down the far side to find himself and Berina thrown together in a swirling tangle of arms and legs. They were in a cup-shaped depression in the center of an upwelling current where the parawaters, having been separated and recooled and reheated, were returned to the pool.

There were no words for his sensations. The uprushing current buoyed them, like heavy corks bobbing on top of a fountain, making swimming unnecessary. And the touch of the desirable body of Berina stormed his senses as powerfully as did the tingling liquid, only in a different manner. They found each other quickly and clung together endlessly, for seconds, or hours, or days, or ages.

Then suddenly the hot-cold was too much. They were satiated. They released each other and attacked the upcurved wall of water around them. They went up and over, carried by the current into the relative calm of the rest of the pool. Lazily they swam ashore.

"Wow!" Keaflyn breathed, catching the towel Berina tossed him. "Do you have many more toys like that?"

"Not many," she replied, drying herself. "The pool's our best one. How's the ache?"

He paused in his toweling for a moment, then reported, "It's gone!"

"I thought it would be, after that," she said.

"Poor Neg!" he laughed. Then: "Hey, that's one way to fight it!"

She nodded, slipping into a brief one-piece costume. "About the most effective way. Mark, you have a choice of remaining aboard if you like. Unfortunately, Sibling business makes it impossible for me to put the *Calcutta* at your disposal to travel to Lumon's Star or to Locus or the other stabilities you plan to investigate. My brother and I have to be elsewhere, and of course we need the ship with us. Will you stay or leave?"

He thought about it as he dressed. "You're quite a temptation, Berina," he said at last, "and so is your pool. But I may have only this lifetime in which to finish my work. I can't stay."

"Okay. Let's go eat," she said. And Keaflyn knew she would not urge him to change his mind. As they turned away from the pool he saw a teenaged couple approaching, the boy tall, dark-skinned and frowning heavily, the girl blonde, picture-pretty and serene.

Berina said, "Mark, this is my brother Bart and his friend Jenvive."

The boy extended his hand. "Ah, the newly-afflicted Mr. Keaflyn," he said, his tone confident but with a touch of tension. "Welcome aboard, Mark. Will you be with us a while?"

"Thank you, Bartok," Keaflyn replied, shaking his head. "No, your sister says the *Calcutta* can go my way only so far, and I have my work to do."

The Junior Sibling nodded gravely. "Okay, but if the going gets too rough, come on back any time. You'll always be welcome."

"Thanks."

"Now, if you'll pardon us, I'm anxious to hit the water," said Bartok.

"Sure," said Keaflyn, and the boy and girl hurried by, shedding clothing as they went.

Grinning thoughtfully as he followed Berina toward the chute tube, Keaflyn finally said, "Forgive my rich kid and toy cracks, Berina. I was slow to catch on to something."

"Oh? What's that?"

"That I'm not the only person in the universe possessed by a Neg."

She nodded. "There are the two of us and you. Bart and I accept it as normal now, after putting up with it for seven lifetimes. Our position makes us constant key figures. When did you start catching on?"

"Not really until I saw Bartok's painful frown," he said. "Just the three of us, you say? What about top government officials? Aren't they in key positions?"

"No. Bart and I have seen to that. We've played politics endlessly, and sometimes not very cleanly, to prevent the development of an interstellar government. With control restricted to systemic or even planetary levels and thus splintered into thousands of autonomous units, no one unit and no one individual is important enough to merit Neg attention. If we had a unified government . . ." She shuddered slightly before continuing, "Well, there were interstellar governments along the backtrack, you know, and some of them began with strength, honesty, and a reasonable degree of sanity. Without exception, they led to the most degraded, shambled societies life has ever experienced."

"Then the Negs would have to be beaten into helplessness before we can have unity," Keaflyn remarked thoughtfully.

"Total defeat of the Negs would mean total triumph for us," she agreed. "Our conquest of the universe would be total, and every atom of matter would be held and guided by a quantum of life-force. And the unity of all life would be automatic and complete, not a mere matter of having one government."

He laughed. "I'm not at all sure I'd like that."

"Nor I," she agreed. "The Negs may be nature's way of telling us, 'Don't go too far.' "

Chapter 5

Keaflyn returned to his own ship a few hours later and continued toward Lumon's Star alone. His Neg did not make its presence felt during the remainder of the trip. Perhaps, he surmised, it was recuperating from the punishment it had received aboard the *Calcutta*.

But when he broke warp one hundred million miles away from Lumon's Star, the now-familiar ache settled once more in his body, bringing with it a sense of despair. He laughed, and that action hurt his chest.

Nevertheless, he pitched into his investigative program, trying to ignore the Neg's effort to bring him to a discouraged halt before he ever began. Perhaps, he mused, his pleasure-impress would be of some help to him now. It seemed to clear a mental area around it from the Neg's influence.

"Kelly," he said to the ship, "launch the Lumon probe."

"Okay, Mark . . . it's on its way."

"Good." Keaflyn was gazing at the magnified image of Lumon's Star on the main viewscreen. It was a white star of approximately the same luminosity as Sol. A planet circling it at Keaflyn's distance could have enjoyed an Earth-type climate, but it had no planets.

Also, it had no sunspots, and thus no sunspot cycle. It was not, so far as the most sensitive instruments could detect, variable. This made it unique among all stars humanity had observed with any closeness.

Lumon's Star was visible from Terra. It was one of the myriad points of light that had filled telescopic photoplates as far back as the twentieth century, when Earth astronomers aimed their big instruments into the glow of the Milky Way. Among so many companions, it had gone unnoticed and untamed.

But just under two light-years away from it was the system of Clevlulex, where humanity in catlike bodies had watched their strange neighbor with intelligent, more-or-less objective eyes for the equivalent of eight thousand terrestrial years. Astrology was an ancient and honored study of the Cl'exians, far more central to their culture than it ever had become among the erect humans of Earth. The learned cats of Clevlulex had observed, recorded, and wondered at the never-changing aspect of the bright star in their northern skies, and had named it for a steadfast mythological character, Lumon.

Only after the exploratory teams from Earth began to arrive was the star's uniqueness in the explored area of the galaxy fully appreciated. Then it was added to the short list of phenomena called stabilities because they showed no signs of being influenced by the processes of change that were at work on everything else within human experience.

There had been some argument about putting Lumon's Star on the list. How could a body that was producing and pouring out a constant flood of energy be a stability? the opponents demanded. Nuclear fusion was going on inside the star, transmuting its elements and therefore changing it. By definition, it could not be a stability.

But Cl'exian records were definite. So far as appearance was concerned, Lumon's Star had acted like a stability for eight thousand years. How could a radiating star be a stability? How could *anything* be a stability? Lumon's proponents retorted. Entropy was doing its work on all normal objects, merely more visibly and spectacularly so in a star than in a cold chunk of stone. Thus, when the arguments were over, the star was on the list.

But the fact that Lumon's Star did radiate, Keaflyn mused, had a lot to do with his decision to start his investigation with it. An active process of energy-production was easier to study than inert matter that insisted on remaining inert.

"All detectors on full, Kelly?" he asked.

"Yes, Mark. The probe is now in the lower corona."

"Report on redundancy?"

"Still one hundred percent for all systems, Mark."

"Good. If hyper-redundancy works as I think it will, that star's going to start giving up some secrets in a very few minutes now."

Stellar probes, resistant against the extreme energies and pressures inside stars, were standard items of astrophysical research. The probes had failed, however, when sent into Lumon's Star. Why they failed nobody knew. They simply quit reporting shortly after entering the star proper, in what was presumed to be an upper layer of turbulent convection.

Keaflyn's probe was not standard. All of its systems featured hyper-redundant circuitry—not two or three duplications of means to handle each necessary function, but on the order of twenty thousand duplications. Each component was in actuality an array of similar minicomponents, any one of which was sufficient to keep the component's function going. And the arrays were joined to each other through in-service-seeking circuitry blocks, so that even if only one of the minicomponents remained operational at each step, the circuitry would seek these out, link them together, and the probe would continue to do its work.

"The probe is now subsurface, Mark," the ship reported.

"Okay." Keaflyn felt a surge of excitement that nullified much of his physical pain and vanquished what lingered of his feeling of despair. He had been working toward this moment, this actual test of a stability, for a long time. This was the payoff, and his emotional response to it was too strong and too positive for his Neg to override.

He studied the readouts with a face-splitting grin, but depended on the *Kelkontar's* summation circuits for interpretation of what he was seeing. "Trace instabilities?" he asked.

"No significant indications," the ship replied. "All turbulence patterns are standing."

He nodded. Standard probes had lasted long enough inside Lumon's Star to report that, in the upper layer, energy was being carried outward by swirling flows of matter. But, unlike the comparable layer of normal stars, these flows seemed permanent, unshifting, unchanging. Unturbulent turbulence, he thought with a chuckle. "Redundancy?"

"Ninety-eight point two percent," the ship replied. "Any pattern in the loss there?"

A pause. "Perhaps . . . yes, Mark, it's more definite now. A definite statistical indication that the destructive agent has a small cross section."

Keaflyn blinked. "You mean our probe is being pin-pricked to death?"

"Yes, in a manner of speaking. Redundancy now eighty-six percent. The destructive cross sections are approximately atomic in size."

"I can't imagine an atom smashing its way through the probe's defenses," said Mark. "But of course a stability-type atom . . . The probe's kinetic sensor is picking up the bombardment, isn't it?"

"No. There is no indication of internal atomic bom-bardment, Mark. Redundancy now seventy-two percent, with probe entering the radiative flow zone."

"Contramatter atoms," Keaflyn hazarded hurriedly, very conscious of the speeded decline of the probe's redundancy. "What energy level inside the probe now?"

"Twelve percent above normal, Mark."

"I must have contramatter on the brain," he muttered. "It can't be that or the probe would be plasma by now." He cast about frantically for some other possible answer, something to check on while the probe was still opera-tional. "Is anything reading unexplainably?" he demanded, hoping he was not asking the question in a manner the ship's computer could not interpret.

"Yes, Mark. The AV shield is drawing decreasing power but is remaining intact. Redundancy thirty-eight percent."

The AV shield? That was a modified warpfield. It could draw less power only if its area were reduced. And that just didn't happen, except when warpfields overlapped each other, as when two ships in warpflight came together for docking or . . .

"Kelly," he snapped, "could those pinpoints be tiny warps of some kind?"

"I don't know, Mark. Warps require power supplies and formulators. Redundancy, nineteen percent."

"*Our* warps do," said Keaflyn, "but tiny, atom-sized warps seem to fit what's destroying the probe. Warpicles! Particle warps! We've used the warp phenomenon for centuries, but have never quantized it! Does that fit what's happening?"

After a hesitation the *Kelkontar* replied, "So far as our probe is equipped to detect events, Mark, that could be the answer."

"Let's try to pin it down," Keaflyn said hurriedly. "Signal the probe to modify by switching the trace-increment monitor into the AV power link."

"I can't, Mark. Redundancy is now zero."

The ache moved back into Keaflyn's body. "The probe's dead?"

"Yes."

"Well . . . maybe when we analyze all the data we did get . . . Did our probe have any detectable effect on the star's behavior?"

"No."

Keaflyn shrugged. That was par for the course. Any ordinary star would show at least a detectable pimple of reaction to the heavy-element content of a probe. Lumon's Star never did.

Which could be important, it occurred to him.

"Kelly, how could a star ignore a cold chunk of heavy elements the size of a probe?" he asked.

"I don't know, Mark."

"It could ignore it by warping a tiny hole through it every time a particle of the star's mass needed to travel through the area occupied by the probe. The particle is preceded by a warp to clear it a path. The more dense the population of particles, the more warpicles there are slashing through the probe, and the faster the probe loses its redundancy."

The ache was easing as Keaflyn exuberantly fitted the pattern together.

"That could even explain how a star can be a stability," he chortled happily. "The main part of the job would be keeping the same balance between hydrogen and helium. It's the change of the H-He ratio that moves a star along its evolutionary track. If a superfluous helium atom is warped away . . . somewhere . . . the instant it is created, and hydrogen atoms are warped in to replace it, the star could go on forever without changing. Right?"

"What you propose seems sound, Mark, granting the existence of the warpicles." After a pause the ship added, "Also, you assume the warpicles are characteristically selective of the kinds of atoms they remove from and bring into the star."

Keaflyn nodded. "I have a notion they would be. A big warp isn't selective, but a warp quantum . . . well, take a light quantum for example. It has a particular wave length, a particular energy level. Ordinary light combines the whole spectrum, from high-energy violet to low-energy red quanta. Or you can produce monochromatic light—all quanta of about the same wavelength. I think we've found the analog of that here . . . warpicles of the right energy to drop hydrogen but pick up any heavier element. I'll have to do some higher-math chicken-tracks to pin it down, of course. And after that . . ."

He hesitated, his forehead frowning while his lips kept their tight smile.

Time! So much, suddenly, to try to do in one lifetime! He had planned to investigate the stabilities at a leisurely pace, taking a couple of centuries, perhaps. Now he might well be limited to less than half a century. Under other circumstances his present body's useful span could be stretched considerably longer than that, but he had to expect physical inroads from the pleasure-impress and from the impinging Neg. Such traumas caused physiological imbalances that speeded the aging process. So . . . fifty years at the most.

"We'd better go to Locus by way of Bensor," he muttered, "so I can get an instrument shop started on putting together a second Lumon probe designed to provide warpicle data. Then, after I finish with Locus we can come back here."

"Are you instructing me to warp for Bensor, Mark?" the ship asked.

Keaflyn hesitated. Was there nothing he could improvise, right now, with which to investigate warpicles? Something that would enable him to save some time?

Not likely, he had to admit. That job was going to require a highly precise, thoroughly specialized, very tough piece of equipment. Something well planned, not something thrown together on the spur of the moment.

He shrugged. "I suppose so, Kelly. Set warp for—"

"Planetary body detected, Mark," the ship interrupted him.

"What?"

"A planetary body," the ship repeated, "orbiting Lumon's Star at ninety million miles. You may observe it on the screen if you like."

Keaflyn turned to stare at the image. "This star has no planets, Kelly," he said reprovingly while reading detector indicators stating that the object was 47.6 million miles from the ship, was of 1.142 Earth-mass, and had an albedo of .493. He chuckled. "That planet isn't there. And why didn't you tell me it was there before now?"

"Because I did not detect it until now, Mark. Presumably, it was not there previous to detection."

"Kelly, I marvel at your incapacity for astonishment," Keaflyn laughed. "A whole planet suddenly turns up out of nowhere and you tell me about it as routinely as if you were notifying me of lunchtime. Planets don't jump about like warping spaceships. Or do they?"

"Not to my knowledge, Mark. Energies required for the establishment of a planetary warp are fourteen orders of magnitude greater than that released by a Sol-type star. The highest energy level usefully harnessed by humanity is only—"

"*Hey! Mark Keaflyn!*"

"Huh? Who said that?"

"It was a call from the planetary body, Mark," the ship reported. "It overrode my vocal circuits and—"

"*Hi, Mark! Come on down!*"

Keaflyn blinked. "Who's calling, and from where?" he demanded, slightly miffed by the speaker's poor comm etiquette.

"You can call me Lafe. As for where I am"—the voice paused for a chuckle—"this place is rivaled only by God in the number of its names. Avalon will do. Tell your ship to bring you down, Mark."

"The . . . the legendary world of Avalon?" Keaflyn stumbled, recalling tales of early spacemen who had claimed inexplicable visits to an elusive world of that name. And even older legends . . .

"This is the place," the voice replied. "Also called Valhalla by some, Paradise by quite a few, and the State of Nirvana by many mystics with an inkling of the truth. Look, are you coming down or aren't you?"

"Sure. Why not?" giggled Keaflyn, his hysteria mounting. "On the other hand, why? I'm a busy man, Lafe."

"If you're interested in stabilities, you ought to look this place over," the voice replied. "Also, we want to take a look at you."

"You mean Avalon's a stability?"

"What else?"

"All right. I'm on my way." To his ship he said, "Head for the planet, Kelly."

Well, why not an Avalon? he mused as he watched the planetary image swell on the viewscreen. Why not a heaven? Earthmen had encountered stranger—and far less anticipated—things than that since achieving interstellar flight. And it made sense that heaven would be a stability, perhaps the key stability as far as his investigation was concerned. Filled with angels who were themselves stabilities, no doubt, and who could answer questions about themselves as phenomena . . .

"Hey, Lafe," he called.

"Yeah?" the voice came back.

"Am I dead?"

"Certainly not! You're just visiting, not staying."

"Good. Suddenly I wasn't sure. Where do I land my ship?"

"Don't worry about that. We'll put an appropriate site under you."

Keaflyn shrugged. "Land anywhere, Kelly," he instructed the ship.

Chapter 6

The site turned out to be a green rolling meadow, complete with sparkling brook and stately groves.

"Environment safety check, Kelly," ordered Keaflyn as the ship touched down.

"Don't be a fuddy-duddy! Come on out!" snorted Lafe.

"Suitable air and climate, Mark," the ship reported.

"Okay," he replied to both of them.

He cycled himself through the lock and stepped down on to the grass. Waiting for him was a heavyset man with a homely, puckish face—a face readily recognizable from photos in numerous histories and textbooks.

"Oh, *that* Lafe," Keaflyn remarked, shaking the pudgy extended hand.

"None other," Lafe said jovially. "We're on a first-name basis here, Mark. Avoids ceremoniousness." He studied Keaflyn keenly. "Hum-um. Quite a combination . . . you, your giggle machine, and the Neg. That Neg is no slouch, either, you may be interested to know. It's quite a guy."

"I wouldn't object to giving up the Neg and the giggle," said Keaflyn.

"Your hint's well-taken," chuckled Lafe, "but we don't interfere to any crucial extent in outside affairs."

"I never thought you, of all people, would pass up a chance to restore a person's sanity," Keaflyn challenged. "When I recognized you, I assumed that was why you asked me to land."

"A hasty conclusion. We merely wanted to look you over. However, we'll keep your intruders repressed while you're here." Lafe turned his head slightly and called out, "Hey, fellers, come on over!"

Keaflyn had not noticed any others around, but now several people strolled up nonchalantly. Most of them were historically famed Earthmen with familiar faces, but extraterrestrial humanity was represented by a couple of furry Kalobangers and a lustrous translucent of Weiglizz. The presence of these three made Keaflyn realize the environment could not be precisely as it seemed. If it were, the Kalobangers would be collapsing from heat exhaustion while the atmosphere poisoned the dioxide-synthesizing Weiglindese. Or perhaps the three weren't really present in body . . . perhaps, for that matter, no one was present in body . . .

"Don't fret over the physics of this place," advised Lafe, obviously having read his thought. "Just accept it and forget it. Let me introduce Siggy, Ben, Albert, Lennie, Klon, Flon, and the ladies Dolly, Zennia, Marilyn, Kathie and Pvlikka."

Keaflyn acknowledged the introductions, noting that Lafe included the Weiglindese translucent among the females. His mind was busy with something else.

"I can't simply accept and forget the physics of this place," he protested. "You say Avalon's a stability, and that's what I'm investigating. My presence here gives me a unique opportunity to conduct a series of tests—"

"No way, handsome," said Zennia, a brunette Keaflyn couldn't quite place. "Lafe's given you the best approach. You'll learn more about this place by relaxing and letting it soak in than by trying to analyze it."

"Oh . . . well, I wondered how you can mingle with Kalobangers and a Weiglindese with nobody shielded . . ."

"It is a wonder to wonder at, at that," remarked Ben.

"Go fly a kite, tubby," sneered Marilyn. Ben grinned, unoffended. He put an arm around her and gave her a squeeze.

Keaflyn saw no answer was forthcoming, so he tried another question. "If you're really wearing bodies . . ." he began.

"Oh, we are, most definitely," said Ben.

"Well, I'm amazed to recognize so many of you," Keaflyn finished.

"That's the way things work on such worlds as Avalon," said Lafe, settling into a lecture pattern. "An ego-field goes along, one trillennium after another, in body after body, leading more or less routine lives. Then comes a lifetime that is anything but routine, a lifetime in which that ego-field achieves its potentials to a startling degree, so much so that any future lives would be anticlimactic. That soul's gone as far as it can go, so nature allows it to quit while it's ahead.

"Thus, it departs from the birth-and-death cycle of ordinary humanity and comes here as a stability. Naturally, its stable bodyform is the one in which it achieved its potential.

"Some of the old Earth religions had a smattering of the truth," Lafe continued, "particularly those that preached reincarnation. They spoke of Nirvana, an exalted state which delivered the soul from continual body-hopping to live through eternity in disembodied bliss. They were wrong about the disembodied condition, of course, and they had some strange notions about how to achieve Nirvana . . ."

"So did you, Lafe," put in Siggy.

But I got here just the same," Lafe grinned, "and I made it without talking about sex all the time."

Siggy shrugged. "You merely broadened upon the base of my pioneering studies into the realm of the mind. And at that, you did not recognize that contralife is the original source of all human aberration, no more than did I."

Lafe sighed and said to Keaflyn: "It is to be expected that all of us are rather hung up in the wins of our final lifetimes. Some of us more than others."

"Will you two shrinks break it off?" snorted Dolly. "I'll swear, you guys are as bad as politicians for arguing!"

"I'm still not clear on what kind of ego-field potential has to be realized to qualify you for—" Keaflyn began.

"Whatever kind of potential a particular ego-field happens to have," said Ben. "Morality has nothing to do with it. For example, Marilyn here . . ."

Albert claimed Keaflyn's attention. "Have you considered the fact that certain principles must be counted as stabilities, Mark?" he asked. "One might mention in this respect the mass-energy relationship, $E=mc^2$ . . . "

"Yes," nodded Keaflyn. "However, in my work I'm concentrating on material rather than abstract stabilities, because abstractions about abstractions are likely to lead into deceptive—"

"A pity old Earth didn't have a stability of its own," said Lennie. "Man might have been spared long ages of ignorance had he developed in constant confrontation with an object such as the Resistant Globe."

"Perhaps," said Keaflyn, "but on the other hand the planet Bensor failed to produce a native humanity, although our geologists tell us there were three abortive—"

"I think morality *should* have something to do with it," said Marilyn heatedly, more to Ben than anyone else. "This place is full of dirty old roués."

"You may be noticing, Mark," said Ben as he cuddled the woman, "that we arrive here with our eccentric personality traits intact. That enriches and invigorates our social life."

"Yes, of course," Keaflyn responded, somewhat dizzy.

A slovenly, heavy-browed man stomped up to the group and glared at the two Kalobangers. "Are you two coming to rehearsal or aren't you?" he demanded stormily.

"Yes, yes, right away, Ludwig," Klon and Flon chorused.

Marilyn pulled away from Ben. "Can I help with anything, Luddy?" she murmured huskily. "I love good music so."

Ludwig frowned at her and replied with a disdainful snort. He whirled and stomped away with the Kalobangers hurrying along behind.

"What was that all about?" asked Keaflyn.

"Oh, Ludwig's still trying to get the first perfect performance of his Ninth Symphony," said Pvlikka.

"A pleasure meeting you, Mark," said Ben, who had reclaimed Marilyn and was now extending his hand to Mark.

"An honor for me," returned Keaflyn, stammering a bit. "I often wondered why some of you never turned up in present-day bodies."

"It ought to be based on morality," said Marilyn.

"That wouldn't work, my pretty," said Ben, leading her away. "That would drain off the cream."

"I think Ben's right about that," commented Lafe. "What good would be a heaven that skimmed off only the strongest and best souls? And as present company amply illustrates, souls of any caliber can fulfill their potentials."

"It doesn't seem that way to me," said Keaflyn, looking over the distinguished company. "I would merely say there's no one-to-one correlation between greatness and morality."

"Handsome, you're a soul after my own soul," Zennia approved.

Albert said, "I have found our discussion most informative," and shook Mark's hand.

"Wait a moment," said Mark as Albert moved away, wondering what discussion there had been for Albert to enjoy. "I wanted to ask you if the Locus-type objects are evenly spaced."

Albert grinned shyly, his large eyes sparkling. "Aha! A trick question! You know of only one Locus, but you ask if the others are evenly spaced. Very good! However, I must decline to answer your question, while advising you that your assumption concerning the existence of other Locus-type objects may or may not be correct."

"Lafe let drop that this isn't the only Avalon-type world," Keaflyn persisted.

"I wondered if you would catch that," said Albert. "Lafe has a less rigorous mind than my own, it seems." He nodded pleasantly and walked away.

"No point in keeping you in complete mystery, the way I see it," Lafe defended himself. "Humanity will explore far enough into the galaxy to find duplicate stabilities in a few hundred years, anyway."

"The sheer homeliness of you Earth creatures is beginning to bug me," said Pvlikka, and she vanished.

"Dolly, who is not at all homely, has promised to model for me," said Lennie. "Come along, fair one."

"We really must be going, too, Kathie," said Siggy, consulting an old-fashioned pocket watch.

"That was a short party," Keaflyn remarked dolefully as the four of them departed.

"They learned what they wanted about you," explained Lafe. "And you're my guest, not theirs. As for Zennia here, I suppose her curiosity about you is still unsatisfied."

Keaflyn was curious about the woman, too, as she was the only Earthsoul in the group he hadn't identified at least tentatively.

She smiled at him. "Why don't we introduce the visitor to the taste of ambrosia, Lafe?" she suggested.

"Why don't you take over my hosting duties and do it yourself?" he replied.

"My pleasure. Come along, Mark."

Keaflyn liked the idea but hesitated to leave such a promising source of information as Lafe. He said to the man, "The Senior Arlan Sibling warned me that I could be a serious danger with my Neg, that I'm in the middle of a cosmic crisis. What do you think, Lafe?"

"I think Berina's right. She's usually been right, though very thoroughly conservative, for the past forty-three trillion years. I would advise you not to let your Neg get the upper hand."

"That's what she said. But what should I do in this crisis?" Keaflyn demanded. "How am I to know what's the right decision for me, and what's wrong?"

Lafe looked thoughtful. "Think of it this way, Mark. Whatever you've been intending to do all along must be right. Otherwise the Neg wouldn't have shown up to try to move you in another direction. It's probably that simple, so don't complicate things in your mind. So long, pal."

"So long." Mark watched him leave regretfully, his mind still brimming with questions of a kind he did not expect Zennia would find interesting. "I suppose Lafe's curiosity was satisfied, too," he muttered.

"Don't feel put out by all the fast departures," she replied, accurately gauging his feelings. "All of us are so fully occupied that we come and go with little ceremony."

"Occupied with what?"

Zennia shrugged, a fetching gesture the way she did it. "That would be impossible to explain. Time and busyness just fit together in a different way here than they do outside. There are no words to describe the difference."

"And I suppose you'll dash off, too, when your curiosity is satisfied," he grunted.

"Very likely," she laughed.

"Okay, ask your question and have done with it."

"No question to ask. You see, Mark, my curiosity about males is strictly physical."

"Oh? And how do you express your curiosity?"

"Very skillfully. Otherwise, I wouldn't be on Avalon. Let's go eat."

What annoyed Keaflyn was that the data he was getting on Avalon was subjective, anecdotal stuff, not at all the hard, measurable observations he needed for his investigation. This was doubly irksome because his mind was temporarily free of Neg and pleasure-impress, and he felt he could do some excellent work if he had the opportunity.

He could only hope the *Kelkontar*, operating without his guidance, was doing better than he. He had, of course, instructed the ship to observe and record all possible data while he was away. But he had a hunch he would leave Avalon with no more solid information than had those pioneer spacemen who had stumbled across this planet and made a legend of it.

He frowned at the thought. Those earlier visitors, he was sure, hadn't found Avalon in orbit around Lumon's Star, although this was certainly the logical place for such a planet. As a stability, it would need a stable sun. But the legends suggested Avalon could hop about freely through the galaxy . . . or perhaps projections of it could.

That thought made him wonder how real his present experiences were.

Maybe his ship could tell him. An urgent desire to find out kept his stay on Avalon from becoming lengthy. Despite his realization that he did not belong and as an outsider would never be able to understand the activities that went on here, he was loving every minute of his sojourn. And he knew somehow, without being told, that the moment he returned to the ship his visit would be over.

But return he did. After cycling himself through the lock he paused, looking inward. No, the act of entering the ship hadn't turned on the giggle and the Neg. The only change he could sense in himself was one of a return to reality from . . . from whatever Avalon was. There was a feeling of loss in that, but it was not overwhelming.

"Kelly, have you been observing and recording?" he asked.

"Yes, Mark. It's all on tape. Lift-off instructions?"

"No lift-off," Keaflyn snapped. "We're going to stay right here while I study your findings. Tell me in general what you have while you run off the summaries."

"Okay. The data indicates this to be an undeveloped Earth-type planet, Mark."

"I know that's what it looks like. But what did you detect that didn't support that appearance?"

"Nothing, Mark."

"Nothing?" Keaflyn pondered this. "What about processes of geologic change? You were here long enough to note their absence."

"They were not absent, Mark. The nearby brook is carrying a normal load of dissolved minerals and fine silt. Also, a two-decimeter segment of its bank caved in and washed away while I was recording."

Keaflyn giggled. "Then this planet must be so stable that it can afford to appear unstable."

"We are no longer on the planet, Mark," the ship reported.

Keaflyn realized that his giggle should have made him suspect as much. "But I told you no lift-off!" he griped.

"I did not lift off," the *Kelkontar* replied. "The planet is no longer here."

"Let me look."

The viewscreen lit up to survey the heavens. Lumon's Star was a glowing sun, just where it should be against the stellar background. But there was no planet. Keaflyn recalled that the spacemen who had claimed visits to Avalon in the past had never been able to find it for a second visit.

He stared at the screen and chuckled. A dream? No, it couldn't have been that, not with all the data the ship had recorded. Also, it didn't have the feel of an ended dream. It was as if he had just finished reading an absorbing, fantastic tale and had closed the book.

Avalon was real, all right, but was not of his reality. Perhaps it was better than his own—more solid in its way, more stable, more senior than the universe he knew. He had coexisted with it for a little while . . . and that was all he had any right to expect. Sojourns in magic lands were of necessity brief.

"Well, back to the mundane, Kelly," he laughed painfully. "Set warp for Bensor."

Chapter 7

There was no point in advertising his return to Bensor, he decided. A call on his parents in his afflicted condition would give them no pleasure and do him no good. And while the Sect Dualers had no special reason to expect him to show up on his home planet at this time, they could probably be alert to that possibility . . . if they were still out to finish him and his Neg.

Thus, Keaflyn did not notify the city directory of Bensor-on-Bensor of his arrival. Instead, he put the *Kelkontar* down at a small ship-park on the outskirts—one patronized mostly by in-system traffic—where he could live aboard during his stay rather than take an apartment. That would keep records of his presence to a minimum.

The Neg, only mildly troublesome during the flight from Lumon's Star, turned on the pain within minutes after his arrival. His grin became a grimace that he was self-conscious about displaying in public—normal people just didn't wear such expressions. But he had to move about the city; his business here was of a kind that almost had to be handled in person.

Attempts to concentrate on keeping a blank face were only partially successful. He could do it only for as long as he *did* concentrate. And a blank face wouldn't solve the problem, anyway—there were so damned many distress-sensitives about. Not full telepaths, of course; Keaflyn wasn't sure a full telepath existed. But many people, such as Tinker and Alo Felston, could catch the peculiar radiations of a sorely troubled mind. Such radiations could not be picked out clearly from any distance in a well-populated city, the way Felston had located him in the isolation of the Sonora Desert. Still, any sensitive he got close to might become troublesomely helpful and inquisitive.

The only thing to do was finish his business as quickly as possible and get back into space.

He debarked from his ship and hailed a robocar.

"Where to, sir?" the car asked as he climbed in.

"Donflannis Instras Corporation, by way of Central Boulevard," he instructed, settling back.

"Yes, sir. A verification message, sir?"

Keaflyn considered the idea. If he arrived at Donflannis Instras without advance notice, he might encounter delaying red tape that would bring him into close contact with several people before he reached John Donflannis. There would be some chance of that at best, since he had made no advance appointment.

"Yes," he said. "Message John Donflannis the Jumblejunk Kid will arrive in (blank) minutes." He giggled over the nickname John Donflannis had stuck on him—a result of the numerous one-of-a-kind devices the corporation had fabricated on Keaflyn's order.

"Nine minutes, sir," responded the robocar, filling in the blank.

"Thank you."

Keaflyn tried to keep himself exteriorized and his distress down by watching the scenery along Central Boulevard. The one-hundred-meter-wide thoroughfare had an urban look almost antiquarian in atmosphere. Massive durastone buildings soared into the clean, sunny air on both sides, interspersed with frequent cross-streets. There was a fair flow of robocar traffic, and Keaflyn could see a number of strolling pedestrians on the walkways.

Unlike most cities, Bensor-on-Bensor was not mobile. It had grown up around the Resistant Globe, at the spot where the Globe had been discovered by the first explorers from Earth. For many years, that gleaming, immovable stability had been the city's prime reason for being, as visitors flocked in to study or merely marvel at the giant mirror-bright object. But the city had long since outgrown its tourist-trap status to become the planetary capital and industrial center.

Being permanently placed was an inconvenience in some respects. The weather was atrocious at times, and no effort was made to control it, since humanity had long ago decided that planetary ecologies were far too easily wrecked by environmental regulation. And unlike such cities as Splendiss-on-Terra, the Bensor capital could not escape winters or drought by following the more pleasant seasons.

Moreover, since the city did not move, neither did the buildings shift about relative to each other; thus the city's heavy, large buildings, many of them no longer ideally suited for their purposes or for their locations with respect to surrounding structures and activities. Many persons remarked that Bensor-on-Bensor was downright backtracky, but Keaflyn considered that an exaggeration. True, an occasional building, too outmoded to meet a present need, stood dark and deserted amid the bustle of midtown activity. And now and then, such a structure would be demolished on the site, to make way for something more useful. But there was no real decay and certainly nothing resembling a slum.

At the most, Keaflyn mused with a chuckle, the city was no more than four centuries backtracky, and you

had to go back twice that far for the really grim filth
and fester.

Central Boulevard ran tangent to Globe Circus, and
he got a quick glimpse of the stability in passing. The
sight brought a question to his mind: When he reached
the stage of his studies where he needed to run tests on
the Globe, how was he going to manage it in his afflicted
condition? Concerned sensitives would be sure to pester
him. And what about the Sect Dualers? He could hardly
set up his instruments on Globe Circus without attracting
entirely too much attention.

Well, that was a problem to think about, but he had
more immediate concerns. Still, he didn't want to leave
the city without paying the Resistant Globe his respects
with more than a passing glance. Perhaps he could come
back by and stop for a while at a time of day when few
people were around.

John Donflannis stepped into the reception court of
Donflannis Instras just as the robocar drove in. He was
grinning as Keaflyn got out.

"Well, well!" he barked, moving lankily forward to
pump Keaflyn's arm. "What kind of no-profit gadget are
you going to bug me with this time, Jumblejunk?" Then
he took a closer look at his visitor and the grin evaporated. "What's wrong with you, Mark?" he asked with
concern.

"Nothing to fret about, John," Keaflyn managed to say
without laughing. "A problem I can't blow, but a couple
of friends of mine are working on it."

"Come on into my office," said Donflannis.

Keaflyn followed him in, was seated, and accepted a
drink. "John, do you have any Sect Dualers working for
you?" he asked.

"Sect Dualers?" Donflannis echoed blankly. "Who? Oh, yes! I remember who they are now. The contralife bunch. No, none of them in the shop that I know of. Why do you ask?"

Keaflyn told him briefly about the impinging Neg and the drastic actions to counter it taken by the Sect Dualer Arnod Smath on Earth. After Donflannis finished exploding with rage, Keaflyn added:

"I'm sure the Neg is really riding me, John, but not the way the Dualists seem to think. All it can do is make me feel lousy, and its aim seems to be to keep me from my work by doing just that. Needless to say, I don't want to run into any more characters like Arnod Smath. I'm trying to keep my presence on Bensor quiet and want to get away as soon as possible. Also"—Keaflyn paused and pulled a sheaf of drawings out of his jacket—"here are the designs for a special Lumon probe I'd like you to build for me. I want it this lifetime, because I understand this may be my last as a capable human. I have to hurry."

"Okay," said Donflannis, glancing rapidly through the drawings. "You said someone was working on this mental problem you have . . . "

"Yes. You remember my talking about Tinker? She's an ego-field therapist and is going to research this pleasure-impress thing. A man named Alo Felston, who's sensitive to lower animals, is working with her. Tinker may be ordering some psionic equipment from you; I gave her your name."

"Sounds like another no-profit job," Donflannis grumbled. "Thanks a lot." He was still examining the drawings. "I'd say from these plans that you think there's a spacewarp inside Lumon's Star. Right?"

Keaflyn laughed. "More like one times ten to the ump-teenth power warps, atom-sized. Quantums of warp. Warpicles. Here, you'd better read my prelim on Lumon's Star so you'll know what the new probe will be dealing with." He brought a tape spool out of his pocket and handed it across the desk.

"Oh, a report all ready for publication," remarked Donflannis, after running the first few frames through his desk viewer.

"Yeah," said Keaflyn, suddenly struck by an idea. "Say, John, the rest of my business on Bensor is to nurse that report through the mill at Science Reporting Service. If I had someone who understood its contents to act as my agent, I could scram right away."

Donflannis gave him a wry look. "Meaning me?"

Keaflyn grinned and nodded.

In a mock-syrupy voice Donflannis said, "What's an old friend for, Mark, except to be imposed upon? Sure, I'll see this into print for you. But let's make sure I know what it's all about first."

"Okay, and many thanks, John."

After a marathon work session that lasted well into the evening, Keaflyn and Donflannis parted, both of them well satisfied that Donflannis had a clear understanding of the probe his company was to make and of the report he was to handle. Keaflyn declined an invitation to the Donflannis home, feeling that his affliction could make him a rather jarring visitor in a household that included two small children.

He stepped out into the semigloom of the company's reception court and discovered it was drizzling rain. At that moment a cruising robocar rolled into the turn-around, and he hailed it, pleased with this minor stroke of luck.

"Where to, sir?" the car asked as he ducked inside.

The late hour and the drizzle, it occurred to him, could make this an ideal opportunity to observe the Resistant Globe without a lot of people around. "Globe Circus," he instructed.

"Yes, sir."

The car pulled out into the street. Keaflyn leaned back, closed his eyes, and tried to relax. The day with Don-flannis had been one of fruitful accomplishment, but his constant effort to conceal the worst of his physical distress while also keeping his hysteria buttoned up had made it a day of strain.

He grimaced. The last few hours had been a minor trauma, he mused unhappily. Something had to be done about his ache . . . but what? Previous bouts with it had been brief, but now it had been on full-power all day.

If only the Arlan Siblings and the *Calcutta's* delightful pool were handy, to make the Neg beat a retreat . . . but the *Calcutta* was probably a week away, in the vicinity of Vega. What else would be pleasurable and was available? Not a thing that seemed impressive at the moment.

What about some old-fashioned medication? It had been centuries since he had taken a painkiller, but it was worth a try. The ship probably had information on how to synthesize aspirin. He decided to ask when he returned to the *Kelkontar*.

Meanwhile, closed eyes were keeping him too interior-ized, making him more aware of the pain. He opened them and looked out at the rain. "Aren't we there yet?" he asked irritably.

"We'll arrive shortly, sir," the car responded.

"Why aren't we on Central Boulevard?"

"We are following the computed route, sir." Keaflyn stared at the nearby buildings, trying to determine his location. When he did, he decided the routing computer was definitely out of order. He was nowhere near Globe Circus. Or maybe the car had misunderstood him.

"I want to go to Globe Circus," he said. "Did you get that right?"

"Yes, sir."

Keaflyn grunted in disgust. There was no point in arguing with an out-of-whack computer. "Stop here," he ordered. "I'll get off here."

"We'll arrive shortly, sir."

"Never mind that! Stop!"

"Well arrive shortly, sir."

"Oh, damn!" Keaflyn yanked at the door handle, planning to leave the car on the move. The handle would not budge.

Only then did it dawn on him that he was being kidnapped. This robocar had obviously been rigged and had been waiting especially for him when he left the Donflannis building. The Sect Dualers!, he realized with a feeling of panic. But who had tipped them off he was there?

Coldly, he pushed down the fear that was making him giggle explosively. If the Sect Dualers were determined enough to grab him, they would have needed no tip-off. They would have had the Donflannis shop—a place

Keaflyn was known to visit frequently when on Bensor—under constant surveillance.

Was there no way out of this damned robocar?

He was searching wildly for some possibility when the car pulled into a building and stopped. A door clanged shut behind it and lights came on. When the car door opened, Keaflyn found himself gazing at two men armed with pistols.

"Get out, please, Mr. Keaflyn," one of them said.

He felt too tired to move. "Why should I bother?" he chuckled. "You guys have some goofy ideas, but you're no more capable of murder than I am. Go ahead and shoot, if you can."

Several seconds passed in silence. Then one of the men shoved his pistol under his belt and motioned his companion to do the same. Then they leaped forward quickly, grabbed Keaflyn by the arms and lifted him bodily from the car.

"This way, Mr. Keaflyn," one said as they hustled him along. He got his feet under him and let them guide him into the depths of the building, realizing that the feeling of overwhelming tiredness had vanished as suddenly as it had appeared.

Keaflyn now perceived, for the first time and with precision, exactly what the Neg was trying to do to him! He laughed loudly and boisterously.

The men led him into a dimly lit room where two more men were seated. One was Arnod Smath.

"Well, we meet again, doctor," laughed Keaflyn. Smath regarded him gravely.

"Regrettably, Mark," he replied, after a moment. "I should have dealt more adequately with the problem the first time. You realize we don't enjoy this?"

"I imagine not," Keaflyn chortled. "I've been told the guilt of the destroyer is as traumatic as the damage to the destroyed. But I'm not inclined to offer my sympathy."

The other seated man spoke up. "We understand you've been aboard the *Calcutta* since Dr. Smath saw you."

Keaflyn grinned at him in silence.

"Why did the Arlans turn you loose?" the man asked.

"Because they know a damn sight more than you guys and are far less sure they know everything," Keaflyn snapped.

"Meaning what?"

"Meaning they didn't know what the Negs' intentions were. Neither did I, until just now."

"Oh? And what are the Negs' intentions?"

"To get me killed. You idiots have been playing the Negs game all along!"

"Interesting, if true. And if untrue, a clever theory for you to advance under the circumstances. What's your evidence?"

"I went to Splendiss-on-Terra, where the local medic just happened to be a Sect Dualer. The Neg picked that moment to hit me with an ache, when my condition would come to the attention of a man who would interpret my symptoms as a reason to derange or kill me.

"After that, the Neg remained more mildly in evidence while I was still on Earth, perhaps hoping for my confinement, in a hospital for instance, as a second-best goal. Once on my ship and away from other people, I wasn't bothered by the Neg until shortly before I boarded the *Calcutta* and entered the presence of other prospective confiners or killers.

"I left the *Calcutta* without a pain in my body and stayed that way until I reached the stability where I meant to conduct some tests. Now, I admit there was nobody around at the time to do me in, so the Negs' efforts there must have been for another purpose. I would think it was trying to discourage me from doing my work. Maybe because Negs are opposed to increased knowledge per se, just as we are opposed to increased ignorance, but more likely because the Negs are skittish about my work in particular. Why else would they want me killed?

"After that, no more pain until I arrived on Bensor," Keaflyn concluded. "It's been giving me a fit ever since, to let the local contingent of Sect Dualers know it's still on the job. And here you are, with the good Dr. Smath hinting that he'll struggle manfully against his humane squeamishness this time in order to do a bang-up job on me and my Neg."

He stopped, then added, "Oh, I almost forgot. When your colleagues pointed their guns at me and ordered me out of the robocar, I was all at once too tired to move. The Neg couldn't have been sure the guns were just a bluff." He chuckled wildly. "I wasn't very damned sure of it myself! Anyway, your pals had to jerk me out of the car."

The seated man glanced at the two men behind Keaflyn for a moment, then nodded.

"So the Neg can make you tired, huh?" he observed.

"Sure. It seems capable of hitting me with any psycho-somatic sensation or unpleasant emotion. But it can't overwhelm me with them. I manage."

"No other indication of its presence?"

"No."

Smath looked questioningly at the other seated man and was given a quick nod. Keaflyn concluded that the exchange had informed the doctor Keaflyn was speaking truthfully, which meant Smath's colleague was a sensitive.

"The Arlan Siblings looked you over and let you go," the man said reflectively, "though you attribute to them data on the Negs that is superior to ours. Why did they free you?"

Keaflyn shrugged. "I'll tell you anything you want to know about myself. If you want to know something about the Arlans, I suggest you ask them. They seem to value their privacy, and I'm not going to violate it."

"We know the Negs would consider them key individuals," the man stated.

"Okay, you know that," replied Keaflyn.

The questioner and Smath huddled for a whispered conversation. Keaflyn waited.

After a couple of minutes they broke it up. The questioner told one of the men behind Keaflyn, "Go ungimmick the robocar." Then to Keaflyn he said, "We're letting you go, Mark. Your interpretation of the Neg's aims concerning you is convincing—at least to the degree that we don't care to risk aiding the enemy's cause in our efforts to hinder it. Also, we are inclined to respect the judgment of the Arlans."

"Glad to hear it," chuckled Keaflyn.

Smath cleared his throat uncomfortably. "There's no way to tell you, Mark, how deeply I regret . . . uh, the damage you sustained at my hands. I was only carrying out . . . well, I felt fully justified . . . "

"Both of us will just have to live with my affliction, won't we?" Keaflyn giggled. Smath winced and turned away.

"We wish you well, Mark," said the questioner.

Keaflyn couldn't honestly say the feeling was mutual, so he merely nodded and turned to the door. The Neg was no longer paining him, he noticed thankfully. Now that he and the Sect Dualers had reached a truce, it evidently had backed away once more from the pleasure-impress. Perhaps, he ruminated, he owed Smath a modicum of gratitude after all . . . but he had no intention of paying it.

The man detailed to ungimmick the robocar was closing the hood as Keaflyn approached. "Will it obey my orders now?" he asked.

The man nodded.

Keaflyn got in the car. "Globe Circus," he commanded.

"Yes, sir."

The car rolled out into the rain, now a hard downpour. Keaflyn watched the car's progress critically until he was sure it was moving in the right direction.

He relaxed, with a strong feeling of relief. Not only had his Neg-induced physical discomforts vanished; gone also was the threat of physical or mental harm from the Sect Dualers. He had not realized until now, until the threat was lifted, just how deeply it had bothered him.

Even the pleasure-impress, though basically as firmly fixed to him as ever, seemed less effective with the other problems eased. That was a normal phenomenon: cure a mind of one thing, and in the sudden ebullience of its release the mind may—temporarily—cure its remaining problems.

In any case, his expression felt like a relaxed smile rather than a taut grin.

"Globe Circus, sir," announced the robocar. Keaflyn looked out at the stability through the constant rain-splatter on the car window.

"Move around to the windward side."

"Yes, sir, if you will indicate which side is windward," replied the robocar. "I am not equipped with sufficient sensors—"

"Of course not," replied Keaflyn, realizing he had given a command beyond a robocar's capabilities. "Turn left and move around the Circus until I say stop."

The car circled the stability until Keaflyn halted it with the rain blowing against its left side and the Resistant Globe on its right.

"Lower the rear window on the right," he instructed. The glass dropped and Keaflyn leaned outward, his eyes fixed in contemplation of one of his favorite sights in the universe: the soaring bulge of the Resistant Globe's dark perfect-mirror surface.

It was not especially huge—forty and a fraction meters in diameter—and its reflectivity gave a fleeting impression of insubstantiality. But no one viewed the Globe for more than a split-second without sensing that here was the essence of solidity, of endurance. It had this quality to a degree that was present in no other known stability. Whereas Lumon's Star was an unfailing light, the Resistant Globe was the unyielding object.

The Rock of Ages, mused Keaflyn, pulling that phrase in from his backtrack. Interesting, he thought, how man back in the Earthbound days had invented religious concepts with characteristics similar to those of stabilities discovered since. Thus a god would be a dependable rock and an ever-shining light . . . but what about the characteristics of Locus? Um-m-m. He couldn't recall a god who made a point of motionlessness . . .

He shrugged these thoughts aside. To modern man, the Resistant Globe was a marvel, but a non-mystical marvel. It was a challenge to his science and his mental powers—a very stubborn challenge.

Scientific investigation of it had yielded practically nothing. Even neutrino beams, the most penetrating energies known, entered-the Globe to a maximum penetration of 1.44 centimeters before bouncing out. Keaflyn's only hope of doing better than that in his study was a rather vague one; he hoped, in the course of analyzing other stabilities, to hit upon a means of probing this one.

Mental investigation of the Globe was only a half-serious game, but one widely played. Earthbound visitors to an old Irish castle had once made a practice of kissing the Blarney Stone; galactic citizens visiting Bensor-on-Bensor made a practice of "nulling" the Resistant Globe.

This ritual was, in a way, a philosophical experiment . . . though maybe a silly one, Keaflyn mused. Theoretically, matter and energy were subservient to thought—that is, all the physical universe and its appurtenances existed because mind considered they did. Thus, if mind said some particular part of the universe had ceased to exist, then that part should vanish.

Mind, however, was myriads of minds—ego-fields strong and ego-fields weak. In order for mind to change, countless individual minds would have to do so. Certainly there would have to be a consensus, or at least a majority opinion, to make an existing reality cease existing—providing, of course, that the theory of the seniority of thought was correct.

Nevertheless, the individual ego-field could nullify an existence from its *own* viewpoint by a simple act of will. The saner, more fully self-determined the ego-field, the more confident its act of nulling. The ego-field could null a wall and move through the space where the wall had been, finding nothing there. Of course, if the ego-field tried to walk its body through the wall, the body would be stopped very abruptly and might contract a bloody nose in the process. Again, if the ego-field depended on information from its body's eyes, it would have data to the effect that the wall had remained solid all the time.

But the ego-field could nullify any object, any energy, for itself as an ego-field. This was a contributing consideration to the theory that a general agreement of mind could cause actual nullity. And that was why visitors to the Resistant Globe, after looking at it as long as they wished, ended their visit by nulling it. Over enough years, every human-grade ego-field in the galaxy or even in the universe might pass that place and tell the Globe: *"Vanish!"*

And perhaps it *would*.

Probably the game was not entirely explainable as a philosophical experiment, Keaflyn ruminated as he continued gazing at the Globe, brightly illuminated through the night by glow-panels concealed in the shrubs around its base. For trillions of years the individual human had known himself as a soon-to-perish entity in a never-ending, ever-surviving universe. That knowing was opposite to fact, as humanity now had learned. But this was recent learning, perhaps recent enough for humans still to harbor a remnant of resentment against the apparently durable universe. And what better object to vent this resentment on than a stability, the Resistant Globe?

Keaflyn stirred. He was ready to return to his ship and get some sleep—sleep that should come easily in his relaxed condition. It was time for the parting ceremony. Even though he had nulled the Globe before, he always repeated the action at the end of each visit.

Vanish! he willed it. It did so. Although his eyes could still see it, his ego-field sense corresponding to sight said nothing was there but empty air. And this sense could examine the far side of Globe Circus through the vacancy, could observe the buildings there and—

Something *aware but alien* was suddenly using that same sense! The Neg was stirring!

Keaflyn twitched with alarm. Was this the Neg's bid to seize control from him, to direct his mind and actions?

He tensed for the struggle, but no contest began. The Neg was not fighting him, not disagreeing with him. It was merely going along with his own thought-processes, verifying and supporting with its own act of will the nullity of the Resistant Globe . . .

Nullity?

Keaflyn's startled attention turned to what his eyes were seeing.

In the center of the Circus, where the sparkling Globe had stood, now hung darkness—darkness that wavered, threatening to become transparent with the complete annihilation of the stability that had once existed there!

A calm corner of Keaflyn's frantic mind was contributing: *Of course contralife entities have their own share of the total mind. And perhaps they can channel a consensus through one individual Neg, which added to the nulling actions of several billion humans who have nulled the Resistant Globe is sufficient to . . .*

Emergency alarms in the city were clanging loudly, he realized. Of course, all sorts of detectors and alarms had long been rigged around the Globe to give notice of any change in its condition. These were sounding now, arousing the city.

And suddenly something previously unknown to Keaflyn's experience but immediately recognizable impinged on his mind: transmitted human thought, powerful enough even for his minute telepathic ability—because this was a thought from thousands in chorus, a thought of distress, a thought seeking him:

(What?) The Resistant Globe! Being nulled!

Oh, no! It can't be!

Universal collapse!

(Who? Where?) Close by! There he is! Mark Keaflyn!

Mark Keaflyn! STOP IT, MARK KEAFLYN!

My God, and we made a game out of this!

Contralife—he's harboring contralife!

Stop him, somebody! Who's close?

SOMEBODY KILL KEAFLYN, FOR GOD'S SAKE!

Keaflyn quivered under the mental impact of frightened hate boiling around him. *I meant no harm!* he tried to reply, but he had no impression that his thought was received. *I'll try to fix it back*, he promised, and stared hard at the place where the Resistant Globe had been. *Be there!* he willed.

The darkness seemed to thicken in response, but no more than that.

—*We'll stop him! We're on our way!*

Keaflyn could sense that they were indeed on their way, converging on Globe Circus with whatever weapons they could lay hands on.

It won't do any good to kill me now! he tried to tell them. *The harm's done, and not by my intention.* But he was too out of agreement with the consensus for his communication to register.

"Get out of here, car!" he yelled hoarsely. "West on Central Boulevard!"

"Yes, sir," the car responded, and began to move.

"Highest legal speed!" he snapped.

"Yes, sir."

The car was on the Boulevard and speeding westward in seconds. A few minutes would take him to the ship-park in the outskirts where he had left the *Kelkontar* . . . if he was not stopped.

And if the Sect Dualers really had unrigged their over-rides on this car's robot . . . After that possibility occurred to Keaflyn, he watched each approaching intersection with anxiety, wondering if the robocar would swerve right or left, carrying him away from his one hope for avoidance of death and degradation.

Chapter 8

In his hurried dash for his ship and the safety of outer space, Keaflyn was at no time really aware of the Insecurity, as that moment in time came to be called. Only upon being told of it later, and thinking back, did he realize that he might have been feeling, during his escape, a threat to far more than his personal being.

But at the time the Neg had turned on the pain again, shortly after Keaflyn ordered his robocar away from the badly compromised Resistant Globe, and had thrown in fear for good measure. Keaflyn had all but forgotten what the physical sensations of gut fear were like, and for several panicky seconds he was nearly unmanned by that all-too-appropriate emotional overresponse to his situation.

He was aware, as the robocar sliced through the rain on Central Boulevard, that the telepathic chorus of the awakened people of the city was dimming, seemingly being left behind as he fled from the center of town. This gave him hope that he was making good his escape. The thought did not occur to him that the populace's attention had been drawn from him by a concern of far more tremendous magnitude and urgency: the nearly nullified Resistant Globe.

That was the Insecurity.

It aroused not only the citizens of Bensor-on-Bensor, but sleeping lifeforms on worlds scattered through an immense range of the galaxy. And on countless worlds, beings who were not sleeping at the time but were busy with their usual pursuits were frozen in mid-action by that same urgent alarm.

Reality seemed to *slip*, as they described the sense of it later. It was somewhat similar to the loss of orientation that comes with intoxication . . . but only somewhat: because this was not the product of a drunken mind's view of the universe; this was slippage of the universe itself.

Sleepers awoke suddenly, to grab (with an instinct they did not know they possessed) at reality and grip it tight.

Walkers halted in their tracks, as suddenly, to concentrate on bearing witness that the ground beneath them and the sky above were thoroughly and definitely *there*.

Swimmers stopped paddling to validate the waters around them.

Fliers stopped flapping. They glided. Many of them crashed to ground, their concentration unbroken.

Indeed, ego-fields that were between lives stopped non-doing briefly in order to do.

Those particular billions of humans who had played the game of Nulling the Resistant Globe did not direct their grip to reality in general. They knew, deeply and non-intellectually, precisely where the Insecurity had struck. Wherever they were on the wide-scattered worlds of humanity, they reached for the Resistant Globe, found it, and hung on.

On the world Danolae, Alo Felston halted in the act of rigging a psionic device on a sad-faced hound dog, and the hound dog halted scratching.

On Terra, the operators of Splendiss stopped mere seconds before they were due to lift that city from its late-summer site in Quebec to its early-autumn spot in the mid-Appalachians. Disaster was missed by that much.

And behind the fleeing Keaflyn in Bensor-on-Bensor, four Sect Dualers in a pursuing robocar were distracted from their grim intent to do their share toward meeting a still grimmer challenge. Their robocar, however, continued westward on Central Boulevard, so Keaflyn gained no ground. Not right then. But when he turned off the thoroughfare at the ship-park where the *Kelkontar* waited, the preoccupied Sect Dualers took no notice and sped on by.

Why was he not involved with the rest of humanity in shoring up the Insecurity erosion? That remained something of a moot question long afterward. Perhaps because he had consciously done all he could, before anyone else, to repair the ruin he and his impinging Neg had triggered by nulling the Resistant Globe. He had withdrawn his nullification and had willed the Globe to *be there!* as forcefully as he could.

Or perhaps he did not participate because, as the being who had done the harm, he was automatically excluded by some unwritten law of mind from trying to help with the mending.

Or perhaps he *did* participate. Among the other concerns his frantic mind held during those few long minutes, the continuation of the Resistant Globe was not missing. He did not cease wanting it to *be there!* Maybe the fact that he alone knew precisely what had happened enabled him to continue other conscious activities while fighting the Insecurity.

He reached his ship feeling much more closely pursued than he actually was, cycled himself hastily through the lock, and yelled "Lift off, Kelly!"

"Okay, Mark," the ship replied. "Now lifting."

"Make it fast, and set warp for . . . for Vega!" That wasn't the first destination that came to his mind. He did not mean it to be his destination at all. He thought of Vega because that was where the Arlan Siblings were, and he named it because he had to move away from Bensor in some direction. After he had thrown pursuers off his trail he could change course—probably for Locus.

He flopped down on a relaxer, feeling weak, shaky, and wrapped in pain.

"Kelly," he groaned, "search your references for data on the formulation of a medication called aspirin."

After a pause the ship replied, "I have the necessary information, Mark."

"Good! Can you make up a batch of it?"

"Yes. In fifteen minutes."

"All right. Get started on it. Are your detectors on full for signs of ships trailing me?"

"No, Mark."

"Well, get them on!" he snapped.

"Okay, Mark . . . There is no indication we are being followed."

"Nothing at all?"

"No. Nothing."

Keaflyn's pain and gut-fear vanished. He laughed as he slumped deeper into the relaxer. "No rush about the aspirin, Kelly."

"All right."

Just as he began to doze off, Keaflyn was snapped awake by the ship's warning: "We're being followed now, Mark."

Keaflyn sat up and tensed himself against the return of pain. Several seconds passed while he waited. Then he chuckled. Could his Neg have exhausted itself? It had really been working long and hard on him, almost

constantly throughout his stay on Bensor, and if impingement was as hard on a Neg as he imagined it must be,
then his invader should be in a worse state of collapse
right now than he was!

"How many ships and what range?"

"One, at extreme range," the ship told him.

Extreme range for the *Kelkontar's* detectors was 2.3
light-months. "Display it," he said.

The viewscreen lit up to show a graphic of pursued
and pursuer, with vector lines of indicated warp velocities and log-plotted scales to right and left to take in the
Bensor system behind and the Vega system days ahead.
A glance showed the *Kelkontar* would be overtaken in a
shade less than six hours.

"You're at max warp, aren't you?" Keaflyn asked,
although he knew the answer.

"Yes."

He let out a giggly sigh. Why had he thought all he
had to do was get into space to be safe? The *Kelkontar*
was a good little ship, but not a racer—and, of course,
not a fighter either.

Evasive tactics?

He shrugged. If he began zigging and zagging he
would merely be overtaken more quickly. The pursuer
could stay on his tail with zig-zags narrower than his
own. And if he doglegged, the distance-gain would be
the pursuer's.

All this business of chasing and being chased was nonsense, anyway. What had happened at the Resistant
Globe was, perhaps, a cataclysmic disaster, but it should
make no difference to the relationship between himself
and the Sect Dualers.

"Kelly, see if you can comm that ship," he requested.

"Yes, Mark . . . Comm established. Do you want visual?"

"Sure."

The viewscreen revealed the faces of Arnod Smath and the man who had questioned Keaflyn back on Bensor.

"Dr. Smath," Keaflyn snickered with a slight bow, "and I never did catch your colleague's name . . ."

"Carmon Daylemon," the man supplied, brusquely. "What do you want, Keaflyn?"

"I want you gentlemen to relax and go home," he laughed. "What else?"

"We'll do so . . . in a few hours, after we have secured the universe against a threat we have allowed to exist too long," Daylemon returned grimly.

"Meaning me and my Neg?"

"What else?"

"I told you before, the Neg is suckering you into playing his game!" Keaflyn snorted. "That hasn't changed."

"Through you," Daylemon returned coldly, "the Neg has already accomplished far more than your death. We're calling a halt to it."

"If the Negs wanted to nullify the Resistant Globe," Keaflyn argued, "they could have done so through any one of the thousands of people who visited the Globe daily. And they could have done it long ago, since we've been playing that nullifying game for centuries. So, the question you guys should be asking yourselves is: Why did they pick me as their medium?"

Daylemon made an impatient gesture. "I can anticipate the answer you're going to hand us to that. The Negs chose you to give us a new motivation to kill you.

I'll grant a possibility—a slim possibility—that you're right, that the prime goal of the Negs is to bring about your death and the stoppage of your research. But there are other more logical interpretations, Keaflyn.

"I would say the most probable of these is that, while the Negs would foresee our reaction to the compromising of the Resistant Globe, they would also anticipate your being able to escape us or to talk us out of our intent. You survived your encounter with Smath on Terra and the one with me a few hours ago on Bensor. The Negs are doubtless pleased with the durability you've displayed. They find you a useful tool indeed. Not only do your plans promise to put you in a position to wreck one stability after another, but you've proved your ability to survive while you do so.

"We're stopping you this time, Keaflyn. That's final."

For a long moment Keaflyn sat silent and grinning, feeling rather foolish. Daylemon's viewpoint, after all, did make sense. The impinging Neg had managed to stir up quite a ruckus. Considering, he now wondered: Had it really been trying to get him killed—or merely make him think that was its mission?

He blinked at that thought. Nothing would make him look out for his survival more thoroughly than the belief that the Neg was trying to kill him. Therefore, it was extremely likely that the Neg would want to make him believe that, as a first order of business, so Keaflyn would guard himself from harm while he carried out the Neg's purposes.

Dully he asked, "If that's what the Neg's up to, why is it letting me become half-convinced that you're right?"

The image of Daylemon stared at him. "I don't know. Doubtless there's a limit to what the Neg can anticipate. We believe they can foresee the future in much the same manner as we can recall the past. If the parallel is exact, it is their own future they would see with some clarity, not ours, just as we cannot know the pasts of others by direct recall but only by hearsay. We cannot be sure whether we overestimate or underestimate the Negs' powers of anticipation.

"But in the present instance," Daylemon continued, "we can easily see what future course of events would be most disastrous to humanity and most helpful to the Negs: the undermining of the stabilities. When we compare that clear and present danger to the vague possibility that we might be stopping the development of desirable knowledge through your research"—he shrugged—"our choice is quite obvious, Keaflyn."

After a moment Keaflyn nodded. "The only flaw I can see in all this is, if you're right, why did my Neg let me get into the predicament I'm in now? You gents seemed determined to finish me off, and damned if I know how to stop you. If it wants me alive, why doesn't my Neg come to my rescue?"

"As I said," returned Daylemon, "the Negs must have their limitations. And when one impinges, it is working in an environment that must be very difficult and puzzling. It has to make mistakes, as yours obviously has."

That, too, made sense to Keaflyn. The fact that his Neg seemed to be conked out at the moment, after its long exertion on Bensor, could exemplify one specific area of limitation.

. . . And maybe if the Neg were on the job right now, keeping him half traumatized and not fully rational, he would not be so receptive to the sound reasoning by which Daylemon was weakening his urge for personal survival.

But, damn it all! he glowered internally, his research project *was* important! He did not want to be stopped! If this was to be his last go-around as a capable human, he wanted to make it count!

On the other hand, he did not want to be instrumental in pulling the whole universe down. "Was the nullification of the Resistant Globe complete?" he asked at last. "I notice you merely said 'compromised.'"

"No, it wasn't complete," said Daylemon thoughtfully. "We've been in comm with Bensor-on-Bensor . . . Something rather puzzling happened. Nobody seems to know just what so far. It was as if an automatic defense mechanism had been triggered. . . ."

"The Globe is still there, then," Keaflyn demanded eagerly, "the same as ever?"

"It's still there," Daylemon admitted. "It *looks* the same as ever, we're told. Whether it really is or not—whether it's still a stability—will have to be learned later."

"Hey! Maybe I did no harm at all!" Keaflyn exclaimed.

"That's the defense a pyromaniac might offer," snorted Daylemon, "after the citizens restored the town he burned down."

"That's a strained analogy," Keaflyn said.

Daylemon did not bother to reply to that. "I see no point in prolonging this discussion. Smath and I have an unpleasant duty to perform, and we would like to keep it as impersonal as possible. If you have nothing further to say . . ."

Keaflyn considered, then said, "Out." The image vanished. There was no chance of talking the Sect Dualers out of their attack on him.

What to do now? He could use some sleep, he knew, but with five and a half hours left in this lifetime, sleeping would be a waste.

Prepare to fight the Sect Dualers? He grimaced. What would he prepare with? The *Kelkontar* was not armed, and such defenses as it had against assault could be activated in full within seconds.

He chuckled. Get on with his work! Of course! Why shouldn't a man spend his final hours living as he had lived? Particularly if he had lived in accord with his desires.

"Kelly, set up the workboard," he ordered. "We'll continue our analysis of the Lumon's Star warpicles."

"Okay, Mark," said the ship. The board opened out of the bulkhead, revealing on its glowing face the mathematical permutations Keaflyn had been formulating before his arrival on Bensor. He sat in the chair at the keyboard while studying the three-channel symbol flows.

"Hum-m-m. Didn't I have an equivalence somewhere in that mess?" he asked.

"Yes." A red indicator flashed around one of the symbols. "Here."

"Oh, sure. Only a third-equivalence, of course. That doesn't simplify matters much. That's as inelegant a concoction of chicken-tracks as any mathematician ever got lost in, Kelly."

"The permutations do seem insolubly complex," the ship agreed.

"We're working with too little hard data about the warpicles, guessing at orders of magnitude where we ought to have precisely measured values," murmured Keaflyn. "About the only assumptions I feel sure of are one, that warpicles exist, and two, that they constitute a spectrum . . . Oh, well. Zoom and elaborate the first block, Kelly."

A segment of the screen full of symbols expanded to crowd off the remainder, and a mass of subscriptural details sprang into view. For several minutes Keaflyn absorbed himself in the math, silent except for snorts and snickers. Then he said, "Make a slow pan to block two." The symbols began a creeping motion from right to left across the screen. Time passed. "On to block three," he directed. " . . . Block four . . . "

When the symbols finally ran out, he straightened in his chair and blinked, surprised with the realization that two hours had passed. Three and a half left.

Urgency pressed in on him. "We can't handle this rigorously, Kelly, because we have no way of knowing what factors out, so I'm going to start throwing out by intuition. Both the non-equivalence channels are beyond redemption and may be meaningless besides. Drop them."

Two-thirds of the symbols vanished.

"Now start running concurrent sums and derives on what we have left."

Equations began to pile up above and below the row across the middle of the screen: a first order, a second order, a third . . . a fourth . . .

"Hold it!" Keaflyn peered at the results for several seconds. "Drop everything but the fourth sum and derive, and show me the Freund's Law warp equation in basic form."

Kelly did so.

After a moment Keaflyn said, "Check me on this if you can, Kelly, but it appears to me that our two equations form brackets, so to speak, that take in only a small portion of the field defined by Freund's Law. Do you need a special program to determine if that's true?"

"My standard programming includes the necessary operations, Mark," said the ship. The symbols on the screen flickered through a rapid series of manipulations, then steadied. "Here's the result, Mark."

"I see. That looks like about a hundredth of a warp field, if Freund's Law is right. It's as if Freund were describing the whole spectrum, and we are describing the blue band in the visible part."

"That could be an apt comparison, Mark," the ship approved.

"But our equations ought to define warps, if they mean anything at all!" snorted Keaflyn. "And if they do, the question is: what the hell is all the rest of that spectrum Freund takes in?"

"I don't know, Mark."

Keaflyn fidgeted. His time was running out, and he would have to do better than this if he wanted get any kind of report on the comm before the Sect Dualers came within attack range.

"We need a meaningfulness check," he griped, "which is to say we need that probe for the Lumon's Star test, but John Donflannis won't have fabricated *that* in less than three years. I don't have that kind of time, Kelly."

"So I've gathered, Mark."

"To hell with it," said Keaflyn, getting up. "Fix me a ham sandwich and coffee."

The ship served him the snack and he carried it back to the viewscreen, where the graphic was still displayed, showing the closing gap between the *Kelkontar* and pursuer.

"Kelly, in a couple of hours, I'm going to suit up and go out to wait on my violently-inclined acquaintances back there. I'll comm them and let them know. Then I want you to go to Danolae and, turn yourself over to Tinker. Her current-lifetime name is Marianne Didorik. Got that?"

"Yes. I will belong to Tinker until your return, Mark."

Keaflyn didn't reply. There was no point in trying to explain to the ship that his upcoming death involved the loss of more than a body . . . that the Mark Keaflyn ego-field was going to lose much as well. Perhaps too much for him to continue as a human. So he merely giggled and continued munching the sandwich.

It was very frustrating. But the blame was his own. He had refused to take the threat of the Sect Dualers seriously enough from the beginning, despite the pleas and warnings of Alo Felston, Tinker, Clav Didorik, and the Splendiss-on-Terra Emergencymen. He had blandly ignored the possibility of ever being involved in a non-sensical, backtrack, space-opera chase such as this . . . the quarry of determined killers.

That, he reflected with a sudden laugh, was the price of being sane. You weren't automatically afraid. You had confidence in yourself and in the universe. You didn't have to be careful. A sane mind was a carefree mind . . . in most cases, his own included. Those Sect Dualers avoided a carefree attitude toward life; they knew of an enemy.

But he, even with an enemy Neg impinging upon him, had refused to recognize danger as fully as he should. And now he was stuck in an indefensible position, in his cozy little ship that was unequipped to fight and too slow to run.

The Arlan Siblings, in their giant *Calcutta* which was probably armored and armed to the teeth, had the realistic approach.

Keaflyn, on the other hand, hadn't even bothered to keep the *Kelkontar's* warp engines precisely tuned for max efficiency.

. . . Tuned warp engines? His jaw stopped munching.

"Kelly," he chuckled, "what would burn out if we channeled your warp energy flow into that bracketed area we came up with?".

The ship replied after a pause, "Nothing should be damaged, Mark. The total flow would be unchanged and would be well within all safety specifications."

"Has anybody ever tried trimming a warp down like that before?"

"Not to my knowledge, Mark. There is no reason why anyone should have. However, in the light of your suppositions concerning warpicles, this would appear to be a useful test of the meaningfulness of your calculations."

"Okay, let's try it," Keaflyn decided.

"Very well. I will need some circuitry changes, specifically, two impeders with cutoffs that could be improvised with little difficulty. Shall I run off specs for you, Mark?"

"Yes, right now!"

Keaflyn spent a busy hour rigging the required components and connecting them into the warp engine circuit according to the *Kelkontar's* directions. At last he rubbed his blackened hands against his tunic and returned to the viewscreen. The Sect Dualers' ship was still fifteen minutes away, the graphic indicated.

"Okay, Kelly," he said, "switch in the gimmicks!"

He heard a soft click as the ship obeyed. For an instant he was not sure what the result was. Could the change have made the warp too specific, producing an ultrafast and fatal mitosis of ship and man by warping certain of their constituent elements while leaving the others behind? Or, perhaps, by warping mass while leaving behind all energies, ego-field included? Or by warping nothing at all, leaving the ship inert in space and subject to immediate attack?

None of these seemed to be happening, he decided with a chuckle. In fact, the only change he could detect was on the screen. The gap between the two ships was widening rapidly.

Keaflyn watched the screen with a calm joy that, for the moment, overrode the false hilarity of his pleasure-impress. He savored the feeling without trying to define it.

Finally he said, "Is this about a hundred times your normal warp speed?"

"It is 78.3 times normal, Mark," the ship replied.

"Our chicken-tracks were pretty close, then, considering our abysmal ignorance," he said with satisfaction. "Well, I'm going to get some sleep. Head for Locus, but stop about two light-years short. And here's a change in standing orders, Kelly: Don't let any ship approach you in space without orders from me. If I'm asleep, just move away from anybody who tries to come closer than a light-week. If whoever it is tries to communicate, wake me as usual."

"All right, Mark."

Keaflyn yawned and climbed into his sleeptank.

Chapter 9

When he woke he remained still for several minutes, examining his sensations. He was experiencing no pain, but he sensed that the Neg was back on the job. This was something new, this awareness of the Neg's presence in his mind, even when the Neg was content to do nothing more than watch.

Probably, he decided, this was a result of the incident at the Resistant Globe. During those seconds when the Neg had acted in parallel with his own mental process, adding its nullification of the Globe to his, it had displayed a . . . a characteristic of itself, a recognizable facet. Not its personality—probably not even a personality trait—but merely a perspective of a segment of a trait, Keaflyn hazarded.

A twisty bitterness was the best verbal description he could find of how this facet of the Neg seemed to him.

He grinned and focused his attention on the twisty bitterness. "Good morning, Neg," he said aloud to it. Its only reaction was a slight shifting, hardly a response to raise hopes of man-Neg communication.

"Good morning, Mark," said the ship with a certain hesitancy, as if not sure who its master was addressing. Keaflyn laughed.

"Where are we, Kelly?" he asked.

"Two light-years from Locus, as you instructed."

"We can really travel now, can't we," Keaflyn said smugly.

"Yes, with unprecedented rapidity, Mark." Keaflyn sat up in the sleeptank. "I want a hell of a big breakfast, Kelly. Eggs, steak, toast and coffee. Have you picked up any comm to or from Locus?"

"No."

Keaflyn hadn't expected an affirmative answer. He guessed that, after the ruckus over the Resistant Globe, the Sect Dualers (and perhaps even the Bensor officials) had sent out warnings that Mark Keaflyn was a dangerous being, particularly not to be allowed in the vicinity of stabilities. But at interstellar distances, psionic comm beams had to be tight. It would have been a fluke for the *Kelkontar* to intercept one two light-years away from a comm terminal.

"Any traffic in or out from Locus?" he asked.

"None within detection range, Mark."

Keaflyn nodded. That, too, was the answer he had expected. A number of people knew he had intended to go to Locus from Lumon's Star, and probably the research stations on the planet had been advised that he might show up. Whole squads of Emergencymen might be on the way, but certainly they could not have arrived yet. His improved warp had brought him here ahead of any special defending forces.

But even so, what did he intend to do?

It was a difficult question, and he tried hard not to let his pleasure-impress cause him to treat it with amusement.

He had seen on Bensor that his Neg definitely could produce disaster. He recalled Berina Arlan's analogy of the Neg as an atom of contramatter in the cloud chamber of the normal universe. That was pretty apt, he decided. The Neg had sure made the particles fly when it tried to nullify the Resistant Globe! For that matter, he guessed, the particles were probably still zinging off that event. Some startling things had happened, such as the telepathic reaction of the Bensor-on-Bensor citizenry to the deed. That was probably what the Sect Dualer Carmon Daylemon had been referring to when he spoke of an automatic defense mechanism being triggered by the compromise of the Globe.

If the Neg could cause trouble on that kind of scale, Keaflyn mused, wouldn't it be wise to give up his research and stay far away from stabilities—particularly if the integrity of the basic fabric of the universe rested on the firm solidity of the stabilities? That must be close to the actual state of things; the stabilities must be crucial to be defended by a previously unknown ego-field instinct that could do something as wild as turning a whole city telepathic!

So . . . maybe the best course was for him to quit. Find himself a raw planet somewhere and hide out. Or better, secretly get in touch with Tinker and Alo Felston and let them use him as an experimental subject in their efforts to discover a process for releasing pleasure-impresses. After all, the advance of mental science was at least as important as the advance of physical science . . . The *Kelkontar* served his breakfast, and he ate with a lively appetite while he continued considering his position.

The decision he faced was far from simple. To quit his research . . . in effect to buy the convincing interpretation of Carmon Daylemon . . . would be the safest course. If he immobilized himself, he would also immobilize the Neg and thus avoid the commission of harmful acts.

But that would also lead to the *omission* of valuable acts. And regardless of the uncertainties always involved in anticipating the value of still-to-be-discovered knowledge, Keaflyn felt strongly the rightness of his long-planned research project. Look how it had already paid off—with a new warpdrive seventy-eight times faster than the old, and more important, a resulting increase in practical range of approximately the same multiple. Why, it would be no trick to explore the entire galaxy with a drive like this! Maybe even a cluster of galaxies!

The crucial question in determining his course was the same as before: Did the Neg want him killed or otherwise stopped, or did it want to use him as a tool with which to undermine the stabilities?

Keaflyn studied that over in detail. He reviewed the events from the time the Neg made its presence felt, at Splendiss-on-Terra, up to the present. As he had told Daylemon and Smath, every instance when the Neg really pushed him hard—except one—was aimed at encouraging someone to kill him, provided the person had a Sect Dualer outlook. The exception was when he was probing Lumon's Star. In that instance, the Neg seemed to be trying to discourage him from his work.

And he had not done anything to undermine Lumon's Star as a stability. If that were the Neg's game, why hadn't it acted then?

The evidence, from his point of view, was overwhelming. The Neg wanted him dead. Its nullification attempt on the Resistant Globe had come much closer to accomplishing Keaflyn's death than to doing real damage to the Globe. Only a rare instance of serendipity had brought him out of that alive.

He finished eating breakfast and making up his mind at about he same time: he would go ahead with his research project.

But he would do so, from now on, with a little more caution. For example, he would find out what kind of opposition he might face before dropping down on Locus.

"Kelly, raise comm with the director of Locus Observatory."

"All right, Mark . . . Comm established."

A man's face appeared on the viewscreen, to regard Keaflyn curiously.

"Hi. I'm Mark Keaflyn. Don't believe we've met in current corpus."

"Halla Penchat," the man responded. "We were told you might show up here, Keaflyn. Didn't expect you so quickly, though."

"Yeah, some acquaintances of mine seem to want to play backtrack games with me," Keaflyn snickered.

"Under the circumstances, I thought I'd check with you on the quality of hospitality Locus has to offer me before I drop down."

"Um. Well, we have received certain suggestions . . . urgently worded suggestions."

"Such as?"

Penchat was frowning. "We've been asked to . . . uh . . . take you in protective custody if we get the opportunity."

Keaflyn grinned at Penchat's discomfiture. "Interference with another's freedom of movement is a code break," he said.

"Of course," agreed Penchat angrily. "I'd follow those suggestions with regret."

"Oh," chuckled Keaflyn, "but you *would* follow them."

"This puts me in a most uncomfortable position, Keaflyn," the man growled. "Some of the sources of that suggestion are also talking about a moratorium on all stability research . . . about closing up such installations as this observatory, and about cordoning all stabilities."

Keaflyn chortled with amazement. "Blackmail is going pretty far, even for Sect Dualers!"

"Wrong on two counts, Keaflyn. We've heard from the Sect Dualers, but we've also heard the same thing from the governments of Bensor, Terra, and a dozen others. Also, from the Arlan Siblings. So don't regard your opposition as the Sect Dualers—unless you agree that the near disaster with the Resistant Globe made Sect Dualers out of everybody . . . "

"Oh come now, Penchat!" Keaflyn snorted. "Such exaggeration from an objective man of science like yourself—"

"I'm not exaggerating," Penchat denied firmly. "The Insecurity gave everyone quite a turn! I confess to having been shaken by the experience, myself. The result is that attitudes toward the stabilities are undergoing urgent reappraisals. That's why you're wrong in assuming the talk of closing this observatory is intended to force me to cooperate in holding you. The stabilities may actually be placed off limits to everyone, and cordoned."

Keaflyn stared at the man's image in mystified silence. The very concepts represented by the words "off limits" and "cordon" were anachronisms, out of place in the year of Grace and Sanity 2842. Yet Penchat was using the words with obvious sincerity.

What the hell had happened?

"You spoke of 'the Insecurity,' " he began, "which doesn't convey a meaning to me. Will you explain it, please?"

"Don't you know? That's what happened when your contralife invader nearly nullified the Resistant Globe. It was a precarious moment, Keaflyn. Everybody had to grab reality and hang on for dear life. It was as if everything was about to slip away from us . . . about to fade out. That theory about the stabilities serving as anchorpoints of cosmic creation is now demonstrated to everyone's subjective satisfaction. Why else do you think everyone would be so concerned over what you may try next?"

"You keep using such words as 'everyone' and 'everything' with a looseness unbecoming to a rigorous mind," Keaflyn said mildly.

"I'm using those words with care, and in the belief they are fully justified," Penchat replied with some stiffness. "Reports we've received indicate the Insecurity was felt on every world known to humanity, by every human, and perhaps by lesser beings as well."

Keaflyn was beginning to get the picture, and guessed he would be appalled if his pleasure-impress had allowed. His Neg had indeed proven itself a contra-atom in a cloud chamber—perhaps a whole mass of contra-atoms!

"Under the circumstances," he murmured, "it would be indiscreet of me to come down for a visit right now, Penchat. Thanks for bringing me up-to-date on the news."

The man nodded. "I'm glad you're being reasonable, Keaflyn. I was afraid the contralife thing wouldn't permit that. Yes, it's best, I think, for you to keep your distance. I'm dispatching a ship to join you, with a few men who can . . . sort of look after you until a squad of Emergencymen arrives."

Keaflyn grinned. "That's not exactly what I had in mind, Penchat. Being in protective custody, my backlife recall assures me, is among the less enjoyable conditions of existence. So I'll be running along now. Thanks again, and goodbye."

"Don't be unrealistic!" Penchat snapped. "You can't get away from . . . " He hesitated in frowning thought, then said, "How did you reach the Locus vicinity so swiftly, Keaflyn? We're over ninety hours from Bensor, and the Insecurity was less than fifteen hours ago."

"Didn't my Sect Dualer pals on Bensor spill that data?" Keaflyn asked. "They were chasing me, after the Insecurity, with murderous intent. Thanks to a bit of serendipity, I pulled away from them as if they were standing still. I thought the news of that would be all over the universe by now."

"I've heard of no such chase," said Penchat, eyeing Keaflyn speculatively.

"Those guys seem to go for the old cloak-and-dagger approach," Keaflyn laughed. "Secretiveness for its own sake. One of my chasers was Arnod Smath of Terra, and another was Carmon Daylemon, probably of Bensor."

"You have an improved spacedrive?" asked Penchat."

"That's putting it mildly!"

"How does it work?"

"Aha! A good question," Keaflyn said with mock slyness. "Pardon me if I'm secretive, too. The habit's catching."

"A better spacedrive is something humanity needs, Keaflyn," said Penchat.

"Right, and humanity can have it, as soon as humanity decides I'm still a member. As things stand, I have a hunch I'm going to need an advantage of speed to stay loose."

"Keaflyn," rumbled Penchat, "it is now clear for the first time, as a result of the Insecurity, that matter is dependent upon mind. It follows that the more humanity knows of the universe, the more understanding we have, the stronger our universe will be. The reality of it will gain to the extent that we gain in our conquest of knowledge. If you hold back information on a spacedrive that would permit us to extend our knowledge and understanding, you will be serving the cause of your contralife invader."

Keaflyn nodded slowly. "Could be, but in that event my Neg has mixed feelings on the subject—because the

Neg also wants me dead or in confinement. I keep my secret and stay free, or I give it to you and we increase our reality . . . or the rest of you increase your reality, because I wouldn't survive in a condition to contribute much. Either way, the Neg loses, so hooray for our side!"

"You aren't making sense, Keaflyn."

"Who is these days?" he snorted. "It would be deplorable if it weren't so amusing, the way one little scare seems to have turned a purportedly sane humanity into one big witch-hunt!"

"Something as positive as a better spacedrive will go far to counter the negative attitude that now seems to prevail concerning you," argued Penchat.

Keaflyn grinned at him in silence for several seconds. "I'll think about it," he said. "In the meantime, I'm going to be discreetly scarce for a while . . . till the heat's off, as we used to say. So long, Penchat. Out!"

His ship broke comm and the screen went blank.

Minutes passed before Keaflyn said, "Kelly, if Locus has poles, there's no way to locate them, is there?"

"There are no poles of rotation, Mark, inasmuch as Locus does not turn," the ship replied. "However, it is possible to define a pole of the ecliptic . . . that is to say, a line perpendicular to the plane in which Locus' sun revolves about the planet."

"I'm not sure that ought to count," said Keaflyn. "Locus' sun isn't a stability, and neither is its orbit. What I want is a direction that has significance in relation to Locus itself. That's hard to come up with for a body that seems to be completely motionless in space. There is its mild magnetic field, but I'd like a more impressive and better defined line than that."

"I know of nothing in that category, Mark. However, the line of Locus' magnetic field has been determined with some precision within the past decade, according to data in my files."

Keaflyn sat up straighter. "It has? Can you give me a display on it?"

"Yes." The screen brightened with a 3D chart of the Locus system, the planet in the center circled by the orbit of its far more massive sun, with neighboring star positions indicated around the edges. A bright blue line appeared, spearing through the planet and extending diagonally off the screen at top and bottom. "That is the line of the magnetic field, Mark."

Keaflyn studied it. In one direction, the line passed through a few hundred light-years of the explored galactic arm before entering a dust area. Beyond the dust, he knew, was another arm, still unexplored, and perhaps the realm of another human society.

In the other direction, the line passed through thinning stars to move out of the galaxy on a slanting course, into the surrounding area of sparse star clusters.

"We're going to follow that line, one way or the other," Keaflyn told the ship. "The question is, which way?"

"I don't have sufficient data concerning your purpose to answer that, Mark."

"Oh. I'm looking for another Locus, one I can study without harassment. Something said back on Avalon indicated that the stabilities we've found in our own little sector of the galaxy are duplicated many, many times in the universe as a whole. There is an Avalon for each realm of humanity, and there may be several realms in this galaxy alone. Probably each realm also has its own

Lumon's Star, its own Resistant Globe, its Whorl, its Forever Ember, and its Sleeping Ghost.

"As for the Locus series, it seems reasonable to assume these objects aren't located by realms, but rather form a grid. They are the motionless objects to which all motions are relative, I would guess. Possibly they are also the source of inertia; the Einsteinian and neo-Einsteinian explanations of inertia as a summation of total universal mass always struck me as clever mathematical inventions rather than descriptions of a natural law.

"In any event, I think it's a fair guess that the Locus type objects are evenly spaced in a geometrically simple configuration, like atoms in a crystal . . . that they provide a foundation of sorts for what we know as the space-time continuum. And like atoms in a crystal, the Locus bodies have attitudinal relationships to the lines of the configuration. If these relationships are simple enough, all we have to do to find another Locus is follow the line of the magnetic field of this Locus in either direction."

"I understand," said the ship. "What do you assume to be the distance of spacing of these bodies, Mark?"

Keaflyn let out a bellowing laugh. "I haven't the slightest idea!" he roared.

"Such an object would be more easily detectable," the ship said, "where there is little other mass in the vicinity. Thus, a search along the line moving away from the galaxy may be preferable."

"Right," Keaflyn managed to reply, getting his pleasure-impress back under some control. "Ordinarily, I might be curious enough about what lies beyond the dust to say go in that direction, but my name is already mud with one human realm and I don't need conflict with

another. Set our new warp to follow the line out from
the galaxy, Kelly."

"Okay, Mark."

Work, exercise, sleep, work, exercise, sleep—the cycle
began to take on the automaticity of routine for Keaflyn
as the *Kelkontar* sped along its course toward a guessed-
at destination of indeterminable distance.

The Neg apparently disapproved.

"You wanted me to stay where the action is, didn't
you, old buddy?" Keaflyn chuckled as he gulped a couple
of aspirins to counter the aches in head and body.

"I had no preference, Mark," said the ship.

"Sorry, Kelly. I was talking to myself, more or less."

Keaflyn wondered just how much of what he was doing
actually got through to the Neg. It was evident that the
mental invader could observe events taking place around
him; for instance, it always seemed to know when other
persons of uncertain intent were around, persons who
might be led by evidence of its presence to harm or in
some manner foil its human host.

And sometimes, when it became obvious that nearby
people were *not* going to harm Keaflyn, it seemed to
know that, too, and relaxed its influence on him.

Could it read his thoughts?

Not exactly, Keaflyn concluded after searching his
memory of the Neg's reactions. But it could identify different thought *processes*. Maybe, right now, it knew he
was thinking analytically, and perhaps it could tell that
it was the subject being analyzed. Probably it could distinguish between his analytic thought and his moments

of creative thought. Those latter moments were apparently very rough on it, because it invariably retreated somewhat at such times.

As to other evidence of its abilities, above all, it had known what he was doing mentally when he had nulled the Resistant Globe.

So it recognized mental actions but did not necessarily follow the content of those actions.

What about his research? Could it understand and perhaps profit from his work, learning of it from his conversations with the ship and from the results displayed on the workboard? Was he feeding the Neg—and through it the contralife universe—data to be used by contralife in the eternal conflict with the universe of humanity?

He laughed when the answer struck him. *Of course not!* Knowledge—any knowledge—was anathema to contralife. The normuniverse and contrauniverse did not seesaw, one expanding while the other contracted. Seesawing is the balancing of similars, whereas the two universes were dissimilars: one positive, one negative. They balanced by rising and falling in unison. And knowledge expanded the reality of either universe—or more precisely, it expanded the reality of both universes.

Since the goal of contralife was contraction to total nonbeing, the Negs would abhor learning with the same instinctive revulsion that normal beings abhorred ignorance. Knowledge was survival, which Negs didn't want. Ignorance was death, which they sought.

Keaflyn grinned with glee. The Negs had been catching some rough going, he suspected, for more than a millennium now—since the Renaissance period on Earth, approximately speaking. They were being plunged into knowledge, just as humanity in the distant past had so often and so inexplicably been plunged into ignorance.

However, the Negs would use their unwanted knowledge in their struggle for nonsurvival. This ability of his Neg to impinge itself on a normuniverse being had to be the result of learning. In an era when the Negs were winning, perhaps they would celebrate a major victory when ignorance advanced to the point where the ability to impinge was lost.

Of course, the flow of battle was not smooth in either direction, Keaflyn mused. Humanity had had its handful of stalwart men of learning in the most ignorant ages. On the other hand, even now, the road toward advancement of knowledge was strewn with pitfalls. He could personally attest to that!

He recalled Berina Arlan's remark that a sure way to learn whether or not a gun is loaded is to pull the trigger—sure but possibly dangerous. Truth-seekers of all times had banged their heads on that wall, on which was written in large but conservative letters: *Beyond this boundary lies knowledge too dangerous for the mind of man.*

Human lore was full of that. Adam and Eve had been punished for eating forbidden fruit—knowledge of good and evil. Prometheus had caught hell for giving man fire. The son of Daedalus, the inventor of manned flight, had fallen to his death. Keaflyn chuckled. Edison had started going deaf before inventing the phonograph. Had that been punishment or preparatory self-protection?

He pushed this intrusion from his pleasure-impress aside. The point was that the bugaboo of deadly knowledge still lingered in his own presumably enlightened age.

Why? Was there in actuality a boundary the mind should not violate? Was the belief in the bugaboo the visible symptom of a deep, unexplored instinct, the purpose of which was to protect humanity from knowledge that would, in fact, be utterly harmful?

That humanity, that life itself had unexplored instincts had been made evident by the startling reaction to the compromising of the Resistant Globe—the Insecurity. That wasn't really surprising, Keaflyn decided. As a physicist, he felt strongly the basic unity of all nature, the tight dovetailing of matter-energy-space-time-positive-negative-knowledge-ignorance-mind. Nobody knew the topography of all the intricate dovetails, all the bindings that preserved the unity.

So, people might play at destroying a stability, but when the stability was seriously threatened, the restoring reaction was immediate and powerful—and also, he felt sure, completely adequate.

Similarly, if there was such a thing as utterly dangerous knowledge, would it not be counteracted as effectively? Would not some factor built into the total unity shout *"No!"* to such knowledge with as telling effect as that by which the destruction of a stability had been overruled?

But if so, why all the concern over acquiring knowledge that obviously fell far short of the forbidden area? Why the old fear that even a little learning was a dangerous thing?

Maybe, he hazarded, because the *No!* that would be given to dangerous knowledge might be, itself, a ruinously painful experience. The mighty, according to the warnings of tradition, fall extremely hard.

Keaflyn snorted at himself for indulging in this lengthy bout of not-very-original wool-gathering. He rose from his chair and went to stare at the viewscreen.

"Detecting anything up ahead, Kelly?" he asked.

"Yes, Mark. Within the next four hundred light-years, our line will pass close by two stars, one of which is beginning to separate into a binary."

"No star clusters near the line?"

"No."

"A Locus body might not be with a star at all. Our line gets less precise every minute. We could shoot by what we're looking for without coming in detection range of it."

"That is true, Mark," the ship agreed.

"Well," said Keaflyn after a pause, "that would be our tough luck. Everything holding up okay?"

"Yes. We are now go for twenty-four days of warp without resupply."

Keaflyn nodded. He would not have to think of turning back for another week.

Chapter 10

The space between galaxies was not devoid of stars; they were merely thinly scattered—so scattered, in fact, that none would have been visible ahead of the ship to Keaflyn's unaided eyes. The *Kelkontar's* sensors were picking up radiation from some two dozen that were bright enough and near enough to detect. These were displayed on the viewscreen.

But compared to the interior of the galaxy, this was emptiness.

If life created the universe, thought Keaflyn with some amusement, why did it put so much space in it? What was it all good for, when life itself showed so strong a preference for the confines of small planets?

"Mark," said the ship, "the binary we're approaching has curvilinear motion."

"You mean, besides the motion of the two stars around each other?" Keaflyn asked hopefully.

"Yes. Their mutual rotation was evident shortly after I detected their separation. And now, after two hundred light-years of approach, it is becoming evident that they are orbiting as a pair, and very slowly, about a still-invisible body."

"Hey! That could be it!" yelped Keaflyn, thinking of Locus, back in the galaxy, and its star, Sol-Locus.

A system containing a Locus type body had to be a prodigy. A star could capture (or be captured by) such a planet, but since a Locus body was stationary in space, the star could not swing it in an orbit. The star itself had to do the orbiting or else move on. It was a case of the tail wagging the dog, and wagging it very slowly. The far more massive star proceeded about its little primary in a barely noticeable creep, completing its circle in something over four thousand Earth-years. The original relative motion of planet and star had to have been almost that slow; otherwise the capture could not have occurred.

Thus, if the binary the ship was now approaching was orbiting something so slowly that the motion had required two hundred years to reveal itself, and the primary was so small as to remain unseen from this distance, then they had probably found a second Locus! Better make that Locus2, Keaflyn decided.

And Locus2 it really was, he discovered as the ship moved into the system. The final light-hours of approach, with sensors studying the small planet, found no slightest indication of motion. Like Locus1, it was an airless globe of stone, approximately Mars-size.

"I presume nobody's around," said Keaflyn, "but try to raise someone on the comm, just to be sure.

"Okay, Mark."

Keaflyn almost hoped someone would respond to the ship's call, even an ardent Sect Dualer. It was one thing to have a high degree of self-sufficiency, but something else to be several thousand light-years from the nearest known living being. True, his ship could talk to him, but a vocal computer was not really company. Neither was his Neg.

He hadn't planned to do his stability-probing in this kind of solitude. Tinker had intended to accompany him. They had planned on it for a couple of lifetimes. But the plan had been disrupted by the *Brobdinagia* disaster. The explosion of that interstellar liner had killed Tinker's nine-year-old body, and even though her ego-field had promptly found itself a new infant, she was still only an eleven-year-old child in her present body. The decade Tinker had lost in the crash left her at least six years short of proper mating age, and thinking back to his meeting with her on Terra, Keaflyn realized that he hadn't been especially disappointed by that at the time.

After all, he had thought then what was a mere six or eight years? He could wait for her to grow up. Also, his pleasure-impress had been influencing him strongly at that time, and he had tended to be entertained by the comic aspects of his and Tinker's predicament.

It seemed less funny now as he gazed out at the lifeless globe of Locus2. He felt isolated. Even if he were back in the galaxy, the drab thought came to him, he would still be a man alone. Except, maybe, for Tinker and Alo Felston. Perhaps they were still friends he could turn to, but after the Resistant Globe debacle he certainly couldn't count on any others, not even the Arlan Siblings, who had promised their aid any time he needed it in fighting his Neg. From what Penchat had told him, the Arlans were now siding with the Sect Dualers.

Why not beat it back to the galaxy right now, to Tinker's home on Danolae? He could at least kiss her and bounce her on his knee and talk to her . . .

"Damn!" he gasped suddenly, starting out of his blue funk. That lousy Neg! It had really found an opening through which to throw an emotional punch at him. It had had him going for a minute there. Self-pity, of all things!

The realization helped him push back the Neg-induced emotion which, as before in a similar circumstance, had tried to stop him from continuing his research project. "Kelly," he said, "pick out a landing site with a reasonable ground temperature and set down. Probably the twilight band, wouldn't you say?"

"Right, Mark. An unshaded twilight area should be suitable. You will not find the radiation from the binary troublesome at this distance."

"Good."

The ship spiraled down to a smooth-surfaced plateau of unbroken stone, while Keaflyn suited up. A slight thud told him when they touched down.

"I'm cycling out, Kelly. Send the supplies and equipment out after me, according to plan."

He went through the lock and stepped down to the stone of Locus2. He wondered briefly if he were the first being ever to touch this world, but that was a question of no importance, and he had work to do. Besides, he now had a severe headache. The Neg, having been thwarted when it hit him with an emotion, was now coming back with a psychosomatic, something more difficult for Keaflyn to think his way out of. And he hadn't bothered to equip his vacsuit to feed him aspirins.

He grimaced and began setting up his temporary shelter and experimental equipment as the *Kelkontar* fed the cases through the lock. The shelter, with its anti-meteor screens, was more elaborate than he expected was needed here. There were no signs that the surface of Locus2 had ever been subject to particle bombardment.

When the job was done, he went back into the ship for aspirin and a ship-cooked meal, then outside once more, to make precise adjustments in preparation for the first test.

"I'm about ready, Kelly," he announced at last. "Take off for my zenith."

"Okay, Mark," the reply sounded inside his helmet.

The *Kelkontar* lifted away, and Keaflyn threw back his head to watch the ship diminish out of sight before turning his attention to the tracking sensors.

When the ship was five light-minutes up, he said, "Okay, Kelly, turn on your light and start the data flow."

"Light and data flow, on, Mark."

Keaflyn waited out the five minutes, then peered upward, wondering if the laser beam from the ship would be bright enough for his eyes to see at this distance. Several more seconds passed. Then an indicator flashed on the control panel at Keaflyn's side. The laser beam had registered. Somewhat more than ten seconds later, the flash went off. Another ten-seconds-plus interval, and it came on again. The cycle repeated a dozen times, then the flash began to flicker uncertainly.

"You're out of range now, Kelly," Keaflyn called. "Head back down."

"Right, Mark. Reversing direction."

The ship, using no warp for the duration of the experiment, would take a while slowing to a standstill and then getting back into range of the instruments. Keaflyn went into the shelter, removed his helmet, and took two more of the aspirins with a glass of Terratea. In a moment he felt better, either from the medication or because the Neg, discovering its inability to defeat him, was slacking off. When the ship was due back in range, he rehelmeted and returned to the control panel outside.

Shortly the ten-second laser beam bursts were being received once more and were precisely measured for frequency and propagation speed. As the ship was now approaching, the bursts lasted for something less than ten seconds at the receiving end.

"Now braking, Mark," the ship announced after a few minutes had passed.

"Okay. Swerve off and get set for the tangent run," Keaflyn directed.

This involved another wait while the *Kelkontar* moved off a few hundred million miles to a position on Keaflyn's horizon, then lined up on a course that would enable it to pass at high speed directly over the observation site.

Once more, measurements would be made of frequency and propagation of a laser beam transmitted by the ship, this time under conditions that would—for a split-second—bring transmitter and receiver to within one hundred meters of each other, and with the transmitter very near the Locus2 surface.

The experiment was carried out as planned, the ship zipping past Keaflyn's position so fast that his senses did not register it at all. "Was it a good run, Kelly, directly overhead?"

"Yes, Mark. I passed fourteen meters to your left at an altitude of ninety-three meters."

"Good enough. Come on in and pick up my data. Then we'll see if we have to do anything over."

Shortly thereafter the ship dropped to the ground by the observation site, and Keaflyn carried his reels of recorded information aboard and fed them into the ship's computers. There his data was compared with information the ship had recorded of its own movements relative to the site. Several minutes passed before the ship announced:

"Calculations are complete, Mark. The results indicate no deviation from straight addition-of-velocities. My velocity corresponded precisely at all times to the difference between the velocity of the received laser signal and the normal speed of light."

"No relativistic effects crept in at all?" demanded Keaflyn. "Not the slightest trace of the time-space contraction?"

"None at all, Mark."

"Humpf! Well, that's that, I suppose," muttered Keaflyn. "No fuzziness in the data?"

"The readings were quite clear, Mark, on the order of two hundred times more precise than in any earlier similar experiment."

Keaflyn nodded. His methodology in the study of stabilities involved, basically, just that: testing with equipment far more precise than previously used, in an effort to find a trace of instability in the stabilities . . . some slight tendency toward the behavior of normal matter-energy objects. He had spent the most of two previous lifetimes searching out those ultra-accurate means of testing and getting the needed equipment fabricated.

And in the case of Locus2, at least, all he had proved was that the stability held up to a couple of additional decimal points.

On that body, light being received from a moving source did not obey the law of relativity. Light speed there was not a constant. If the source were approaching the planet, its light would have the additional velocity of the approach. If the source were moving away, its speed would be subtracted from that of its light.

Why?

Well, that was the way this particular stability worked. No better explanation than that had been found. Presumably it had something to do with the motionlessness of Locus; it was fixed in space. Other objects moved relative to Locus, but Locus moved relative to nothing. So, no relative motion, no relativistic effects.

Probably, Keaflyn mused, his experiment had proved just how firmly fixed in position Locus2 really was.

And, come to think about it, his methodology of seeking traces of instability had not worked on Lumon's Star, either. What he had discovered there—warpicles—

pertained to the nature of that particular stability, not to its limitations.

But completely unintentionally, he had been instrumental in revealing a limit to the resistance of the Resistant Globe of Bensor-on-Bensor. The Globe could be nulled by mind, provided both contralife and normlife mind were included in the action.

"One thing we did find out, Kelly," he consoled himself, "is that there is more than one Locus, and there could be a whole gridwork of them." He paused in his work of repacking his test equipment. "By the way, does this one have a magnetic field?"

"Yes, Mark."

"Pointed back at Locus1, I bet."

"No. The magnetic poles form a line perpendicular to our line of approach," the ship said.

"Um. That makes sense, I suppose. If the poles were in line, that would indicate nothing more than a string of Locuses. But if every other one has its poles at a 90–degree angle, that implies squares and cubes . . . a grid, in short. Tell you what, Kelly. After we get you loaded, we'll follow up the magnetic line of this one, and see if we can hit a Locus3 at the same distance as Locus1. That'll prove we have a three-dimensional grid, won't it?"

"Not beyond argument, Mark.."

"But substantially." Keaflyn worked in silence for several minutes. Then he said, "The proof would be more substantial if we found a Locus3 at the proper distance on a line perpendicular to the magnetic fields of both Locus1 and Locus2. Right?"

"Yes, that would be more convincing."

"Then that's the line we'll take, straight out from this one's magnetic equator, and ninety degrees away from our line of approach from Locus."

Locus3 was there, where he had predicted it would be. It was fortunate that the *Kelkontar* knew the precise line to follow and the distance at which to search, because this Locus had no sun and could easily have been missed if they had not known just where to look.

Again Keaflyn spent a few hours on the ground, running a series of tests similar to those done on Locus2, to verify that this dark little world was a true Locus body.

When he was aboard the ship once more, he said, "That's enough Locuses to satisfy me, Kelly, and by the time we get back to civilization you'll be about due for a check-up and resupply. So head for home."

"For Bensor, Mark?"

"From this distance, it wouldn't matter by many degrees which system you aimed at," chuckled Keaflyn. "No . . . not Bensor. Let's go to Danolae."

"Okay, Mark."

Getting his ship checked out and its consumables replenished was going to require cooperation—something the average citizen could take for granted on any known world of humanity. But Keaflyn had a hunch he was going to need the help of special friends to get that chore handled.

And certainly Tinker and Alo Felston were still friends. If they weren't . . .

He shrugged and giggled. Of course they were his friends! They had to be.

He dismissed the thought, gulped two aspirins, and got busy putting his findings on the Locuses into publishable form.

Chapter 11

But as he neared the Danolae system, he had second thoughts.

Granted that Tinker and Felston were people who would do everything they could to help him. He knew that, but the trouble was, so did everyone else. He had to assume, until he discovered differently, that most of humanity was still upset over the Resistant Globe affair and would be eager to confine him, or give him another dose of the Sect Dualers' treatment.

So, wouldn't his known friends be under close observation? Would they not, in fact, be the bait of cleverly concealed traps by this time?

Keaflyn grunted his annoyance. His mind just wasn't geared for scheming, nor for anticipating schemes. That was an antiquated approach to personal relationships, one that bespoke a distrust of one's fellows and the universe that was hardly appropriate in 29th-century society. Except, of course, for the Sect Dualers who, even though they were technically sane, had something of a wartime psychology because of their constant mindfulness of the contralife threat.

But even in backtrack ages, Keaflyn mused dolefully, he had never been an able schemer. He had always been the unsuspecting patsy, the artless scholar, the maker of the politically unwise remark, the revealer of sensitive information, the blind walker into traps, the tool of the clever and unscrupulous . . .

There was, for instance, that life back in the 20th Century, when he had tried to found an electronics company to develop and produce a couple of items he had invented. His money-men had taken him mercilessly—so badly, in fact, that that was one of his very few lives that had ended in suicide.

Damn it, he had to wise up! he told himself grimly. Be as underhanded and a thousand times as clever as a Shakespearean villain! If he were to stay alive and keep his freedom of action against the wishes of everybody else, he would have to make a point of out-scheming the schemers.

Yet, even as he told himself this, he knew it was useless. He simply lacked the knack for that kind of thinking. He had thought that he had kept his recent visit to Bensor a secret, that be could handle his business there and be gone before the Sect Dualers became aware of his presence. But he had reckoned without a true grasp of the painstakingness of experienced plotters. It had never occurred to him that the Dualers would be keeping a lookout for him at the plant of Donflannis Instras Corporation. So he had gone to confer with his friend John Donflannis, and the Sect Dualers had grabbed him as soon as he left the plant.

He would always overlook some such possibility as that, he suspected, because he was a no-talent amateur at this game, up against professionals. To them, the cleverest trick he could think of would probably be obvious and hackneyed, maybe even stupid.

Like the idea he was thinking about now: Instead of trying to contact Tinker directly, he would call her father, Clav Didorik. Didorik would certainly not be considered an ally of Keaflyn's but might be trusted to be neutral. In any event, Didorik was not likely to be bait in a trap.

And perhaps, came the hopeful thought, the schemers would not really believe their quarry was stupid enough to come to Danolae at all . . .

"Kelly, raise comm with Clav Didorik of Danolae for me," he directed. "If he wants to know who's calling, tell him Spence Spargon." Keaflyn invented the Spargon name on the spur of the moment.

Several seconds later Didorik's hard and heavy face appeared on the screen. He blinked when he saw who "Spence Spargon" was, and then studied him in silence a moment before saying, "What can I do for you, Mr. Spargon?"

"I'm not sure, Mr. Didorik," Keaflyn replied. "I'd like to discuss a number of possibilities with you, privately."

"Sure. Come on down. I'll give your ship my location code."

"Would it be too much of an imposition to ask you to come up to my ship?" Keaflyn asked.

"Um. Well. Up to your ship, huh? I suppose I can do that. I have a one-man launch here. I'll call your ship back for a guidebeam as soon as I'm aboard. In five minutes."

Keaflyn nodded. Didorik apparently understood his feeling of need for caution. "That'll be fine. See you soon."

Some seventy minutes later Didorik cycled aboard the *Kelkontar*, flipped his helmet off and removed a spaceglove before extending a hand to Keaflyn.

"Well, Mark, you've made a name for yourself in a few short weeks," he commented with a cold smile.

"Not quite the way I intended, Clav. Thanks for coming up," Keaflyn replied, shaking the hand. "The name I've made seems to be mud."

Didorik gave a short affirming nod. "Just what the hell were you trying to do to the Resistant Globe, anyway?" he asked.

"Nothing, really. That is, I wasn't experimenting on it. I merely nulled it, the way I've done a dozen times before, and the way about every sightseer who comes to Bensor-on-Bensor does. What happened was that my Neg invader suddenly did the same thing, and that caused all the ruckus."

"Couldn't you keep any control over the Neg?" Didorik demanded.

"Not on that, I couldn't. You see, I gave him an opening. All he had to do was agree with what I was doing. It wasn't a matter of his taking control or my denying control."

"*Can* he—or it—take control?" Didorik asked pointedly.

"No. He can give me a bad moment emotionally now and then or keep me in nearly constant pain. He can't guide my thoughts or actions."

Didorik found himself a seat. "Enough pain can control action, by paralysis," he remarked.

"I've thought of that," said Keaflyn. "The answer must be that it's beyond his power to hit me with that much pain. His purpose is to kill me. He could do that by paralyzing me any time I put on a vacsuit. I'd be helpless, and my ship would be unable to help me. He could hold me there until I starved to death."

"You seem sure his purpose is to kill you. Why?"

"Because of my stabilities research," shrugged Keaflyn. "If our gains of knowledge are defeats for the Negs, I've already given them a pretty hard time." He giggled.

"Well, you won't do much more," Didorik grunted. "You've been blocked away from every stability for the past couple of weeks, I hear. Where have you been, Mark? Drifting in space, waiting for the heat to die down?"

Keaflyn laughed. "Believe it or not, I've been probing two previously undiscovered stabilities. I call them Locus2 and Locus3. In fact, I have a paper about them here. If I can't visit Tinker, I'd like for you to pass it along to her, with instructions that she steer it through Science Reporting Service in my behalf."

He handed Didorik the manuscript and waited while the man flipped curiously through its pages. "Two more Locuses, huh?" Didorik murmured, sounding impressed.

"An infinite number of Locuses," Keaflyn beamed.

"What about the other stabilities? An infinite number of all of them?"

"I think so. That's the impression I got from a hint dropped on Avalon. Of course the others aren't necessarily evenly spaced in a gridwork, and I can't find them easily, but—"

"You've been on Avalon?" bleated Didorik.

"Yes," Keaflyn replied, smiling broadly.

"You really get around." Didorik sounded a bit overwhelmed.

"All in the line of the job," Keaflyn said, feeling flippant. "Avalon is itself a stability, and the ego-fields who live on it are. You know, the ones people are always wondering what became of: like Einstein, Beethoven, Marie Curie, to mention a few of the more famous.

"You met them?"

"Those three, and a dozen or so more."

"That means the ancient religionists were right," mused Didorik. "There is a heaven for sufficiently righteous souls."

"Not exactly. An ego-field winds up on Avalon as a result of a lifetime in which it fulfills whatever potential it has. Any more lives after that would be anticlimactic —a sort of waste. So the ego-field goes to Avalon and no longer participates in the birth-death cycle. Righteousness has nothing to do with it."

"I see." For a minute Didorik sat silent, frowning in thought. Then he straightened up and looked Keaflyn in the eye.

"I'll do whatever I can to help you, Mark," he said, "despite the fact that your constant tittering annoys the hell out of me and you seem too damned proud of yourself. Maybe that pleasure-impress is responsible for the giggle, and the Neg might be doing something to make you act conceited. But too many centuries have passed since a mob was allowed to interfere with an individual's freedom for me to condone any backsliding now! Besides, I'm impressed by what you've accomplished. Is it true you found a way to improve the warpdrive, and this ship can now run circles around anything else in space?"

"It can practically *englobe* anything else!" snorted Keaflyn, then caught himself. "Sorry, Clav. You're right. That Neg is trying to make me insufferable right now. It's back under control. Thanks for calling my attention to it."

"Okay. Forget it. Now, about this warpdrive: I can see why you have to keep a monopoly on it for the time being. But don't keep it too secret. If something happens to you, the drive shouldn't be lost."

"Right. My ship knows all about it, and if I get knocked off, the ship is instructed to turn itself over to Tinker."

"Not good enough. The way things stand, you and your ship could be vaporized at the same instant," Didorik told him.

Keaflyn grimaced at this bald verification of danger.

"Damn it," he sniveled, "Don't they realize I can't take dying in my condition? A death would be the ruin of me as an ego-field!"

"Not only do they know it; they're counting on it," Didorik told him harshly. "Now, snap out of it and let's figure something out on this warpdrive of yours!"

Keaflyn realized the Neg had been trying another emotional gambit on him. He sat up straight. "Right. I see your point, but that's not the kind of problem I'm good at. What do you suggest, Clav?"

"Well, I don't suggest you give me the secret," Didorik grunted. "And I forbid you to give it to my daughter. With everybody so upset, some fanatic might try torturing the secret out of her. In fact, you'd better not even talk to her, so nobody will get the idea that you *might* have told her about the drive."

Keaflyn considered this and nodded reluctantly. "I can't understand why people are suddenly afflicted with so much emotional thinking about me," he complained. "After all, the Resistant Globe wasn't really damaged, was it?"

"No, evidently it wasn't," said Didorik, "but that's not the point. The way I analyze it, there are two reasons. One, you showed everybody that a stability *can* be damaged, can even be obliterated, and that we have enemies whom nobody but the Sect Dualers took seriously before, but who are nearly powerful enough to do the obliterating. Our universe is suddenly less secure than we thought, and that shakes a man.

"Two, the Insecurity triggered a stimulus-response reaction in everybody. For the first time in centuries, people found themselves taking an unreasoned action. They were fighting to put down the Insecurity on an instinctive level, and after it was over with that bothered them. It bothered me! A sane man expects to keep control of himself. That's what sanity is, basically.

"What it boils down to is that you've undermined people's confidence in their universe and in themselves, Mark. You've shown them—us—that some very important unknowns still exist, and that what we don't know can hurt us."

"And that makes me a public enemy," said Keaflyn.

"Sure it does! What's so strange about that? Hell, the men who have invented steam engines from time to time and deprived people of the security of being slave laborers were public enemies. So were the doctors who described microbes, invisible carriers of death. And the astronomers who announced that their home planet wasn't the stationary center of a revolving universe. It's happened plenty of times!"

"Perhaps so," argued Keaflyn, "but people are supposed to be sane today. Take yourself, for example, Clav. You're reacting rationally, so why can't everybody else?"

Didorik gave him a hard stare. "The hell I'm reacting rationally!" he growled. "I'd kill you right now, Mark, if I thought it would do a damned bit of good!"

Keaflyn sat back, startled. "The point is, though, that you do know it wouldn't do any good," he countered.

"No, I don't know that. It's merely my opinion," said Didorik. "And I can see how others could differ with my opinion."

Keaflyn gave a dazed titter, and sat in silence for a long while. Finally he said tentatively, "You wanted to decide something about my new warpdrive."

"Yeah," grunted Didorik "Look. You wouldn't be doing anybody a favor—anybody you could trust to keep your secret—by giving it to them. So that's not the solution. How about this: couldn't you disclose something about the theory behind the new drive, maybe even send it to Science Reporting Service? Don't tell how it works or how it's made but just enough of the theory so that in time someone else could duplicate the application you've made of it."

Keaflyn laughed. "An excellent solution, Clav! Leave it to me. Thanks!"

"Don't put off doing it," Didorik warned.

"I won't," said Keaflyn. He was vastly amused, because they had been worrying over a problem that he had already solved. The report on his investigation of

Lumon's Star, which he had turned over to John Don-flannis back on Bensor, gave all the theoretical data any competent warp engineer would need for the development of his improved drive. Especially if the engineer knew in advance that such a drive had probably been based on that theory.

"You would prefer that I not talk to Tinker," he said.

"Under the circumstances it could be ill-advised," Didorik said firmly.

"Has she started her research on the pleasure-impress yet?"

"Yes, like a ball of fire! Your ex-cowpoke pal, Alo Felston, is working with her—a big help, she says. And since the Insecurity she's recruited a number of others—people who are interested in the 'Keaflyn problem,' as I've heard them call it."

"Any results yet?"

"Don't know. Probably nothing that would help you. They're working with animals, and the idea seems to be to peel off traumas from animal ego-fields until they come to a pleasure-impress like yours, and then see what they can do with it. So far as I know, they're still in the peeling stage."

"I'm not counting on help from them," Keaflyn said. "In the first place, it's only educated guesswork that extremely old pleasure-impresses are a cause of all the animal-level ego-fields in existence: And unburdening an animal, with its limitations of nervous system, of backlife traumas is a major research project in itself. Also even if they do succeed in uncovering a pleasure-impress, the big job of finding a way to break it will remain."

He paused, then chuckled. "That's why I've got to stay loose, Didorik. Tomorrow I may be a camel."

Didorik frowned. "That's an exaggeration," he protested.

"Maybe so, but death traumas fasten onto pleasure-impresses," said Keaflyn, "and fasten tight. I'll be a somewhat degraded ego-field in my next lifetime, perhaps too degraded to claim a human body against the stiff competition of able ego-fields. So I might wind up in an animal body and get loaded with another death trauma when that body dies, then on to another animal body, and so on down the ladder. Tinker's the expert in that field, and she didn't offer me any hope of another human lifetime.

"So anything I accomplish as a human, I accomplish now. And I need help getting my ship checked and resupplied."

"Oh." Didorik thought about it a moment, then said, "I can't promise you total safety, Mark, but if you want to take the chance of landing at my place, I can service your ship."

"I can't ask a better offer than that. Thanks. Maybe if I stay aboard and out of sight . . . "

"That would help," Didorik nodded. "The ship can do its own loading and storing. Only a couple of maintenance technicians will have to come aboard, and I have two good men for that. Both of them took the Insecurity business in a levelheaded way, so I think you can trust them."

"Then it should all go without a hitch," Keaflyn said happily.

Didorik frowned. "I didn't say that. My plantation's ship terminal is a pretty busy place. A good many people will see your ship and wonder why you, whoever you are, stay hidden inside. They'll wonder why you came to me for servicing, rather than to a public spaceport. Somebody might recognize your ship by its make. Anyway, enough suspicion will be aroused to catch the attention of the Sect Dualers or Arlan Siblings pretty soon, but your ship should be serviced and you on your way even sooner."

"That could result in reprisals against you," Keaflyn protested.

"I doubt it. We haven't slid that far backtrack. Not yet. And if it comes to that," Didorik grinned wolfishly, "I can take care of myself." He pulled his glove on and picked up his helmet. "So consider it settled. Have your ship tail me down."

Keaflyn nodded, and Didorik cycled out to his small launch.

The *Kelkontar* spent less than five hours on Danolae, and Keaflyn saw no more of the planet than was visible on his screens. It was something of a treat for him to chat with the maintenance technicians Didorik sent aboard, even though the Neg pestered him the whole time. He had been missing human companionship.

Didorik came in again shortly before the sere icing was completed.

"I don't want to know where you're going from here," he said, "but if you want some advice, stay away from the stabilities. All of them are heavily guarded now. I realize your ship can outrun trouble, but what's the point? You're not going to be left alone around a stability long enough to run any of your tests. And every time you get chased away from one, there'll be more public static. I'd say, go to ground somewhere in an isolated spot and let the whole affair cool off for a few years."

That was sensible advice, Keaflyn thought, nodding slowly. The catch was that "a few years" no longer had the same meaning for him as for Didorik . . . like a drink of water would be nothing to a man standing beside a clear, pure lake, but everything to a man stranded on a desert.

"Thank, Clav," he said. "I'll think it over." Didorik understood and shrugged.

"Have you told Tinker I'm here?" Keaflyn asked.

"No. Thought it best not to, until you're gone. But I told Felston, just in case they might have been ready to take a crack at your pleasure-impress. They aren't. He sends his regards."

"Give him mine, and Tinker my love."

"I will. And I'll give her your write-up on the Locuses."

"Okay. Thanks for everything, Clav."

"Sure. Now, get out of here, man!" A few minutes later, Keaflyn did.

Chapter 12

The Whorl was a . . .

Keaflyn stopped the mental verbalization in mid-sentence. Bad semantics? Could it be accurately stated that the Whorl *was* or *is* anything?

Well, yes. The Whorl was a *condition* in space. That was vague enough to get by.

This condition had form and motion. It was roughly lenticular, twenty light-minutes in diameter and three light-minutes thick at its center. Its round faces were not smooth. They had irregularities that were spiral in shape. The semblance was thus that of a small, three-dimensional "shadow" of a galaxy. The spiral aspect gave the condition its name, the Whorl.

It was not visible in the ordinary sense. It obscured stars behind it but reflected absolutely no light (or so earlier tests indicated). Its form had been revealed only by exploding bombs of radioactive tracerdust in its vicinity and then mapping the "surface" of vanishment of the dust particles.

The Whorl revolved about the center of the galaxy, but in the direction opposite the galaxy's rotation. It moved face first, and all matter and energy coming in contact with that face disappeared from existence. Three stars had vanished in the Whorl while humans had been watching, the first two witnessed only by distant astronomers and the third—coming after the development of interstellar travel—observed close-up by shiploads of scientists.

Not that they had learned a hell of a lot, Keaflyn snickered. The star had simply been gulped down by the Whorl. No informative outbursts of peculiar radiation, no gravitational phenomena other than what might obviously be expected when a star ceased existing, no indigestive burpings from the Whorl afterward.

"What really puzzles me, Kelly," Keaflyn remarked, "is the purpose of the Whorl. The other stabilities can be understood generally as anchors of universal normality—the enduring curtain-rods on which the flimsy fabric of reality flutters." He chuckled at himself and continued, "But I can't fit the Whorl into the curtain-rod pattern. Why should there be a stability that annihilates?"

"I don't know, Mark," replied the ship.

"It's a philosophical question," said Keaflyn, "which means we don't know enough to treat it as a scientific question."

The Neg was working on him, making him feel giddy. That feeling, coupled with the effects of the pleasure-impress, was resulting in something closely akin to drunken irresponsibility. This could be dangerous, he knew, but it was so comfortable and relaxing that he was reluctant to fight it.

Also, he guessed, it was an activity the Neg would not be able to sustain for long, since it produced pleasure rather than pain. Nonetheless, while it lasted it might prove far more effective than the Neg's usual tactics, for that very reason.

Maybe, he thought lazily, he should simply drift in space until the Neg became tired. On second thought, that hardly seemed necessary. He was approaching the Whorl and had his plans all made. Following through should be simple enough despite his carefree condition.

The ship was proceeding under normal warp velocity, so as not to give away Keaflyn's identity. "How many cordoning ships can you pick up?" the man asked.

"I've detected seventeen, Mark. If their stationing pattern is uniform, nine others are out of range behind the Whorl, making a total of twenty-six."

"All right. Move in and make like number twenty-seven," Keaflyn giggled. "You have your speeches all set."

"Okay, Mark."

The *Kelkontar* reduced speed and finally broke out of warp to edge slowly closer to the loose assembly of ships. Keaflyn monitored the call it sent out:

"This is the approaching Condor Quarto, Series 2600–50. My owner, who prefers to be anonymous, volunteers our service for cordon duties and requests assignments."

"Comm received," the reply came a few seconds later. "Stand by for reply."

Keaflyn grinned. "They've got to huddle and think it over."

Minutes passed before a stern, half-angry face appeared on the screen. "Am I in comm with the owner of the Condor Quarto?" he demanded.

"My owner prefers to be anonymous," said the *Kelkontar.*

"Nuts to that noise!" snapped the face. "We're not playing games out here! I'm informing your owner that if he wishes to assist he must identify himself and permit an inspection of his ship before he receives instructions. Also, I'm informing your owner to do so quickly, because his ship happens to be the make and model of Mark Keaflyn's."

"Thank you, sir," replied the *Kelkontar.* "My owner apologizes for taking your attention and time and regrets he cannot accept your conditions on his assistance. Therefore we will withdraw. Out."

"You will *not* withdraw!" the man snarled. "You will remain where you are for boarding and inspection!"

"My owner regrets, but he declines to cooperate," said the *Kelkontar.* "Out."

"Beautiful!" Keaflyn applauded. "Move away at normal warp maximum."

His ship complied, and a moment later the situation graphic on the screen showed four cordon ships start moving in pursuit. It was soon evident that they were closing the gap. They were faster ships than the *Kelkontar's* normal maximum.

"Break off ninety degrees," chuckled Keaflyn, "and increase velocity thirty-five percent."

"Right, Mark."

The ship broke warp and immediately assumed a new course at a right angle to the old and slightly more than one-third faster. Instantly eleven more cordon ships responded by taking up the chase. "They know who I am now," Keaflyn glowed. "The only uncertainty about all this is, do they know how fast we can really move? I'm counting on them thinking the info on the new warp-drive has been greatly exaggerated. If they don't they won't bother to chase me."

"The cordon leader is on the comm again, Mark."

"Okay. Let's see him."

The man's face appeared on the screen. "We know it's you, Keaflyn!" he barked. "Believe me, we don't want to blast you and your ship, but if you don't halt and place yourself in custody we'll have no choice."

"Give him visual," Keaflyn told the ship, then responded, "Thanks for the warning, friend. I'll consider it . . . when and if you get within blasting distance of me. Not before. Out."

The man's eyes widened momentarily. He replied, "Don't be too sure we're not within blasting distance right now, Keaflyn."

"Cut him off, Kelly. Start doing evasive zig-zags."

"Right, Mark."

Evasive action, rather than a straight-line retreat from the Whorl vicinity, would allow the defending ships to close up on him somewhat. And now his identity was definitely established for them. Keaflyn watched the situation graphic eagerly. Soon more of the guarding ships were under warp.

"How many are after us now, Kelly? My count is twenty."

"There are nineteen, Mark."

"Well, we want to do better than that. Fit the evasive pattern into a large circle around the Whorl, if you can. Don't get any further away from it right now."

"Okay, Mark."

Minutes passed, then the ship said, "I now count twenty-six ships in pursuit, Mark."

"Good!" he gloated. "Gradually narrow the zig-zags, on a course away from the Whorl."

"Right, Mark."

"When we start pulling away from them, stutter the warp, as if we're having technical problems with it, until they catch up. I don't want them to get discouraged and go back."

Keaflyn left the viewscreen and had some lunch. The chase had become a routine the ship could handle alone, so he took advantage of his Neg-induced giddy relaxation by taking a nap. His opportunities for easy sleep came seldom and unpredictably. He didn't want this one to get away from him.

The situation had not changed when he woke, except that the Neg was apparently taking a break. He could not detect the twisty bitterness of its presence.

"Just you, me, and my pleasure-impress, Kelly," he remarked through a yawning chuckle.

"Yes, Mark," said the ship.

He moved up to count the pursuers on the situation graphic. They were all still there. "Some kind of gauntlet should be shaping up somewhere ahead by this time," he said. "No sign of it yet?"

"No. I detect no activity ahead, Mark."

"Well, the moment you do, scoot back to the Whorl as fast as our new drive will take us." Keaflyn ate breakfast, and lingered over a glass of cold Terratea.

"Kelly," he asked suddenly, "what do you think of my personal situation?"

"That is not a matter to which I have given computational attention, Mark," the ship replied.

"No, I guess you haven't," the man said musingly. "The day is long gone when people were so inept with their life-problems that they sought the advice of computers, fortune-tellers, astrologers, and even Terratea leaves. Now we're content to let you handle warp matrix configurations, supply-demand semi-equations, observational summations, and the like. But do you know, Kelly, that people once tried to use computers to find mates for themselves?"

"That historical data is available to me, Mark."

Keaflyn sipped his tea for a while. Then he asked, "But you are aware of my personal situation, aren't you? The fact that I'm no longer totally sane, since the Sect Dualers loaded me with a pleasure-impress—you know about that from hearing me discuss it with others, even though I've never told you about it directly."

"Yes, Mark. That data is stored. I have made no computational use of it."

"And that a contralife entity . . . a Neg . . . has impinged itself on my mind. And that my life is in danger, and I can't afford to die, because the pleasure-impress will produce accumulative life-to-life degradation?"

"Yes, I am aware of all that, Mark."

· "All that, and much more," Keaflyn said. "That is true, Mark."

After a silence, the ship said, "You asked me what I think of your personal situation, Mark. Does that mean you wish me to attempt a computation on the data we've discussed, and offer an extrapolation?"

Keaflyn stared at his empty glass.

Advice from his ship? Funny, he had never considered that before, and the *Kelkontar* had been with him for two and a half lifetimes. But what he had said was true: people didn't need that kind of advice from computers . . . or didn't want it. A life was not something to reduce to an equation—if, indeed, that could be done. Living was more interesting and exciting as an art than it would be as an exact science. A life should be an adventure, not a formula.

But hell, his life had become too damned much of an adventure to suit him! If computer advice would assist him to continue his work . . .

No generalized predictions, he decided firmly, not from *Kelkontar*. He had confidence in his ship and would be too inclined to accept the ship's predictions as gospel . . . perhaps to the point of not trying to think for himself. But maybe, in dealing with specific situations . . .

"Go ahead and compute, Kelly," he said, "but hold up on offering me your extrapolations. I'll ask you specific and limited questions from time to time, as occasions arise. For a start, tell me if you would have advised tactics other than those we're using to lure the cordon away from the Whorl."

"Assuming I had advised proceeding with your planned test of the Whorl—" the ship began.

"Yes, assuming that."

"Then the tactics used would meet my approval, Mark."

"Good! Then you think we'll gain enough uninterrupted time at the Whorl to conduct the test?"

"The probability is that we will. However, to maximize that probability we should turn back to the Whorl immediately, without waiting for indications of ships ahead."

Keaflyn saw the point instantly. "Of course! You're taking in the possibility that ships could be mobilized from areas nearer the Whorl than we are, for a new cordon, long before our pursuers could get back. I thought of that but didn't include it in my planning because I didn't know if it had much likelihood. Okay. Head back for the Whorl right now, full speed!"

"As for the advisability of conducting the planned test—" began the ship.

"Never mind," Keaflyn broke in quickly with a loud giggle. "I want you to limit your answers to questions in this area to specifically what I ask. Otherwise I might depend too heavily on you. Okay?"

"Very well, Mark. Now on course for the Whorl. The cordon ships are out of detection range."

***

When they were again near the star-obscuring presence of the Whorl, Keaflyn asked, "Anybody else around?"

"No ships are detected, Mark."

"All right. Get as close as you consider safe to the face of the Whorl and release a tracerdust bomb."

The ship complied. After a pause, the bomb exploded with a brief bright flare and space glowed with fluorescent particles.

"The Whorl boundary surface is now detectable, Mark," the ship reported. "I can close to within five meters."

"Okay. Do it."

The ship eased closer to the black presence. Keaflyn felt a tenseness at that awesome, threatening nearness, a feeling that was not Neg-inspired, as far as he could tell. The Neg was apparently still off-duty.

"We are in position, Mark," the ship reported.

"Okay. Open up the flare bay and turn on your receptor cellbanks. Everything clear?"

"No, Mark. There are still traces of dust from our bomb between our receptors and the surface."

"Oh. Well, let's hold up until they thin out. Dust motes would put too much noise level over whatever reflection we might receive."

They waited, Keaflyn slightly annoyed with himself for not foreseeing so elementary a problem as this. "There's no way you can put a repulsing electric charge on your outer hull?" he asked.

"Not immediately, Mark. In perhaps two hours you could assemble a simple electrostatic generator and condenser. By then, however, the dust will have dispersed."

"So we just sit here a while," said Keaflyn, gazing at the blank blackness of the Whorl on the viewscreen. "I hope we don't drift into that thing in the meantime, or it doesn't drift into us."

"Our motion relative to the Whorl was established at under two millimeters per minute while the particles were rendering its boundary detectable, Mark," the ship assured him.

"Okay," Keaflyn chuckled, still staring at the screen. After a few minutes of silent contemplation he said, "Kelly, I have a childish desire to suit up, go outside, and poke that thing with a stick. That's the way primitive creatures investigate unknown objects that look dangerous. The Whorl seems to bring out the animal in me."

"Analogous tests of the Whorl have, as you know, been performed," said the ship. "However, a sufficiently sophisticated version could provide possible data."

"No kidding?" laughed the man. He thought about it, then said: "You mean poke the stick in, then yank it out a sophisticatedly small sliver of a second later, hopefully before the Whorl has time *to* destroy the part that was inside?"

"In essence, yes," the ship said.

"That shouldn't be difficult to set up," Keaflyn mused, "with equipment we could improvise. Probably the quickest way to poke something in and out would be with a warp, wouldn't you say?"

"That is correct, Mark. That has been tried before, without successful recovery of any of the stick material, so to speak—"

"But that was using the horse-and-buggy warp of last month," Keaflyn chortled. "We can do it almost two orders of magnitude more nimbly."

"Correct, Mark."

"Okay, we'll try it, after we finish this light-reflection experiment . . . provided we don't have company before then."

Finally the drifting dust had thinned to the point where *Kelkontar* calculated it would offer no critical interference.

"Then it's time to hit the beacon and see what bounces," said Keaflyn. "Go ahead."

There was a soft hum as the ship's power plant ran at capacity for several seconds, creating and storing energy. Then the hum gave way to an abrupt click as a high-load switch closed, letting the pent-up energy flow in one swift surge through the flash-filaments exposed by the open flare bay. For a split second an intense flood of light lashed the Whorl's surface before the power was spent and the filaments vaporized.

As far as Keaflyn could tell from watching the viewscreen, nothing had happened.

"What results, Kelly?" he asked eagerly. "Coming right up, Mark," the ship replied, and the blankness of the screen gave way to a lined graph. Trailing across it was a jagged path that, about midway, suddenly dropped to the bottom and stayed there.

"This is a summary of the intensity readings of the reflection receptors, with time plotted from left to right," the ship explained needlessly. "You will note that while the burst of light was passing through the space between us and the Whorl, there was some backflash, partially from drifting atoms but more from turbulent interactions between the photons themselves—a phenomenon to be expected in beams of the intensity we used. Then, when the burst of light reached the Whorl, all reflection ended, as the abrupt fall of the line indicates."

"Aw, hell," Keaflyn grunted drably. "Another great big zero."

"Yes. If the Whorl is reflective, it is so to a degree immeasurably small," said the ship.

"In a universe where there are more than two sides to every question," griped Keaflyn, "where nothing is all black or all white, this Whorl keeps insisting it's totally black! It bugs me, Kelly."

The ship said nothing and Keaflyn went on, "That's the way all the stabilities seem to behave. Lumon's Star is an *absolutely* unfailing light, and I suppose we have to take the word of the inhabitants of Avalon that they and their world are *absolutely* eternal. The Locuses are *absolutely* motionless, the Whorl is *absolutely* black, and the Resistant Globe is . . . well . . . thought made a dint in it, but just the same from the physical standpoint I imagine it will prove *absolutely* resistant.

"Kelly, I might as well face it. My whole investigative approach—trying to find trace instabilities in the stabilities in order to get them on a gradient scale and thus refute the concept of absolutism—it's a flop. I'm barking up the wrong tree."

"We have obtained data, Mark, though not of the type you were seeking," the ship conceded.

"Right, and you know, Kelly, the thought just occurred to me that I was looking for trace instabilities because that's what I wanted to find. I wanted to make the stabilities philosophically acceptable to myself." He giggled. "That wasn't especially scientific of me. This idea of taking an ultra-quick poke at the Whorl with a stick would just be more of the same, wouldn't it?"

"Basically, it would be," said the ship.

Keaflyn laughed. "What the hell, we may as well try it, anyway. But while we're improvising the gear for it, Kelly, let's move a couple of light-hours away from the Whorl. It's not a comfortable thing to be this near."

"Very well, Mark."

The ship went into a brief warp that reduced the Whorl to an undisturbingly small black disc against the starry background.

"Now let's—" Keaflyn began, but halted when he felt the ship go into warp again. "What's up, Kelly?"

"A fleet of eighteen ships just came into detection, Mark. One of them is of worldship mass."

"Okay, let's scram," Keaflyn grunted, then chuckled. "I wasn't too enthused about that experiment, anyway. The big ship in that bunch must be the Arlan Siblings' *Calcutta*. I don't know of anything else of worldship mass still in use."

"I presume you're right, Mark."

"Too bad the Arlans couldn't stay my pals," Keaflyn murmured. "I'd enjoy visiting with the Senior Sibling Berina again . . . You've run out of detection range by now, I suppose."

"No, Mark. They are keeping pace with us," came the surprising answer. "The worldship seems to have slightly more speed than the others. It is in the lead, pursuing us at a distance of 2.1 light-months."

"Then it must be closing on us!" yelped Keaflyn in astonishment.

"Yes. At current velocities, the worldship will overtake us in forty-six minutes, fourteen seconds."

"But how could they . . . ?" Keaflyn began, then fell silent.

How could they, indeed! As he had realized while talking to Clav Didorik back on Danolae, he had disclosed all the theoretical information necessary to the development of his faster warpdrive.

The Arlans were fast workers, with plentiful resources. No doubt they had not waited for his report on Lumon's Star to go through all the prepublication routine at Science Reporting Service. Probably a copy of his findings had been in their hands within a week after he turned it over to John Donflannis. Shortly after when Keaflyn's ship had shown a sudden capacity for outrunning anything else in space, the Arlans would have wasted no time getting a team of top-quality engineers to work, going over that report of his.

Not surprisingly, they had been able not only to duplicate his own application, but to refine it to the point where it was somewhat better than his own drive. They were, after all, engineers, which he was not. And they had the assistance of computers larger and brainier than *Kelkontar*.

Keaflyn suddenly bellowed with laughter. "Where's my hat, Kelly?"

"Your hat, Mark?"

"Hat. Check your dictionary. It's an obsolete term for headwear."

"Except for your helmet, Mark, I know of no head-wear aboard."

"Too bad. I need my hat to pull a rabbit out of."

But the only change in Keaflyn's situation during the next forty-five minutes was entrance of the Neg into his mind. The twisty bitterness came through to him distinctly at the instant it ended what was presumably a rest period and returned to duty. He sat tensely for a couple of minutes, waiting to see what its line of attack would be this time. However, it seemed content to observe.

Its presence was actually helpful in a way, Keaflyn noted. It tempered his laughing jag, enabling him to regard his position with less hysteria. Not that it mattered, because serious thinking wasn't going to open any escape hatch for him this time. He sighed. This was the end, and all he could do was to separate body and ego-field with the ego-field in as clean a condition as he could keep it. That meant he could not allow himself to be captured.

"Kelly, I hate to do this to a good ship like you," he said, "but I'll have to force those Sect Dualers to blast us. You can understand my reason for that, can't you?"

"Yes, Mark."

"Can you find a way out of this situation that doesn't require either the destruction of both you and my body or my capture and degradation preceding the loss of my body?"

"Assuming the intentions of our pursuers are such as recent data indicates, I can propose no third alternative, Mark," the ship replied.

"You're not really alive, are you?" Keaflyn asked urgently.

"No, Mark."

He tittered. "Thanks, Kelly. I needed that. I knew it, of course, but you *seem* alive to me much of the time. Okay, then, we go out fighting. And the only way I know to use you for a weapon, is to attempt to ram."

"Assuming the pursuers are armed, ramming will not succeed," said the ship. "Long before we could maneuver into proper position they would have aligned their blastbeams and—"

"I know," interrupted Keaflyn, "but that's okay. I don't want to kill anybody, anyway. Just make them kill me promptly."

"Then an attempt to ram should prove effective, Mark."

"Good. That's what we'll do. Not the worldship, though. Its hull's too tough for them to take a ramming seriously. One of the smaller ships."

The worldship was now close enough for definite identification as the *Calcutta*. It was not directly behind Keaflyn's ship, but off to starboard. When it pulled abreast, its distance was a little over a light-minute. It made no effort to close this gap; instead, it continued on course, gradually gaining a lead on the *Kelkontar*.

"Where do they think they're going?" Keaflyn muttered. "Unless they think I've cooked up a weapon and prefer for me to try it on the smaller ships . . ." He chortled at the idea.

"The *Calcutta*'s on the comm, Mark," his ship said.

"Okay. Put it through."

Once more he heard the slightly over-mellow male voice of the Arlan Siblings' flagship:

"The Senior Sibling's compliments, Mr. Keaflyn, and the following message: You have doubtless considered the alternatives now available to you. These are limited to suicide, which is intended to include suicidal attack, or capture. Suicide would be the less disturbing choice for everyone concerned. However, if your decision is for capture, you should choose your captors thoughtfully. The Senior Sibling makes the point that, aboard the *Calcutta,* your condition is understood."

Keaflyn did not reply immediately. He did not know what to say. Instead, he cut transmission and spoke to his ship.

"What the hell was that supposed to mean, Kelly? First she tells me to go ahead and get myself killed, and make everybody happy. And then that business about understanding me. Could the whole thing be a disguised offer of asylum aboard the *Calcutta?*"

His ship replied, "The possible implications of the message defy my analytical abilities, Mark. If the Arlan Siblings do wish to offer you asylum, they could not do so openly without displeasing their presumably Sect Dualer allies in the other pursuing ships. Conversely, the message could be a verbal trap, intended to lure you into captivity with minimal risk of violent resistance.

"Since the message defies clear interpretation, Mark," the ship continued, "the best course may be to base your decision on such nonverbal evidence as you have."

"Well, I was treated hospitably the other time I was aboard the *Calcutta,*" Keaflyn murmured. "That's about the only solid piece of nonverbal evidence I have." He stared at the situation graphic, which showed the *Calcutta* holding position off his starboard, no longer pulling ahead, while the remaining pursuers were rapidly closing in from behind.

He made up his mind. "Oh, what the hell! Where there's life there's hope. Tell the *Calcutta* I'll come aboard."

The worldship responded by swerving toward the *Kelkontar*. As the ships came together Keaflyn saw the *Calcutta* had opened a large hangar bay, and when grapple fields suddenly clamped on the *Kelkontar*, it was into this bay the smaller ship was drawn.

In his earlier visit, his ship hadn't been taken inboard this way. The suggestion was that this time he had come to stay for a while. But so what? He had expected that.

"Air pressure is up outside, Mark," said *Kelkontar*.

"Okay." Keaflyn went to the lock. "See you later, Kelly, I hope."

"Okay, Mark."

Out in the bay, he was met by the same guide, dressed in an old-time naval officer's uniform, who had greeted him on his earlier visit to the worldship.

"Please follow me, Mr. Keaflyn," the man said.

The interior of the *Calcutta* struck Keaflyn as even more spacious and luxurious than it had before . . . probably, he guessed, because he had spent so long in the close and rather Spartan confines of his own ship. He hadn't been on an Earth-type planet since . . . well, since Danolae, and that shouldn't count because he had stayed aboard the whole time he was there. So the last time he was really *on* a living planet had been Bensor just a few weeks back, but it seemed a long time.

The *Calcutta* could give one the sensation of being on a planet. Its widely spaced decks, frequently bright with growing trees and shrubs, and with high, sky-like overheads, made the ship feel like a world—although that was not the reason it was called a worldship. Such giant vessels had originally been built and used for colonization purposes, and had been designed so that enough colonists could be packed into the hive-like interior of one such ship to man a new-world colony; hence the coinage "worldship."

Of those giants, only the vastly remodeled *Calcutta* had survived. Colonization on the massive scale for which they were built required an overpopulated home planet, mused Keaflyn as a chute tube carried him and his guide up past several quickly-glimpsed deck-levels. With no overpopulated planets, worldships were outmoded. Only individuals with the extreme wealth and special needs of the Arlan Siblings could put one to practical use.

Keaflyn giggled. He shared the special needs of the Arlans but lacked their extreme wealth.

His guide led him from the chute tube onto what he guessed must be one of the ship's highest decks. Here the planetary verisimilitude was carried to the extent of having a building—complete with roof, walls, and even windows—standing among the shrubs and fronted by a neatly trimmed lawn. Giggling, he followed the guide up the walk and through the front door.

The hallway was short. One doorway stood open. The guide pointed to it. "The Senior Sibling is waiting for you in there, Mr. Keaflyn."

Keaflyn nodded, and advanced through the door, which closed behind him. He found himself in a large, rather bare, office. The Senior Sibling was seated behind an uncluttered desk.

"Hello, Mark," she said.

"Hi, Berina," he returned, unmindful until an instant later of the cold danger in her tone of voice. He stiffened, and that physical tension probably told the Neg something, because it pounced hard and viciously. He grimaced with the sudden pain blasting his head and body. "If you had spoken to me on comm yourself," he snickered, "I would have declined your invitation."

"Sit down, Mark," she said.

He flopped in the armchair, suddenly too tired to stand. Realizing the Neg had induced the tiredness that led to his quick obedience, he tried to stand up again. He could not. Shackles had clamped across his wrists, anchoring them tightly to the chairarms. And when he stopped struggling, a duraplas belt snaked across his stomach to complete his confinement.

He stared at the lovely woman across the desk. She returned his gaze somberly. A slight frown wrinkled her forehead, suggesting that her Neg was on the job, too.

"Berina," he chuckled inanely, "your hospitality has simply gone to hell since my last visit."

She winced. "Lay off, Mark, for heaven's sake!" she snapped in irritation. "You won't gain anything by making this more difficult for me. I'm going to do what has to be done, regardless of how I detest the job!"

"Sorry," Keaflyn laughed. "I was just trying to bring a touch of lightness into what is shaping up as a melodramatically grim situation."

"Well, don't!" she lashed at him. "Those ignorant Sect Dualers! Your touches of lightness, as you call them, are

the result of that pleasure-impress Arnod Smath
inflicted. That's been your ruination, Mark! I warned
you, a Neg is an enemy, to be kept under control at all
times, which requires constant mental discipline.

"Without the pleasure-impress," she went on moodily,
"perhaps you would have heeded my warning. But you
did not. Instead, you gave the Neg an opening to attack
the Resistant Globe—pure scatterminded thought-
lessness on your part! If you had been thinking halfway
seriously, with the caution a Neg carrier must never lose,
you would have realized that null-the-Globe game was
not for you.

"And your experience with the Globe taught you nothing! You've continued to flit blithely about from one stability to another, very carefree and all too willing to give
a trial to any idea that pops into your head. The fact that
you've done no more damage I'll chalk up to pure good
fortune. In any event, you can't be allowed to continue
your careless antics. They're done with, as of now!"

Smiling with amusement at her angry tirade, Keaflyn
shrugged. "Okay, I'll go along with you. Fact is, I had
just come to the conclusion, after running my experiment
on the Whorl, that my whole research approach was off
target, anyway. The things I've discovered—the warpicles and the additional Locuses—were by chance, not
my brilliant design. And I seem to have run out of serendipity. So I'm willing to quit and let the citizenry recover
their peace of mind."

His face twisted with pain. "Look, Berina, now that
we've got that settled. how about telling your pet chair
to let go? My Neg is acting up, and I guess from your
frown yours is, too. Let's go take the cure in your lake."

She continued to gaze silently at him after he finished. Finally she shifted uncomfortably and said, "Mark, what has to be done has to be done. Putting it off won't change its necessity or make it any easier when the putting-off has to end. Instead, it would make it much harder for me to do, because I could become attached to you awfully quickly if I allowed myself to do so."

Keaflyn was not sure the feeling was completely mutual, but Berina had an attractive way of wearing a body, to say the least.

"I wonder if we've ever been mates," he murmured.

"Stop that!" she yelped.

He chuckled. "Sorry, again . . . and what can I say, dear, after I say I'm sorry?"

Berina touched a button on her desk and the walls on either side of the office began folding into the ceiling.

"I can't delay any longer," she said with studied briskness. "As the *Calcutta* told you, in suggesting that you surrender to me, your condition is understood here. And understanding brings knowledge of what must be done. Shortly, the Neg will find you are no longer useful to it."

A twisted smile on his face, Keaflyn looked at the equipment being exposed by the lifting walls. There were about a half-dozen major complexes in the enlarged room. And although he had not seen their like for several hundred thousand years—such equipment never having been used on Earth—his backtrack memories enabled him to recognize them immediately.

Electronic torture devices: instrumentation that bypassed the body to hammer and slash the ego-field itself!

He couldn't quit laughing as his chair suddenly went into motion, carrying him toward one of the complexes.

It was all very funny, after all, his mind gibbered at him. He had grown more or less accustomed to the idea that the pleasure-impress would degrade his ego-field to a point where, in his next life, he couldn't expect to be human. He had been thinking in terms of coming back as one of Alo Felston's cows.

But after Berina and her torture machines got through with him and permitted him to escape his body—hell, he'd be lucky to wind up as a fly, swatted at by the tails of Felston's cows!

Chapter 13

In one of his more lucid moments while the machines under Berina Arlan's direction slammed him, twisted him, attenuated him, compacted him, drained him, flooded him and discredited him, the thought came to Keaflyn: *Nature is kind.*

The normal forces at work in the universe *never* harmed an ego-field—a soul, a spirit, a life-force. Not directly, the way Berina's hellish gadgets were doing him.

No. Nature was rough only on bodies, and thus indirectly on ego-fields—to the degree the ego-fields became fixated on or in bodies. The worst nature could do to an ego-field was tear a body away from it, either the body the ego happened to be inhabiting, or the cherished body of a loved one.

Or it could give a fixated ego-field some solid grief by denying it the favors of a desired lover. Unrequited sexual desire was about as severe as any torture nature dished out, and even that was indirect, requiring fixation on a body.

That was why he hadn't really been bothered when Tinker showed up in a pre-sex eleven-year-old body for their this-lifetime reunion, his thoughts ran on sometime later, in another lucid moment. He loved Tinker, but with a love that was more and less than fixation. Fixations were for the not-sane, and besides, you couldn't very well get fixated on one body during a marriage such as his and Tinker's, which had lasted through several lifetimes . . .

What was it he had been thinking about? Oh, yes—Tinker! It helped to think about Tinker. Think about her even when he could open his eyes enough to see the beautiful but grim Berina Arlan at the control board of one murderous machine after another. . . .

Tinker! Mustn't forget Tinker . . . and the kindness of nature—that was part of it, too. Like the reason Tinker was only eleven years old, instead of in a body compatible with his own in age. She had been killed while in a nine-year-old-body—which *would* have been compatible in age—in the *Brobdinagia* disaster. A freak accident of some sort, evidently an in-space collision, had blown up the spaceliner *Brobdinagia* with the whole crew and all passengers, including Tinker.

A sudden, unexpected death like that was the worst kind, because it could catch an ego-field by surprise and have a stunning effect. But Tinker's present lifetime father, Clav Didorik, said she got over it by the time she was two years old. So, even at its worst, nature was kind . . .

What was that nice thought I was thinking? Got to find it quick! Stabilities? Kelly? *What was it?* Oh. Oh, yes. Tinker. Find something else to think about Tinker before the Senior Sibling gets the next machine lined up on me. Helps a lot to have a thought like that. To hang onto.

But what's Berina up to now? Taking a break or something? Just standing there . . .

The Senior Sibling moved forward and did something to his chair. Then she asked him something, but she ran her words together and no meaning came through. He didn't care what she had asked, anyway. He didn't feel like talking to anybody, much less to such a frightful monster as she. Still, he was going to get a grip on himself and stop shaking like a leaf and stop being afraid . . .

Berina asked the same question again.

This time he looked up at her, annoyed because the sight of a beautiful woman could make him flinch with a sudden surge of abject terror.

I'm not going to be cowed! he told himself determinedly. *Oh, yes, I am!* came a responding thought from the vicinity of the pleasure-impress—*I'm going to be cowed, horsed, dogged, rabbited, and even cockroached!* But that thought wasn't him, and in spite of everything, he could still speak for himself.

"What goofy language is that?" he growled at her.

Berina replied, "I asked if you can stand up now. But I spoke too rapidly for you to understand. Can you stand up?"

"I guess so, but why should I bother? Let your damned chair carry me where you want me. Am I supposed to go to your execution chamber under my own power or something?"

He noticed she was no longer frowning, but she looked unhappy nevertheless. Not nearly as unhappy, though, as he would like to see her. "I'm discontinuing the procedure for a while," she replied. "Something has come up. I want you to go to the quarters I've assigned you, and wait."

Terror hit him. "You mean there's more of this still to come?" he yammered.

Her face creased as if she were going to cry, but the expression was gone almost before he noticed it. "Perhaps not," she said, looking away. "Judging from your verbalization speed, your IQ is now about one hundred and twenty. The Neg will have no further use for you."

"Verbalization speed?" Keaflyn asked in puzzlement.

"Yes. That's why you couldn't understand me when I first spoke a moment ago. I had forgotten to slow down for you, until I heard you speak."

"Oh. Oh yeah," he muttered distractedly. A slower mental tempo was one of the characteristics of a degraded mind. That was the reason why books from the old Earthbound times were still read and enjoyed, while films from that same era were unwatchable. The actors took forever getting a couple of words said.

"Will you please go to your quarters, Mark?" she asked, sounding impatient.

"Any change would be an improvement!" he growled, pushing up from the chair. His body felt clumsy and his mind foggy. Berina's estimate of a 120 IQ was probably about right, he figured dazedly.

"The guide is waiting for you outside," she said. He approached the door, and it opened with such haste that he jumped. "You ought to get your door fixed," he complained without looking back. He went through it and into the hall before the thought came that there was nothing wrong with the door. It had merely seemed to snap open twice as fast as it should, because he was sensing only half as fast as before.

Half as fast! That much? The realization was a stunning shock.

"Plecflomemistrkefln," the guide waiting for him said. Which probably meant "Please follow me, Mr. Keaflyn," or something to the same effect. It didn't matter. The guide was supposed to lead him to his room, and he was supposed to follow the guide. Talk was not necessary.

They walked to the chute tube at a pace only slightly too fast for comfort. The velocity of gross body movements was, after all, a matter governed mostly by size and musculature, not by reaction time. And entering and leaving the tube was not too bad. It required an instant of planned exertion and nimbleness, but he got in and out of the moving tube without stumbling or losing his balance.

The deck the guide took him to had a number of small buildings. Keaflyn was led to the door of one of these. The guide turned and spoke. "Ulstaeremistrkefln comfrwatuned."

"If that's something I need to know, tell it to me slowly," he snapped.

The guide blinked in surprise and stared at him. When he didn't speak, Keaflyn shrugged and went inside.

It was a small, well-appointed apartment. He explored it nervously, then returned to the door. It did not open for him. Well, that was to be expected. This was his prison cell until the Senior Sibling was ready to work on him some more.

Escape?

He giggled at the thought. Even with all his wits about him he couldn't have gotten out of the *Calcutta* against the Siblings' wishes. And now that he was the equivalent of the old-fashioned village idiot . . .

One good thing: That was his first giggle since before Berina had worked him over. His pleasure-impress was encysted now in the middle of so much additional mental junk that it could no longer force itself into expression.

That additional junk could, though. Curiously, he looked around for a mirror and found one on the wall in the sanitizer. He stared at length at his face in it.

It was a backtrack face. His, of course, but changed. There was no glow in the skin, which had a definite pallor. The eyes were dull. And the expression . . .

Well, he had grown accustomed to the reflection of his mouth drawn up in a smile of false glee. Not in the weeks since the pleasure-impress had been forced on him had his face been serene.

But this was far worse. This was a face with the quivering tension of a madman.

I'm not that far gone! he protested silently and desperately. I'm still more or less rational!

Consciously, he tried to make his face relax. Unclenching the jaws helped. Then he worked his mouth until the muscles around his lips loosened. This did not bring his expression back to normal, but it made an improvement.

The realization came that the startling expression was not due to total insanity, but the result of the shock he was still in from the Senior Sibling's torture chamber. He was still tight with terror from that . . . and from the knowledge that more of the same might be forthcoming.

He stumbled away from the mirror and slumped down on a relaxer. When he stretched out he realized how exhausted he was. He wondered doubtfully if he could go to sleep, jumpy as he was. How many lifetimes had it been since he had experienced this kind of physical and mental anguish?

And to think, only a few hours ago he had been bothered by the trivial little torments that the Neg was able to inflict him with!

He dropped into fitful slumber.

And woke to dullness. He had slept off the worst of the shock, and his mind was no longer in turmoil. A mild feeling of hunger was all that made getting up seem worth the effort.

The autocate annoyed him when he ordered breakfast. It had no trouble understanding his slow speech, but seemed incapable of slowing down itself and making itself understandable. But no matter. It fed him what he asked for.

Afterwards he returned to the relaxer for a series of broken dozes, ended at last by a tapping on the door.

He sat up. "Come in!" he yelled, angry and frightened.

The door opened and the Junior Sibling, Bartok Arlan, stepped inside. Keaflyn noted, with mild interest, that his mind's first identification of Bartok was the one word "Negro," whereas on his earlier visit to the *Calcutta* he had merely noted dark skin among the identifying features of Bartok's present body. Maybe low intelligence was the reason for racial prejudice back in the old days, he mused.

"Hi, Bartok," he said.

"Hello, Mark," the young man replied, speaking barely slow enough for Keaflyn to understand. "I'm taking you to your ship and releasing you. I don't expect interference, but try to move as rapidly as you can. Let's go!"

Keaflyn stared, then said, "You're helping me escape?"

"Right. Come on!"

Keaflyn followed him out of the apartment and trotted to keep up as they headed for the chute tube. "What's going on?" he asked, keeping his voice low. "Are you bucking Berina?"

"In a way, yes. Berina's ambivalent concerning you at the moment. But I'm not sure she would release you, now or later. I'm not waiting for her to decide."

Keaflyn noticed Bartok wore a frown of pain, indicating his Neg was working hard on him. "I wish she could have felt ambivalent about me earlier," he complained.

"Don't ask questions—they take too much time—and I'll explain," replied Bartok. "Berina was in the process of traumatizing you with her machines when she suddenly realized that her Neg had ceased bothering her. It took her a while to notice that, because her own actions were disturbing to her. When she did notice, she ended the torture immediately and sent you to recuperate."

Keaflyn started to speak but Bartok waved him to silence and continued: "We've learned that inactivity of a Neg means, more often than not, that the Neg approves of what we're doing at the time, and ceases its interference. Berina was surprised to find hers inactive, but she's not sure what it means. A Neg can be tricky. Hers might have backed off to make her think it approved her actions when it violently disapproved. So she's taking time to reconsider before doing anything more.

"In the meantime, I'm getting you out of here, because I never approved of this from the beginning," Bartok went on grimly. "Berina's practical and conservative; I tend to be idealistic and progressive. That balances out nicely over the long term. Any policy we can maintain consistently, as each of us in turn is Senior Sibling, has to be reasonably sound, to have the approval of both of us. But in an emergency action, especially one not covered by established Sibling policy, the Junior Sibling may be obliged to sabotage the Senior Sibling's decision. It has happened a few times before this."

Keaflyn stumbled and nearly fell getting into the chute tube. He was having to concentrate to follow Bartok's words, because the Junior Sibling was talking a bit too fast for him.

"What happened to the Resistant Globe—the Insecurity—was very disturbing to a person of Berina's protective inclination," the young man continued. "She was mindful of the potential value of your research, but even more mindful of the damage your loosely-controlled Neg could do. Did she make the comparison to you of a Neg impinging on this universe and an atom of contramatter in a cloud chamber?"

"Yes," Keaflyn gasped, trying to catch his breath.

"It's an apt analogy," the Junior Sibling said. "I can understand my sister's concern. An impinging Neg has the theoretical potential to wreck our universe quite thoroughly. Berina felt that you, handicapped by the pleasure-impress, were letting yours get more and more out of hand. She saw no recourse but to render you too dull a tool for the Neg's purposes.

"I can't abide her decision!" the young man said with angry determination as they exited from the chute tube. "If idealism counts for anything at all, it must insist on the sanctity of the human spirit! No consideration of practical danger is sufficient to justify the degradation of a single ego-field.

"That's why I'm helping you escape, Mark, while Berina is in her sleep period. I've already given your ship data on how it can deliver you secretly to your friends Alo Felston and Tinker on Danolae, and they will be advised of your coming. I urge you to reach them as quickly and quietly as possible, Mark. Put yourself in Tinker's care and let her clean out the mess Berina's loaded you with. Okay?"

Keaflyn nodded dazedly. "Okay," he said. He had felt a surge of relief when Bartok indicated that Berina was asleep. Now he was getting the shakes again at the thought of her waking before he made good his escape. "What about the Sect Dualer fleet that was with you?" he asked.

"They've broken up and gone to their homes," said Bartok. "When Berina lured you aboard, taking the responsibility for doing what they thought needed to be done, they were glad enough to wash their hands of the whole affair and scram. They didn't kid themselves about the dirtiness of their business. Just move quietly, Mark, and you won't have to worry about Sect Dualers."

"Right. And thanks, Bartok," agreed Keaflyn, halting at the lock of his ship and facing the Junior Sibling. There were things he wanted to say . . .

"Thanks is enough!" the young man said swiftly, urging him toward the lock. "Good luck, Mark."

Keaflyn allowed himself to be hurried aboard. "Kelly," he told his ship, "get out of here as soon as the bay opens. Warp for Danolae."

"Okamrk mistarlngavme—"

"*Stop!*" squawked Keaflyn. "If you can't talk as slowly as I do, Kelly, there's no use in talking at all!"

After several seconds of silence, during which Keaflyn felt the ship move out of the bay and go into warp, *Kelkontar* replied, "This should be a satisfactory adjustment of my speech, Mark."

"Yeah. That's better. Now, what were you saying before?"

"That Mr. Arlan gave me data for a rendezvous with Tinker and Alo Felston in an isolated portion of the planet Danolae."

"Fine. And we're supposed to get there quietly, without attracting attention."

"He explained that, also, Mark."

Keaflyn took a chair and tried to relax, but the knots in his nerves and muscles stayed tight. He thought of asking for aspirin, but that remedy seemed insufficient for his need. What were the old cures for this kind of feeling?

"Kelly, fix me an alcoholic drink. Do you have the data for something like bourbon on ice?"

"My historic chemistry files include that data, Mark," the ship replied. "The drink will be ready in five minutes."

"You may as well mix up a good-sized batch of the bourbon while you're at it. Say half a gallon."

The five minutes seemed long to Keaflyn, but the drink finally rose on a serving pedestal beside his chair. He picked up the glass, took a couple of tentative sips, then quickly drank it all.

"Wow! That's better," he laughed. "That loosens me up! Pour me another, Kelly old pal."

"All right, Mark." The pedestal retreated into the deck, to return promptly with a fresh drink. Keaflyn downed half of it and then decided he could drink more slowly.

"We're through probing stabilities, Kelly," he said, feeling a little sad about it. "All through."

"Okay, Mark."

"It's a shame in a way, even if I was on the wrong track. I had my heart set on poking that stupid Whorl with a stick."

"The idea did have promise, Mark."

"It sure as hell did!" he said with belligerent emphasis. "It had a damned hell of a lot of promise!" He had a large swallow of bourbon. "We might've got somewhere yet, if we didn't have to quit. Dirty shame." He drained the glass. "Fill 'er up again, Kelly."

The new drink came and he nursed it morosely. "Three lousy lifetimes I spent getting set up to crack them stabilities wide open, Kelly. Three lousy lifetimes! It's not fair!"

"I can grasp that you have reasons for disappointment, Mark," the ship allowed.

"Damned right I do," he glowered. "Who do they think they are, anyway, making me stop? You know what Bartok Arlan told me, Kelly? He said the sanctity of the human spirit wasn't to be trifled with! Bartok's an idealist. Damned good one, too! They better listen to that guy! He knows what it's all about. And he said my spirit wasn't to be trifled with, like they been doing. What do you think of that, Kelly?"

"Debasement of an ego-field is most emphatically in violation of the human code, Mark."

"Right! They've got no business tryin' to put me down!" His new drink was about gone, so he drained the rest of it, then slammed the glass down with a determined gesture. "They ain't goin' to get away with it, Kelly. They can't push *me* around! We out of detectin' range of the *Calcutta?*"

"Presumably so, Mark, by a large margin. The *Calcutta* was on course for the Terra Sector, while our warp toward Danolae is one hundred thirty-eight degrees away from Terra."

"Put me up a graphic on the screen. Show me us and Danolae and where you figure the *Calcutta* is and the Whorl."

The graphic flashed on, and Keaflyn studied it owlishly. The Whorl lay off at a slight angle from *Kelkontar's* line of flight.

"Kelly old pal," he announced, "we're going to make a little side-trip, just long enough to poke that old Whorl with a stick. Right?"

"Whatever you say, Mark."

"Right! Set warp for the Whorl, and let's get busy makin' ourselves a super-duper pokin' stick!"

Chapter 14

The new course had been established no more than a few seconds when the ship reported, "There's a hey-you call on the comm, Mark."

Keaflyn frowned in alarm. "Aimed at us?"

"Evidently so."

"Well, let's hear it," he snapped.

The comm screen remained dark, but the voice cut chillingly through Keaflyn's alcoholic daze. It was the voice of the Senior Sibling:

"Hey-you! IQ 120! Resume and maintain your original course, or you're in trouble!"

"H-h-how far away is she?" Keaflyn managed to ask, fighting to stave off the terror Berina's voice aroused.

The graphic changed in response to his question. He studied it intently. "That witch must've been awake the whole time," he muttered. "She's been trailin' us, to make sure we did like Bartok told us. But we can beat her to the Whorl, can't we?"

"Yes, Mark, by some eight minutes," *Kelkontar* replied.

"And I better get to work on our stick. You got the plans ready?"

"You will find them on the workbench," said the ship.

Keaflyn hurried to the bench and peered at the three pages of specs. The stick, he saw after some study, was to be a small ball of steel with a tiny one-shot warp drive imbedded in its center. The drive unit looked awfully complex to him.

"We got a drive unit like this in stock?" he asked.

"Not assembled, Mark. We have the components for it. I am laying them out on the bench for you."

Mark watched stupidly as one tiny package after another plopped out of the bench's supply tube. Dozens of them.

Well, time to get busy. He began opening the packages and lining up their contents, trying to recognize each item as he did so and remember how it fitted in the diagrams he had just looked at. He couldn't place them all without referring back to the specs.

He muttered in annoyance. This job was more complicated than it looked!

"You better consult your files again, Kelly, and find something to sober me up. I got problems here."

"All right, Mark. The remedy is ready for you, since I anticipated this as a possible need."

"Good for you! Thanks!" Keaflyn grabbed the cup of dark liquid and emptied it with hurried gulps. He gagged over it for a few seconds. The taste of the stuff alone was bad enough to have a sobering effect.

Kelkontar said, "There is another hey-you from the Senior Sibling, Mark."

Keaflyn hesitated, staring at the components on the workbench. He was going to have all he could handle, getting the stick assembled, without being thrown into one tizzy after another by the voice of Berina Arlan. But . . . he had to know what she was saying.

He sighed. "Okay, Kelly, let's hear it."

Berina's voice came through: "Hey-you! IQ 120! Unless you resume your former course at once, I will be obliged to assume you are totally out of control of yourself. I will act on that assumption! Last warning! Out."

It was some relief to hear she wouldn't call again. Out of control of himself? Obviously she meant the Neg had taken him over completely and was guiding his actions.

Was she right?

Keaflyn considered the question as he worked frantically and clumsily at the task of assembling the stick. The Neg was not in evidence. He could not sense the twisty bitterness by which he had previously been able to detect its presence. But that "feel" of the Neg had been a subtle sensation; maybe his mind was now too dull to detect it.

And although he was beginning to feel awful, he was familiar enough with the kind of somatics the Neg hit him with to know this was different. This was very plainly the beginnings of a hangover.

He did regret his decision to have one final go at the Whorl, now that he was sober. That decision had been brought on by the booze, not by the Neg. But what could he gain by backing down? He had already shown Berina Arlan that he could not be trusted to behave in what she considered a responsible manner. She would not again feign sleep while the Junior Sibling helped him escape . . . if indeed young Bartok would help him a second time.

Probably she would not even take him prisoner again. Whether he went to the Whorl or changed course for Danolae, Berina would probably blow him out of space when the *Calcutta* came within blast-beam range.

"We are now approaching the Whorl, Mark," his ship announced, "and will arrive on testing station in twenty-five seconds."

Keaflyn blinked and stared in frustration at the half-completed tangle of components on the bench. *IQ 120, indeed!* he thought with chagrin. In other words, just plain stupid! The task of assembling the stick—ordinarily little more than a dexterity game for an infant—was too much for his benumbed mind and ineffectively directed hands.

So . . . he was defeated even in his drunken gesture of defiance.

He walked away from the bench and returned to the chair at the viewscreen. "I can't put it together in time, Kelly," he said tiredly as he collapsed in the chair.

"Okay, Mark. What are your orders?" asked the ship. What orders?

A good question. What orders could he give that would prevent man and ship from being blasted to dust within a very few minutes?

Not that he would ordinarily object too strenuously to being killed. That had happened thousands of times before. Bodies were destroyed, and new bodies were inhabited.

But his ego-field was now degraded far past the point where he could hope to inhabit a human body, with the nervous system necessary for intellectual activity, ever again. Death would add one more trauma to the load he already bore, pushing him still lower. His next life would be as an animal, and the life and death of the animal body would contain traumas to debase him further, so that the following life would be as a still lower animal, the traumas of which would bring him down to a still more degraded condition . . .

A long downward spiral into darkness. An eternity of pain and ignorance.

It was easy to see—the thought passed through Keaflyn's mind—where the ancients got their concept of hell. That, precisely, was what he faced.

Nothingness would be infinitely preferable. But ego-fields did not vanish into nothingness. They were indestructible. An ego-field went on and on, while universes were created and destroyed. Perhaps, after sufficient eons of sufficiently brutal torture and humiliation, an ego-field could be squeezed down to near-nothing, to almost-extinction. That was what Alo Felston and Tinker thought, and they were experts. Alo by instinct, and Tinker by training and experience.

In other words, an ego-field's approach to nothingness was asymptotic—coming nearer and nearer but never quite reaching it. There would always remain a tiny little knot of hurting awareness that had once been Mark Keaflyn . . .

"Is there *no* way out?" he gibbered frantically. Call Berina and beg for mercy? Even if granted, it would merely delay his descent into the deeper reaches of hell by a few meaninglessly brief years.

The pleasure-impress alone had assured his doom; Berina's torture machines had subsequently brought home with intimidating clarity just how horrible that doom was.

The blackness of the Whorl on the viewscreen seemed symbolic of the darkness of his fate. But it was a pale

symbol, because the Whorl had the blackness of nothingness, while he . . .

"Kelly," he demanded suddenly, "haven't ships gone
into the Whorl?"

"It is presumed that three ships were lost in that manner when the Whorl was first discovered, Mark, and
before its boundaries were accurately—"

"What about the crews?" he broke in impatiently.
"Were they ever heard from? I mean, did they have lives
after that?"

The ship was silent for several seconds. Then it
reported, "A thorough search of my files finds no report
of a past-life entry into the Whorl, Mark."

"Which means the crew members didn't get back as
ego-fields," Keaflyn babbled hurriedly, "which means
they didn't even *survive* as such! Kelly, the Whorl
destroys *everything* that enters it, including life-entities!"

"That is one possibility, Mark. There could be alternative explanations for—"

"Never mind. the alternatives! I'm going for nothingness! *Warp into the Whorl!*"

"Okay, Mark."

For a brief lucid instant Keaflyn was amused by the
unsurprised, routine manner in which his ship accepted
this ultimately outrageous order. And then . . .

Then the *Kelkontar* warped into the Whorl.

Strangeness and wrenching pain, but not nothingness.

"Oh, damn," grunted Keaflyn in despair, the words
hurting his vocal cords in a peculiar manner. "Turn
around and get out of here, Kelly. No! DON'T!"

His last two words were screams as the ship began to shift its course. The pain had nearly torn him apart.

"K-keep going straight ahead," he managed to say when the pain eased. "What kind of p-place *is* this?"

"The characteristics are similar to those experienced by pre-warp interstellar vessels, Mark," *Kelkontar* replied, its own voice sounding tinny and distorted. "As those ships approached the speed of light via straight-power acceleration, they and their crews discovered that relativistic contractions of time-space were experiential, as well as observable, phenomena. These effects placed a lower-than-expected limit on endurable warpless velocities and delayed frequent interstellar travel until the redevelopment of the warp in the year 2158 by—"

"Okay, I know about that," grumbled Keaflyn. "Can you get our warp working again?"

"Our warp is functioning, Mark, apparently normally," the ship told him.

"If we're in warp, why do we feel contractions?" Keaflyn asked, wishing he could think of fewer words to ask the question with. Every utterance was a pain.

"The contraction we're experiencing is imposed from outside, Mark. Also, it is characteristic of acceleration at a right angle to our line of warped flight. The indication is that this acceleration is moving us laterally through the disc of the Whorl. Meanwhile, our warp is, presumably, continuing us on course through the thickness of the disc."

But the Whorl was only a few light-minutes thick, Keaflyn protested silently. If the warpdrive were working right in this peculiar Whorl-space, they ought to have

emerged on the other side a split second after they
entered. And this seemed to be lasting forever!

Relativistic contractions, huh? He knew about them,
knew how surprised everybody had been when they were
experienced on ships approaching light-speed. Like the
attainment of nonexistence by an ego-field, the speed of
light was an asymptote for a ship under normal acceleration. It was unreachable, and the contractions were
symptomatic of that. The accelerating ship would
shorten; a yardstick pointed fore and aft would be less
in length as the ship went faster and faster. Time, too,
would contract; a second aboard a ship near the speed
of light could be a minute in the normal universe.

Thus, the ship would measure each added increment
to its velocity—since acceleration is determined by feet
per second per second—by multiplying a constantly
shortening length by a constantly slowing unit of time,
with a resultantly smaller gain in real velocity.

Beneath his misery, Keaflyn took a modicum of pleasure from the fact that, stupefied though his mind obviously was, he could still understand the workings of
relativity. Then he remembered that lots of 20th century
men had understood that, so he had no cause for self-
congratulation.

If the ship was being carried laterally by the Whorl-
induced acceleration, that meant he was currently about
as thick as a sheet of tissue paper from side to side . . .
or was it head to toe? In any event, it wasn't from front
to back, since that was the direction in which the warp
was working. Presumably working, that is. Maybe
although the warp was doing its job, the time contraction

was making what should be a split-second stretch out into endlessness.

Did a sidewise time contraction work like that? He tried to figure it out, but decided his 120 intelligence quotient wasn't quite as capable of handling relativity as he had thought. He could ask *Kelkontar,* but knowing the answer hardly seemed worth the pain of speaking.

The trick was to be as motionless as possible. Any movement involved some turning, some change of portions of his body to the orientation of the lateral contraction, some strange stretching and twisting of muscles, bones, and nerve fibers. The beating of his heart and his careful shallow breathing were more than enough movement.

How long would this go on? Did the ship have enough consumables to get them through? Let's see . . . fuel and oxygen and so on had been adequate for five weeks in full warp . . . food, too—not that he was likely to try eating anything! So the ship had fuel to keep going far longer than he was likely to stay alive.

Staying alive! That same old problem again, even here in the Whorl, where he had looked for nonexistence.

Neg thinking . . . that was what he was doing. Negs were supposed to be seeking nonexistence, just as normlife sought enhanced and extended existence. Which spoke pretty damn highly of Berina Arlan's skill as an ego-field degrader. In just a few hours she had pushed him so far down that his entire system of basic values could become inverted. Even awareness of that didn't keep nonexistence from seeming like a very desirable state . . .

Wasn't *anything* happening?

"Sense anything outside?" he asked the ship.

"No, Mark."

Keaflyn was suddenly aware that he was beginning to sense something *inside* the ship. It came as a desire to look over his shoulder, a feeling of other presences nearby. There was nothing mysterious about this sensation; it merely indicated that one was not alone, that someone else, whether in a body or not, was near.

But . . . in the Whorl? Ego-fields here? Dozens of them?

Why not? As *Kelkontar* had reminded him, ships had accidentally entered the Whorl, and the crew members had not made their presences known in civilization since. And as he had learned, the Whorl did not destroy an ego-field. So, the crews were still trapped here, and had now impinged themselves aboard his ship, to take a look at the newest rat in the trap.

Hi fellers, he thought at them, not really expecting them to get the message. But he was sure they were there.

All of them, he guessed, had left their bodies behind long ago. Strange though the behavior of time might be in this weird environment, physiological processes struggled to continue, and bodies doubtless wore and starved themselves to death within a very few subjective days.

Days? It seemed to Keaflyn he had been here for weeks already! On the other hand, in terms of breaths and heartbeats, he knew hardly an hour had passed. But to his ego-field visitors—deprived of bodies to serve them as clocks, their inherent time sense doubtless as twisted by their surroundings as was his own—how long had their three or four trapped centuries seemed?

Endless. What other word was there for it?

Far more endless than the stars glittering at him from the viewscreen . . . More endless than the stabilities themselves . . . More endless than the power of thought to conceive of startings and stoppings.

Stars glittering on the viewscreen . . .

Keaflyn gasped. "Kelly We're out!"

"That is correct, Mark. We have exited from the face of the Whorl opposite to our point of entry." He sat stunned for a moment, taking in his escape. He sensed he still had company . . . the ego-fields had ridden the ship out with him. Probably they had come aboard in hopes of just that. He had hardly finished the thought when the awareness came that he was now alone. His passengers had debarked.

"Change course for Danolâe, Kelly," he ordered, "and go all out! Maybe we can get out of deteetion range while the *Calcutta* is still on the other side of the Whorl."

"I doubt that the *Calcutta* is anywhere in the vicinity, Mark," the ship said.

"Why not? We probably weren't inside the Whorl as much as a second!"

"The position of the Whorl relative to the nearer stars indicates otherwise, Mark. Its relative movement since our entry is a distance requiring the passage of twelve years and five months."

Keaflyn's mouth gaped open. "You're sure of that?"

"I'm checking other stellar position changes now, Mark . . . Yes. It is now verified. By Earth reckoning, we are now in June of the year 2855."

Well, what do you know!" exclaimed Keaflyn with a grin. "The Whorl's a time machine!"

"Only in the loosest sense, Mark," the ship reproved.

"Yeah, I know. But anyway, we learned something about it, didn't we?"

"Yes, Mark."

"I guess I'll never figure out exactly what it was we learned. That'll take a better mind than I've got left. But by damn, we showed 'em, Kelly! I can write a report on the Whorl . . . or you write it. You can do it better than I can now. And Kelly—"

"What is it, Mark?"

"Tinker's twenty-three years old! Marriageable age and more!"

"That is correct, Mark."

Chapter 15

The *Kelkontar's* report on the trip through the Whorl was completed a few minutes later, and Keaflyn tried to read it. It was a frustrating experience.

There were entire pages that left him feeling blank, and these were, he realized, the most important pages. That is, they contained the ship's mathematical analysis of the Whorl phenomenon. Keaflyn could recognize the symbols, could even define the meaning of each, but their relationships within a complex mathematical statement were a mystery to him.

Was his intelligence *that* far down?, he asked himself with a sick feeling.

"Kelly, let me see the report I did on Lumon's Star."

The ship displayed the earlier paper, one he had written himself . . . and he had the same problem with the math. He could no longer comprehend equations he had originated.

"I can't follow the math we've been using, Kelly," he admitted. "I suppose yours is all right. I can't criticize it, in any event."

"I understand, Mark. However, you must sign my report if it is to receive publication."

"Oh, yes. Computer reports aren't acceptable, are they?" Keaflyn considered the matter for several minutes. It would not be honest for him to pretend authorship of the *Kelkontar* report, and he had always been scrupulous in matters of scientific authorship. Besides, if his mental condition was public knowledge, and it might be after twelve years, everyone would know the report was beyond his capacity.

"Let's do it like this, Kelly," he decided at last. "Put my name at the top of the report, and add an opening paragraph that says: 'On Jan. 17, 2843, entry was made into the stability known as the Whorl by myself aboard my ship the *Kelkontar*, traveling under the impetus of the high-velocity warp drive developed a few weeks prior to that date. Inside we encountered a condition of extreme relativistic contraction, which endured throughout our stay inside the Whorl. Various factors would make any subjective estimate of the time spent inside unreliable.' No, leave that sentence out, Kelly. No need to go into that. Just say, 'Following is an analysis and summation of the phenomena encountered, as reported by my ship.' If Science Reporting Service won't accept that, to hell with them."

"Okay, Mark."

"And put this at the end: 'Postscript by Keaflyn: During the final moments of our stay inside the Whorl, I received a subjective awareness of several presences aboard the ship. This awareness continued until a few seconds after return to normal space, at which time the presences seemingly departed. My supposition is that these presences included crewmembers of ships previously lost in the Whorl and unable to escape. I am including this subjective material here for the purpose of apprising the public of the existence of these ego-fields, and to suggest that their long entrapment could have left them in a burdened condition.'"

"All right, Mark. I will prepare the report with those additions," said the ship.

Keaflyn nodded and sat gazing at nothing. "Of course," he said after a while, "if the report is rejected, I can redo it myself after Tinker cleans the rubbish out of my mind. But that might take a while, and I like to be prompt about reports. Kelly, have you made any guesses about what the Whorl really is? Its purpose, I mean?"

"No, Mark. Your comment to the effect that it's a time machine could be accurate to a degree. I cannot propose a purpose of value for such a time machine, if that is the case."

"Well, one of the few things I grasped in your report," Keaflyn said, "is that normal material entering the Whorl—material not being pushed along as we were by a warp drive—would take an almost meaningless number of years to drift all the way through—something on the order of 10^{21} or 10^{23} years, you said."

"That is what I calculated, Mark, on the basis of average encounter velocities between the Whorl and the material in overtakes and engulfs."

"That's not billions or trillions, or even quadrillions of years!" Keaflyn continued. "A star going into the Whorl today would come out so far in the future that . . . well, it's meaningless."

The ship did not reply.

After a long pause Keaflyn added, "Unless its purpose is to distribute matter and energy throughout time. Maybe the Whorl will eject a galaxy—a small galaxy—all those years from now, when everything else is long gone. And that galaxy will be the seed for a new universe or a whole series of universes."

"Such a seed will not grow, Mark, without the presence of creative life-forces," said the ship.

"Oh." Keaflyn was distressed as the realization hit him. By traversing the Whorl, he had provided a means of escape for life-energies which, in the natural order of things, might have been the builders of that distant-future universe. "Looks like I've put my foot in the jelly-jar again, Kelly," he mumbled.

"That could be, Mark. However, there are presumably other Whorls in existence. Also, there should be numerous additional occasions for the one we traversed to entrap life-entities."

Keaflyn considered this and nodded. "You know, Kelly, I think it's a good thing to learn about such possibilities as this future-universe thing. If humanity knows the purpose, or the possible purpose, of something like the Whorl, they'll know how to avoid interfering with it. If they don't know, they might interfere time and again, out of ignorance.

"In the same way, it's worth knowing that thought can nullify the Resistant Globe and probably can nullify any stability, for that matter. If we know what the bad possibilities are, we'll know to avoid them. Maybe I've done something that's worth a little bit. I've shown everybody there are some rocks in the path by stubbing my toe on them."

"Shall I include your supposition concerning the Whorl's purpose in the report, Mark?"

"Might as well, although it could be something a normally intelligent person would see right off. Just say something like, 'Keaflyn's tentative conclusion of the Whorl's function is . . . such-and-such.' Put it in your own words, Kelly. My words are sounding clumsy to me."

"Okay, Mark."

They continued the flight toward Danolae in silence, Keaflyn wondering morosely what the reaction to his return would be.

Doubtless he had been considered out of existence for twelve years. The *Calcutta* had been close enough to witness his entry into the Whorl, and no one had ever come out of that stability before.

Would his return signal a renewal of the chase by the Sect Dualers and the Arlan Siblings? Probably so, he guessed glumly. Maybe some of them would have cooled off by now, but not the diehards. And if he remained as slow-wilted as he was now, he could not hope to escape them for long, or, when captured, to convince them that his Neg was gone for good.

So the first order of business was to get Tinker to use therapy on him, to restore his mind to what it was before Berina Arlan had put him under her machines. Then he would at least be able to go on as he had before, not hopelessly handicapped by galloping stupidity.

It would be good to be with Tinker again. He hoped she wouldn't spoil things by feeling a lot of pity for him. She might be inclined to do just that, and pity was the last thing he wanted from her.

He would soon be able to see her reaction for himself, he noted, glancing at the viewscreen. His ship was approaching the Danolae system.

At that moment the ship reported, "I have a shielding malfunction, Mark."

"Huh? What's the trouble?"

"The problem is atypical and may require lengthy analysis," the ship replied. "While shifting into an approach warp, several thousand particles of gas and dust with low relative momentum passed through the shieldscreens and impacted on the hull."

"Sure," shrugged Keaflyn. "That's normal, isn't it, Kelly? The shields keep out the high-velocity stuff that could do damage and let the harmless stuff alone. When you go out of warp near a planetary system, even for a split second, you get some of that stuff coming through." Keaflyn wondered if his ship was beginning to reflect his own stupidity, bringing up such a trivial matter and calling it a problem.

"That is correct, Mark," *Kelkontar* agreed. "However, these particles are exploding energetically when they strike the hull. The damage sustained during the brief exit from warp was minor. However, a long-duration exit from warp, before the cause of this condition is determined and corrected, could be destructive."

"Oh. Well, do you have any idea what the trouble is?" Keaflyn asked, irritated by the possibility of a delay in reaching Tinker.

"I checked and eliminated the possibility of improper shieldscreen performance before calling the problem to your attention, Mark," the ship replied. "The shield is functioning normally. Observation discloses no abnormality in the Danolae system that would produce highly reactive dust. The remaining possibility is that we are ourselves the source of the atypicality. Our substance, including my hull, is reactive in contact with normal matter."

A contra-atom in a cloud chamber, the thought flashed through Keaflyn's mind. But that was impossible! He wasn't a Neg! Or . . . was he?

It took him several seconds to shake off the sense of unreality this thought inspired, along with a fantasy of his Neg, having been forced to give up on his ego-field, turning its attention to his body and his ship and converting them into something similar to contramatter.

But a Neg couldn't possibly do that!

"H-how do you suppose we got reactive?" he asked.

"I believe I must reassess the phenomena of the Whorl in the light of this new data, Mark," the ship said. "No event other than our passage through that stability has transpired to account for our atypical condition. Some theoretical work has been done, as you know, on temporal energy. It is possible that we left the Whorl carrying a charge of such energy."

Keaflyn nodded slowly. He had read of those theories. The basic idea was that any object displaced in time would be energized into a condition incompatible with its surroundings. This was an energy of tension—the *desire*, so to speak, of the temporally displaced object to snap back to the time in which it belonged. All this was hypothetical, as no means of achieving temporal displacement had been developed.

"Relativistic contractions don't cause displacement in time . . . at least not in a way that left ships charged with energy," Keaflyn remarked.

"That is true," replied the ship. "Thus, I suggest that we encountered phenomena other than relativistic contraction inside the Whorl."

"Something for which the contractions were merely symptomatic?" asked Keaflyn.

"Perhaps, Mark. In any event, and as you noted in my report, the contractions alone could account for very little of the twelve-plus years of lapsed universal time during our traversal of the Whorl."

Keaflyn had missed that point in the report completely, he realized. "Well," he demanded impatiently, "if we're charged up with some kind of time-energy, how do we blow it? I gather we can't land on Danolae or anywhere else in this condition."

"Indeed we cannot, Mark. And I have no data on how we can achieve compatibility with the universe of this date."

"What the hell do we do, then?" Keaflyn snapped.

"I don't know, Mark."

Keaflyn paced the deck, feeling ultimately trapped. "Are you absolutely sure you're right about our condition?" he asked. "Shouldn't we verify it instead of depending on what a few thousand stray dust particles did? They could have drifted in from anywhere."

"A verifying experiment could be informative, Mark," the ship agreed.

"Okay. As I recall, this system has a Plutonian asteroid belt. How would it be to toss a small chunk of metal at one of the asteroids, and see what happens?"

"That would be a satisfactory test, Mark. Shall I warp toward the asteroid belt?"

"Sure! Let's get this test over with!"

Several minutes later the ship positioned itself a quarter of a million miles from a barren chunk of rock in the belt. The sun of Danolae was, at this distance, hardly more than an unusually bright star.

"I have launched a centigram pellet of steel toward the asteroid, Mark," the ship reported. "Is a centigram enough to tell us anything?" Keaflyn asked.

"It should be, Mark."

"Are you still getting hull reactions every time you take us out of warp?"

"Yes, Mark."

The asteroid test was doubtless a waste of time, Keaflyn thought fretfully, being conducted solely because he hated to face an obvious truth: he was isolated in his ship, isolated until death, which wouldn't be long in coming—just as long as it took to exhaust the ship's vital consumables.

What was the old saying of scientific researchers? Somebody's law they called it. Oh, yes. Murphy's Law. To the effect that "If something can go wrong, it will."

Well, Murphy hadn't loused up his stability probes in particular, but the law had applied with a vengeance to his personal affairs of this lifetime!

First the Neg had invaded him; then the Sect Dualers had loaded him with a pleasure-impress, thinking that would counter the Neg; then Tinker had turned up in an eleven-year-old body; then the Insecurity of the Resistant Globe had turned half the human population into a modern lynch mob; then the Senior Arlan Sibling had finished the job the Sect Dualers had started, by burdening him down to a backtrack level of mentality; and then . . . *this*.

Of course, some desirable things had happened, too. He had made some discoveries he considered important, whether anybody else did or not. And others would *have* to recognize the value of his improved warpdrive. But none of the desirable events had disturbed the vector of the undesirable—a vector carrying him straight to death and total degradation.

A brilliant burst of radiation flowered for an instant on the viewscreen and was gone.

"Was that it?" he asked.

"Yes, Mark. Our steel pellet proved to be reactive," said the ship.

"The explosion seemed awfully energetic, to look that bright at a quarter of a million miles, and to be created by just a centigram of steel. Something on the level of total annihilation of matter."

"It was on that order of magnitude, Mark. The asteroid was, of course, vaporized."

"Well, that's that."

"Yes, Mark."

After a long pause, Keaflyn said dejectedly, "I suppose I should call Tinker, anyway. No, maybe it would be better if I talked to her father again. Have you finished revising your Whorl report?"

"Yes, Mark."

"Okay. I'll get him to let you feed it to one of his computers. So, get him on the comm. Clav Didorik, I mean."

"Right, Mark."

But a few seconds later, the face that appeared on the screen was that of Alo Felston. The former cowpoke's eyes bugged when he saw who was calling.

"Mark, old pardner!" he exclaimed.

"In the moldering flesh," Keaflyn returned with an effort at lightness. Felston, he saw, carried his thirteen additional years gracefully. He had lost some of his leanness but otherwise seemed to have aged very little. Felston's face wore a look of shock. "Why the stoned expression?" Keaflyn asked him.

Felston shrugged and chuckled tightly. "Well, you got to admit, pardner, this is a combination of meeting an old friend, seeing a ghost, and bumping into the hero of the age all at the same time!"

"How did that hero bit get in there?" asked Keaflyn, surprised to find himself feeling almost good, just from talking to a fellow human again. "The last I heard, I figured to qualify for the job of villain."

"Folks have had time to reconsider . . . Where've you been, anyhow, old buddy? You look mighty done in."

"I'm just a few hours out of the Whorl. I time-traveled over twelve years going through that thing. My ship's got a report on all that, to feed Didorik's computer, since I can't land. The report tells why I can't land. How is it you're answering Didorik's comm for him, Alo?"

"Clav's off-planet on business, and I came back to Danolae to look after things for him. Usually I'm on Rimni these days. That's a center of ego-field research, you know. Tinker and I moved our project there about ten years back, so we could get in the thick of things."

"Oh," Keaflyn nodded, feeling that he was missing something. Probably his lowered IQ was making him insensitive to conversational nuances—to high-comm. "Seems to me old Clav would have picked a relative for his take-over guy," he remarked.

"He did, Mark. I'm his son-in-law."

"No kidding? And I didn't even know Tinker had a sister!"

"She doesn't, Mark."

So . . . that was the point he had been missing. The way Felston had said "Tinker and I" . . . it was all there in the phrasing and inflection.

Keaflyn tried to stop himself from reacting badly to the news. After all, Tinker had ample reason to consider him gone beyond return. Why expect her to wait for a man who wouldn't be coming back? Who for all practical purposes actually had not come back? He was here, in the Danolae system, talking to Alo Felston, but he could never touch the surface of a planet again, much less the flesh of his beloved Tinker . . .

So, this was no new defeat for him. No new loss. Nothing to be so upset about. How could this be a loss, when he had already lost everything?

Slowly his quivering stopped. He gave a rueful little laugh.

"As I recall the Wild West stories," he said, "the straight-shootin' cowpoke always got the girl. I wish both of you the best, Alo."

"Thanks, Mark." There was understanding in Felston's acknowledgement. Understanding, but—mercifully—no pity. More like . . . admiration?

"I suppose Tinker's on Rimni . . . or is she with you?" Keaflyn asked.

"On Rimni. Our project's grown into a sizable operation, with about two dozen investigators and maybe fifty other full-time people involved. Rimni's quite a place for ego-field studies."

Keaflyn nodded. "I guess Tinker had been there before," he said. "The *Brobdinagia* disaster was in the Rimni system, I recall."

"That's right," said Felston. "She was in school on Rimni in her nine-year life. That's how she happened to be on the *Brobdinagia.* She was headed home for a vacation. So in this lifetime she knew what the planet had to offer a project like ours."

There was a break in the conversation, an uncomfortable one for Keaflyn. He was constraining himself from asking if Tinker had turned into as beautiful a woman as she usually did. But, hell, he didn't need to ask that! He had seen her as an eleven-year-old. It had been obvious then that she was going to blossom into enchanting love-liness.

He searched for something else to say. "You're the first person or computer I've run into, since Berina Arlan worked me over, whom I didn't have to ask to talk slowly," he said.

Felston grinned. "Something I picked up in researching animal ego-fields, Mark. It's funny people would miss something as simple as that for so long—the necessity of slowing down their communication in dealing with animals. Just that one thing could've enabled men to talk with their pets long ago!"

"The project's making headway, then," said Keaflyn.

"It sure is! Look, Mark. You say you have a report on the Whorl to feed Clav's computer. Since you're twelve years out of date, why don't I feed a summary of what's been going on to your ship, at the same time—with emphasis on what Tinker and I have been up to, and on the upshot of your own work?"

"Okay. That 'hero' remark of yours has roused my curiosity, I admit. If I've been getting some pats on the back in my absence, I'd certainly like to feel them now!"

He was ashamed of that maudlin comment immediately, but Felston seemed tactfully unaware that he had made it.

"People started good-mouthing you just a few weeks after you disappeared in the Whorl, Mark. Your super-duper warp drive made the physicists take a look at your report on Lumon's Star, which they decided was a terrific piece of work. Some of them objected to the subjective stuff about Avalon you had in that report, but—"

"That was factual reporting about Avalon," Keaflyn interrupted, irritated. "I visited that planet and reported what I saw and heard."

"Don't jump on me about it," grinned Felston. "They said it was subjective because your ship's recording instruments showed Avalon to be nothing more than an undeveloped Terra-type world. You know how physicists are, Mark, being one yourself. They trust their instruments more than their senses. If you say you discovered the heaven-world and hobnobbed with some famous backtrackers there, I'll take your word for it."

"Well . . . physicists do have to maintain rigorous standards of proof," Keaflyn agreed, conscious that he wasn't behaving at all gracefully. "Of course I was aware while on Avalon that my senses were reporting on a level of reality other than that of the normal universe, but that isn't the same as saying my senses were deceived. The inhabitants of Avalon are stabilities, and the planet is something of a stability itself. It's real, and they're real, but not on our level of reality or my ship's. So I hardly felt a need to limit my report to those scanty observations my ship could verify."

Felston nodded agreeably. "The criticism over that didn't last long, anyway. You really opened up some horizons, pardner! You broadened our views so much that . . . well, you can read the details in the stuff I'm feeding to your ship. I don't want to talk you to death, with you looking so damned poorly." His voice took on a tone of concern. "You could use some therapy, man."

"That's why I came—one reason, anyway. And found out after I got here that I can't land. I figured Tinker could clean out a lot of that mess the Senior Sibling loaded me with."

"Tinker could," nodded Felston. "What's this about not being able to land?"

"Kelly and I came out of the Whorl carrying a twelve-year charge of temporal energy," Keaflyn replied tonelessly. "That's enough to make us a few hundred times as reactive as a fusion bomb of the same mass." He described the effects of dust on the ship's hull and the experimental destruction of the asteroid.

"All that's in the report you're feeding down?" Felston asked.

"Yeah. Kelly put in all the pertinent data."

"Well," said Felston, "I'll get that report into distribution right away. Maybe somebody can figure something out from it."

"You think you can get it through Science Reporting Service?" Keaflyn asked anxiously.

Felston laughed. "Who's going to fool with Science Reporting Service?" he snorted. "Who do you think you aren't, old buddy? Anything from Mark Keaflyn, or his ship, rates top priority on the triple-A comm circuit!"

Keaflyn blinked and shook his head. Presumably Felston knew what he was talking about, but the former cowpoke's words stirred feelings of unreality in him. Dazedly, he said, "Handle it however you think best, Alo. In the meantime, do you have any suggestions on what I ought to do?"

"Yeah. Just one. If your ship's consumables are in good enough shape, hightail it to Rimni and let Tinker get to work on you! You don't have to land. She can do pretty competent therapy via comm, if you're not too far away."

"Any hope of reaching and blowing my pleasure-impress?" Keaflyn asked—although he was reasonably certain he knew the answer already from Felston's speech nuances.

Felston verified that: "No. We've made real progress, Mark, but that goal still looks a couple of lifetimes of hard research away."

Keaflyn shrugged. At best, then, all he could expect from therapy was that the speed of his degradation would be slowed. It would be a halfway measure, in a situation where such measures were of little help. But at least he would be in comm with Tinker, and therapy would make his remaining weeks in this lifetime endurable.

"Okay," he agreed. "I'm off to Rimni, as soon as our computers complete their exchange of information."

"The   exchange   is   complete,   Mark," the   ship
informed him.

"Thanks. Alo . . . "

"Yes, Mark?"

He forced a smile. "Be kind to dumb animals, Alo.
One of them might be your wife's ex-husband."

Felston returned the smile. "I will, Mark. So will Tinker. Out."

"Out."

After a moment Keaflyn said, "Warp for the Rimni
system, Kelly. And let me have some aspirin."

Chapter 16

He slept for several hours, then ate breakfast. After that,
he began reading the material Felston had fed to his ship.

Much of it was beyond his comprehension—the
research reports on stability investigations in particular.
But it was gratifying to learn that such investigations had
been made in great number. And nearly every one cited
his papers on Lumon's Star and the Loci as key references. Obviously, he had started something . . .

The reports on Tinker's ego-field research were,
superficially, more understandable. At least they did not
include page after page of involved mathematics. But
after wading through the ones of most recent date,
Keaflyn gave up on them as well. He had gathered that
the investigators had achieved the rather remarkable goal
of lifting certain types of trauma from the ego-fields of
such animals as dogs, pigs, and goats—quite a feat, considering that means of communicating with these animals
had to be established first.

Maybe there was a glimmer of hope there . . . if he could remain a fairly high-type animal for a few lifetimes. Maybe he could hang on in that manner until a way of blowing pleasure-impresses was discovered, and then get himself into an animal being treated by Tinker's investigators. Obviously, with trillions of animals in existence, that would take more than a little luck. But it was a hope to hang onto; purely for the sake of hope.

Finally he turned to the popular accounts Felston had included and was chagrined to find these over his head, too. Even lowest-common-denominator expositions were too heavy for his restricted intelligence. But after a struggle, he gleaned a few salient points and began to grasp the change that twelve years and five months had brought:

—Exploration of the galaxy as a whole. With the fast and more efficient warp drive, ships had gone far from the galactic arm segment he had known. Five other human realms had been found and communication established with them. Much was written about resulting cross-cultural progression that Keaflyn could not follow at all.

—General recognition of Negs and the contrauniverse as forces in opposition to enhanced existence and reality. The Sect Dualers, Keaflyn gathered vaguely, had disbanded.

—Enhanced reality? That, as near as he could make out, was what several of the accounts were talking about. It had something to do with conscious endorsement of the universe and particularly of the stabilities. The old game of Null the Globe had never been resumed. Just the opposite kind of game—Validate the Globe—was now the custom on Bensor.

—Mind over matter. This fit in with enhanced reality, he gathered, and with the recognition that mind was indeed senior to the physical universe, even senior to the stabilities. The whole field of "psi" abilities was being replotted and expanded.

All of that from nothing more than his hurried and harried probings of a few stabilities? he wondered in astonishment. So it seemed. Time after time he found himself mentioned in the accounts, in such phrases as " . . . the pioneering studies of Mark Keaflyn . . . " or " . . . was suggested by Keaflyn's findings on . . . " or " . . . of course draws heavily on Keaflyn's speculations concerning . . . "

He recalled Alo Felston's amused reaction to his anxiety over whether his Whorl report would be accepted for publication. "Who do you think you aren't?" Felston had demanded joshingly.

"I aren't that Mark Keaflyn," he now replied aloud.

"Was that addressed to me, Mark?" his ship asked.

"No, Kelly. Just my extremely retarded reply to something Alo Felston said yesterday."

Indeed, he wasn't that Mark Keaflyn. Not any longer. That Mark Keaflyn was *dead,* in the old, finalistic, backtrack sense of the word. He no longer existed. The present Mark Keaflyn was a shrunken thing, too reduced to understand, much less find gratification from the accomplishments of his former self.

How, for example, was he to comprehend "enhanced reality?" He stared about the cabin of his ship, at the bulkheads, the instruments, the viewscreen, the glass of bourbon he had ordered but decided not to drink. Was anything enhanced?

"Give me a clear view, Kelly," he said.

The viewscreen blackened and sparkled with stars as the *Kelkontar* duplicated on it a naked-eye view of the stars visible from the ship's present location on the way to Rimni. Keaflyn gazed at the image long and thoughtfully.

Well, perhaps the effect *was* somehow different than he had ever noticed before. Though the stars were still points of light, those points had a feel of solidity—of huge masses the stars really were, scattered through the depths of space.

He was not sure, but the impression came to him that the most ignorant savage, gazing up from a wilderness world at a sky like that, could never mistake it for a light-spangled roof around his world, a few thousand miles up. It was a sky of depth, a sky that went on and on and on . . .

He looked away from it, half intimidated by the sight. He had gained a glimmering of what "enhanced reality" meant.

At the edge of the Rimni system, light-hours away from the central planets, he halted the ship. "We'd better park out here, where the dust is thin," he said to his ship. "Get . . . get Tinker on comm . . . Mrs. Marianne Felston, I suppose that is . . ."

Moments later her face appeared on the screen. Her eyes—beautiful eyes—widened with concern as she studied him. "Oh, Mark! What a mess you are!"

"Yeah, I've picked up a few problems, Tinker," he said, feeling extremely dull-witted and aware, for the first time, that the sluggishness of his speech and clumsiness of his gestures must make him the least sexually-attractive man in existence.

She had called him Mark, whereas Jack had been his mate-name through all his lives with Tinker. He didn't need more IQ than he had to understand that. Tinker was no longer, his—except perhaps as a therapist.

"Mark, if I had known you were alive and would be returning in any shape or form, I would have waited," she was saying. "You know that, don't you?"

He shrugged, angry without knowing why. "It doesn't matter, Tinker—Marianne—because I'm not really back," he said thickly. "Didn't Alo comm you about the temporal charge I'm carrying?"

"Yes, and of course I got the complete explanation from the triple-A comm circuit. Everybody did, Mark! Thousands of scientists are hard at work right now, on hundreds of worlds, trying to find a way to help you. So please don't go on thinking your position is hopeless. It isn't!"

He thought about it and found some encouragement. If so many able people were so concerned about his fate, well, maybe they could do something. It was comforting to have his betters looking after him. He might as well let them do the worrying . . . except for one thing. In their way, his betters were even slower than he was!

Sure, thousands were trying to find a way to deal with temporal charge; sure, Tinker and Alo and their outfit were digging for techniques that would break a pleasure-impress . . . but with what deadlines in mind?

No deadlines at all!

He remembered how it had been at Bensor-on-Bensor. Only because Keaflyn was an old friend had John Donflannis agreed—grudgingly—to try to complete a special probe for the examination of the Lumon's Star warpicles within three years. And that was a fairly straightforward job of engineering! Donflannis would have preferred to take three decades instead of three years . . . or carry the project over to the next lifetime. Keaflyn had found it necessary to point out that for him this lifetime was *it!*

People who had all the time there was just couldn't gear themselves to the schedule imposed upon a one-lifetime man. They could not grasp the sense of urgency he lived with. Certainly not in dealing with such a marvelous intellectual challenge as temporal charge.

He could imagine some distinguished thinker reproving him, as he gasped on the last whiff of oxygen left in the *Kelkontar:* "Patience, Mr. Keaflyn, patience! Scientific enquiry mustn't be rushed."

Oh yes, they were looking for the answer to his problem and might find it in a century or two!

To Tinker he said, "Maybe I should take another turn through the Whorl, a slow trip that'll consume a hundred years."

She looked thoughtful, as if she were seriously considering his suggestion.

"That was a joke," he added, annoyed. "I don't think I could take the Whorl again."

"I understood, Mark. My thought was of the lack of haste your joke was aimed at. I do all I can to spur people along."

"I'm sure you do, T—uh—Marianne, and I appreciate it. But I doubt if you can have much effect on them."

"Yes, I can, too, on some of them . . . I'm still Tinker, Mark."

"Okay, you're Tinker," he snapped back. "But I'm no longer Jack."

"You're no longer Jack, but only because you are so entirely Mark Keaflyn. Jack had to be crowded out and left behind, Mark."

Keaflyn shook his head in puzzlement. Tinker's eyes flared angrily.

"What am I supposed to do, Mark? Apologize for thinking you were wiped out?" she demanded stingingly. "Do you want me to come wipe your nose and change your diaper? You're so damned busy being traumatized and sorry for yourself that you can't understand a thing you're told! Snap out of it!"

"Don't you think I'm trying?" he glared back.

"Not very hard, you're not! Men lived with trauma and confronting death for trillions of years without going to pieces. Or is courage too much to ask?"

He was startled, both by Tinker's manner and her remark. Courage? Hell, he hadn't even heard that word used in three hundred years! Who needed to think about courage when everyone had it? Or had an absence of fear, which came to the same thing?

But it was something he needed now. Fear had been pounded into him—a little of it when the Sect Dualers stuck him with a pleasure-impress and an overwhelming burden of it when Berina Arlan had put him through her torture mill. He needed to look wherever it was untold generations of men had looked, each man isolated within

himself and constricted within the brief span from birth
and death, imprisoned in ignorance. They had found the
will to carry on with the business of life and had managed
to cling to their hard-pressed sanity while they were
doing it.

They had looked and found courage. Keaflyn looked
now and found the same. Guts. Grit. A proud stubbornness. It was there, this something that boomed deeply
and soundlessly: *I am man! Defeat me, and I remain
man!*

He raised his face to the viewscreen. "Okay, Tinker.
I came to ask you for therapy, and you just gave me the
first dose. I'm ready to continue when you are."

"Good, Mark!" she applauded. "Just one more matter,
concerning our personal relationship, to clear away
before we begin. Alo Felston is a very gentle, lovable,
and remarkable man. He and I work well together . . .
and love well together. What he and I have isn't what
you and I had and might have again. But I want you to
understand this, Mark: you're not going to get me back
without working at it and working hard! I'm quite content with Alo, and if you want to shrug your shoulders
and walk away, I'll stay content. All clear?"

He grinned. "Sure! I've got to woo you to win you.
That's fair enough. It was fun the last time I tried it."

She smiled at him. "It was for me, too. Okay, let's get
to work."

Not until later did Keaflyn realize that the talk of woo-
ing-and-winning had led him to set aside, for the
moment, the tremendous barriers that lay between the
present and that hypothetical idyllic future in which his
most serious problem would be of a romantic nature.

Tinker had dangled a carrot in front of him, but from across a deep chasm. In so doing, she had succeeded in pulling his attention up from the depths of that chasm—precisely what she had intended to do.

She asked, "Are you ready to look at your second visit aboard the *Calcutta*?"

He winced. "Yeah."

"Good. When does it start?"

"Well, there's no point in looking at going aboard. That was all harmless enough. It started in Berina Arlan's office. I went in and knew I walked into a trap as soon as she spoke. She had mayhem in her voice." Keaflyn was aware that he was starting to quiver as he recounted the experience. That was good, he thought approvingly. *You have to re-experience these things to blow them. Can't just see them from a safe distance* . . .

"When she told me to sit down, my damned Neg made me too tired to keep standing. So I sat, and the chair strapped me down before I could get up again. I ought to have told her my Neg was giving her a hand, but that might not have impressed her. Anyway, I didn't think of it at the time . . . "

"Go on," Tinker encouraged.

"Well, we talked for a while. She dressed me down for being irresponsible, for giving the Neg one opportunity after another to attack stabilities. I said I'd leave the stabilities alone, quit my research, and said she should cut out the backtrack stuff and let's go for a swim. She said"—Keaflyn frowned in an effort to concentrate. Recall was becoming more difficult, the closer he came to the moment he was placed in the field of the first of the machines—"she said that would just be postponing what had to be done. I can't see anything after that. but I know what happened."

"Okay. Just tell me what happened till you get to a point where you can see it again," suggested Tinker.

He told of his chair carrying him from machine to machine, his voice a dull monotone.

"Then it stopped, and she was just standing there." He shuddered. "I can see this part, but I don't like it."

"All right," said Tinker. "Go ahead."

"It scared me to look at her . . . Ugh . . . She said something too fast for me to understand. Then she said it again, and I said something back to her. After that she talked more slowly, and . . . God! It's awful to feel as helpless as I did! She said she was stopping the procedure for a while because something had come up. What she meant was that she had just noticed her Neg hadn't been bugging her during all this, as if it approved of what she did. I found out that later, though."

"Her Neg?" asked Tinker.

"Sure. Didn't know that, did you? The Arlans have been Neg-ridden for several lifetimes. That's how important the Negs think they are."

"Go on," Tinker said.

"Well, nothing much after that, except being in a state of terror. I was taken to an apartment where I was confined. I got some sleep, then the Junior Sibling came and helped me escape. I started to go to Danolae, to get you to do this, but after having a few drinks to ease my nerves, I decided to take one last crack at the Whorl. When I changed course I found out the Arlans had been tailing me, out of my detector range. I wound up diving into the Whorl because I thought it might wipe me out, ego-field and all . . . and here I am."

"Good," approved Tinker. "Now, let's look at it again, from the time you entered the room where the Senior Sibling was."

Keaflyn sighed and fidgeted. He knew that in the course of therapy he was going to have to face each instant of the torture of those horrible machines. The prospect was utterly depressing.

"I thought you and Alo had found better ways of doing things than this," he protested. "If you can strip the traumas of dogs and goats you must use a method that's easier on the patient."

"That's true," said Tinker, "but I can't use our new methods on you—first because they have to be done at arm's length, not via comm, and second, because they require the use of drugs you don't have and that are too complex for your ship to manufacture."

"Kelly can make aspirin," Keaflyn countered. "How do you know he can't make your drugs?"

"I'm quite sure Kelly doesn't carry the necessary ingredients," she replied. "I'll feed your ship the data on the drugs, if you like, just to make sure."

"Good!" exclaimed Keaflyn in relief. "I'll take a coffee break in the meantime." He started to stand.

"No," she ruled firmly, but with a smile. "We'll keep working in the meantime."

"I'll do better after a little rest," he argued.

"Didn't I hear someone being caustic a short while ago about the leisurely pace of everyone else?" she purred.

"Okay, so I'm scared!" he flared. "It's not good therapy to use a patient's words against him!"

"I know," she agreed. "But I also know in your case I can get away with it."

He gave a bark of a laugh. "You win, Tinker. Let's get on with it."

Two hours later, when she decided he had done enough for one day, they had hardly smoothed down the surfaces of the machine-installed impresses.

And thus it continued, two or three hours a day, for more than a week.

"Damn it," he fretted once, "there was uglier stuff than this on my backtrack that I blew with nothing like this kind of struggle!"

"Yes, but your backtrack impresses weren't attached to a basic pleasure-impress."

"Oh, yeah," he nodded, remembering.

Pleasure-impresses would not yield to any known therapy because of the fundamental reluctance of an ego-field to relinquish pleasure—even pleasure intensified to the level of debilitating pain. And traumas experienced later tended to attach to the pleasure-impress. Given sufficient therapeutic attention, these later incidents could be deintensified somewhat but could never be blown completely as long as that underlying pleasure-impress was in place.

"We can't clean this stuff out completely," he said.

"No, but we're making progress," replied Tinker. "Why don't you ask your ship about your verbalization speed?"

Keaflyn blinked. "What's she talking about, Kelly?" he asked.

"Tinker is doubtless referring to the fact that your speech has been approaching normal tempo during the period you have been receiving treatment," the ship replied.

"No kidding? How much gain?"

"Formerly your verbalization speed averaged forty-two percent of the norm," the ship told him. "Now it is seventy-one percent of the norm."

"Then my IQ's gone up accordingly," he said eagerly.

"Presumably so, Mark."

"Hey, that's great! Maybe now I can make some sense out of those reports I was trying to read—find out what's been going on!"

"Sure," Tinker approved, "but right now let's concentrate on getting you in even better shape."

So the sessions continued.

Finally the point was reached where Keaflyn could look at any instant under Berina Arlan's machines without terror or flinching. He could see them, with distaste and cold dread, but he could not rid himself of them.

"It's all up at the conscious level now," he told Tinker. "I can examine the whole experience from every angle. I can analyze the hell out of it. But it sticks right where it is."

Tinker nodded gravely. "We'll end therapy here, Mark," she said. "That's all we can do."

"Until you find a way to deal with the pleasure-impress?" he prompted.

Tinker nodded. "Yes. Until then."

"When will that be?"

"I wish I knew, Mark. We have some procedures in mind that look awfully promising to us. If only we had a human subject to work with here on Rimni! Ego-fields in animal forms are so difficult to reach . . . "

He stared at her. His high-comm ability had returned sufficiently for him to know she was leading up to something, but he could not fathom what. Unless . . . "Are you hinting that there's hope of my landing on Rimni?" he asked. "In this lifetime? What is it, Tinker?"

"An acquaintance of yours commed me this morning," said Tinker. "She thinks she can help. Are you ready to talk to her?"

Berina Arlan!

The thought did not turn him to jelly, he noted gratefully, but neither did it inspire much delight. "Berina thinks she can help?" he asked dubiously.

"Yes. The Arlan Siblings probably have more technological skills at their command than anyone else, Mark, and of course they've been working on the temporal charge problem. Berina thinks they've solved it."

After a moment, Keaflyn nodded. "I'll talk to her."

Chapter 17

For some reason he had expected the Senior Sibling to be unchanged—or very slightly changed. He was surprised to observe the signs of age on her face.

She read his look and smiled humorlessly. "This has been an excellent body, Mark," she said, "as I'm sure you'll agree. It held up beautifully, but it's seen its best days now. Another two years and I suspect Bartok will be Senior Sibling."

He nodded, not quite trusting himself to speak. He guessed her body was about sixty years old, and the

Arlans did not cling to bodies once the infirmities of age began to show. Come to think about it, a Neg-ridden ego-field had problems enough without trying to cope with the additional ones of a worn-out body.

"Mark, I'm sorry," she said. "Telling you that may not help very much."

"It doesn't," he replied in a toneless voice.

"Well . . . to business. Our people have devised an approach for removing the temporal charge from you and your ship. This will require some special equipment that you must build yourself. We have a large volume of data to feed to your ship on that. Shall we proceed?"

"Yeah. Go ahead. Kelly's ready to receive, aren't you, Kelly?"

"Yes, Mark."

"Good," said Berina. "The data's being fed. Meanwhile, I'll describe briefly what we have worked out, based on theory derived from your report on the Whorl.

"What you've referred to as temporal charge or energy bears about as much relationship to what we think of as time as an electrostatic charge bears to, say, a magnetically-caused motion. The relationship exists, but it is not direct. The Whorl is a complex time-connected phenomenon that involves temporal charge, movement through time, and seemingly various other characteristics related to these. Perhaps the purpose of the Whorl is, as you speculated, the transferal of seed material for universes to an unimaginably distant future. Or, as some of my technicians prefer, it may be a means of thinning over-materialized eras and thickening times of under-materialization. Which is, of course a generalization of your speculation.

"In considering your present problem," Berina continued, "the thought occurred to Bartok that the warp spacedrive also involves the time phenomena, insofar as it circumvents relativistic time contractions at velocities many multiples the speed of light. Bartok suggested that some particular segment of the warpicle spectrum could be modulated to produce a field that would 'leak' temporal energy. After a great deal of investigation, a team of theorists working with him have concluded that's correct. The data now going into your ship's computer gives the theory and application in detail."

Keaflyn was grinning. Of course! He would have thought of that himself if he'd had his wits at full strength! He could guess now, without being told, which segment of the warpicle spectrum was the one to be used, and the manner of using it.

"The modulation would be a time-vibration, wouldn't it?" he asked.

"Yes . . . time-travel, in a sense. Time would be the medium through which the modulation moved, or better, in which you and your ship would resonate."

"And where in time would I wind up when the temporal energy was all leaked away?"

"Here-and-now, presumably. The amplitude of your modulation would be proportional to the charge you're carrying. And since you are a forward-in-time anachronism, the range covered by your time-vibrations would be backward in time from now. In other words you would resonate between this year, 2855 and 2830."

"And I wouldn't wind up in 2843–the midpoint of the vibratory range where I started from—when the charge was leaked away?"

"Not according to our theory," Berina said positively. "The vibration doesn't damp. The amplitude stays the same; only the charge damps out. You wind up here-and-now because, despite the charge you're carrying, this is the time in which you are fixed. The data given to your ship should explain that better than I can, because I don't really comprehend some of the technical aspects of all this."

"Never mind. I get the picture," he said, smiling with satisfaction. "It all fits together beautifully, Berina. My congratulations to Bartok and the people who worked with him on this. It'll work! I'm more confident of that than I was of the improved spacewarp before it was tested. By the way, lacking an object with a temporal charge to experiment with, I presume you haven't tested this idea."

"No, we haven't," said Berina. "We regret that, Mark. We could run a test only by sending an unmanned ship through the Whorl, to accumulate a charge. That would require more time than you have. We realize the urgency of your situation. That's why I'm presenting the data now, untested."

Keaflyn laughed. "Thanks for not waiting! I'll get to work on it right away."

"Fine . . . And good luck, Mark."

"Thanks." Keaflyn hesitated, eager to end this conversation and get to work, but feeling there was more that needed saying. He gazed at the image of the elderly woman on the screen, thinking of the pleasure and pain he had experienced from her, and of the motivation that had prompted her actions in relation to himself.

A conservative she was—as he had been told by Lafe on Avalon, as he knew from his own experience, and also as her brother Bartok had verified. She was a preserver of what was—a resister of change until she was totally convinced the change was for the better. And she took plenty of convincing.

A feminine trait, in a way. Women were holders; men were reachers, very loosely speaking. Thinking back to the night of the Insecurity when the weakening of the Resistant Globe had roused a mass telepathic response in the populace of the city of Bensor-on-Bensor, Keaflyn took conscious note for the first time that the most distressed and "loudest" thoughts in that flood of mental protest had come from feminine minds.

As to Berina, not only feminine but the self-appointed champion and defender of humanity against the reductive forces of the contrauniverse . . . well, how else might he have expected her to react to such a shaking event as the Insecurity? He had to admit that now, since the passage of twelve years had convinced her the changes wrought by his stability probings had been for the best, she was working hard to heal the damage he had suffered.

"No grudges, Berina," he said, and meant it.

She smiled, and for an instant her face echoed the youthful beauty he remembered. "Thanks, Mark. Out."

Feeling more himself than he had since that distant-seeming morning when he had awakened at Splendiss-on-Terra aching with Neg-created somatics, Keaflyn dug into the job of assembling the charge-leak field generator.

He realized his intelligence level was still below normal, though not nearly as much as it had been before Tinker's therapy. This made the job of building the generator more difficult, but he didn't mind that. Instead, he liked the challenge the chore presented.

His Neg had not reappeared, and he guessed it was gone for good this time. It may have departed during his bout with Berina Arlan and her machines, no doubt assuming such degradation would end his stability research; if not then, his time-jumping journey through the Whorl had lost it.

And another possibility was that, since he had achieved the research results the Neg was trying to prevent despite its interference, the Neg no longer had any reason to impinge upon him. He was, in short, no longer a key individual in the Neg-Norm conflict.

That did not mean his stabilities research was over and done with, Keaflyn decided as he worked with the generator components. By no means! Particularly not if Tinker and Alo Felston succeeded in lifting his pleasure-impress. If they did, he could conduct his project as he originally intended to—at a leisurely, thoughtful pace over a period of two or three lifetimes.

In any case, for the moment, the pleasure-impress was not bothering him, blanketed as it was by a deintensified shell of more recent trauma. He did not have to laugh or giggle, and the face that looked back at him from the mirror no longer wore a crazy fixed smile.

"It occurs to me, Kelly," he said cheerfully, "that creativity is self-protective."

"I construe that as a philosophically rather than scientifically based statement, Mark," the ship replied.

"I'll go along with that. Just the same, take a look at my vastly improved position and the reason why it is improved. I intended to do some creative research and ran into a barrage of obstacles—but I wasn't stopped by any of them, not even when I was reduced to a backtrack intelligence level and soused to the gills!

"And now my creativity is paying off by solving the problems I accumulated along the way. This gadget we're working on is a result of my trip through the Whorl. The helpfulness of everyone, including Berina Arlan, is motivated by appreciation of our achievements. I wouldn't be at all surprised if the results Tinker and Alo have, when they go to work on my pleasure-impress, will be favorably influenced by enhanced reality.

"In the final analysis, I was really creating solutions to my own problems, even though that wasn't my conscious intention."

"Your argument lacks rigor, Mark," the ship said. "One obvious flaw concerns your purpose for entering the Whorl. You stated to me earlier that you did so in search of total nonexistence, not for continuation of your research activities."

Keaflyn laughed. "Oh, well. It was an attractive notion, whether it was true or not. Anyway, Kelly, it's going to feel very good to be a normal man again, in normal situations."

"The events of recent weeks have confronted you with hazards to a degree the human individual tends to find overwhelming," the ship agreed.

"And how! I've had some moments I wouldn't wish upon a Neg! But we're coming out of the tunnel now, Kelly."

This being a statement the ship could neither verify nor deny, it remained silent.

Out of the tunnel and into the light, mused Keaflyn. Of course, there were difficulties still to handle before he had his life back into optimum channels once more. Getting rid of his temporal charge was the first of these, and the successful completion of his ego-field therapy was second. Then the winning back of Tinker.

But he was supremely confident these difficulties would not stop him . . . simply because he would not allow them to stop him. He sensed, in fact, that in this universe of 2855—more glowing, more optimistic, more life-imbued than had been the universe of 2842—difficulties would be stopping hardly anybody!

"In view of my limited intelligence, Kelly," he said, "you'd better check the functioning of this generator before we go into action with it. I don't think there's anything wrong with it—it comes pretty close to standard warpdrive technology with mostly standard components. But run some checks on it, just the same."

"Okay, Mark."

Keaflyn had a sandwich while the ship tested the generator's circuitry.

"All characteristics are optimal, Mark," the *Kelkontar* reported.

"Good." Keaflyn paused. Should he call Tinker first? No. The charge-leaking process would take only a matter of minutes in lapsed present time as well as in ship subjective time. He would call Tinker when he had the good news to tell her that he was heading down for a landing on Rimni.

He glanced at the viewscreen. He was still on the outskirts of the Rimni system, not having moved far since the test detonation of the Plutonian asteroid.

"This is as good a place for it as any, Kelly," he decided. "Activate the charge-leak field generator.

"Very well. Mark."

The feel was, as he had expected, much like going into warp or changing warp vector. The viewscreen told the main difference: the stars were not shifting across it noticeably as they did when the ship was under drive. They remained firmly in position . . .

No . . . there was some movement of one of them. Rimni's sun was moving, but not with great rapidity.

"We're shifting position slightly, Kelly," he remarked.

"Yes, a certain amount of spacedrift was predicted theoretically, Mark. Our movement is parallel to the plane of the system's ecliptic and ninety-two light-minutes above it. We will not intersect the orbit of any known astronomical object."

"That's okay, then."

Keaflyn watched the screen as the ship's drift carried it sunward. Long before reaching a point above the center of the system, however, the direction of the drift reversed.

"We have completed half a cycle of our time-vibration pattern," the ship told him.

"We're heading back now from the year 2830, then?"

"That is correct, Mark."

Two minutes passed, and the ship said, "One complete vibratory cycle now, Mark. Beginning the second."

"Okay." The screen showed they were not beginning the second swing back through time from the same position as the first. There had been a sideways motion of perhaps ten light-minutes.

Once more Rimni's sun swung closer until they reached the point of nearest approach . . .

And there was another ship.

It was not moving at warp velocity, being powered by a drive of 2830 vintage that had required a sizable distance from a massive gravitating body for safe warp activation.

The relative motion through space of the two ships was sufficiently small for Keaflyn to catch an instant glimpse of the other vessel's lines and its name glowing around its prow.

It was a large passenger liner. Its name was . . . *Brobdinagia!*

Perhaps the two ships collided. Or perhaps the interaction was between protective shieldscreens—one of which carried temporal charge—rather than between masses of reactive matter.

Brobdinagia and *Kelkontar* exploded into a flare of energy and rapidly dispersing vapor. They were destroyed with all hands.

Chapter 18

Just when everything was working out so beautifully, too!

Why such a *wildly* improbable event as a collision in space, of all things? Was some jealous and elemental force of nature behind it—some Principle that resented this latest display of overweening cockiness by humanity in general and by Mark Keaflyn in particular?

He had been cocky, all right. No denying that. And proud as a peacock! All that talk to his ship about his "creative research"! Downright boastfulness!

But was the collision really a wild coincidence? Not on second thought. It was an event obviously destined to happen, even predictable, if men had bothered to be as wise as they were intelligent . . .

There was a project for somebody to work on—a study on how humans should go about acquiring wisdom. Most people doubtless thought intelligence and sanity were enough . . . or perhaps they thought wisdom automatically came enclosed in the same package.

But it did not, as he knew all too damned well. Wisdom came from . . . making mistakes? Well, it could, provided one learned the right things from the mistakes.

He certainly hadn't learned the proper lessons from his own! He hadn't even learned to consider all the obviously pertinent data in a situation before taking action. He could add two plus two, but he had not learned to add twelve years and five months to twelve years and five months and subtract the sum from 2855 and come up with the answer: the year in which the liner *Brobdinagia* mysteriously exploded in the vicinity of Rimni.

Killing a nine-year-old girl-body inhabited by his beloved Tinker!

That wasn't incredible coincidence—it was incredible irony!

Because if Tinker had continued to live in that body, and had been waiting for him when he arrived at Splendiss-on-Terra, according to plan—well, this whole misbegotten mess would have never come to pass. Tinker was a competent medic as well as an ego-field therapist. So, when the Neg impinged on him and started pestering him with somatics, he would have had no reason to comm the local medic at Splendiss—a medic who happened to be a Sect Dualer and who thought a pleasure-impress was the way to exorcise a Neg!

No, Tinker would have handled his problem very differently than Dr. Arnod Smath . . . probably by devising a means that would allow him to live with his Neg in reasonable comfort, the way the Arlan Siblings lived with theirs. After treatment he would have gone on with the work the Neg was trying to prevent, and when the work was completed the Neg would have departed in defeat, and he and Tinker would have lived happily ever after.

So he had to go back in time to destroy the *Brobdinagia*—as well as himself—for all the rest of it to happen.

It was over now, and his doom was sealed. He had added a real shocker of a death-trauma to his growing burden of garbage. And he couldn't even *find* that trauma, much less blow it. Whatever kind of body he had moved into must have a very primitive nervous system, to keep him from seeing that death trauma.

What kind of body was it?

Judging from the relaxed way he was sprawled on the ground (it felt mossy) he might be a worm or a caterpillar. But no, he was on his back, not his belly. Worms did not sprawl on their backs.

Also, he had two arms and two legs. He could feel them . . .

Mark Keaflyn opened his eyes and looked up, through the sunglow on fluttering leaves of oak and maple, at the patches of blue sky. It was a beautiful and vivid sight. He reveled in it for several minutes before taking much note of anything else.

Then he noticed the ground *was* mossy, and it sloped down to the small, shaded pool of a spring, just a few feet away. The smell of springy vegetation and the tinkle of water were delightful. Whatever kind of body he was in, it seemed to benefit from enhanced existence, he decided.

He looked at his body.

It was his own. It was the body of Mark Keaflyn, born twenty-six subjective years ago on Bensor.

"What the hell . . . " he muttered in surprise. Could he possibly have been rescued from the collision with the *Brobdinagia?* That just wasn't reasonable!

He rose and walked to the spring, to stare down at his reflection in the still surface of the little pool. Yes, it was his face, all right, and more glowing and serene than he had ever seen it. Now he realized why he couldn't find the death trauma. This was the face of a man with no traumas at all—the outward aspect of a totally clean ego-field.

Curious and curiouser, he thought interestedly.

"Ah, there, Mark! You made it!"

He whirled to face the source of the vaguely familiar voice. He recognized the bluff, pudgy man at once.

"Hi, Lafe. What are you doing here?"

Lafe chortled. "Where would I be but here on Avalon, old son? Where did you think you were?"

"I hadn't gotten around to thinking about that yet," Keaflyn mumbled, in a daze. "Avalon?"

"Sure! Your reward for a climactic life, Mark! No more marching around and around the old birth-and-death treadmill for you, man! Onward and upward! And we've got quite a welcoming celebration planned for you!"

Keaflyn stood in silence, gazing at Lafe's jovial smile. Finally he shook his head. "This takes a while to get used to, Lafe. I was just thinking, a little while ago, what a conceited ass I was, but I was never conceited enough to anticipate this!"

"Not many who make it are, Mark," Lafe replied.

"And . . . and I wasn't ready for this!" Keaflyn protested. "My stabilities research wasn't finished!"

"So, what?" shrugged Lafe. "There are plenty of others to put on the final touches."

"And Tinker! This separates me from Tinker!"

Lafe gave a showy snort of disgust. "It never ceases to amaze me, the penchant we humans have for griping! Here you are, more fortunate than a soul in an early Christian heaven, and you start complaining about the broad you left behind! Oh, well, never mind. She'll be along shortly, anyway."

"You mean, Tinker will be here?" Keaflyn demanded.

"Sure. Couldn't you see she was working herself into a climactic life, too?"

"Oh . . . her research on the pleasure-impress," muttered Keaflyn.

"Yep. I may as well tell you, since you'll soon be able to see the near-future parts of the universe for yourself. She doesn't succeed with her research, not to the extent of blowing pleasure-impresses. Her work with animal-level ego-fields is pretty impressive, though.

"However, what will really get her here is that she's going to install a pleasure-impress on herself, to provide a human subject for testing. The tests will be flops."

"But that's . . . that's awful!"

"It would be if she weren't coming here," agreed Lafe. "She'll die with the same expectation you had, of eternal degradation."

Slowly Keaflyn nodded. "If you're sure she'll make it to here, I suppose it's all right."

"I'm sure," Lafe told him, chuckling. "Now come on, old son! A welcoming party is waiting for you."

But Keaflyn still stood in awed silence. Finally he laughed. "Sorry to be so slow on the uptake, Lafe. I think I'm with you now. It's just that I never thought of my life as climactic."

"Let me put it to you like this," said Lafe as they moved away. "If you had another lifetime, how would you make it more climactic than the one you just finished without pulling the poor old universe apart at the seams?"

Which was, Keaflyn had to agree, a pertinent question.

Ten Percent of Glory

Ah, Miss Krimsby, I'm glad to see you on the job so promptly. While I was alive, I always believed in giving the old job a full day's effort. That's a policy I intend to maintain here in the realm of the spirit I feel we owe that to our clients . . . Hum? . . . Yes, Miss Krimsby. I'll be busy going over the preliminaries for our explorers campaign, but not too busy to accept important calls . . .

. . . What now, Miss Krimsby? . . . Certainly, I'll talk to him. Put him on . . .

Well, Senator, I'm honored to hear from you. We met on Earth once . . . No, I didn't vote for you, but only because my home was in Connecticut. I was rooting for you all the way, Senator . . . Thank you, Senator. I hope

you're getting accustomed to the place . . . Good. If I can
be of any help . . .

Oh? Why, certainly, the firm would be honored to
have you as a client . . . How's that? . . . I see. Well, that's
your decision to make, Senator. Of course we would
prefer to sign you on immediately, and get busy on a
long-term program for you, but you're the boss. I might
add, though, that we're prepared to accept you now on
a straight commission basis, and later on we may have
to start you on the fee system at a time when you will
have far less remembrance-power than now. Those fees
can dip pretty deep into a soul's capital, so to speak.
Heh-heh-heh . . .

Now, Senator . . . Please, Mr. Senator . . . Look Senator, baby, don't take it that way! This is a respected
remembrance agency dedicated to the best interests of
our clients. We *earn* our commissions and fees! How
long do you think we could hold our reputation if we
tried to bilk every new soul that wanders in? . . .

Let me explain the situation, Senator, before you say
another word. First, look about you at the other souls in
the realm. You'll notice that, on the average, they just
don't compare with you in brilliance and radiating power.
The reason is, as you must have learned by now, that
these are average souls, souls-in-the-street we might say.
They are remembered, at the most, by a hundred or so
relatives and friends, and for only a few decades. After
that, they draw what little brilliance they display from
the background of remembrance-power that is spread
through the realm.

You're not like them, Senator, baby, not like them at
all. You're a member of the Lustrous Company, the

greats of history at whom remembrance-power is constantly being directed by millions of the living! That's what sets the Lustrous apart from the ordinary, what gives you high-magnitude radiance.

Now you've been mingling since you arrived with the Lustrous set, Senator, baby. Tell me this: how many of them are Senators who died more than twenty years ago? . . . Right! And how many Senators who've been dead fifty years? . . . Of course you haven't met one yet, because there aren't any to meet, except a few like Hank Clay who're best remembered for other reasons.

I'll tell you why that is, Senator. Most politicians arrive here in a blaze of glory, riding on a surge of remembrance brought on by their funerals. The first thing they know they're mingling with boys like Bill Shakespeare, Julie the Caesar, Genghis Khan, Ben Franklin, Johnny Bach, and so on. Now I don't mean this critically, baby, but politicians have a good opinion of themselves to begin with. When they get here and are slapped on the back by old G. Washington himself, *nobody* can tell them they're not all set for eternity!

Then, five or ten years later, it's pouf! Down the drain. For most of them. The people back on Earth have quit thinking about them, and they shrink down to normal soul size.

That's when most of them come running to me or some other remembrance agent, but it's too late then, baby! They don't bring us enough to work with, more often than not You have to understand, Senator, baby, that it's a thousand times easier to keep your memory alive than to rebuild it from nothing.

So you can accuse me, if you like, of trying to bilk you out of ten per cent of the remembrance-power that's coming in now, and that you achieved without my help. If you want to keep that attitude, all I can say is good luck to you, baby! Gleam it up for the next few years! You've won that privilege. But if you want to start thinking about the long term—and up here, baby, the long term is *long*—then we can talk business. Get the picture? . . .

Who's trying to rush you? Not me! Any time within the next week will be fine with us. Talk it over with your acquaintances in the Lustrous Company. See what they say . . . How's that? . . . I'd rather not, Senator, baby . . . No, I don't mingle with the Lustrous myself, although I don't mind admitting that my remembrance-power commissions give me a fair magnitude. A good remembrance agent, like a good press agent back on Earth, is one who keeps himself out of the limelight. You do the shining, and I'll keep my light hidden under a bushel. Heh-heh-heh . . . No, I'm afraid I'm too busy to meet you personally, and there's no need of that, anyway, as the mode of communication we're using now is quite adequate. Although I do appreciate your asking me . . .

. . . Very well, Senator, baby. But remember: don't wait too long. Two weeks at the most, and that's more for your own good than mine. Every day you delay is going to work against you . . . Goodbye . . .

Are you there, Miss Krimsby? . . . Okay, make a note to turn the Senator over to Lanny if he calls back and wants to be taken on . . . Yeah, within two weeks. The best we can do for him, I'm afraid, is the folk-hero routine. Lanny's doing a good job on the Davy Crockett account, and maybe he can use the same techniques to keep this new pigeon flying for a century or so . . . No, no long-term potential at all. Carry on, Miss Krimsby . . .

. . . Yes? . . . Who? . . . Oh, Ludwig, baby! How are ya? What's on your deep and sonorous mind today, baby?

Oh, come on, now Ludwig! I can't believe the great Beethoven is jealous of such a minor composer as-what did you say his name is, Luddy, baby? . . . Jean Sibelius? Oh, sure, I remember him now, a guy recently from Finland. Well, you got to remember he *is* recent, and was a national hero when he came across to us. He'll start fading soon, and you'll still be right up there, Luddy, baby . . . Oh yes, we're working hard on your account all the time—after all, you're just about the biggest we've got . . .

Hum? . . . Well, we're prompting more and more performances of the Ninth Symphony-we're letting the Fifth and Seventh rest for a few decades right now. Also, we're doing something rather experimental with comic strips for you. The idea is to by-pass the formal education systems (which are in a confused mess at the moment, anyway) and use other media to plant your name in the retentive minds of millions of children . . .

No, that won't counter Sibelius' national hero status, not immediately, anyhow. But in the long pull . . . Well, if it's bothering you, Luddy, baby, I'll try to come up with something. Hey, here's an idea. Rebels are the "in" thing on Earth right now, so why not inspire one of the turned-on writers to give you a build-up along those lines? Something like: *Beethoven, Fighter for Self-Expression?* How does that hit you, baby? . . . Okay, the agency will get right to work on it . . . Right I'll keep in touch, Luddy, baby. Goodbye . . .

(Eech! What a grouch!) . . . Miss Krimsby? That Sibelius fella might have potential. Beethoven's in a stew over him, which must mean something. What's the latest info on him? . . . Still the strong, silent type, hah? Well, if he's not talking to anybody, chances are he's still unrepresented. Put a couple of the boys on him. When he starts talking, I want him to talk to us first . . .

Oh, you've already done that, Miss Krimsby? . . . Fine! That's what I like to see, sweety—intelligent initiative. Keep up the good work . . .

Who? . . . Yes, but don't call him Mark Twain even when he calls himself that. Let him know you're aware he's Mr. Clemens . . .

Hi, Sam, what's the good word? . . . Why, thanks, Sam, I appreciate that. Thoughtful of you to mention it. What can I do for you today? . . . Nothing? What . . . You mean to say you called just to congratulate me on my promotion to managing partner of the agency? . . . Sam, you-you've got me all choked up! If there were such things as angels, you'd sure as hell be one, Sam. If all our clients were like you . . . Sorry, Sam, I didn't mean to go mushy like that, but you caught me by surprise . . .

Well, since you're one guy I can speak frankly to, Sam, I don't mind telling you I feel pretty damn smug over the whole thing. Of course I give the senior partners in the firm a lot of credit. They've been in business a long time, but they're on their toes every minute, and they didn't take long in grasping the advantages of having a modern public relations man like myself running things. Nothing stodgy about those guys! . . .

Oh, no, Sam, I'm no genius. Of course I have a bright idea occasionally, and I'm glad that one turned out so well. The hard part was to find just the right actor to portray you. Once we found the Holbrook lad, all we had to do was pour the inspiration to him . . . heh-heh-heh! Yeah, Sam, I bet you're collecting far more remembrance-power than you ever did royalties. That's often the way it is with the true greats, Sam . . . Thanks, and if you want anything from us, all you have to do . . . Okay, Sam. So long. ..

. . . Miss Krimsby, were you listening to that? . . . Then I don't have to explain why I'd like us to do something special for Sam Clemens, and I've got an idea . . . An international build-up is what I have in mind-new translations of Sawyer and Finn, written to appeal to modern minds. We'll want European translators who'll work a background of passionate sex into the stories (maybe Tom and Becky could fool around while they're lost in that cave) and the editions for the communist countries ought to be given a socialist ring. The boys in our international letters department can work out the details . . .

How's that again, Miss Krimsby? . . . Say, that's a good idea. Put the boys to work on that, too. You are really earning that last raise you received, Miss Krimsby, and at this rate the next one won't be long in coming . . . Heh-heh-heh! It's a pleasure working with you, Miss Krimsby! . . .

. . . Well, I might as well talk to him. Put him on . . . How are you today, President Fillmore? . . . I'm sorry to hear that . . . That's too bad, but you have to see the situation like it is, Milly, baby, and the truth is that ex-Presidents are a dime a dozen . . . Oh, sure, there are exceptions, but not many . . .

Don't be that way, Milly, baby. It's just the way the universe cycles, and we all have to accept it. Look at the vast majority of Roman emperors—they're merely touched upon in history books today, almost completely forgotten. That's true of former crowned heads the world over. There's just so damned many ex-rulers, Milly, baby! If you could have gotten yourself assassinated, or could have won or lost a war, things might be different for you. But you just didn't provide us much to work with, Milly, baby . . .

That's always your privilege, if you think some other firm can handle you better, Milly, baby. Of course, we'll keep working hard for you, but I really can't promise any improvement. And if some other agency is promising you anything like that—well, just bear in mind that we've always been honest with you, even when honesty hurt . . . Milly, baby, if you fall for a fee-basis arrangement, you'll be down to soul-in-the-street magnitude in no time at all! If you insist on changing agents, insist on your new man giving you a straight ten percent commission deal . . .

That's more like it, Milly, baby . . . Sure, I understand. If I were in your shoes, I'd get impatient at times myself, seeing my magnitude almost lost in the glare of so many newcomers who, despite the tremendous remembrance-power they're drawing, are basically trivial souls . . . That's right, all those disreputable actors and mounte-banks, Milly, baby, but they always fade fast. They haven't got the staying power—the security-that you have, even though they outshine you temporarily . . . Right. Call me any time, Milly, baby . . .

. . . Miss Krimsby . . . Send a memo to accounting, will you? I want a comparative-profit study on all the American President accounts previous to—make it previous to Teddy Roosevelt, and excluding Washington and Lincoln . . . That's right. I think it may be time to trim some deadwood off our client list. But they're still our clients in the meantime, so instruct operations to inspire a television special titled *Our Forgotten Presidents*. That ought to brighten them up for a while, and keep them off my back . . .

. . . *He's* calling *me?* . . . Did—did he say what it's about? . . . Not even a hint? . . . Yes, yes, Miss Krimsby, put him on. Mustn't keep the senior partner waiting . . . And don't monitor this one . . .

. . . Niccolo! I'm flattered that you called . . . How are you today, sir? . . . A personnel matter? Certainly I'll give it my immediate attention, sir . . . What? . . . Not Miss *Krimsby*, sir! Why, I can hardly believe . . . She did? . . . She did? . . . Oh, no! That's awful, sir! . . .

No, sir, she can have no possible excuse. Our entire staff is thoroughly briefed on the necessity of never showing themselves in public. And being right at the center of our activities, she would be even more aware than the others that we can't afford to be seen, outshining as we do all but the brightest members of the Luminous Company . . .

Ah? . . . I see, sir . . . A crush on Clark Gable, huh? I knew she was ambitious for some reason, but I assumed her motivation was the same as my own, and the firm's other loyal members . . . So she had to show off in his presence . . .

Yes, Niccolo, she'll be drained and discharged immediately, but I'm afraid the matter doesn't end there. The Luminous Company is going to be in an uproar over this. Our agency will almost certainly be investigated, and all of us will have to appear personally . . . No, sir, it won't be sufficient to have her confess the embezzlement of working remembrance-power from the agency. Although that's a necessary first step . . .

No, sir, I'm afraid we don't have that much time. You see, sir, a newly-arrived American Senator—a prospective client—was talking with me earlier today, and he was suspiciously persistent about interviewing me in person before he made his decision . . . Yes, I draw the same conclusion as you, sir, that the news of Miss Krimsby's disastrous indiscretion is already getting around . . .

Thank you for your confidence in my ability to deal with this emergency, sir. What I propose is this: all partners and staff members will drain their accumulated magnitude down to levels appropriate for the firm's image. For myself and the other partners, except yourself, sir, I believe a Ben Franklin magnitude would be about right. For the staff people—perhaps the Gracie Allen size would be suitable.

These magnitudes are high enough to demand respect, you will note, sir, but not so high as to seem out of line. They will bear out our claim that we operate on a tight margin of profit, converting almost all of our earnings into inspiration which is expended in behalf of our clients . . .

Your magnitude, sir? . . . Since you mingle with the Luminous, sir, we couldn't change yours if we wanted to. Also, you have been more prudent than the rest of us in your participation in the firm's success, and have increased your magnitude no more than might be explained by the popularity of your book, *The Prince* . . .

Where do we drain to? That is a problem, sir. We can't simply drain into the firm's working capital of remembrance-power. That will surely be investigated, too. I'm afraid we'll actually have to expend the overage in inspiration, sir, and pour it out on Earth . . .

No, it will be no problem to dump that much inspiration on Earth without producing effects the investigators would notice. I'll make it inspiration for peace, and as you know, sir, the living take delight in *fighting* for peace. The inspiration will be practically invisible, heh-heh! . . . No, sir, it won't be enough to start a war—at least not a major one . . .

I agree, sir. This depletion of capital is going to set the firm back at least five centuries, and believe me, you can't be as heartbroken about it as I. To think, this had to happen under my management! . . . Well—yes, sir, we have to take these things in stride . . . you can count on me to handle the whole affair with discretion and dispatch, sir. Goodbye . . .

Miss Krimsby! . . . Miss Krimsby, why in the name of all the mythological gods and devils—why *did you have to go prancing out in public, outshining the Virgin Mary?*

Bowerbird

Even in an age when technology had reduced almost all gemstones to baubles, the Alversen Diamonds were beyond man's power to duplicate. They were priceless, and astonishing in beauty. And their theft from the National Space Museum in Houston was little short of a national calamity.

Two weeks later the FBI was still looking for its first useful clue. And the President was turning on the heat and making "suggestions."

"Try to see this the President's way," urged Attorney General Larkle. "Congress is acting salty, the TV comics are making jokes, and the public is annoyed. Maybe the public is frightened, too. A theft like this is enough to make anybody feel unsafe! It's only natural for the President to want somebody he has faith in on the case."

FBI Director Caude retorted angrily, "Sure, but the President doesn't have to work with Otto Hoffmann! He doesn't know what an unbearable bitchtard that guy is! Damn it, I've never run into a criminal who could touch Hoffmann for pure despicability!"

"I know," the Attorney General nodded glumly. "I've worked with him before, myself. But we have to admit, Caude, that Hoffmann has shown he can make sense out of situations that stump everybody else. Anyway, the President says get him, so why fight it?"

"Oh, I'm not fighting it! Fact is, I ordered him brought in last night, and word came a couple of hours ago that my agents have located him and are bringing him in now. But I'll be damned if this makes sense to me. We lose maybe half a dozen starships a year, plus a lot of good men, and nobody turns a hair. But let a couple of gaudy rocks get stolen and the whole country's in a swivet!" He paused, and then brightened. "Say, maybe Hoffmann will refuse the assignment. He was pretty burned up at me the last time he did an FBI job."

"Don't count on it," said the Attorney General. "I hear he's hurting for money and his ex-wife's bugging him for back alimony."

At that moment the door opened and Otto Hoffmann himself, with the form and demeanor of an enraged grizzly bear, lumbered in to stand before Caude's desk.

"Okay, fuzz-master," he snarled. "What now?"

Hoffman's face, like the faces of many people, wore a perpetual scowl. But whereas most scowls come from squinting in the sun too long, or from long hours of brow-puckering thought, Hoffmann's scowl was the genuine article—the exterior display of a loathing (and therefore loathful) inner man.

His small pig-eyes were nearly lost in the vast, ugly, booze-bloated face that hunched above an equally booze-bloated body. Nor did the scars of numerous brawls enhance his appearance, although these disfigurements were old and faded. Hoffman had gained a reputation as a "mean drunk," and bar-room habitués had learned not to tangle with him.

But he was a man of rare ability. The story was that his gift came from an unusual upbringing, from a crack-pot father who had taught him at an early age that man's greatest sin was self-deception. As a result Hoffmann saw the world with eyes unobscured by man's stock of comforting fantasies, and this made him very wise. He saw himself the same way, and this made him very bitter.

"Good morning, Mr. Hoffmann," Caude said, trying to be pleasant. "I hope my agents didn't interrupt—I—"

"Skip the small-talk, fuzz!" barked Hoffmann. "What's the deal?"

"We, er, wish to engage your services on a case—"

"My fee is one million dollars, payable in advance."

"*A million? In advance?*" gasped Attorney General Larkle. "Surely you must be joking, Hoffmann! The amount is out of the question, and payment in advance is against regulations!"

"Look, tumble-tongue, the last time you guys suckered me to do your work for you, I waited ten months for my pay, and then had to go to court to get it. This time *I* don't start until I have Uncle Skinflint's check certified and deposited. Otherwise, you figure out for yourself what happened to the Alversen Diamonds."

Caude's eyes narrowed. "Who told you this was about the Alversen Diamonds?" he demanded.

Hoffmann sneered, "Try to hide your imbecility, fuzz. If I had to be told why you needed me, I'd be too stupid to do the job in the first place. Well, speak up! I'm not going to stand here all day!"

The men glared at him for an instant, then Larkle said, "I'm prepared to give you a check for five hundred thousand now, and the remaining five hundred thousand will be paid upon your successful solution of the case."

"Okay," said Hoffmann.

"Okay?" asked Larkle in surprise.

"Sure. Give me the check. As soon as it's deposited in my account I'll be ready to go to work. But I know damn well *I'll* never see that second half-million!"

Feeling as if he had been had, Larkle complied. Was this all Hoffmann had *expected* to get? he wondered. No matter. Hoffmann had probably guessed the FBI would never have brought him in except for orders from On High, so the dickering advantage had been on Hoffmann's side.

With the check in his beefy hand, Hoffmann said, "I'll be back in half an hour. Get the case file out for me to go over. And bring Alversen in for a conference this afternoon."

"Bring Mr. Alversen *in?* We couldn't do *that!*"

"Why not? Your strong-arm goons didn't apologize about dragging *me* out of bed."

"But—but we—he's *Hank Alversen!*" sputtered Caude.

"And the law is a respecter of persons!" snarled Hoffmann. "Oh, never mind! If you won't bring him in, arrange for us to go to him. This afternoon." He stuffed the check in a pocket and stomped out of the office.

"He's right about one thing," Larkle growled. "He'll never see that second five hundred thousand, the arrogant S.O.B.!"

"Hell! He put you over a barrel as it was," complained Caude in disgust. "Do you realize *I* don't earn five hundred thousand in ten years?"

Larkle nodded and grinned. "Don't take it too hard, Caude. I don't mean to let him keep that money."

"Oh," said Caude, and he grinned, too.

When Otto Hoffmann returned from the bank he settled his bulk behind a vacant desk and read through the file on the Alversen Diamonds theft. This, thought Caude, was a waste of time, because there was precious little in the file that had not been in the newscasts.

And everyone knew the story of the gems and their great discoverer, Henry Alversen.

While still in his early twenties, Alversen had been the first man to penetrate the asteroid belt beyond Mars. Afterward, the young NSA pilot had gone on to be the first explorer of the Jovian satellites, and still later he had captained the initial expedition to Saturn.

He was only thirty-five when the starship drive was developed, but he gracefully stepped aside to allow other men the glory of leading the long voyages to the stars. Much remained to be explored within the sun's own system, and Alversen was content to follow through the work he had begun. He surveyed hundreds of the bare rocks and metallic chunks of the asteroid belt. And he set a record for the closest orbital approach to the surface of Jupiter—a record that still stood unchallenged thirty years later.

He found the diamonds in the course of these explorations. The find made him a millionaire many times over, but the discovery had its frustrating side. His report told the story:

He was surveying a small but unusually dense chunk in the asteroid belt when a glittering reflection from deep in a metallic crevice caught his eye. Fascinated and curious, he put a ramjack in the crevice and pried the walls apart, breaking loose a large section of the brittle planetoid in the process. He drifted down to the source of the glitter, and found the partially exposed surface of a globe only a few feet in diameter, a globe with a curiously "manufactured" look. Certainly there was no doubt that the large gems studding its surface had been cut and faceted by some intelligent being.

Two of the gems were loose enough for him to pick free and stow in his pouch. But as he studied the task of releasing the entire globe from the mass of the planetoid, he became aware that the section he had pried free in opening the crevice was drifting away quite rapidly, and his ship was anchored to that chunk.

He dived after his ship, but several minutes passed before he caught up with it. By the time he had boarded it and released the anchor, his treasure trove had drifted out of sight in a direction he could not guess. He spiraled his ship in the vicinity for days of futile search before giving up.

The loss was deplorable, not merely because of the unique qualities of the two diamonds he did bring back, but because the globe was almost certainly a relic of a highly-advanced civilization. There had been speculation since the first telescopic sightings of the asteroids that these fragments were the remains of a planet, perhaps bearing life, that had once occupied the wide orbital gap between Mars and Jupiter. But no fossils or other relics had been found, which made Alversen's Diamonds, and his report of the object they had decorated, of unique interest. Also, no semblance of intelligent life had been found within the seven-parsec sphere of space explored by the starships. The diamonds were man's only evidence that he was not totally alone in all space and time.

And the diamonds had a feature far beyond man's power to duplicate: the planes of their crystalline structure were not flat. The plane that had paralleled the surface of their globular mounting had a positive curvature approximating that of the globe's surface. The diamonds had, in effect, been "wrapped around" the small segments of the globe they had covered. How that curving had been achieved was a matter of considerable scientific debate. Most experts agreed that nothing less than a gravitational field too concentrated to be found in nature—so intense that it created a closed spacewarp in its vicinity—would yield an environment in which such "bent" diamonds could crystallize. The creatures who produced this gravitational field must have been highly advanced, indeed.

The loss of the major portion of his find seemed to take the drive out of Alversen. He returned to Earth, sold the diamonds to the U.S. government, and never ventured into space again. A man of wealth as a result of the sale, and of immense prestige, he lived in pleasant (if perhaps melancholy) retirement.

As for the diamonds, they had been studied, marveled at, speculated over, and finally installed in a special gallery on the top floor of the National Space Museum. Millions of people filed past the well-protected display case to gaze at their clear, wondrous beauty. And then one night they were stolen.

It was strictly a space-age theft, one that would have been impossible a very few decades earlier. Even now, the FBI's experts were hard-pressed to explain just what types of equipment had been used to nullify the surveillance systems, and to muffle the noise made when a gaping hole was torn through the museum's roof.

At last Otto Hoffmann tossed the file aside with a disdainful snort. He got up and stomped into Caude's office. "I'm going to drink some lunch, fuzz," he said. "When I get back I want to go see old Heroic Hank."

"You can eat on the clopter," said Caude, rising. "I've been in touch with Mr. Alversen. He said to come whenever we wished."

He led the way to the roof where a large-cabin clopter was waiting. The Attorney General was already aboard, and the clopter was quickly in the air speeding westward. Ninety minutes later it drifted down on the Alversen estate in the Rockies. The three men were ushered into the spacious, cheerful living room where Alversen himself made them welcome.

Now in his seventies, Alversen still had the warm sincerity that had always endeared him to close friends, casual acquaintances, and to the public at large. Age had, if anything, actually improved him by contributing a quiet dignity to his bearing.

Larkle and Caude, grumpy and morose from their long clopter ride with the unbearable Hoffmann, brightened immediately in the warmth of Alversen's presence. Hoffmann sulked while they chatted gaily with their host.

Finally they got down to business. "As Caude told you on the phone, Hank," said Larkle, "we have asked Mr. Hoffmann to assist us in the diamond theft case, and he wishes to ask you some questions."

Alversen nodded and smiled at Hoffmann. "I'll be most happy to tell you anything I know, Mr. Hoffmann," he said, "but frankly, I don't see how I can be of much help in this deplorable matter."

"Thanks," Hoffmann said ungraciously. "Suppose you start by telling me how you came by the diamonds in the first place."

Alversen looked briefly startled, then said, "Very well, though I doubt if I can recall, after all these years, anything more than you will find in the published reports. But here goes: I was conducting a sampling-survey in the asteroid belt, time-space coordinates T24F13 something-or-other, QQ700651 dash 445K, when I spotted a planetoid roughly two hundred meters long by—

"*Hold it!*" Hoffmann snapped peevishly, waving his arms. "I know that bilboesque yarn as well as you do. It's time to come clean, Alversen. Let's have the real poop!"

"*Bilboesque?*" hissed the scandalized Attorney General. "*Come clean?* Really, Hoffmann! We didn't bring you out here to insult Mr. Alversen! Hank, I must apologize, but perhaps you know something of Hoffmann by repute. He's ... he's ... " The Attorney General stopped, unequal to the task of finding words to define the obnoxiousness of Otto Hoffmann.

"He's a *realist!*" Hoffmann himself supplied. "That's what I am, Alversen, a realist! I'm a man with damn few illusions—about the universe or my stinking fellow-man. I was a realist even as a child, the first time I ever heard your fairy tale about finding those diamonds. Let's have the facts this time!"

Alversen was displaying the shocked puzzlement with which the innocent often react to absurd accusations. "I don't ... " he began, "I ... I really don't know what to say to you, Mr. Hoffmann. I can only tell you what happened. I can't *invent* a different story for you!"

"Sure you could," sneered Hoffmann. "You're a good inventor of stories. Listen to me, Alversen! The human race acts foolishly enough when it has accurate knowledge for a guide. When its knowledge is wrong, it acts like a damned idiot. And you've handed the world a hunk of nonsense that could make us behave stupidly enough to get ourselves killed!" He stared disgustedly at the old spaceman and added, "If you don't tell your story straight, I will. It'll sound better coming from you."

Alversen glanced helplessly at the others and shrugged, "What do I say to this? Is this some kind of joke?"

"Not one we're in on, I assure you!" huffed Larkle. "Hoffmann, if this is the best you can do—"

"Keep your cool, mouthpiece," growled Hoffmann. "I know what I'm doing! Maybe you guys don't know about bowerbirds."

"Bowerbirds?"

"Yeah. They live in Australia and New Guinea. Very amusing animals, and instructive to observe. They get their name from the male bird's habit of building a grass bower in mating season. Then he decorates his bower with bright flowers, leaves, pebbles, pieces of glass-anything that might catch the females' fancy. A lot of ornament stealing goes on, and the sharpest cock winds up with the pick of the decorations in his bower. That gives him the pick of the hens, which makes the system practical."

The FBI Director was glaring fiercely, at him. "Hoffmann," he stormed, "if you're trying to tell us a bowerbird stole the Alversen Diamonds, I swear I'll have you committed!"

"You're close, fuzz, close!" leered Hoffmann with mock approval. "I'm telling you that a creature which frequently displays bowerbird-like behavior stole the diamonds. Of course an ordinary bowerbird couldn't have done it, but this creature could."

"What creature?".

Hoffmann flicked a thumb toward Alversen. "That one."

"This is ridiculous!" protested Alversen. "I haven't been near the Space Museum in five years!"

"Who said you had?" demanded Hoffmann. "You didn't steal the diamonds from the museum. Nobody did."

" What?" yelped the Attorney General. "That's nonsense! They're gone, aren't they?"

Hoffmann shrugged and looked sourer than usual. Finally he said, "Gents, I'm going to kick some of your most cherished beliefs to death, so steel yourselves to bear up under the grief.

"First, Heroic Hank here is no incorruptible paragon. The bowerbird in his soul was too much for him! But don't think too unkindly of him. Each of us contains a touch of bowerbird, along with touches of mouse, skunk, snake, peacock, and so on. Sometimes I wonder if the difference between man and the lower animals is merely that man can choose, from one moment to the next, which other animal's instinctive behavior would best suit his needs." Hoffmann grinned crookedly and added, "For example, I am now copying the hawk, or maybe the buzzard.

"Second, we don't have this neck of the universe to ourselves, as everybody likes to think—though Alversen knows better! In reality we're a minor lifeform around here."

"Our ships have explored the planets of dozens of stars," the Attorney General observed ponderously, "and have found no trace of past or present intelligent life."

"Naturally not!" snapped Hoffmann impatiently. "Why should superior life hang around something as undependable as a star? *They* wouldn't be living on planets at all. Look. You know there are more dwarf stars than giant stars. Right? And it follows there are more sub-dwarfs than dwarfs. The smaller stellar bodies are, the more numerous they're likely to be. Within five light-years of the sun is only one other bright-star system, Alpha Centauri, but there has to be dozens of small stars closer than that—stars too small to radiate noticeable light, but big enough to have slow nuclear fission processes in their interiors to provide them with warm surfaces and atmospheres.

"I'm not making all this up! Sub-dwarfs are in astronomy textbooks—not mentioned often, I admit, but that's because man isn't much interested in little dark stars that have enough gravity and atmosphere to crush him. But life could evolve on such a world and find it quite satisfactory . . . plenty of surface on a world that size to let a society spread itself out! And plenty of similar worlds just light-weeks away, to colonize or to trade with. And a very stable energy situation, because a world like that could outlast two or three suns.

"That's where *The* People live in this neck of the universe, gents. *The* People! We, a particular breed of animals, live in what The People must consider barren waste, on a cold little clinker near a scorching ball of gas that throws all sorts of deadly radiation at us. A fit place for bowerbirds, maybe, but not for The People."

Alversen smiled. "What you say about the existence of sub-dwarfs is accurate enough, Mr. Hoffmann. But when you speak of these so-called People, I'm afraid you're fantasizing."

"No, I'm *real*-izing," countered Hoffmann. "I don't miss on telling reality from non-reality, Alversen. Do you think the FBI hired me for my personal charm? You're licked, Heroic Hank! Why don't you give up and confess?"

Alversen chuckled uncomfortably. "It's your story," he shrugged. "Go on with it."

"Okay. The People would be curious enough to explore some of our planets, and naturally, they would be most interested in planets that came closest to offering them a livable environment. If they sent a research team to the sun's system, the team would probably go to Jupiter, our biggest planet. The weather would be chilly for them, but the gravity and air pressure would be almost enough for comfort.

"But one thing would be the same for them and us—the economics of spaceflight. They wouldn't land their spaceship on Jupiter. They would leave it in orbit, and go down to the surface in small shuttle-ships."

He eyed Alversen coldly. "That's where you found the diamonds, Alversen-in a ship they left in orbit around Jupiter! Aside from fooling around in the asteroids, you're also the man who made the closest fly-by of the Jovian surface. Close enough to find their parked spaceship. You went aboard, found the diamonds, stole them, and came home with that innocent tale of a relic on an asteroid.

"That tale had to be nonsense! Maybe a diamond would survive a billion years in an asteroid, practically exposed to open space, but it wouldn't wind up looking like it had been cut yesterday, with all its facets smooth and shiny. Nobody should have believed your story for a minute, but it was *your* story, and you were the unblemished hero! Besides, your tale put this frightening supercivilization a comforting billion years in the past. So everybody politely pushed reality aside to make way for your fantasy."

"This is the wildest thing I've ever heard!" laughed Alversen, getting to his feet. "Who would like a drink?"

Larkle and Caude declined numbly, but Hoffmann said, "If that invitation extends to me, I could do with a shot."

"Certainly," smiled Alversen, going to his bar. "I'm not the thin-skinned sort who would take this personally, Mr. Hoffmann. You were hired to do an important and difficult job for our country, and I sympathize with the vigor and, I'm sure, the sincerity, with which you're trying to do it." He downed a stiff jolt of bourbon, then refilled his glass and brought it, along with Hoffmann's drink, over from the bar. "But there are one or two points in your version that don't jibe with what I would call reality. You say I boarded an alien spaceship, swiped some diamonds, and scurried home. Mr. Hoffmann, surely you realize that the knowledge I could have gained aboard such a ship would be worth far more than all the diamonds I could carry."

Hoffmann nodded and slurped his drink. "That's true, but I'm not criticizing you for taking the diamonds instead. I probably couldn't have done much better myself. That ship must have been incomprehensible, and terrifying. The diamonds were probably the only things you saw that had any meaning to you. In your fright, you couldn't have done much thinking, anyway. You could only react, and with the diamonds staring you in the face, you reacted like a bowerbird."

"I see," grinned Alversen. "Then why didn't these aliens come after me to get their diamonds back?"

"They did. That's why I said the diamonds weren't stolen from the museum. They were reclaimed by their rightful owners!"

"If that's true, why did they do it so sneakily?"

"Not sneakily, but gently, when nobody was in the museum to get hurt," said Hoffmann. "Suppose an Australian rancher is out in his yard, looking at something through a magnifying glass. He leaves the glass there, and the next time he needs it he looks in the yard for it and it's gone. He's seen bowerbirds around, and reasons that one of them took it. This doesn't make him mad at the birds. He understands their instincts. So he goes to the area where the local birds have their bowers, and since his glass was a top prize that would have found its way into the top cock's bower, he gently pulls back the wall of that bower, takes his glass, and goes his way.

"That's what happened to the diamonds. When The People were ready to use their ship again, they saw the diamonds were gone (and I would guess the diamonds weren't there for looks but were parts of the ship's working gear). The People would have noticed us, of course, and watched us as we do bowerbirds, with amusement and mild curiosity. So they would have known the NSA was a sort of pluralized top cock in our society, and would have gone straight to NSA's bower, the Space Museum, to retrieve the diamonds."

Hoffmann finished his drink and looked around at Larkle and Caude, as if studying the effect of his words on them. He sneered at what he saw in their faces.

The Attorney General said in a tight voice, "I'll be a long time apologizing satisfactorily for exposing you to this arrogant nonsense, Hank. I'm truly sorry! May I use your phone for an urgent call?"

"Of course," smiled Alversen, looking a bit saddened.

Larkle went to the phone and punched a number. The screen lighted to display the face of the president of the bank in which Hoffmann had deposited his check. The banker smiled in recognition.

"Hi, Pete," he said.

"Hello, Tony," said the Attorney General. "Tony, you have an account for one Otto Hoffmann. I'm hereby impounding that account, on the grounds that Hoffmann defrauded the government out of the five hundred thousand he deposited earlier today."

"All right, Pete. Put through the official notice within six hours, won't you?"

"Okay. But do you mind checking to make sure you have the account?"

"Just a second." The face disappeared briefly, then came back to say, "Yes, we have it. Name of Otto Hoffmann, with a federal check that size deposited today."

"That's the one! Impound it!"

"Right . . . But Pete . . . One thing . . . "

"What's that?" asked Larkle.

"There's only two thousand in the account. Hoffmann made the deposit, and then wrote checks to cover almost the whole amount. Three hundred thousand to Internal Revenue Service, one hundred and twenty thousand to a prepayment trust for a Mrs. Stella Ebert Hoffmann (sounds like he's paying alimony, doesn't it?), and there's one check marked 'one year's rent,' and another for a twelve-month triple-A dining card, and several marked 'payment of account in full.' Only two thousand left. But I'll impound that."

"Forget the whole thing!" bawled the Attorney General, slapping the phone off with a furious gesture.

Hoffmann grinned with gloating triumph. "Let's see you start, big shyster," he snickered, "by conning IRS out of three hundred thousand!"

"Go to hell!" grated the Attorney General.

"Hadn't we better leave?" Caude murmured to him.

"Yeah, let's get this S.O.B. outta here!" Larkle barked. "Again, Hank, my deepest apologies."

Alversen nodded and smiled forgivingly.

"Just one more thing," said Hoffmann. "Alversen, I want to remind you of something I said a while ago. You've got the world believing a dangerous lie, one that could get the whole human race smeared but good! Let's get back to that Australian rancher. When he went to recover his property the first time, he was good-humored about it. But suppose the next time it happened he was badly inconvenienced and got angry. The bowerbirds would no longer be a bunch of amusing goofs; they would suddenly be a damned nuisance. He would go after them with his gun."

Hoffmann rose and lumbered toward the door. "Well, so long, Heroic Hank! Sleep well tonight. One of the billions of lives you're endangering is mine, if you want a cheerful thought to sleep on."

"Wait," said Alversen quietly. They turned to look at him.

"The damned S.O.B.'s right," he gritted. "He's mixed up on some of the details—but he's right. I did lie about the diamonds, and I suppose the rightful owners took them from the museum. It's hard to explain any other way."

Larkle and Caude sat down again, looking stunned.

"My God!" said Caude at last. "We can't let this get out. It would ruin Hank completely!"

Alversen lowered his head. "Thanks for considering me, but at my age it doesn't matter so much. I made the mistake, and I'm ready to pay for it."

Hoffmann snorted caustically but didn't speak.

"But this could play hell with morale, Hank!" protested Larkle. "The public needs heroes, and it needs them untarnished. I think we'd better hush the whole thing. Hoffmann's talking malarky about the danger, anyway, so there's no need to issue a warning about the aliens. If Hoffmann's summary is true, as you say it is, Hank, then the aliens have shown themselves to be highly civilized and, um, forebearing. If a human should offend them again, surely they will merely get in touch with us, to warn us."

Alversen shook his head. "We can't be sure of that, and the risk is too great to take."

"Some slight risk perhaps," argued the Attorney General. "But isn't it far more likely that they would prefer to talk it out with us?"

Hoffmann sneered and helped himself to some more of Alversen's liquor. "Tell me, big shyster," he demanded. "How likely are *you* to start a conversation with a *bowerbird?*"

The silence that followed was long and uncomfortable.

Man Off A White Horse

This was the real thing. Barfield was gloriously sure of that. Not just a dream, like it had been a thousand times before. This time he was really astride a powerful white stallion, drawing looks of admiration, fear, and respect from hundreds of upturned faces as he rode through Central Park.

It couldn't be a dream, because he never thought to wonder about that when he was dreaming. And a dream wasn't this real.

Just to make sure, he studied the reins gripped lightly in his right hand. Genuine leather, all right, with blood-red rubies attached in little square silver mountings that were pointy at the corners. Certainly no dream contained detailed stuff like that.

Was he going to fall off? Not in a hundred years! The dream intensifier had finally worked, and simply by dreaming of riding, he had learned to ride.

A family of picnickers scattered in all directions as he galloped his horse over their spread cloth. He roared with laughter to see them jump, their faces pale with terror. He towered over them for a moment, then rode on . . .

. . . Into a swarm of high-society chicks having a lawn party. He picked a choice one and swept her up in front of him.

"Barfield!" she exclaimed, recognizing him.

"Yeah." He knew who she was, too—Jacqueline Onassis' granddaughter—but he wasn't going to give her the pleasure of letting her know he knew.

He stood in the stirrups and quickly had his satisfaction with her. Then he let her slide from the horse to sprawl panting and indecent on the grass.

His horse was now climbing a hill, going up fast in powerful lunges. All the world lay below him, below the magnificent Barfield.

They topped the hill crest. The down slope on the other side was dizzyingly steep. Barfield gasped and cringed back. His left foot lost the stirrup and . . .

. . . He was falling!

"Ugh!" he grunted as his body gave a jerk. He opened his eyes and gazed dully at the captive across the room for a moment.

"Something wrong?" the man asked in that annoyingly confident voice of his.

"I must've dozed off," said Barfield.

He stood up, feeling as short, dumpy, and ineffectual as he knew he looked, and walked over to check the captive's cuffs and blindfold.

"We haven't been properly introduced," the man said pleasantly. "My name's Paxton . . . G. Donald Paxton."

"Never mind the chitchat, Body," Barfield growled. Usually a captive would show fear when addressed as "Body," but this guy didn't turn a hair.

He saw the cuffs were still tight on wrists and ankles, and returned to his chair, his mind returning to his dream. Funny how real it had seemed, and how sure he had been of it. Looks like that high-society party would have been a dead giveaway. Everybody knew upper-crust chicks didn't fool around in places like Central Park. Besides, there'd been something on the tube about that girl dreaming herself up a judo black belt. Nobody was going to grab *her* up on a horse and get away with it.

But it had been a good dream—all but the last part.

"I hate to be a nuisance," said Paxton, "but I need to go to the bathroom."

Barfield got up. "No sweat, Body." He got out his keys and removed the cuffs from Paxton's ankles. "Stand up." Paxton stood, and Barfield guided him into the bathroom, where he refastened his ankles and freed his wrists.

"I'm gonna close the door, and then you can take off the blindfold," he instructed. "When you're through, put the blindfold back on and call me. Try something funny, and there ain't enough ransom in the bank to keep you alive. Got it?"

"Yes. Thanks very much, Friend," said Paxton.

Barfield thought a few cuss words. What kind of nut was this guy, Paxton? Acting like he didn't have a care in the world, which was no way for a kidnap victim to act.

Presently Paxton called him, and Barfield opened the door and returned the man to his seat.

When they were settled down Barfield said, "You don't catch on, do you, Body? You stand a good chance of getting conked. You dig that?"

"Of course," Paxton nodded, cheerful as ever. "As an attorney, I'm quite familiar with the kidnap racket and its practices. I believe the general rule is to kill one out of four victims, to keep the public aware you mean business."

"One out of three," Barfield corrected, grimly. If Paxton had said one out of three, he would have replied one out of two. But again the victim showed no sign of intimidation. "You figure the odds are in your favor, huh, Body?"

Paxton shrugged. "If not, everybody's got to die some time, Friend," he replied with a mild chuckle.

"Well, if I don't hear soon that the payoff's bein' made, your time's comin' pretty damn soon," Barfield glowered. He looked at his watch and blinked. Five hours had passed since Stony Stan and the other guys had brought Paxton in. He ought to have heard from Stony long before now.

Paxton seemed to realize that. "I'm afraid I have enemies as well as friends," he said. "That could delay the payoff."

"Friends?" grunted Barfield. "What about your family?"

"No family. The ransom will be collected from my friends, or business associates might be more accurate."

Barfield frowned. Stony Stan never told him more than he had to know about a job, which was damn near nothing. Barfield's job was to baby-sit the victims, and then drive them to the release or conk-out point. So maybe this wasn't an unusual job, so far as he knew. But it seemed risky to expect a payoff from a guy's buddies instead of his relatives.

"What kind of line you in?" he asked.

"I'm an attorney, as I think I mentioned. Actually, my position is general secretary of a union."

"Big operator, huh?" glowered Barfield. "I got a hunch you're goin' to be the one out of three, Body." He stared at the blindfolded man in resentful silence for a while. A damned union boss, and Barfield couldn't even get into a union as a member!

"Which union?" he finally asked.

"American Bar Association."

That didn't win any sympathy from Barfield. He knew several barkeeps, and thought most of them were jerks.

"Your friends better come through pretty damn quick," he said.

After a silence Paxton asked, "Do you know you talk in your sleep?"

"Huh?" Barfield sat up. "What did I say?"

"It sounded as if you were talking to a horse. Were you having a dream about riding?"

"Yeah." Barfield's thoughts returned to the dream.

"It sounded like a good one, except perhaps at the end," Paxton said.

"I fell off the damn gluepot," Barfield said in injured tones. "I always do."

"I do a little riding," Paxton said modestly. "It's very pleasant exercise, don't you agree?"

"Me, I couldn't say, Body," Barfield retorted. "I can't stay on top of a damn pony."

"Oh? That's too bad. Why don't you get an intensifier and let your dreams teach you how to ride?"

"Look, I already told you," Barfield snapped, "I keep fallin' off at the end of the dream!"

"Oh, yes. That would invalidate the dream-learning procedure, wouldn't it?" Paxton said.

Barfield grunted.

"That's said to be why there are so few levitators," Paxton went on thoughtfully. "Many people have dreams of floating through the air, but the overwhelming majority of those dreams end in crash landings." He chuckled. "Of course when someone has that dream under an intensifier, the technique of levitation becomes clear to them, but the crash at the end becomes equally realistic, and traumatic. As a result, they actually have the waking skill of levitation, but the trauma is a total block that keeps them from ever using the skill. It never occurred to me that the same condition would apply to dream-learning how to ride a horse, but I can see now why it might. Effortless motion is involved in both—suddenly becoming very effortful."

"How come a mouthpiece knows so much about dream-learnin'?" Barfield demanded.

"An attorney has to know a little about a lot of things," replied Paxton. "I've never used dream-learning myself—never felt the need for it, really—but I have several acquaintances in the dream-psychology field, and have discussed the subject with them frequently. Just a couple of weeks ago—"

Paxton's voice trailed off. Barfield was thinking of Stony Stan, who could levitate. That ability of the gang's chief was very useful in pulling kidnappings. In fact, it was their secret of success. But just the same, Barfield cherished the hope that some day Stan would lose control and fall to the ground and burst open like a rotten apple. That would be fun to see happen. If what this guy Paxton was saying was right, Stan had never dreamed of falling, didn't know the helpless terror of it, and the damn bossy bastard had it coming to him.

Barfield blinked suspiciously. "Yeah? What about two weeks ago?"

"I beg your pardon?" Paxton smiled brightly.

"You said something about two weeks ago, and then shut up. What is it?"

"Oh, nothing. I merely decided I was boring you with all my chatter about dream-psychology."

"The hell you say," growled Barfield. "You're tryin' to hold somethin' out on me! Start talkin', Body, or I'll conk you right now!"

"Well . . . it was just something this acquaintance was telling me about recent research on the fall-syndrome. Really, Friend, I don't think you want to hear this."

"Keep talkin'," Barfield commanded. He wasn't sure he wanted to hear any more about falling, either, but making victims obey him was one of the pleasant things about being in this racket.

"If you insist," Paxton shrugged. "He said they've discovered the cause of the fall-syndrome."

Barfield started. "Is that the straight stuff?" he demanded.

"Oh, yes. The man I'm speaking about is one of the top experts in the field. I'm sure he was right."

"I mean are you givin' it to me straight?" yelped Barfield in exasperation.

"I have a precise memory of the conversation," replied Paxton. "An attorney has to have a—"

"I mean, are you tellin' me the truth?" hissed Barfield.

"Oh. Yes, of course. Sorry I didn't catch your meaning sooner, Friend."

Barfield sat back in his chair. He was inclined to believe this guy. "What does cause it?"

"The fall-syndrome? Fear . . . but oddly enough, not usually fear of falling. That's why it stumped the dream-learning specialists for so long. It can be fear of almost anything, but is usually a realistic fear, based on feelings of guilt."

"Hah! I ain't afraid of anything! Except fallin'."

"Well, it can be fear of falling, of course," said Paxton, "but is usually something else. I suppose, then, you have a fear of high places—acrophobia, it's called."

"Hell, no," grunted Barfield.

Paxton paused, looking surprised. "You're sure of that?"

"Sure I'm sure!"

"Well . . . that doesn't jibe with a fear of falling," Paxton murmured, as if to himself. "So it must be . . . well . . . never mind."

"Must be what, Body?" Barfield yelled, rising and walking forward to stand menacingly over the captive.

"It must be a fear you can't let yourself know about," said Paxton rapidly, cowering.

"Yeah? And what's that?"

"I have no way of knowing, Friend," Paxton babbled. "Possibly a man in your . . . your profession would have a fear of getting caught. Other than that, I honestly don't know."

"Me afraid of the cops! Haw!" Barfield strode away to stand close to the phone. He wished it would ring and Stan would tell him the job was going according to schedule. Had something happened?

He decided he needed a drink. When he picked up the bottle he noticed his hand was shaking. He stared at it.

Hell. Paxton was right.

"Anybody who ain't in with the law is scared of gettin' caught," he said defensively, "but that ain't one of them phobia things. It's just common sense! I got good reasons to be scared of cops."

Paxton brightened. "Why, certainly. That's it, then. This acquaintance said it usually would be a realistic fear, one well-justified by the person's circumstances."

"But Stan . . . " Barfield hesitated. "This guy I know who can levitate. The cops would like to get the goods on him, too. How come he don't fall?"

"I'm really not an expert in all this, Friend. But I would suppose the person you speak of is insensitive. Others might consider him extremely brave, but the truth could be that he is insensitive to fear, even when being afraid is quite sensible."

"Yeah, that's him, all right," mumbled Barfield.

"A dangerous man to the people around him."

"Yeah?" Barfield looked up. "Why?"

"Because, being without fear, he might take risks that endanger others as well as himself."

Barfield looked at his watch. Damn that Stony Stan, anyway! If something had gone wrong with the job, to hold up the action this long, why didn't he phone and call it? Or maybe Stan was gambling, just like Paxton said. But would Stan get caught if something went wrong? Oh, no, not him, the damned levitator! He would sail away, leaving Barfield and the other guys to take the rap.

The sensible thing to do was scram out of this place right now. Just leave Paxton where he was. Damn if that wasn't exactly what he was going to do!

With the decision made, Barfield felt better, and his mind turned again to the talk about the fall-syndrome.

"A good shrink could get rid of a guy's fear, and then he wouldn't fall no more in his dreams. Right?"

Paxton shook his head. "No. That's why I didn't want to talk about all this. A psychoanalyst can't help."

"Why the hell not?"

"Because they deal with irrational responses, and often can relieve them. But when a fear is rational, based on a clear recognition of a real danger, an analyst can do nothing."

Barfield's shoulders drooped. There went his hope of ever sitting tall on a horse in real life. For a little while this Paxton guy had really had him stirred up. Right now, the thing to do was lam out of here fast while he had the opportunity.

"The only solution," Paxton was saying, "would be to remove the need to feel fear, to change one's actual circumstances so as to eliminate—"

At the door, Barfield turned and came back. "What are you mumblin' about, Body?"

"Nothing you would find helpful, I'm sorry to say. For you to get rid of your fear of the police, it would be necessary for you to clear yourself with them. I'm sure you find that out of the question."

"I don't find nothin' out of the question!" Barfield stormed.

"You mean you'd have the nerve to give yourself up, turn state's-evidence against your associates, and depend upon the gratitude of the police and perhaps the goodwill of certain highly-placed individuals such as myself? Really, my friend, I can't buy that. Not with your fear of the police."

There was a drawn-out silence. "You say you'd pull strings for me?" asked Barfield.

"Certainly. That would be the least I could do."

Barfield's hands were shaking so much he could hardly unlock the cuffs on Paxton's wrists and ankles, but he ignored the shaking with grim determination. He had to do this, or his dream would never come true.

"O.K., Bod . . . uh, Mr. Paxton, let's go talk to the cops," he quavered.

Amid the bustle of the police station, the interrogation of Barfield, the hurried and successful efforts to round up Stony Stan and the rest of the gang, almost two hours passed before Paxton and his younger law partner, Fred Jarman, could have a quiet word together. They were alone in the captain's office, Paxton having a cup of the captain's coffee.

"I hope I handled things right, Don," Jarman said, a trifle uneasily. "I hated to put you in increased danger by holding back on the ransom, but knowing you I assumed that was what you wanted—time to handle the situation yourself."

"You did exactly right, Fred," Paxton assured him. "I admit it was touch and go with Barfield for a while. I had to lie a couple of times, telling him I've never used dream-learning, and promising to pull strings for him. Barfield is quite stupid, you know, and a stupid man is often harder to deal with than an intelligent man." He chuckled. "The poor dope is so uninformed that he didn't even know who I was."

"He didn't know you're presidential timber?"

Paxton shook his head.

"That's why I'm grateful, Fred," he said, "that you handled things the way you did from your end. The public image of a kidnap victim—helpless, intimidated—is inappropriate for a man who aspires to a position of high leadership. A leader must be viewed as a person who can control any situation that confronts him. That's what the public wants."

"But not from on top of a horse," grinned Jarman.

"Never from on top of a horse," said Paxton. "That's something else I lied to Barfield about. I said I rode. Can you imagine what the press would do with a photo of me sitting tall in a saddle?"

"I can see the caption now: 'The Modern Napoleon'," snickered Jarman.

"Or some even less-fondly remembered dictator," Paxton said.

"Well, I'm glad it's all over, Don, and you're safe," Jarman said, becoming serious. "This business gave me a very trying afternoon."

"I'm glad to know my partner appreciates me," Paxton smiled, sipping his coffee.

"I do," said Jarman. "I'd love to have your ability . . . to talk anybody into anything—" He halted and glanced about uncomfortably.

"It's O.K., Fred. This office isn't bugged," said Paxton.

"Good. What I started to say is, that while I don't have the ability to talk anybody into anything, it's great to have a partner who can."

Paxton nodded slowly. "Dream-learning isn't a democratic process, Fred. First, you have to have the dream . . . repeatedly. Otherwise, there's nothing to work with. And nobody can choose the subject matter of his dreams. It's a matter of luck, essentially. I was fortunate enough to have grown up having my dreams of influencing people with my spoken words, and—"

He fell silent as the door opened and the police captain entered. The officer wore a concerned expression.

"How are things going, Captain?" asked Paxton.

"Generally O.K.," the officer replied. "I'm wondering if there's going to be a problem later on, though."

"Oh? What's that?"

"Barfield insists that you're going to pressure the courts into turning him loose. I want to know where we stand with you, Mr. Paxton."

Paxton shrugged. "I'm afraid I did promise to pull strings for him, Captain. If I hadn't, I probably wouldn't have remained alive to bring the Stony Stan gang to justice."

The officer eyed him grimly. "Then you're going to get him off," he said.

Paxton stared down at his feet, looking torn with indecision. Suddenly he looked up at the policeman.

"No, Captain," he snapped. "Barfield's all yours. When it comes to a choice between breaking my word to a criminal, or compromising the judicial procedures of our country, my course is clear."

The police captain beamed approval at him. "Thanks, Mr. Paxton. I'll see to it that this stays out of the press, of course." He hurried out of the office.

"You handled that beautifully, Don," said Jarman as they rose to leave.

"Of course," said Paxton.

Soul Affrighted

Dellbar slowed as he approached his driveway, giving himself a moment to send out his usual earnest but randomly aimed prayer.

Please, make her be here this time. Make her be home. Let me see her car when I turn in.

He swung into the drive, and could see into both sides of the garage. Her car wasn't there.

He hadn't really expected it to be. But every evening he managed to hope until he could see into the garage.

He parked and went around to the front of the house to pick up the newspaper and mail, then unlocked the door and went inside. A quick glance around, into the bedroom, bathroom, and kitchen, told him Margitte hadn't been in all day. And she hadn't been there last night, or for much of the previous day.

Dellbar dropped tiredly to the couch, and sat slumped forward. His depression was a numb ache he had learned to tolerate during his two years of marriage, but he had a feeling it was wearing him down. It stayed with him now even when he was at work, and that was bad for the job. The other guys at the lab were beginning to wonder about him. The department supervisor had asked him a couple of days ago if he felt okay.

Where was she this time? Tripping out on acid? Or had she gone on to the really hard stuff? Or maybe it was booze and sex—although she had sworn she saved all her sex for him, he couldn't quite believe that. How could she put that one restriction on herself, and no others?

He found himself staring at his dim reflection on the dusty face of the television screen.

"You're the world's most mismated man," he told himself aloud.

Then why don't you unmate? he replied silently.

"That's why I say the *most* mismated. It wouldn't be that bad if I could break it off."

You're stubborn, or stupid, or a sucker for punishment.

"All three. Also, I still love her, but maybe that's covered by 'stupid.' "

It is.

Dellbar stood up, annoyed. These solo dialogues didn't accomplish anything.

A drink? No. If he had a drink he would mope around all evening, feeling worse and worse. The only thing that would distract him, even a little, was work. So . . . get some supper, and then to the workshop.

Something had spoiled in one of the kitchen bins, making a stink that killed what little appetite he had. He hunted around till he found what it was—a large paper bag containing one very rotten onion. He carried it out to the garbage can. Then he gulped down a cheese sandwich and a glass of milk.

The sandwich felt heavy in his stomach as he went down the basement steps and into his workshop. For several minutes he perched motionless on the stool at his bench, gazing at the visualizer he had built while he tried to put thoughts of everything else out of his mind.

That was hard to do. There was too much relating the visualizer and Margitte. He had built it for her, although she didn't know that. And it, like his marriage, was a failure.

What was wrong with it? Was his idea that such a device could be made fallacious? Or was it something less basic? Maybe nothing more than a failure of one of the junk electronic components he used in building it? Or perhaps an overlooked imbalance in the circuitry?

Intellectually, the visualizer was a strangely conceived device—half of it straight electronic engineering, and the other half modern-day witchcraft. Dellbar had, at first, been surprised after getting his degree and taking a job to learn of the "dark technology"—the weird and unexplainable effects that could be produced by such-and-such arrangements of electronic gear. None of this was to be found in textbooks; it passed by word of mouth when engineers got together over a few drinks. It was the folklore of electronics technicians, unsupported by scientific theory, unannounced to the public, and spoken of among the engineers themselves in low voices, and seldom then until their tongues were loosened by drug or drink.

Dellbar had listened, and disbelieved. Then after his wife had begun straying out and he needed business for lonely hands, he set up his basement workshop and tested the dark technology himself. After that, he believed.

But so far, the visualizer had not worked.

Could he, himself, be the faulty component? He grimaced. The visualizer was supposed to reveal, on its second-hand color-TV screen, whatever the user wanted to see—not necessarily his favorite TV show, but *anything*. That meant the user was, in truth, part of the visualizer circuit, the tuner, the channel selector.

But that meant he had to *want* to see something. And the mood he had been in recently left him with very little desire to look at anything.

Not that he didn't see the world around him; it was there, and he had no choice but to be aware of it. But to actually will to see something more than that, something he didn't have to see . . .

He braced himself and turned on the visualizer. The place to attack this problem was at its root. He was afraid of the sight—and knowledge—of what Margitte was doing, what had stolen her away from him. Okay, what he had to do was face up to that sight squarely, painful though he knew it would be. Know and see the worst, and then he could look at other things without fear.

I want to see Margitte.

His heart thudded as he built this decision in his mind, and his eyes stared at the blank screen.

But it was no longer blank. The image was foggy but her face was vividly clear.

A hard shiver ran the length of his spine, and his hair stirred. His concentration skittered away and the screen was blank again.

All he had seen, he realized, was the expression on her face. It was a look he had never seen her wear, not even when they were in bed together. To see that was plenty, without seeing the cause of it. He heaved a quaking sigh and turned off the visualizer.

At any rate, he knew the device worked. Maybe it would give Margitte the sensual stimulation she seemed to live for while keeping her at home. Anything, real or imagined, that she wanted to see, without the bad-trip risk that went with acid of things she didn't want to see.

The visualizer ought to work well for her, with her sensual hunger, though it hardly worked at all for him because . . . well, because he was too scared to look. The feeling he experienced when his concentration on her image shattered made that obvious.

Still, there should be something he wanted to see, that wouldn't frighten him. Something intellectual instead of emotional. Something impersonal.

Reality! That was it. Not the routine reality of daily life, of biology, of electronic theory, of the physical laws of the universe, but the *underlying* reality—the realm of basic cause, of which all things man knew were merely effects. The reality philosophers sought after . . .

That he could look at, if it was there to see. He could face reality.

He turned the visualizer on once more, and concentrated. The screen went jet black, then some formless thing swirled on it, nearly breaking Dellbar's concentration again, but he hung on grimly. The swirl steadied and shaped itself into a man's face.

And the man was looking at Dellbar. He was aware of him.

"Well!" the man chuckled with amusement. "One of you has penetrated! Very clever!"

"Yes." That grunt was all the response Dellbar could make without breaking his concentration.

"Oh, relax!" said the man. "I'll maintain the connection for you." Dellbar did so, feeling caved in. The image stayed solid.

The man asked, "In what form do you see me?"

"As a man. An older man, with white hair. Clean shaven."

"That's appropriate enough, I suppose. Were you looking for God?"

"I-I don't know. Maybe I was," Dellbar mumbled. Then he pulled his mind together and said, "I was looking for the underlying reality."

"Aha! Why?"

Dellbar hesitated. "Because . . . I want to understand."

"I see. You think you can face understanding?"

"I don't know. I'm willing to try. I need to know there's something more than . . . well, I need to know if there's a purpose."

The image on the screen studied him with a slight smile. "There is a purpose, all right, but you flatter yourself if you think you can understand it. The closest you can come is to regard your reality as a combination kindergarten, campground, and insane asylum. It has features of each of these."

Dellbar tried to find the significance of that. "Then it is in preparation for something else," he guessed.

"Of course! How would you define 'purpose' other than as intention to prepare? But you want to know more than generalities. Here. Look at this and tell me what you see."

The image changed. Dellbar squinted his eyes.

"Boxes," he said. "Millions of boxes, stacked high, in rows. They look empty."

"They *are* empty. Every one of them. So you see them as boxes. That's close enough. They are storage bins for what you think of as souls."

"Oh." So souls were real. "Why are they all empty?" Dellbar asked.

"Why do you think?" the voice chuckled. "Consider conditions in your world today."

Dellbar did so, then hazarded, "The population explosion?"

"Obviously! The demand for souls has far exceeded the supply."

"But . . . but how can that be?" Dellbar protested. "How could there be more people than souls?"

"Very simple. Billions of people don't have souls. It is an unusual situation, of course, but no reason for that alarmed expression you're wearing. Such conditions are self-correcting."

"But that means a lot of people aren't *human!*"

The boxes vanished and the face reappeared to say, "You could put it that way. Or you might say with more accuracy, a lot of people are not *more* than human."

"They're not zombies?"

"By no means. The unsouled are distinguishable from the souled by their lack of high purpose. Take yourself, for example. You wouldn't have been interested enough to ask about underlying purpose if you had no soul. And you wouldn't have dared ask the question unless you were unconsciously certain a purpose really existed. Right?"

Dellbar nodded.

"Thus, you have a soul. Now, you tell me, how would an unsouled person think and act, in contrast to yourself."

"I suppose . . . without . . . without whatever purpose a soul has. Whatever a soul is supposed to do . . ."

"The kindergarten, campground, insane asylum program," approved the image. "Correct. The unsouled person would find random motivation for activities—mostly based on exaggerations of the normal needs of the physical body. The acquiring of more territory or mates than can be used, the consuming of more food than the body can handle, the search for sensual pleasure . . . all these are symptomatic of the unsouled."

"But there were people like that before the population explosion," Dellbar objected.

"Yes. For various reasons, not all bodies are suited as habitats for souls. But normally the unsouled persons are a small minority of the population. If present growth trends continue, they will become a majority. But as I told you, the condition is self-correcting."

"How so?"

The image shrugged. "Who do you think is more likely to start a war, or to pollute your environment . . . the souled or the unsouled man?"

"I guess the unsouled."

"So, there you have it. A self-correcting condition."

Dellbar remarked sharply, "You don't seem to care if we have a war. Are you so indifferent to human suffering?"

The image laughed at him. "You're mistaking me for one of your legendary merciful gods. I'm really just an administrator. And the general happiness or unhappiness of humanity is neither here nor there, so far as basic purpose is concerned."

"And you don't give a damn," grated Dellbar, "that I'm married to an unsouled woman—a sensual pleasure-seeker—and she keeps me in continual torment."

"Not the slightest damn," the image smiled. "However, that will change now, as a result of this conversation. Your soul is ready to move on. This doesn't mean death, so don't turn so pale. You will merely complete your existence as an unsouled person."

"You mean I'm ready to . . . to graduate from this reality?" asked Dellbar in awe.

"By no means! I mean that, having glimpsed as much of the underlying reality as you have, and as much as you can ever tolerate, you have exhausted the scope of purposive activity of your present personality. You, or rather your soul, will begin a new life in a new body. Graduation, as you call it, is several thousand lifetimes away for all you humans."

Dellbar's mind was a frantic whirl. How much of him was soul and how much was unsouled human? What would be left of him if his soul were pulled away? Not much, he was sure. Could he actually go on living in such a condition?

"What can I do with ..." he began to protest, then he saw the screen had gone blank.

He shrugged. What was the point of arguing, anyway ... especially over some nonsensical business about a soul, and with a character who had to be a figment of his imagination?

His trouble was that he had let that damned wench of his, Margitte, get him in such a stew that he was taking a bad trip without the benefit of acid. There were better uses for the visualizer than that. Why, hell, with this gadget he had invented he could become the richest man in the country! He could listen in on corporate board meetings, for instance, and get enough inside scoop to make countless killings in the stock market.

And as for women, he would be able to buy any woman he wanted, so what the hell!

But right now he was tired from working and worrying too hard. So, take it easy for a few days, and have some fun with his visualizer.

Dellbar went upstairs, made a pitcher of martinis, and returned with it to his workshop. He pulled a comfortable chair around to face the visualizer screen, poured himself a drink, relaxed, and tuned in a pornographic movie.

THE ULTIMO NOVO

The Infinity Sense

The world opened for Starn of Pack Foser one day when he was eight years old.

He had gone nearly a mile down the creek from the Compound, into a swampy tangle far from the farmed land and grazes, in hope of getting away from the other boys. Maybe Huill or Rob wouldn't bother to follow him so far, or, if they did, maybe he could guard his thoughts so they couldn't find him.

The young telepaths seldom left him in peace. The fact that Starn was large for his age, and much taller and stronger than any other eight- or nine-year-old in the Pack, seemed to give them all the more delight in their little tortures.

Starn was not a telepath, or much of anything else. His father Virnce was a pretty fair perceptor, and his mother Becca premoted now and then, but Starn couldn't do hardly anything. His only trace of a Novo ability was a sense of danger that was too weak to amount to much. So he had to control his thoughts in the swamp if he wanted to avoid discovery. He had to think things that most anybody would think, and avoid thoughts that could be identified as coming especially from him. Adults were good at doing that, after years of experience, but it was exceedingly hard for Starn.

So as he sat by the creek fishing he busied his mind by reading the book "Sacred Genetic Law" which his father had given him the year before. Lots of people read religious books if they had time to spare in the afternoons, so if he kept his mind on the book he figured he would be fairly safe. He would rather have thought about other things while he fished—of growing up to be a great raider, and leading unbelievably successful attacks on enemy Packs, and pillages of Olsapern trading posts, or even taking a whole army through the Hard Line and slaughtering hundreds of Olsapern infidels in their own country. But Huill or Rob would know if he thought things like that. So he read.

Book-English, the language in which all writing was done, was a funny language. It left out a lot of r's, especially before n's where they most always came in common talk. And it put in a lot of d's, and used m's to begin many words that really started with an n sound. It seemed to Starn that it would be better to write Book-English the way people really talked, but the Pack teacher had explained that if that were done, the religious texts would have to be revised into the new writing or people would forget how to read them. And nobody would *ever* revise the religious writings.

It was hard to believe the Olsaperns actually talked the way Book-English was written, but they did. All the kids laughed the time the teacher spoke some Olsapern to show them how it sounded. She had called Starn "Stan"—and that was something else Huill and Rob wouldn't let lie. They were always yelling "Stan, Stan, the Olsapan!" at him, and making like he really was an Olsapern because of his size and lack of Novo senses.

Perhaps this identifying thought was what gave him away, but when he sensed trouble it was too late to escape. Huill, Rob, and another boy named Houg were almost upon him. They had sneaked through the bushes, and when he detected their presence and turned they were running at him full speed. It didn't take telepathy to know they meant to push him into the creek.

Frantically Starn thought of using his fishing pole to punch them away, but that wouldn't work because they could read him and dodge the way they always did. Or he could grab a rock and . . . but that wouldn't work either.

At the last split-second, without thinking about it, Starn flopped sideways to hug the ground. Huill stumbled over him and fell down the bank. He hit the cold water with a yell. Rob was also thrown off balance and skidded down the bank on his belly, managing to stop at the water's edge. He was liberally smeared with mud.

Houg, who wasn't a telepath but a perceptor, was not caught so badly off guard. But when Starn sat up and glared at him, Houg backed off. Without the help of his telepathic buddies, he was no match for Starn and he knew it.

"T-that was a dirty trick!" shivered Huill, climbing out of the creek with his buckskins dripping, and close to tears. "You done that and didn't *think* it!"

Starn was as startled as they were. He wasn't sure just how it had happened, or if he could do it again, or . . .

"Push him in, Houg!" yelled Rob. "I'll tell you what he's thinking!"

Houg grinned and started toward Starn, who thought of flopping on his other side and jerking Houg past him, or getting up and fighting it out despite the coaching Houg would get. But Rob was spouting his plans faster than he could make them so . . .

Without planning, Starn swished his pole back over his shoulder, as if landing a fish, and dealt Houg a lashing blow on the top of his head. Houg bellowed and hastily scampered away, feeling his stinging scalp for blood.

Despite his size, Starn had never won a fight before. He felt confident and elated. "Come on! Just try something!" he challenged fiercely.

"You wait till my mamma finds out!" whined Rob, trying to rub the mud from his clothing. "Look what a mess you made!"

"Your ma'll just whip you for being a *clumsy oaf!*" retorted Starn, delighting in using the epithet that had so often been used on him.

"I'm going home!" quavered Huill.

"Me, too," said Houg.

"O.K.," giggled Starn. "Huill, you're wet anyhow, so you carry my fish! And Rob . . . well, a little mud won't hurt my fish-pole. And Houg, carry my Book-English book!"

"I ain't carrying your junk!" Rob yelled.

Starn's fist flew up suddenly and hit him in the nose. "You take that pole!" he ordered.

Rob sniffled, and obeyed, as did Huill and Houg.

But Starn gave in to their pleas before they got back to the Compound, and did not force them to humble themselves by carrying his stuff in front of the adults of the Pack. But in an isolated community of less than two hundred souls, with one out of every half-dozen a telepath, the full story wasn't long in getting around. The fact that Starn had outmaneuvered two telepaths was widely discussed around many hearths that night. Such a deed was unheard of, and there was ample speculation on the nature of the sense Starn had suddenly learned to use.

Starn basked in this new experience of adult approval, and resolved to heed the advice of his father to give his new sense a lot of exercise and make it strong.

The Foser himself visited Virnce's hut that evening, and he spoke to Starn for the first time the boy could remember.

To his parents the Pack chief said, "You must be mighty proud of your lad."

"Indeed we are!" beamed Becca, and Virnce nodded. Starn decided The Foser was awful good to say something like that about him, especially in front of the neighbors who had dropped in to talk.

Turning to the boy's father the Pack chief said, "Virnce, I'm told you have some interesting thoughts on the significance of all this. I'd like to hear them."

Virnce looked uncomfortable. "A man's thinking about his own children suffers from immodesty, Foser," he protested.

The Foser shook his head. "You were never a man to hold false pride, Virnce. And you understand and abide by the teaching of the Sacred Gene as well as any man in the Pack."

"Well," Virnce began slowly, "we are sometimes troubled at heart by false beliefs of the Olsapern kind, that we of the Packs are not the chosen of the Sacred Gene. The infidels claim that when Science fell long centuries ago, the whole of humanity suffered a deep spiritual shock of such potency that the very chromosomes of our forebears cowered in despair, and beat an evolutionary retreat.

"Thus, they pretend, we of the Packs are not a people far advanced toward the Ultimate Novo, but rather are throwbacks toward the ancestral man of a million years ago. They would have us believe that, far from leading us onward, the Sacred Gene has not simply forsaken us but has pushed us backward into savagery! They choose to ignore, or to explain away, our durable if humble civilization, the continued literacy of our children, and above all our blessed Novo senses.

"But there is, in the Novo sense my son has revealed today, something the Olsaperns cannot explain away! We know the early prophets, even in the days before Science fell, were aware of traces of telepathy, premonition, perception and the various other Novo senses in certain people of their own time. We need not believe the evil theories of the Olsaperns, that these senses were present even in the most primitive men, were perhaps even prevalent at the dawn of humankind. We need not believe this, but we have been hard put to disprove it!

"However," and here Virnce's eyes glinted triumphantly, "even the oldest of prophets and commentators make no mention of such a sense as Starn's! Nothing like it has ever been known before! It is new—Novo without question! And it is a clear manifestation of the logic and balance with which the Sacred Gene leads us forward to the Ultimate, in that it provides a desirable foil and counter to the telepathic sense he has previously bestowed on us!

"I cannot help but believe, Foser," Virnce concluded solemnly, "that in my young son the Sacred Gene not only sends us another bountiful blessing, but that he is giving his people a convincing reaffirmation: The Gene is with us; he is with us indeed!"

At that inappropriate instant Huill's mother Nari rushed into the hut and hugged Starn's mother. "Oh, Becca!" she gushed, "I'm so happy for you and Virnce! We've all felt such sympathy for you, and for poor little Starn! And now it turns out that he has this marvelous instinct!"

"*Instinct?*" flared Becca, pushing Nari away in anger. "What kind of Olsapern talk is that? As if Starn were an *animal*! Honestly, Nari, you are the most exasperating woman in the whole Pack!"

"Oh, I'm so sorry, Becca!" Nari apologized. "The word just slipped out!"

"I'll bet it did!" huffed Becca.

"Easy, Becca," soothed Virnce, putting a hand on his wife's shoulder. He looked at The Foser, at Starn, at the others, gathered before his fire, and said, "Perhaps the whole Pack has been engaging in Olsapern talk tonight, like a group of proud, senseless scientists trying to explain a new star, or a new kind of fruit. I perhaps more than the rest of you have been guilty. In our first excitement over Starn, we can pray this was a forgivable error."

In a voice of impressive depth he finished, "But we must not persist in this! Hereafter my wife and I will seek to see Starn as what he is—a blessing from the Sacred Gene to be accepted humbly and gratefully, with no questions, no attempts to pit our meager wisdom against that of the Sacred Gene himself!"

"Amen!" exclaimed Becca, with a final glare at Nari. And the others, The Foser included, echoed the word.

Good things kept happening to Starn after that. A few months later, for instance, the Pack chose his father as the Gene's Voice for the Tenthday services.

But the boy was too fascinated with his newfound sense to give more than the required amount of devotion to its mighty Bestower. He spent an hour or two every day working with Huill or Rob in mock contests, learning to act effectively, and without thinking, to meet the challenges produced by his telepathic friends. There wasn't really much to learn, except to do it. That was the right way, anyhow, because as his father had said, it would be wrong to try to figure out how the sense worked. That was the Sacred Gene's business, not his.

Starn made the most of the world which had opened to him that day by the creek. Because his sense was superbly useful in battle, especially in the raids and

counter-raids on traditional enemy Packs that had telepaths to be outwitted, his childhood dream of being a
great warrior promised to come true. In fact, at the age
of nineteen he was elected Raid Leader of the Pack.
Even at that age he was the tallest of The Foser's men,
and had physical strength to match his impressively rugged appearance.

Another high moment came when he was twenty-two.
That was when he found his wife, Cytherni, at the annual
spring parley of Packs allied to the Fosers.

Cytherni was a lovely girl, and as he had suspected
from their first meeting she was not basically the timid
person she appeared. Her initial shyness with him, and
later with the entire Pack when he brought her home,
was real, but he could guess its cause easily enough.

In fact, part of her attraction for him was a sense of
similarity—a feeling that "there, but for the grace of the
Sacred Gene, go I." Like himself, Cytherni had displayed
little Novo capability as a child; but unlike him, she had
never revealed such talents later on. Starn could readily
imagine himself growing up, without his "surprise
sense," into a person much like Cytherni. It gave him
deep pleasure to see her bloom, with fears and self-
doubts forgotten, when they were alone together.

But just four months after their marriage, Starn's
bright, open world began closing.

2

The trader Nagister Nornt was known by repute to every
Pack east of the mountains. Many people said he was

the closest man to the Ultimate Novo—the goal man of the future—then alive. Without question, his powerful Novo abilities made him someone to be feared and hated. He was a dangerous man.

But he was also a trader of unusual scope, trafficking in many goods the Packs needed—salt from the coast, bulletlead perhaps from the ruins of some ancient city, and fine, but honest, cloth from Packs far to the south who had maintained the arts of weaving. Thus, when word came that Nagister Nornt was heading their way, the people of Pack Foser were both pleased and disturbed.

The point was carefully drilled into the children that Nornt was a man to be hated, because that was the best defense against a telehypnotist who could invade and enslave an unwary mind. And they were warned not to take even the briefest nap during the several hours Nornt would be in or near the Compound, because they couldn't hate him while they slept, and could wake up with their wills in his control, doomed to be Nornt's slavies for the rest of their lives.

The trader arrived one midmorning with his vacant-eyed slavies and his heavy-loaded train of mule-drawn wagons. The Foser greeted him ceremoniously, at the same time making it clear that Nornt was to conclude his business there by midafternoon and be at least three miles away by nightfall. Nornt agreed, showing his protruding yellow teeth in an ugly grin, and proceeded to display his wares in the Compound yard.

He was a hunched, heavy man, better described as hairy-faced rather than bearded. He looked as if he had

grown bald-jowled and had left untrimmed the few strag-
gling facial hairs that remained. He smelled unclean.
Nornt was, indeed, an easy man to abhor. Starn wondered, as he made his rounds to assure himself that the
Pack's men were all armed and alert for trouble, why
the trader didn't fix himself up a bit. Surely, if hating
Nornt was a good defense against him, the trader
shouldn't make the hating so easy for everybody. But
then the Sacred Gene had made Nornt's personality what
it was, and perhaps the man was unable to change his
ways.

Nornt glanced at him and chuckled, evidently amused
at Starn's thoughts. Starn regarded him coldly before
moving away.

But Nornt had beautiful cloth, and Starn had a young
and lovely wife. It was necessary for them to do business.

When Starn returned with Cytherni, the trader was a
few yards from the cloth display with his back turned,
haggling with one of the older wives over a skin of salt.
Cytherni fingered a swath of light-blue fabric under the
dull but watchful eyes of a slavie.

"How much prime leather for the blue?" Starn asked.

"Trader trades," the slavie said tonelessly.

Starn shrugged and reconciled himself to dealing
directly with Nagister Nornt.

Nornt soon concluded the deal for the salt and turned
to face Starn and Cytherni. He did not move toward
them but stood motionless, his eyes examining the young
woman with uncouth interest.

Huill hurried to Starn's side. "Watch out!" he warned.
"He's yenning for Cytherni!"

"I can see that!" growled Starn.

"*But he means to have her!*" the telepath hissed urgently.

Starn swept a rapid glance over the slavies and found them reaching for their knives, pistols, or long-guns. "*Hold it, Nornt!*" he yelled. "Start anything here and you're a dead trader!"

"I think not!" cackled the trader. "Your men don't have—"

In a flash Starn whipped his throwing knife from its sheath. It zinged through the air to plunge deep into Nornt's right shoulder. The trader screamed and fell, and his slavies lost interest in their weapons.

"He read us that you could do things like that," Huill explained excitedly, "but he didn't believe you could fool him!"

The Foser came hurrying up. "*Trading's over!*" he bellowed. "All you women and kids go home! Get inside! Nagister Nornt, pack up and get out!" All moved to obey except Cytherni, who seemed afraid to stray from Starn's side.

Grimacing horribly, Nornt got to his feet. One of his slavies pulled the knife from his shoulder and helped him to a comfortable seat, where another removed his filthy jacket and bandaged the wound. Meanwhile the other slavies began repacking the wares and hitching the mules.

Within fifteen minutes Nornt was helped onto a wagon seat and the train started out of the Compound. The trader turned to direct a final baleful stare at Starn as he departed.

"Holy somes!" cursed Huill. "He's raving mad! I never read such hate in my life! He's not through with you, Starn! He means to even things up, and get Cytherni!"

"Let him try!" said Starn grimly. "He'll just get more of the same!"

"I don't know, Starn," said the worried telepath. "You caught him at a disadvantage today."

"No I didn't! His slavies had their weapons drawn!"

"Yeah, but to his way of thinking, he was still at a disadvantage! He was *here*, where he could be attacked, and he didn't have to be! What if he'd been waiting half a mile away, and had sent his slavies to take Cytherni or anything else he wanted? He can do that, you know! And slavies are cheap to him!"

Starn frowned. "Let's not think more about it while he's in reading range," he said. "Are you all right, Cythie?"

His wife wore a sick expression, but she nodded.

"His looks revolted her," Huill said helpfully.

"I'd better get you home," Starn told her.

That night the Pack's chief men met by The Foser's fire. Nagister Nornt, the telepaths reported, was camping for the night five miles west, and intended to continue in that direction, trading with the mountain Packs, for several weeks before turning back. But he did mean to return to Foser Compound.

"We won't let him get close!" growled Starn.

"Don't underestimate him," warned The Foser. "Huill, what do you make of his attack strategy?"

"It isn't clear," said the telepath. "He can control his thoughts unusually well, and has avoided thinking about his plans. But the picture I got was of him waiting in some safe place, and sending his slavies up to read us—he can use them as telepathic relays, you know—and to snipe our scouts and sentries. If we go out to fight, the slavies kill some of us while we're killing them, and if we don't go out they besiege the Compound. We'd have to go out."

With an unhappy expression Huill continued, "But, if we do kill his slavies, he'll just recruit more from Packs that aren't alert for trouble, or from farms that can't keep telepathic guards out all night. Thirty slavies at a time is about all he can control without straining, but he can get new ones faster than we can kill the old ones, and after each battle there'll be fewer of us left for the next fight. He means to get what he wants if he has to wipe out Pack Foser to do it!"

Starn bolted to his feet. "This is between Nornt and myself!" he snapped. "It's my fault for not finishing him today, and I'm going after him right now!"

"Sit down," said The Foser sternly. "Sit down and listen to me!" It was an order, and Starn grudgingly obeyed.

"Nagister Nornt was taken by surprise today," the Pack chief said, "because he didn't believe in your sense. Now he's seen you in action, and he won't be off guard a second time, tonight or later. He's a wily man, Starn, who's survived many battles and knows how to protect his skin. His slavies would come at you singly and in bunches, and you would have to kill them all before you got a crack at him! Don't forget that every one of those men is under his complete command! Their bodies are his, as if his brain was in each of them! Don't let the dull look of their eyes fool you!

"As for this being your fight and not the Pack's," The Foser continued, "you know better than that! You know no Pack can let an enemy demand and get his choice of its women or children! A Pack that sells out the least of its people is soon no Pack at all, but the timid prey of any raider who comes along!

"Neither the Pack nor your wife can spare you, to get yourself killed in a foolish one-man venture against Nornt! You'll defend your wife as a leader of the Pack!"

Starn snorted. "Defend her *how*? You heard what Huill said! How do we beat Nornt against that kind of strategy, and with guns no better, if as good, as his slavies have?"

"That's why we need you," The Foser explained. "Your sense will provide the answer if anything will."

Starn grunted and stalked unhappily around the fire. "My sense will help me, but in a long series of scattered skirmishes I can lose a lot of good friends, and the Pack a lot of good men, while I'm engaged elsewhere! The only way we could win would be to push through to Nornt himself, no matter what kind of defenses he threw up! We'll waste many men doing that—unless we have weapons far better than anything in the slavies' hands!"

After a moment The Foser said, "Well?"

"Well," Starn replied angrily, "we'll have to get the weapons we need! We'll have to raid the Olsaperns first, so we can fight Nagister Nornt!"

3

A raid on an Olsapern trading post wouldn't have helped. The posts were not defended by any weapons worth stealing. Starn wondered about this sometimes. Why were the Olsaperns so unconcerned about their trading posts being pillaged? Of course about the only goods they stocked were basic rations, which were freely stolen during drought years and long winters to keep the Packs alive, and such items as books and artificial fabrics, both of which the Packs disdained in favor of the honest cloth and books certain Packs produced for trading. The fact that the trading posts stayed well-stocked and practically defenseless was just one more example of the idiocy of the Olsaperns.

But the Olsaperns did have a few outposts in Pack country that were heavily defended, with the kind of weapons the Pack needed. The only such installation close to Pack Foser was a copper mine twenty miles northwest of the Compound. The mine would have to be raided.

This was not necessarily a desperate risk. The Olsaperns were a cowardly lot who seldom chose to expose themselves to battle. Trading-post keepers invariably deserted their stations when under attack, to scoot away like frightened birds in their flying machines, seldom stopping before they were safely behind the Hard Line hundreds of miles to the north.

But the mine's defenses were automated and could prove deadly effective, Starn was well aware. Perhaps the Olsaperns didn't much care about their trading posts, but they obviously cared about the tons of ore they

removed from the mine each day, to carry off in giant
flying wagons. Not since the days of Starn's great-grand-
parents had the mine's perimeter been tested by Pack
raiders, and that attack had been a disaster. Ten raiders
had been killed, and twenty-eight captured and sub-
jected to the Treatment.

Of course the long decades of peace following that
raid could have lulled the Olsaperns into letting the
defenses fall into disrepair. That could be hoped. Nevertheless, Starn laid his plans with strict care to minimize
potential losses and to put his men at the best possible
advantage. With Huill's help he questioned the Pack's
oldest members, to get the most direct accounts available
of what the long-ago raid had encountered.

What he learned made him delay the attack for three
weeks, fretting over the possibility that Nornt might
return earlier than expected, but convinced that the raid
would be far more likely to succeed if carried out in
the right kind of weather. When at last the premonitors
advised him a day-long rainstorm was due, he led his
thirty-man party forth to the attack.

They approached the mine complex in a heavy downpour, and were thoroughly soaked beneath their hard-
leather armor and face masks.

Starn intended no broad frontal attack. Against automatic defenses that would probably do nothing but
increase the casualties among his men. What he hoped
for was a point penetration, the driving of a hole through
the perimeter defenses, by which all could enter and
defeat any last-ditch stand of the Olsapern miners.

The task of making the penetration he reserved for
himself. His men gave him argument about this, but they

had to admit that he was best equipped for the job. Though there were no telepathic defenders for his special sense to surprise, his ability to act instantaneously and effectively served him well in any tight spot where there was little time for thought.

The first barrier was a fence of steel mesh, intended mainly to keep animals and hunters from straying onto dangerous ground. The party quickly chopped a slit in the mesh, and Starn stalked forward through the forest which continued for several hundred feet inside the fence. With him were Huill and a perceptor, Jaco. Six more men followed twenty yards behind, spreading out only slightly to explore the sides of the route and under urgent orders to take no chances. Their essential duties were to mark the trail clearly and to back up the three-man point, protecting its rear and coming to the rescue if that proved necessary. At intervals behind them followed two four-man squads, and then a string of two-man teams.

This needle of men was wide open to flank attack, but with defenses automated Starn expected no such counter. The unmanned weapons along their flanks would almost certainly stay poised for a frontal assault, and the only defenses the raiders needed to worry about were those almost directly ahead of them.

Have we sprung a warning system yet? Starn wondered.

"No," hissed Huill. "The Olsaperns are still thinking about their work, not about us."

Starn looked a question at Jaco, who shrugged an answer. He was percepting nothing worth reporting.

They came to the edge of the forest. Beyond lay what was once a clearing but now had grown a fair amount of cover in the form of bushes and young evergreens—a promising sign of neglect. The buildings clustered at the mine shaft rose into view no more than two hundred yards away. The only visible barrier was another fence, this a high one of strung barbed wire, some distance inside the old clearing. The scene looked dreary and deserted under the thick clouds and hard-blowing rain.

"Slowly," warned Starn, and he moved forward with Huill and Jaco close behind. Suddenly his long-gun pushed back against his chest, stopping him in his tracks.

"We're at the Metal-Stopper," he hissed over his shoulder. "I'm going to try to push through." He got a firm purchase with his cleated boots and shoved forcefully against his long-gun. It broke clear of the unseen barrier and he fell forward a few inches, to be stopped by the knife and hatchet attached to his belt. Another hard lunge put these metal objects past the barrier also.

As he had theorized, the Metal-Stopper was electromagnetic, and whatever electrical fields supported it were partially shorted out by the heavy rain. Beyond this point the earlier raiders had gone armed only with stone and wooden weapons.

"Try to get through," he told his companions.

"They know we're out here now!" Huill reported as he, too, pushed his ironware past the barrier, with Jaco close behind.

"WARNING TO INTRUDERS!" a mechanical voice bellowed in Book-English. "YOU ARE TRESPASSING ON A HEAVILY-DEFENDED INSTALLATION OF . . . OMBINE! RETU . . . EDIATELY, OR WE

WILL NOT . . . SEQUENCES! REPEATING! WARN
. . . UDER . . . ARE   TRESPASS . . . FENDED
INSTALL . . . "

"That's scaring them more than it is us!" chuckled
Huill. "They think if their loudspeakers are out of whack,
their weapons might be, too!"

"What are the weapons like?"

"They don't know. They were all installed before their
day, and are kept secret from them so telepaths can't
read them. But they're wishing they had some really
good stuff out here!"

Starn nodded. "Let's move on."

They walked forward slowly, Starn not bothering to
stay under cover of the bushes, which he figured would
be a waste of time and add dangerous footage to the
length of their trail.

"Something's moving!" Jaco hissed.

"*Down!*" yelled Starn, hitting the dirt. A split-second
later a fearsome *tat-tat-tat!* startled them, and twigs and
leaves were shredded over their heads.

"That's a rapid-fire gun!" yelled Huill.

"Where is it?" Starn shouted back.

"Beyond the barbed wire!"

We could use something like that, thought Starn. He
motioned to the others and began crawling forward on
his belly. He had not gone far when the gun's chatter
ceased.

"It's jammed," reported Jaco.

"Anything else moving up there?"

"No."

Cautiously Starn rose to his feet. Nothing happened,
so he walked on toward the fence.

"Ferrik in the back-up didn't duck fast enough," said Huill. "Bad flesh wound in the shoulder. He's being tended."

Starn nodded and kept moving. The fence, he saw, was of horizontal heavy-gauge, single-strand barbed wire, the strands about a foot apart. This was as far as the long-ago raiders had gotten, because the wire was electrified and they had lacked the means of attacking it. They had spread out along it in search of a weak spot, and that had cost them dearly.

The electricity was on, as Starn could tell from steam rising from the wet insulators on the fence posts. The rain was helping them again by shorting the wires to some degree.

"Did Houg get that chain through?" he asked.

"Yes," reported Huill.

"Tell him to bring it up."

Houg came warily forward from the back-up group, lugging a length of heavy chain.

"Put it down here," said Starn, "and all of you move back a little." As they did so, he picked up the chain, swung it in his hand to get the feel of it, and then tossed it into the barbed wire. A noisy uproar of sparks erupted as the iron links looped over the lower four strands and shorted them into the soggy ground.

"*Wow!*" complained Houg.

Starn's expectation was that the sparks would burn through the wire strands, or at least weaken them enough for him to finish the job with a quick, fairly safe swipe of his hatchet. After watching the sparks briefly, he decided the hatchet would be necessary to part the heat-resistant wire.

He wiped the hatchet handle as dry as he could get it and moved up to kneel carefully beside the dancing chain, ignoring the sparks leaping about him. He leaned forward on his left arm, took precise aim at the wires and brought the hatchet down in a firm stroke.

There was an instant of elation as he felt the blade slice through the strands, but after that a sudden nightmare of pain and confusion. The loose ends of the wire whipped and coiled like unleashed spring-steel snakes. One caught him murderously in the groin, shredding his protective leather and his flesh like so much wet paper, before jerking away to roll into a tight coil against the nearest post. Another grabbed his left forearm and didn't let go. It wrapped the arm in a tearing, bone-snapping grip, and dragged him hard into the post.

Dimly he heard Huill shouting something about "Memory Metal," and felt his companions tugging at him. *I know about things like that*, he thought in a strangely detached way. A rubber band that goes back to its original shape after it has been stretched a long time. But who would have thought a coil of wire could be made with such a strong memory, and one that would last for so many decades!

He pulled his mind back to the job and ordered, "Never mind me! Go get that gun! And other weapons!"

He didn't know if the order was obeyed or not.

4

The bed fabrics felt sleekly soft to his hands, and the bed itself strangely smooth. When he opened his eyes the flat whiteness of the ceiling overhead told him he definitely was not in Foser Compound.

An Olsapern hospital-prison? He had heard of such places from certain elderly Pack men who had been in them after being wounded and captured in skirmishes with the Olsaperns. They had been healed, given the Treatment, and released.

Suddenly remembering the slashing barbed wire, he lifted his left arm to examine it. It was strong and whole. But it wasn't his arm. A graft. He wondered who it had belonged to as he studied it, comparing its fingers—a little too long and thin—to those of his right hand.

But he had received another injury. He quickly reached under the cover to explore with anxious fingers. What he didn't find left him with a dismal empty feeling.

Despite his father's position as the Gene's Voice of Pack Foser, Starn had never been overly occupied with the forms of religion, but his faith was deep nevertheless. There was for him an essential rightness in the concept of the Ultimate Novo, the completely-sensed man of the future, the reason beyond reasons for man's existence in his present confused, troubled, and unfulfilled shapes. He was *trending* toward the Ultimate; that was his highest task.

And Starn had been specially blessed with a new sense, one that he had expected—with what he hoped was due humility—would be preserved in his offspring to bring the Ultimate Novo into being far sooner than most people would dare hope—perhaps while the name of Starn of Pack Foser was still recalled in the legends.

But he would produce no offspring now! That strand of barbed wire had seen to that!

The realization was numbingly bitter. Had the Sacred Gene forsaken him for unworthy pride? Or was his special sense of no value after all, something that should not be passed on?

And what of his wife, whose expectation of children was, if possible, stronger than his own?

But of course, he realized with a start, childlessness was a price he would have had to pay, regardless of that barbed wire, once he fell into the infidel hands of the Olsaperns. It was part of the Treatment. The Olsaperns did two things to men of the Packs taken in battle. They installed a psychological block that would prevent a released man from fighting the Olsaperns again. And they performed an operation to render him sterile, so he could breed no new enemies to attack their sons.

There was a certain comfort in this thought, because the danger of the Treatment was one that had to be faced by any man dedicated to the armed support of his Pack. That dedication made the danger acceptable, even to a special individual like Starn, because the Pack's heritable potential was more important to the Ultimate than that of any one of the Pack's members.

The door of the hospital room opened and an Olsapern walked in—one of the few Starn had ever seen in the flesh, so he studied him curiously. He looked human enough, except that he was closely shaven instead of trimmed, which gave him an odd young-old look. Other than that and his pure-white clothing, he might have passed for a Pack man—a little large, perhaps, but so was Starn.

"Awake at last, huh?" grunted the Olsapern. "I'll get you some breakfast." He left without waiting for a reply.

Starn decided that, thanks to the skills of the Olsapern medics, he felt like getting up. He found clothing, and managed to figure out how to dress himself before the orderly returned.

The food was good despite its unfamiliar taste. When he had eaten he prowled around the windowless room, tried the door and found it locked, and finally sat down on the bed. He did not rise when the door opened to let in a middle-aged man, somewhat taller than himself, in gray jacket and trousers.

"You're Raid Leader Starn of Pack Foser," the man said, not making it a question.

Starn nodded.

"My name's Higgins. I'm Director of Domestic Defense," the visitor said.

The title meant little to Starn, except that he could not recall any ex-prisoners of the Olsaperns telling of encountering such a person. He said nothing.

"That raid of yours made a real glom!" the older man finally remarked.

After a pause, Starn said, in the best Book-English he could muster, "I was not conscious to witness the outcome."

"Speak your dialect!" Higgins said impatiently. "I can understand it. As for the outcome of your raid, none of your men got much farther than you did. Two of them, named Jaco and Houg, were killed, and another besides yourself was captured. His name is Huill. He was questioned and Treated and returned to your Pack a week ago."

"Seven days?" asked Starn. "How long have I been here?"

"About three weeks."

A long time to be unconscious! thought Starn.

"You really glommed things!" Higgins grunted.

Crossly Starn responded, "What's your complaint? You beat us off, didn't you?"

"Yeah, we beat *you* off, but not before you softened the mine's outer defenses, and spied some of our interior layout! And you Pack people, with your lousy telepaths, can't keep secrets! So when Nagister Nornt came along a day later he helped himself to weapons none of you should have, much less Nagister Nornt!"

Startled, Starn asked, "What has he done with the weapons?"

"For one thing he's forced your Pack to hand over your wife! And he shot up two of our trading posts!"

Starn sat in stiff silence, trying to conceal his sick dismay.

"One consoling thought for you," the Olsapern added, "is that your wife was already pregnant."

"Cytherni pregnant?" gasped Starn.

"She was waiting until after the raid to tell you, and the telepaths were keeping her secret. Nornt will not make a slavie out of her as long as she's cooperative."

"You got this from Huill?"

"Partly. We made him talk freely."

"Where's Nornt now?"

"If I knew, I might not be here!" growled Higgins. "We've got to recover those weapons! And kill him if we get the chance! He's trouble now, and could be *big* trouble in the future!"

***

Starn had been about to demand his immediate release, so he could hunt Nornt down and rescue Cytherni. But the words "big trouble in the future" made him pause.

Yes, the Ultimate Novo would definitely be "big trouble in the future" for Higgins and all the obsolete Olsaperns! And though Starn wanted Cytherni back, and wanted to be the known father of his unborn child, the fact remained that he could give Cytherni no more children. And Nornt, distasteful though the thought might be, could! Also, Nornt could very well be in direct line to the Ultimate! Personal animosity had to be thrust aside for such a profound religious consideration.

He saw that Higgins was watching him with an air of almost friendly expectancy. A very clever fellow, this Higgins! The way he seemed to take for granted that Starn was his ally against Nornt was so convincing that Starn had been almost taken in! But Higgins had let slip a telling reminder that he was an Olsapern, while Starn and Nornt were Pack men.

It was a mistake, Starn decided, to even converse with this man. So he sat in silence.

Higgins fidgeted and growled, "No trafficking with the enemy, huh? O.K., if you're the kind who'll let his only child be destroyed by that creature Nornt, there's no point in talking!" He started for the door.

"*Hold it!*" snarled Starn. "Nornt won't destroy my child!"

Higgins turned. "No? Do you think he'll let your child grow up to challenge his own brood? Nornt believes in his own bloodline, not yours!"

"That's absurd! It's against the creed of the Sacred Gene!"

Higgins shrugged. "All I know is what I was told by the men who returned your friend Huill to Foser Compound. They parleyed with your Pack chief, who told them what Nornt had thought when he discovered his prize was pregnant. He doesn't mean to let your child grow up, creed or no creed! Oh, he'll make a pretense for a few years, to keep the child's mother content. But when the child's about six . . . well, it will 'wander off' some day and never be found! And not being a telepath, your wife won't learn the truth from Nornt!"

"That's the kind of lie I ought to expect from degraded infidel scum!" roared Starn, surging to his feet and facing the bigger man.

But Higgins showed no anger nor intention to fight. He smiled, and shook his head sadly.

"I don't wish to argue religion with you, Raid Leader," he said. "That would only raise animosity between us, and stir up side issues at a time when we ought to work together for a common cause. But let me point out a couple of facts. One, if I'm lying, you'll find that out soon enough when you return to your Compound, so the lies would have gained me nothing. Two, if Nagister Nornt is a step toward where your Sacred Gene wants humanity to go, then your Gene has chosen a most despicable vessel!"

"The ways of the Gene are mysterious to the eyes of man," Starn quoted sternly.

"They are that!" sighed Higgins. "So mysterious that he can lead you in reverse for centuries and you still think you're going forward!"

"The way of the Gene has no turning!" snapped Starn. He stared at the Olsapern in disgust. "Even your primitive Science should tell you that! The ancients knew that evolution moved steadily ahead, as relentless as death and time!"

"That was one of the errors of the Science Age," said Higgins easily. "They knew so much that they didn't know how much was still unknown! Don't try to tie me down to the beliefs of Science, Raid Leader! That age fell under its own weight, and good riddance! It was just another experience men should learn from, although many men, including your own ancestors, learned less than they should!

"There are relationships, Raid Leader, that ancient scientists never recognized. They specialized too much to see the broad interweavings of nature. For example, they never observed the linkages between certain unconscious levels of the mind and the information of heredity which is coded in DNA molecules. Consequently, they would have denied as readily as you do that the profound psychological shock which hit the human race when the Science Age toppled could have any direct effect on our evolutionary process. They would have said the extreme change in environment would make certain traits more suitable for survival than if the Science Age had continued, but this would merely be a change in the selection vector, not in the evolutionary force itself.

"But we know differently today, Raid Leader. The state of the human mind *can* communicate with the genetic code structure, thereby changing the structure. And the collapse of human morale that went with the collapse of Science was a clear message—a signal to retreat!—to the codons of the vast majority of the race! About the only people who escaped the reversal were the few who realized that the Science Age *should* fall, that despite its victories it had turned reactionary and anticreative."

Higgins paused, then concluded thoughtfully, "I hope history will call our own time the Creative Age. Science could have been that, but despite its lip service it never really loved creativity, nor fostered the creative personality. Probably not one of its adults in a hundred was allowed to develop into effective creativity, and that alone was enough to doom the Science Age!"

Trembling with rage, Starn forced himself to sit down on the bed again. Such heresy was hard to endure! Especially that absurdity about the human mind influencing—actually changing!—DNA! As if the humble human intellect could not only *enter* the inviolable abode of the Sacred Gene in man, but could *pillage* there!

Still, Higgins had been right about one thing: the futility of religious argument between Pack man and Olsapern. And he might be right in his estimation of Nagister Nornt. The telehypnotic trader would indeed be a despicable vessel for the will of the Sacred Gene, particularly if he meant to subvert that will by murdering Starn's child.

At last Starn growled, "If you Olsaperns are so creative, why don't you create a way to catch Nagister Nornt?"

"Self-restraint," answered Higgins. "I'm not going to explain that, because it's something you shouldn't know.

I'll only say that we limit ourselves, in our relations with the Pack people, in the materials and techniques we use. I'm pretty sure you won't believe that; otherwise I wouldn't have said even that much!"

"You're right, I don't!" grumbled Starn. "But never mind. You want me to find Nornt and kill him, don't you?"

Higgins nodded. "I'm prepared to give you a little help if you'll try."

"What kind of help?"

"Have you ever noticed that Treated men are poor hunters and fighters?" asked Higgins.

"No. The only ones I know are old men."

"Well, they are. The psychological block that keeps them from fighting us can't be strictly contained. It dims their combative spark generally. If you're going up against Nagister Nornt, you'll have a better chance if you're left Untreated. So here's my offer, Raid Leader: I'll release you without Treatment in return for your solemn oath to never participate in hostile action against normal—against the Old Sapiens as you call us—in the future."

Starn gave a grunt of disbelief. "You can't break your rules like that!"

"Rules are useful in ordinary situations," replied Higgins. "They are meant to be broken when an emergency demands radical action."

This was a strange attitude toward rules, but it was of no concern to Starn. The offer was one he felt he could honestly accept. "I solemnly promise not to war against the Olsaperns in the future," he said.

"Good! Now let's get you home! And this time, for pity's sake, follow your own ideas when you go after Nornt! Don't let anybody sidetrack you the way they did before!"

"Huh? Who sidetracked me? How?" demanded Starn.

"Your Pack chief. He insisted that you work with the Pack instead of going after Nornt as soon as you were aware of the danger! From what I've learned of this so-called 'surprise sense' of yours, I'm pretty sure you could have killed him then, while he was wounded and confused. All this glom would have been avoided!"

Starn stared at the man. Higgins was full of surprises, himself! He all but admitted the Olsaperns' inability to track down Nornt; he broke a basic rule to help Starn do the job instead; and now he seemed to be half-praising a Novo sense! But then the Olsaperns lacked a religion of their own, in opposition to that of the Packs. They had a sort of nonreligion. And maybe a nonreligion wasn't of much help in keeping a man's thinking straight. Or maybe the Olsaperns were finally falling apart, as they were destined to do sooner or later, anyway.

But Starn found Higgins' advice in accord with his own thinking, so he nodded. "I wished many times that I had gone after Nornt immediately. If I had settled everything then, Cytherni and I would still be like we were."

"I don't know about that," frowned Higgins. "I think you could have killed him, but he would probably have finished you while you were doing it! What I'm saying is that this whole glom would have been avoided, which would have suited me fine!"

5

Starn returned to Foser Compound for two days, just long enough to pay his respects to his parents and The Foser and to rearm himself. He needed a telepathic companion, and was pleased when Huill volunteered. He had learned that Huill had been captured by the Olsaperns because he had stayed at the electric fence, trying to free Starn, until it was too late to escape. Even though Huill had been Treated, Starn felt high confidence in him.

They set out on horseback, following Nornt to the south. Trailing the trader, which the Olsaperns had found all but impossible, was no job at all for them. They could ask friendly questions and get friendly answers from the folk who lived along the way. Nornt was not trying to conceal his tracks. He was trading as he went, in his usual manner. The telepaths Huill communicated with generally knew where Nornt intended to make his next few stops, but he was avoiding thoughts of his winter destination.

"He's worrying everybody," remarked Huill after they were several days on the road. "They don't like the way he's thinking. He wants . . . *everything!* He was vaguely like that all along, but since he captured those Olsapern weapons and took Cytherni, he's much worse! He thinks about having children who will be telehypnotics like himself, and about getting craftsmen together who can copy those weapons. He's figuring his sons and weapons will make him king of the world!"

Starn nodded grimly. "The Olsaperns seem to be afraid of something like that," he agreed.

"I thought they'd never quit probing at me about him and his Novo ability," complained Huill. It went on for hours, and they got more worried, the more I told them! They made me talk a lot about you, too."

"I can imagine," said Starn.

"But your Novo ability didn't worry them. It just aroused their curiosity, because it was something they had never heard of before."

"Isn't Nornt's a new one, too?" Starn asked.

"They don't think so . . . well, of course, you know they don't think *any* Novo senses are really new, and that people had them back when we were still almost like the apes a million years ago. But they think there have been people with a little of what Nornt has in historical times—a combination of telepathy and hypnotic force. They think men like Alexander, Hitler, Rasputin, Barstokee and Quillet had touches of it."

"All those men were supposed to be crazy," Starn remarked.

"And you think Nornt isn't!" said Huill. "The Olsaperns call him a megalomaniac."

"They seem to know all about him, except how to catch him," Starn remarked wryly.

"They're a knowing bunch of people," replied Huill seriously. "Of course, they're wrong about a lot of things, too, like thinking we're subhuman and that the Novo senses aren't worth studying, much less having. But you know what, Starn?"

"What?"

"One of the Olsaperns who questioned me would be a telepath if he could let himself. He had the sense; I could feel the shape of it in him. But, somehow, he couldn't use it at all. I guess because if he could, that would've made him a Pack man."

The mountains slanted eastward to the south and Nornt's trail gradually climbed into the higher foothills. Starn had been thinking for days about possible strategies of attack, but as he and Huill approached maximum telepathic range of the trader he dropped these thoughts. Instead, he concentrated on getting into a position where he and Huill would have flexibility of action—where his special sense would have plenty of room in which to work.

The foothills seemed right for this. They were almost empty of people, and provided a variety of covers and obstacles, without fettering choices the way high mountains could.

He was under no delusion that victory was assured. Nornt had around twenty slavies to throw into the fight, and he would not hesitate to expose them to any risk imaginable to save himself.

But in compensation, Starn had his advantage of surprise. This was no small thing in conflicts where full telepathic knowledge of the opponents' plans and strategies was taken for granted. As Raid Leader of Pack Foser, Starn's unanticipated actions and decisions had often given his men a more than momentary advantage, because of the time required for the enemy to shift forces to meet a totally unexpected situation.

They were riding up a thickly-wooded valley, following the bed of an ancient highway, when Huill made contact with Nornt's rear guard. "Three of them!" he reported. "About half a mile ahead of us and a mile behind the main train with one telepathic relay between them! They're on horseback!"

"Let's take them!" snapped Starn, pushing his mount into a gallop.

Huill stayed alongside him. He chuckled. "Nornt didn't expect us! He's in a panic ... Something about getting to Pile-Up Mountain ... Hey, guess what? He premotes the Olsaperns are in this with us! Instead of running he's driving his wagons off the road to get them out of sight of Olsapern fliers!"

"Why does he think that? Can't he read us?"

"Yeah, but he thinks we could be leading the Olsaperns to him without us knowing about it! He figures they made you trackable somehow while you were captured!"

It was a strange but possible notion which Starn wondered about briefly and dismissed. There were more urgent matters to think of.

"Can we overtake the rear guard before they reach the wagons?" he asked.

"I think so. He's making them slow up to hold us back while he fortifies himself. He's trying to get the Olsapern guns set up! Hey, the rear guard's turned off to the west! Nornt figures we'll either have to follow them down or take a chance of having them come in behind us!"

"He's right," said Starn grimly. "We follow the rear guards. Lead the way!"

A short distance farther Huill swung off to the right in the track of the three riders. Meanwhile, he reported, Nornt was deploying his men in defensive positions.

"Can you read Cytherni?" asked Stare.

"Indirectly, yes. She's all right. He's still leaving her alone in return for her good behavior. She doesn't know what's scaring him ... doesn't know you're here."

"What about the men we're chasing?"

"They're riding hard, and Nornt's looking for a good place for them to make a stand." A few minutes passed. "Stop!" yelled Huill.

"They've ridden out of range! No need to chase them any farther."

"How'd they outdistance us?" Starn demanded.

"Not us! I mean they're out of Nornt's range! They're not his men any longer! And not our enemies . . . not much use to themselves either!" Huill looked a bit sick from what he was seeing in the ex-slavies' minds. "They'll die soon if somebody doesn't find them and take them in."

"Let's head back," Starn ordered. They turned their horses and he asked, "Why did he let them get away?"

"He didn't intend to. It's hard to judge telepathic range when you travel twisted roads like these. He's down to seventeen men now."

Starn nodded, wondering if he and Huill would have to fight them all before getting at Nornt.

"He sure means for us to!" said Huill. "He's trying to locate ten of them out where they can close in on us no matter where we strike!" He described the terrain between them and Nornt, and the placement of the defenders.

They were less than a mile from the wagons when Starn noticed a trail angling off to the left and apparently up a low ridge that paralleled the road. Without hesitation he swung his mount into the trail and up the ridge.

"He didn't notice this trail," informed Huill.

"I hoped he hadn't. How many men are in front of us?"

"Just four on the ridge. But those across the road are moving over to head us off . . . A steep bank in the road-cut's blocking them! They can't get up in time!"

Starn grinned. His sense was working with its usual success! "Nornt's crazy-mad!" Huill reported gleefully. "You ought to read the things he's thinking about us! He's going to fight his men like maniacs!"

"Be ready to yell and jump for cover the instant one of them sees us," warned Starn.

Their horses galloped along the silent ridge, both men sharply alert.

"Jump!" Huill yelled suddenly.

Starn tensed but didn't jump. Instead he spurred his horse into a sudden sprint forward.

Gunfire spurted from the bushes ahead, and Starn heard an answering bark from Huill's long-gun. His surprise maneuver had fooled the defenders, though. At least two of them fired where he would have been if he had jumped, and the other two had shot at Huill. Before they could cock and re-aim he had ridden past them and leaped from his horse. They were caught between an enemy in front and an enemy behind.

His first shot downed the only slavie in plain sight, while Huill yelled hoarsely, telling him there were two left and their locations. Starn stayed low, making swift moves as his sense inspired him. The slavies took several shots, all aimed at him as far as he could tell. Huill's gun spoke twice more giving him covering fire. Finally he brought a slavie into plain view and shot him through the chest as he was raising his gun.

"The last one's taking off down the south slope!" called Huill in a tight voice.

Is Huill hurt? Starn wondered, dashing after the slavie.

"In the leg, just as I jumped!" Huill yelled the reply. "Get him and hurry back!"

Starn put caution aside as he dashed after his quarry. When he was halfway down the hillside and approaching a rocky bald area he heard Huill's distant bellow. *"To your left!"*

Starn dropped on his backside to slide down a pebbly stretch while his eyes searched for the enemy. A spurt of gunfire, aimed too high, revealed the man, and Starn threw a pistol shot at him. The man rolled out of his hiding place with dying hands clutching his stomach.

"They're up the bank!" Starn heard Huill's dim call.

Hurriedly he started back, losing his footing once on the loose pebbles. He had not gone far when he heard Huill shout, *"They're on me!"* A volley of shots rang out.

"Huill!" he called in the ensuing silence.

No answer.

Without hesitation but with deep sorrow, Starn turned left toward the wagons, fighting his way through the undergrowth at a dead run. Telepathically blind now, his only hope was to bull and sense his way through to Nornt, and kill the man before the slavies could kill him. From what Huill had said of the terrain, the wagons and their master had to be somewhere below the south end of the ridge. If he could find a high spot that overlooked them . . .

He could hear the slavies thrashing through the woods some distance to his rear and to his right. At best, he had only a half-minute lead on them. He would have to hurry if he—

A long-gun spurted from behind a tree just ahead of him and a slug hit his left shoulder, knocking him sprawling. He clung to his rifle but was lying on top of it. Before he could get it into action the slavie stepped out of hiding and shot him in the right forearm.

"I gave your friend a clean death, Starn the Olsaperns' eunuch!" said the slavie, voicing Nornt's thoughts with an expressionless face. "He was a mere telepath who never did me any real harm. But you and that quick knife of yours have caused me much pain! During the next few minutes, before you die, you're going to suffer as much as I have in the past two months!"

The slavie's gun fired again, and the slug tore into Starn's left ankle. The other slavies had arrived by then, and a couple of them got out their knives and began methodically slashing and stabbing Starn's limbs and body, careful not to deliver any immediately fatal wounds, and pausing when he almost blacked out.

"You should see yourself, eunuch!" said the first slavie. "What a revolting shambles you are! Even your friends the Olsaperns couldn't patch your body now! Especially after we break your spine in a few places! Try to stay with us for this, eunuch! I don't want you to miss any of the fun!"

But when something heavy struck him in the small of the back, the torture ended for Starn.

6

He was shocked into sudden wakefulness. Overhead was a white ceiling he had seen before, and at one side was the remembered face of the Olsapern Higgins. Two white-clad medics were detaching electrodes from his chest and wheeling a machine away from his bedside.

"Sorry we couldn't get there fast enough to save more of you, Starn," said Higgins. "And there was nothing we could do for your friend Huill. He was shot through the head. But we arrived in time to keep them from damaging your brain, and everything else is replaceable."

Starn regarded him steadily and replied, "I'm not grateful for this, Olsapern."

Higgins muttered "I suppose not," and turned away for a moment. Then he asked, "How do you feel?"

"Like I ought to be dead," grunted Starn. But he sat up with a feeling of dreamy detachment and looked down at his bare body.

No, not his body, but a fair copy. At least it wasn't the patchwork of grafts he expected to see. But on the other hand, it was not quite real human flesh. And it definitely did not *feel* real. The sensations of touch, when he experimentally squeezed his left arm, were strange. His brain got the message all right: that his forearm was being squeezed by his right hand. But it was as if the message was in a new language with a new sound. There was no suggestion of pain, for one thing.

"What is this?" he asked.

"Your body? It's an artificial structure, a sort of machine of pseudo-flesh and bone. I'm sorry it has to be artificial. We can regenerate your entire body—your brain contains all the information needed for that, of course—but that takes time we don't have. Nagister Nornt is still at large, and your wife is still in his hands."

"She can stay there," retorted Starn dully. "He defeated me in a fair fight—his Novo abilities against mine. That ends it."

Higgins frowned thoughtfully. "You mean he's proved himself your superior, and has earned the privilege of mating with your wife, and destroying your own child, without further interference from you," he said.

Starn winced but nodded.

"That's the will of your Sacred Gene, so to speak."

Again Starn nodded.

Higgins grunted in disgust. "I halfway anticipated this! How do you like that? I anticipated your attitude without being a premonitor! Get some clothes on! I'm sending you on a little trip!"

A few minutes later Starn was put aboard a flier which carried him south almost to the Hard Line that guarded the Olsapern border. The craft set down at a small complex of buildings and the pilot ushered him into one of them. An older Olsapern than Starn had seen before greeted him.

"My name's Richhold, and I'm an anthropologist if that means anything to you," the man said. "I understand I'm supposed to give you an illustrated lecture, in the company of an old friend of yours. Holden, send that telepath in."

The pilot went out and a few moments later Rob of Pack Foser entered.

"Rob!" exclaimed Starn. "It's good to see you!"

Rob stared at him, gasped, and backed away. "W-what are you?" he stuttered in terror.

"Why . . . I'm Starn, Rob! I know I don't look exactly like I did, but I'm still me!".

"But I c-can't read you! I can't even know you're there!"

"You mean I'm a blank?" asked Starn in amazement.

Rob gulped and nodded.

Starn could guess what must have happened. The Olsaperns had some means of screening a brain against telepathy, and they had built the screen into his artificial skull. This was a numbing thought, because Starn had never heard of such a thing, and was, therefore, inclined to doubt if it could have come out of the Science Age. If it had, it would have been used before now, and there would be legends about it.

And it was completely unacceptable that either the ancient scientists or their diehard followers, the Olsaperns, had devised a counter to telepathy that even outdid his own Gene-given sense!

The Olsapern Richhold fidgeted impatiently while Starn and Rob discussed these thoughts. "Never mind that!" the old man snapped at last. "You don't know what you're talking about, anyway! You're here to learn a few things, and this telepath was talked into coming so he could verify that what I tell you is the truth, so far as I know it. So let's get started!"

He waved his hand and a wall of the room vanished to display a series of projections and exhibits. Richhold spoke boredly about what was being shown, as if this were elementary stuff that he had recounted a hundred times before.

The lecture proceeded backward through the history of man, starting with a typical Olsapern figure and modifying it step by step, back to a creature Richhold called "the link." Each modification was justified by the replica of a skeleton which he said originated in the era being described.

"You don't see people today who look like the link," said Richhold when the backward journey was completed. "But let's come forward and look again at some later models."

The projection revealed a squat, scraggly-haired creature with a near-gorilla face and a sharply-receding forehead. "Higgins said he wanted you to take a good look at this one. Resemble anyone you know?"

Starn grimaced with annoyance but nodded. Higgins' intentions in exposing him to this lecture were obvious, because the projection looked like Nornt, except Nornt's forehead was higher and straighter.

"All right," said Richhold, "let's move several thousand years closer to the present." He chuckled and glanced at Rob when the new image appeared.

"My head's not that low!" snarled the telepath.

"True," agreed Richhold, "but look at the shape of your jaw, and the form and stance of your body!"

"Hold on!" said Starn. "People come in all shapes and sizes, and you know it! Higgins is a large man; you're small! The pilot who brought me here is thin; one of the men at the hospital is fat! And your faces and heads have different shapes!"

"We're dealing with averages!" snapped Richhold crossly.

"But that's not all!" said Starn. "How do you get off calling us apemen when you can see our brains are much bigger than those you've been showing us?"

Richhold shrugged. "Cave bats go blind in a comparatively few generations, but keep their eyes much longer. Land animals which return to live in the sea keep vestiges of their legs for millions of years, and seldom lose their lungs at all. So in man the brain grew and developed slowly as he became more advanced; now the portion of the race that is regressing isn't losing its big brain immediately. You won't be exactly the same on the way down as you were on the way up. You'll carry remembrances of what you were. But the big brain will finally go."

"You claim to be so all-knowing about the direction we're going," sneered Starn, "but your whole theory depends on that stupid idea Higgins told me about—that the unconscious mind can communicate with the chromosomes. How do you know that nuclear radiation didn't cause the mutations of the Pack men, aside from the ones authored by the Sacred Gene to give us our senses? There was radiation when Science fell, wasn't there?"

"Radiation had its effects, certainly," rapped Richhold, "but they were doubtless random in direction, seldom even viable. Don't argue with facts, young man! There is evidence in plenty that Pack mutations have been in a regressive direction.

"As for that 'stupid idea' as you call it, of a linkage between the unconscious and the genetic structure, its existence has been rigorously demonstrated by a means I can't expect you to understand. The ancients almost discovered it, but they were looking in the wrong direction and for something else at that time. They were trying to find a cure for the aging process, of all things!"

"They discovered that the cells of normal human tissue can subdivide through only sixty cell-generations or thereabouts, before the cells lose their functionality and die out. They were very interested in discovering the reason for this, hoping thereby to make their cells, and thus themselves, practically immortal.

"The reason is obvious, of course, to anyone who knows communication theory. In repeated transmissions any message suffers a loss of information. That's entropy, young man, and it's unavoidable. When a cell divides, it must, in a real sense, transmit its genetic message to both new cells. The information loss is unimportant through many subdivisions, but becomes critical in human cells after about fifty generations. After that the cells, the tissues, the human body in general, must go downhill at a rather rapid rate.

"But instead of asking why human cells deteriorate, the ancients should have been asking a far more important question: Why do other types of living cells fail to deteriorate? Why do one-celled animals go on subdividing for millions of years without apparent loss of genetic information? Is the code transmission mechanism in these creatures perfectly error-free?

"The answer is that it can't be; no such process is perfect! There has to be a corrective agent, something completely outside all the redundancies and other corrective processes of the transmission mechanism itself, something that 'knows' when the message is getting garbled, and can step in and clear it up.

"The word 'consciousness' is as good a description for that agent as I can expect you to understand. One-celled animals have it. So do many kinds of cells in plants, and in other animals.

"But it is missing in the cells of humans, and in other animals that stop growing when they reach maturity. Why is it missing? Because in these creatures 'consciousness' has become concentrated in special organs, to serve the needs of the animal as a whole. This is a kind of sacrifice cells are often called on to make when they become components of a more complex organism. They give up their abilities to respond as individuals to environmental stimuli—to light, to heat, to contact, even to the presence of nourishment.

"But that old cellular consciousness of the genetic message is not completely lost when the consciousness becomes concentrated. It is still there, almost totally buried in the unconscious mind of the human, but functional to a limited extent. The mind can direct it at times, provided the mind maintains the same desire with sufficient intensity through a sufficiency of human generations.

"Thus, when the post-Science environment told the average human 'Retreat!' the message got through. And your genes retreated! Back to primitivism!"

Starn gazed at Richhold for a long moment after the scientist fell silent. Then he said, "This 'consciousness' you speak of sounds to me like an Olsapern version of the Sacred Gene. What does it do that the Sacred Gene cannot?"

"Nothing," shrugged Richhold. "The only difference is that the 'consciousness' is real. Probably so!"

Starn glanced a question at Rob, but got no response. He had forgotten the telepath couldn't read him. "Does he believe all that nonsense?" he had to ask aloud.

Rob nodded. "As far as he knows, he's telling it straight. And the Olsaperns think he's very wise about such things." His voice took on a whining tone. "He's got me all confused! I can't go back to the Pack halfway believing the stuff he's said! They'd kick me out!"

"We're not novices in dealing with such trivial mental problems!" snorted Richhold. "You'll be hypnoed into forgetting everything you've experienced here! It's a shame in a way to send you back as ignorant as you came, but that's our policy, and a necessary one."

Rob looked relieved.

The stunning thing to Starn was not that Rob had found the mind of Richhold honest, but that, after looking behind the man's thoughts as they were expressed, the telepath had been forced to believe them!—or if not to believe, then at least to doubt the eternal truths of the Sacred Gene and the Ultimate Novo!

The whole matter was so completely absurd!

In a mental turmoil, he scarcely realized his interview with Richhold was over, and that Rob was rather nervously shaking his hand and saying, "Great Gene, Starn, I'm glad I won't have to remember this, or seeing you all vacant inside!"

He remained in a distracted state all the way back to the hospital-prison, where he was vaguely relieved not to find Higgins waiting for him in his room. He was in no condition to talk to the Olsapern or to anybody else.

7

Higgins stayed away for two days, until Starn came out of his shocked stupor. When he appeared, Starn glowered at him.

"I've got one question to ask you Olsaperns, Higgins: *Where do you think you're going?* You have no belief in the Gene, so how do you find any purpose or direction in your lives? What are you good for?"

Higgins smiled at him. "Old Richhold really shook you up, didn't he? Where are we going? The same place you think you are! Toward a more advanced human species! The difference is that we define the superman quite a bit differently than you.

"Take these Novo senses, for instance. Did Richhold tell you the theory that apemen had some of them a million years ago?"

"I've heard that one before," growled Starn.

"Of course, it's only a theory and can't be proved. Some of Richhold's colleagues say the Novo senses are just make-work activity for your left-over big brains, but others suspect that the dawn men needed those special senses to survive in a savage environment, full of enemies stronger and faster—and at that time probably just as bright—than they were.

"That may be right. At any rate, the Novo senses can't be the next step up for man, because they make a specialist out of him! Man's whole strength is his *lack* of specialty, his ability to find ways to live anywhere, eat anything, do anything! Specialists are so loaded with their special equipment that they can't change! They're static, inflexible!

"What would your Ultimate Novo be, Starn? Telepathic, premonitorial, perceptional, and maybe hypnotic like Nornt? All right, what would he *do* with all those abilities? Would he use them to build a marvelous civilization?"

"Certainly!" replied Starn.

"I'm not so sure he would," chuckled Higgins, "but let's say you're right. He builds his Ultimate civilization, but what does he do *then?*"

"He *lives* in it, naturally!"

"Forever?"

"Well . . . " Starn hesitated, suspecting a trap.

"Ah, there's the rub!" trumpeted Higgins. "Forever's a long time! And what will keep your Ultimate Novo from asking himself the same question you asked me? Where will *he* be going, Starn?"

"Perhaps there will be more Novo senses to develop, senses we don't know about now," Starn replied.

"Ah! Then he won't be the Ultimate until he's acquired them all! You're begging the question! Once the *ultimate* Ultimate comes, where does he go from there?"

"Why do you think he'll have to go anywhere?" stormed Starn. "We don't know what he'll be like! Maybe he wouldn't *need* a purpose in life of the kind we understand!"

"Very good!" approved Higgins wryly. "That's the kind of unanswerable supposition that makes further debate futile! But it leaves one question open: Is such an unstriving Ultimate man the kind of goal you striving Pack people consider worthy of your centuries of toil and deprivation? Can you really devote yourself to achieving that kind of result?"

Starn shrugged. What was the use of arguing with an Olsapern who thought he knew all the answers?

After a pause Higgins went on: "Striving, like generalizing, is a basic feature of man, Starn. Make man a specialist and he'll be less than human. And if something ever stopped him from striving the same thing would happen.

"You call us infidels because we don't take your Sacred Gene seriously, except as a scientific principle. And you consider us obsolete, partly because we don't have Novo senses but more because we refuse to disdain the Science Age as an era of rampant evil. Certainly the Science Age brought its own destruction with it, and nearly destroyed man in the process! But that was because it was too much like the civilization you dream of for your Ultimate Novo! It built itself a super structure of interdependent techniques and specialties, social orders, and economic mores that had to become increasingly rigid simply to support itself, the bigger and more complex it grew. It couldn't *create* answers to the kinds of problems it faced because it was unable to accept those problems. Its rigidity led to its final ruin when it had to change, but couldn't.

"We're not trying to recreate the Science Age, Starn! We know of too many things that were wrong with it! But we do recognize that science was a tremendous step forward for man. Whereas your people have opted for its total rejection, we have tried to retain it, not as a divine revelation or a way of life never to be modified, but as what it was—a step forward.

"In the last analysis, Starn, the mistake of the Science Age was the same one you're guilty of, and the same one the Christian priests made in pre-Science times—the same one practically all civilization-builders have made. You strive for an end to strife—for permanence, either now or in some dreamed-of future, despite the fact that permanence is against the nature of man and the world."

Starn remarked, "Then you think man's real future lies in ceaseless change?"

"Yes."

"But you're opposed to change in man himself!" Starn shot back. "You find excuses to treat Novo senses as a dead end, and you refuse to see them when you have them yourselves! You may be right about a lot of things, but you're wrong about the Packs being subhuman, and Novo senses worthless!"

"*Why* are we wrong? Where's the flaw in our picture?"

"I don't know," Starn admitted angrily, "*but the flaw is there somewhere!*"

Higgins laughed and replied patiently, "What's the better means of communication, Starn, a language or telepathy? Remember that telepathy has no privacy, as Nornt recently demonstrated to your Pack's dismay. Remember, too, that language can be transmitted over vast distances, and that if it is well-structured and effectively used, it can carry almost precisely the message the sender intends, with no unwanted and perhaps embarrassing side-disclosures."

Starn recalled with a slight wince the anguish of his childhood, when he had to force himself to control his odd thoughts and wild daydreams to avoid the censuring laughter of his telepathic playmates. Of course his childish thoughts were probably worthless, but . . .

But Higgins was continuing: "What's the better means of exploring your surroundings, Starn, special devices we can imagine and create, or your perception? You've noticed, I suppose, that a perceptor detects only objects in motion, and usually only objects moving toward him. Did you know that your weak 'danger sense' is a form of perception that works only when something is moving up behind you? You're not much of a Novo, Starn, with just that one weak sense."

Starn tended to forget his "danger sense" because it proved useful to him so seldom. But Higgins was wrong in saying that was his only Novo sense. He was about to protest when Higgins again interrupted his train of thought.

"And what about premonition? Isn't it far better to understand the functionings of man and nature, so well as to predict what they are likely to do next, than to depend on the spotty, over-emotionalized glimpses of the future your premonitors can produce?

"And the same is true, I think, of any other Novo sense you might propose. With a little effort and creative imagination, we can come up with something better! And with us, it's an open-ended process! Creative imagination knows no ultimate limit, Starn, and has no ultimate goal. It just keeps going! If anything can give man unending existence in a changing universe, his creative mind will do it!"

When Starn finally replied, his question sounded like a non sequitur, but Higgins did not treat it as such.

"Why didn't you let me die?"

The Olsapern smiled. "Because I was using my creative imagination! Sure, we could dream up some means of hunting Nornt down without your help, but that sort of dreaming can take time, and we want Nornt stopped quickly.

"As I told you before, there are methods we refrain from using. I suppose I can explain that to you now. We try not to reveal our capabilities too fully to the Pack people. We use almost nothing in our defenses that was not known to the Science Age, and the only members of our society who allow themselves within reading distance of your telepaths are . . . well, they're our lower-intelligence citizens who don't know—and don't care to learn—just what our capabilities are. You remember that Rob's memories of contact with Richhold had to be erased? Also, it would be bad for the Packs to learn of your artificial body.

"The reason for all this is that we don't want to give the Pack people's morale another shock that would hasten their evolutionary retreat! The past has made them all too susceptible to that kind of damage!

"So you can see why you're the weapon we need, Starn. If you kill Nornt, we will not need to display ourselves to the detriment of the Pack people. Also, we won't run the risk of making a martyr of that madman, which is something else we want to avoid!

"We think your wife and child are worth saving, Starn. Are you with us?"

Starn was tempted. He realized that his religious faith had been seriously eroded by Richhold and Higgins. He no longer felt he would be morally wrong in continuing his battle with a man who had once defeated him fairly. And the sense of deep depression with which he had awakened in his artificial body was giving away to a restlessness, a desire to be doing *something*—anything at all.

But he shrugged. "What would be the use? What happened before would happen again. I'm the same man Nornt has proved he can beat."

"Not quite," replied Higgins. "Rob couldn't read you, remember! You were a blank to him. You would be the same to Nornt and his slavies! He wouldn't even know you were around unless someone was eyeballing you! And he'll find this body of yours isn't easy to kill!"

Starn considered this. What Higgins said was probably true, and that would make a fight with Nornt a very unusual affair! It would be more like a hunt than a battle. The old woodman skills of following sign and tracking would be more critical, perhaps, than the Novo senses. To a man who had always enjoyed hunting, it was an appealing picture.

Slowly he nodded.

"Fine!" exclaimed Higgins. "Now, there's just one problem that can't be solved the way we did before. Your people won't accept you now, because you can't be read—and we don't want them in contact with you, anyway. So the question is; how do we locate Nornt?"

"I think I know where he is," said Starn thoughtfully. "Something Huill caught from his thoughts when we first came in range and frightened him. He thought about Pile-Up Mountain. I'll look for him there."

8

Pile-Up Mountain was a lonely peak at the end of a minor offshoot of the main range. It stood above a low rolling countryside that, while thickly wooded and certainly fertile, was seldom trod by men. The area had an evil repute, and was the subject of numerous ugly legends. Probably some time in the dim centuries of the past, perhaps all the way back in the years of terror following the fall of Science, deeds of great horror had happened thereabouts.

In the pre-dawn of a crisp winter morning a dark Olsapern flier dropped onto a bald strip of old roadway three miles from the mountain, and Starn leaped to the ground. The flier soared away, to follow, from great altitude, Starn's fortunes through special devices included in his artificial body.

Starn walked rapidly toward the mountain, taking advantage of what darkness was left to get close while there was little risk of being seen. The old roadway brought him close under the mountain's steep eastern slope, where he turned into the thick underbrush and began a slow ascent. By then there was enough light to disclose footprints or other signs of man. He did not unsling his long gun, but carried at the ready the weapon he preferred under the circumstances: a powerful bow.

He reached the sheer rockwall that stood around the summit without seeing a trace of human trail. This was not surprising; assuming that Nornt really was somewhere about, he would have no need to send his slavies out on sentry patrols. He could trust telepathy to detect any nearby intruders, with perhaps one lookout on the summit to watch for fires and smoke beyond telepathic range.

There would be a trail somewhere, through a break in the rockwall, leading to the summit. Starn began working his way along the foot of the cliff.

He circled almost halfway around the peak before hitting the path. Then he paused in thought. Should he climb to the summit and kill the lookout? If nothing else, the mysterious death of the slavie would scare Nornt, and a frightened opponent was seldom a clever opponent.

The decision was taken out of his hands by the sound of footsteps coming up the trail—the morning relief on his way up to replace the night lookout. Starn readied his bow, crouched out of sight behind some brush, and waited.

Starn did not shoot at first sight. He waited until he recognized the slack emptiness of face that marked the man for what he was. Then Starn put an arrow through his throat. The slavie fell, tumbled a few yards down the slope, and lay still.

Starn readied another arrow and waited. Only a few minutes passed before the lookout came rushing down the path, sent by Nornt to learn what accident had befallen his relief. Starn waited until he reached the fallen man, and stood gazing down at him, before zinging an arrow at his back. But this slavie—or perhaps Nornt himself through his presence in the slavie's mind—had a danger sense similar to Starn's. The slavie jumped sideways almost as soon as the arrow flew and took it in his sleeve. He whirled with long gun raised and fired at Starn, who had dropped to the ground as he brought his own gun into play.

The slavie did not shoot a second time. He simply stared at Starn until a slug smashed through his heart.

Nornt was just as shocked as Rob had been, Starn guessed, to see a blank man, particularly an enemy probably presumed dead who rose from the ground to kill his slavies. The thing to do was give him no time to recover his wits. With long paces Starn hurried down the trail.

Ghosts were not prominent in Pack religion, since it was not based on expectations of a surviving personal soul. But there were tales of certain spirits of departed men, particularly men whose deaths had been unusually painful and brutal, which walked in evil places on the earth. And Pile-Up Mountain was supposedly an evil place. Nornt probably had little belief in such tales; else he would not have chosen the spot as his hideaway. But if he could be made uncertain, just for a little while, the result could be most important to Starn.

He rounded a curve in the trail and confronted two slavies. He raised his gun and fired, killing one, then leaped sideways. But Nornt had learned something from his previous brushes with Starn. The other slavie did not shoot immediately, but waited until the leap was completed. His slug ploughed into Starn's chest, knocking him backwards. With his gun recocked, he sat up and plugged the slavie in the act of rushing forward.

Starn had little time for curiosity about his wound, from which a blood-red oil was oozing. The point was that he was still functioning, so no vital part had been hit. The Olsaperns had provided some sticky repair patches for such eventualities, so he pressed one over the hole and continued down the trail.

As soon as the terrain opened enough he left the path and crept through the brush, to guard against being caught in an ambush. Moving slowly, he went some three hundred yards before his danger sense awakened suddenly to make him whirl and hit the dirt. He had bypassed an ambush, and now the slavies were spreading out through the woods behind him. He could not see them, but the crackling of bushes told the story. Cautiously he readied his bow and waited until the one headed in his direction came into view. He shot him through the heart.

The noise of the other slavies increased as their search became more frantic, but, as Starn had hoped, they did not close in on his position. Since telepathy was only roughly directional, it could actually be confusing when people were spread out and hidden from each other in unfamiliar surroundings. Neither Nornt nor the other slavies knew just where the dead one had been in relation to them, and Starn's silent arrow had not betrayed his position.

Cautiously he crept away from the sound of the hunt, and continued in the direction he had been going, roughly parallel to the trail.

The path curved back to him, and after peering up and down he stepped into the open and increased his speed. The slavies he had slipped past would soon be brought scurrying back to provide Nornt a close defense, and he had to stay ahead of them.

He came upon the tunnel mouth suddenly, and sprinted for cover through a hail of slugs that spurted from an Olsapern weapon concealed within the dark opening. He was hit three times, twice in the body and once in the left arm. The arm was obviously broken, and he had no time for complicated repairs. He discarded his bow—useless to a one-armed man—and edged with a stumbling gait to a spot from which he could approach the tunnel from the side, unseen until he stepped into the opening itself. This maneuver would have brought defenders hurrying into the open if he had been readable, but as a telepathic blank he got away with it.

He entered the tunnel in a staggering run and pushed past the Olsapern weapon and the slavie operating it, collecting two more slugs in the lower part of his body. He shot the slavie down and hastily examined the weapon. The Olsaperns had explained the functioning of these automatic guns to him, and it was easy to adjust this one to fire at anybody approaching or entering the tunnel.

He noticed he was leaking red oil quite rapidly now, and his legs were working erratically. Something in his body had been damaged by those last slugs. But he had escaped head wounds, and he guessed his strange body-machine would keep working in some fashion as long as his brain was undamaged. He turned and limped deeper into the tunnel, which was dimly lit by occasional oil lamps perched in recesses high in the walls.

"*Starn of Pack Foser!*" the voice of a female slavie called from some distance ahead. "*Leave immediately or I will kill your pregnant wife!*"

"That will unite her with me, Nagister Nornt!" he responded hollowly. "Go ahead!"

The voice blasphemed the Sacred Gene and fell silent. Starn moved ahead as fast as he could, his eyes and ears alert for possible attacks from the dark side tunnels. Evidently the carved-out underground labyrinth was huge, and he could not guess its original purpose. He followed the lamps which lighted the portion Nornt was using, guessing they would lead him finally to his enemy. A muffled rattle came from the Olsapern weapon back at the entrance, presumably halting the slavies who had followed him down the trail.

But there was enough trouble waiting for him just ahead, where he rounded an oblique turn and faced Nornt and his final line of defense less than one hundred feet away.

Two Olsapern guns opened fire and the slugs knocked him flat on his back. He had caught a glimpse of two slavie women operating them, of a third female armed with an ordinary long-gun, of the wild face of Nagister Nornt glaring hate at him, and behind them all a huddled form which he guessed was Cytherni.

He had rolled behind the angle in the wall, out of range of the guns. His body was riddled with holes! And the tunnel was totally silent, which hardly seemed likely, so his hearing was obviously knocked out. With a clumsy right hand he explored his head and found a gaping hole through his forehead. A slug had passed through the center of his skull, and even yet he was functioning after a fashion!

The Olsaperns must have placed his brain elsewhere in his body, but where he had no idea. He didn't seem to have enough unpunctured area *anywhere* to contain a cat's brain!

His sight was flickering on and off, and he knew he had little time left. He managed to drag himself erect and lurch forward, his long gun up and ready for one final shot, and his body leaning into the hail of bullets.

He stumbled toward the spurting gunfire, forcing himself to keep moving as the slugs tore at his artificial flesh.

He raised his wavering gun to aim at Nornt's frantic form, then hesitated as his sight flicked off. When his eyes came on again he adjusted his aim, but suddenly fell forward on his face when the Olsapern weapons stopped spurting at him. He was having trouble moving any part of himself, but finally managed to twist his head around so he could see what was happening.

The slavie women were slumped like discarded dolls behind their weapons. Nornt's mouth was open and frothy with screams Starn could not hear, and he cowered back in terror when Starn's eyes stared at him. Cytherni was moving. She took a long-gun from a limp slavie woman, raised it, and shot Nornt down. Then she gazed in horror at Starn for an instant before crumpling.

Starn tried to call out to her, but his voice was gone. Soon whatever life his artificial form had ever held was gone as well.

9

The dreams went on and on.

Sometimes there were scenes; sometimes there were thoughts that strung themselves together into patterns that seemed to hold astonishing power, but these patterns were elusive. They were suddenly unrememberable when a dim awareness attempted to grasp and hold them.

Scenes and thoughts came and went.

He was fishing on the creekbank, and whirled to confront an approaching danger, and there was Nagister Nornt screaming soundlessly . . . A snake of steel was crumpling his left arm . . , His father was preaching at the Tenthday service and was shouting: "Where is the flaw in our reasoning?" (No, it wasn't his father, it was Higgins.) He stood up and started to answer the question but couldn't remember what the question was . . . His body was being flexed—was this a dream—while it hung suspended between six glowing suns . . . He was with Huill swimming in the river and the water—so warm—swirled against his bare skin . . . He was arguing with Higgins . . . His mother was cooking breakfast, but he was too tired and sleepy to get out of bed . . . Music was weaving strange patterns and somebody was talking in Book-English . . .

There were more scenes, and some returned again and again. The elusive answers and the flexing and the music and the swirling water. The face of Higgins loomed over him against a smooth white ceiling and it said, "You're awake now."

Starn sat up in bed, wondering how many more times this was going to happen in dream or reality, and realized that indeed he was awake.

He stared around the hospital room, trying to get the fantasies in his mind labeled as such and thrust aside, and to remember his last real moment of consciousness. It had to be in the tunnel, when Cytherni had killed Nornt, but that seemed so long ago! He had been in an artificial body which Nornt's slavies had shot up, and—

He looked up at Higgins with a sudden question. "Where was my brain?"

"Here in this building," the Olsapern replied. He grinned. "We finally got a bright idea on how to defeat a telepath! Nornt couldn't read a mind that wasn't even there! So we kept your brain safely bedded down here, but directing your body through a highly redundant system of transceivers. Nornt must have thought he was fighting a ghost!"

"That's what I tried to make him think," said Starn. "Otherwise he might have killed Cytherni. Is she all right?"

"Oh yes, she's fine! She and the baby will be in to see you shortly, but I wanted to look you over first. Do you feel normal now?"

"I suppose so," shrugged Starn.

"Still a faithful sheep of the Sacred Gene?"

. Starn growled at the frivolous tone of the question, "After the way you've used me, Olsapern, I don't even have faith in my own death anymore!"

"Don't take it too hard, lad!" chuckled Higgins. "That's done with now! I'm not unsympathetic about your state of mind. You've lived through more weirdness than an ordinary Pack man could possibly endure. I'm not sure I could have stood it myself! But you've got an innate flexibility of mind, lad, that couldn't be stiffened by all the rigidities of Pack law and religion! Frankly, I envy you more than I sympathize with you!"

Starn shook his head at this puzzling speech. He got out of bed and looked around for clothes. "If you're through with me," he grumbled, "I want to get back to Foser Compound. Bring in my wife and ... *baby did you say?*"

"That's right," nodded Higgins.

"But ... but Cytherni was only ... five months gone!"

"And your baby is now nearly a year old," agreed Higgins. "Quit hunting for clothes and go take a look at yourself in the mirror."

✦✦✦

Starn glared at him, and then strode to the full-length mirror on the door. He gazed at his image for several minutes without speaking.

It was his own body, in perfect condition. He had his own left arm back, and . . . and he was a whole man again.

He realized Higgins once remarking that the brain contained all the information needed to reconstruct its body. No wonder those dreams had seemed so endless! They had lasted more than a year while his body was building.

The wonder of his discovery lessened as he stood gazing at his reflection, but his elation grew. He was beginning to remember—and grasp—some of those thoughts that had eluded him during his long dream-state. What he saw in the mirror fit those thoughts precisely.

So far as his appearance was concerned, the kids in the Pack had been right. His posture was too erect, his shoulders too horizontal, his belly too flat, and his head too big for him to look like a Pack man. Physically, even allowing some spread for individual differences, he was thoroughly Olsapern!

And it didn't matter! Except that it supported his new thoughts. After all, he had two Novo senses, one major and one minor.

He thought of Cytherni's figure and frowned. In a purely feminine way, her form departed from the Pack norm in the same direction as his. She had shown no Novo senses . . . but then not every individual had to be living proof of his theory.

Almost to himself he remarked, "She couldn't have given Nornt children that resembled him."

"Your wife?" said Higgins. "Probably true. I have a theory that something deep in Nornt's genetic structure knew he had to be defeated. That Sacred Gene of yours abhors regression in the final analysis, and is trying to block wrong-way evolution among the Pack people. The combination of factors leading to environmental and psychosomatic shock when the Science Age collapsed is breaking up now, as the existence of you and your wife and son amply testify. Anyway, when Nornt chose his mate, something right in all his wrongness led him to pick a woman who could not possibly give birth to a telehypnotist. As I told you before, a rapport exists between genetic information and certain unconscious levels of the mind, so—"

"You always have a theory, don't you, Higgins?" Starn broke in impatiently. "A theory, and a framework of facts to hang it on. But somehow, Higgins, your theories always seem to know more than your facts do!"

Higgins shrugged. "That's the way knowledge advances, Starn. A lot of old information, plus a new bit or two, plus a few guesses about how the new bits fit in and what they mean. We keep in mind that our theories are just guesses. They don't get in the way of recognition of new information when it comes along. Not anymore. We stay flexible."

"You do, do you?" grunted Starn disdainfully. "Then tell me this: How is it that you've never theorized that the genetic shock effects of the fall of Science didn't end quickly, within a couple of generations after the event? The fall wouldn't be much of a shock to people who had no personal memory of it, would it? But as Richhold said, genetic changes don't come and go in one generation. If the Pack people were thrown back then, we could still be showing the effects in our shapes today."

Higgins looked a little surprised, but after a moment he nodded. "An expert in the field might argue with you on that. But I know no objection to the idea. Not that it matters either way . . . "

"No? Well, tell me this, Higgins. Have your people ever made a study of Pack people's traits, from generation to generation, to see if physical indications of regression are rising or falling at the same rate as the Novo senses?"

"I doubt it," said Higgins.

"Then how, in the name of the Sacred Gene or the objective knowledge you pretend to worship, can you tie the two things together? You've failed to make the kind of study that would provide real evidence for or against your belief that the Novo senses and the regressive signs have the same source! You have no use for the Novo senses, just like the ancient scientists. But you can't deny their existence like they did, so instead you put your evidence together in a way that says 'Novo senses are primitive, and no good!'

"What's more, you've overlooked something important about this connection you say exists between the genetic structures and the unconscious mind. The Pack people have been seeking stronger Novo senses for hundreds of years! Our unconscious minds must be as aware of that as they were of the fall of Science! Why don't you admit that this desire might be getting through to our chromosomes, Higgins? Is it because that would be admitting the Pack people are making progress in a very real way, and in a way you haven't touched with all your miraculous gadgetry?"

"Nonsense!" Higgins exploded. "Of all the absurd, self-justifying pieces of warped reasoning I've ever heard—"

"Don't get so red in the face, Higgins," Starn chided him icily. "After all, I was merely presenting a theory."

"Umpf!" grunted Higgins, obviously annoyed at himself over his loss of temper. He simmered down. "I'm sorry I blew up that way, Starn. As you say, you were merely presenting a theory—an extremely childish one, I must say, but . . . "

"Where's the flaw?" asked Starn.

"Let's see if I have this straight," said Higgins. "Your idea is that the fall of Science did have a regressive effect on the Pack people, but that this had nothing to do with the Novo senses, which received their stimulus later on, and from another source."

"That's about it. Where's the flaw?"

"Well, I can't say right off. But *there has to be one there somewhere!* Something wrong in another way, though, is your motivation for producing such a theory. You have a deep emotional need for it to be true, Starn! The truth of a theory with such a motivation is necessarily suspect."

"And doesn't that apply to Olsapern theories that make Pack men degenerates?" demanded Starn.

"Absolutely not! We have no ill will toward the Pack people. Our trading posts, which we keep going solely to relieve hardships within the Packs, should make that clear."

"Solely for that reason?" Starn countered. "Don't you think helping the poor Pack savages gives you another reason to feel superior? Or that you might actually be trying to keep us inferior by making us dependent?"

Higgins grimaced angrily and strode off across the room to gaze out a window. Starn smiled. He had the Olsapern on the run.

"Don't ignore the lesson of this fight with Nagister Nornt, Higgins," he continued relentlessly. "Your science didn't stop him, and our Novo senses didn't stop him. He was beaten by the *combination* of the two, working together! We needed your talents and you needed ours! You can't keep pretending the Novo senses are worthless, and beneath the attention and understanding of your scientists, when you find them very worthwhile indeed when you're face to face with a dangerous enemy.

"And one final point, which my father made years ago: What about my own special sense, Higgins? I know you Olsaperns are fascinated and puzzled by it. Why? Because it is without precedent! You can't find a single slim thread of evidence tying it to ancestral man! That disturbs you, doesn't it? You're afraid it is something completely new, something leading directly toward the Ultimate Novo!"

He fell silent and eyed Higgins expectantly, waiting for the man to turn and face him. But when Higgins turned, the smile on his face was not one of gracious surrender. It was, startlingly, a smile of triumph.

"Starn, lad," he chuckled, "how can you be so sure you're right about everything else when you're so totally wrong about *yourself!* A special Novo sense? Hell, boy! You have no such thing! What you have is a *creative mind,* and a fine one even if it is overloaded with non-sense! That 'special sense' is something you created, to meet a critical need of your boyhood, to make you the equal or better of your telepathic playmates!"

Starn shook his head. "It was nothing I did. It was just there."

"Not when you first needed it. Not until you were eight years old. You needed it before then. Novo senses don't wait that late to appear, do they?"

Starn frowned but didn't speak as Higgins continued, "We know quite a bit about the creative process, lad. It's our stock in trade, after all. One thing we know is that it isn't a conscious process entirely. The key activity is unconscious. Of course you have to be aware of a problem that urgently needs solving. Also, it helps to cast around consciously for an answer, or for data and ideas that might help supply one, but this is only to feed the unconscious mind, and to focus its attention. The creative solution doesn't come from reasoning and the use of logic. It suddenly just flashes up from the unconscious! Then all you have to do is make it work.

"In your case, you had to have a defense against tele-paths, and your unconscious went to work on the problem. When you were fishing that day and needed the solution, the unconscious had finished its job and gave you the answer! Of course you couldn't understand that it was something you had created—that was part of the solution. You had to think it was a Novo sense, because nothing else would have made you normal and acceptable."

Higgins beamed at him. "Why do you think we've gone to such expenditure of effort and resources to grow you a new and genuine body, now that Nornt is disposed of? Out of sheer gratitude? Not that we're ungrateful for your valuable collaboration in a critical matter, but . . . well, gratitude isn't that strong a motivation.

"We did it because of the unique quality of your *mind,* your creative potential. We don't know of any mind ever displaying such flexibility, or such immediate or total rapport between conscious and unconscious as that 'special sense' of yours requires. Your wife has more than a touch of it, herself, and your son—well, we'll have to watch him and see. The point is, you've got the seeds of greatness in you, Starn!"

Feeling stunned, Starn slumped on the bed. He had found reason to reject many Olsapern theories, and those objections still held good whether Higgins accepted them or not. But so far as the nature of his own, highly-prized special sense was concerned, the Olsaperns were obviously and damnably right!

Novo senses did *not* wait until the age of eight to suddenly appear. And there were his strange dream experiences, while his new body was growing, in which hundreds of thoughts and clues had milled around, finally fitting themselves together into answers to the puzzling mysteries that had plagued him for so long—answers that came readily to conscious recall after he woke. The experience fitted Higgins' description of creative thinking with appalling accuracy.

"Then there is nothing special about me," Starn muttered. "No special sense."

"The only special sense anybody needs," Higgins beamed cheerily. "The infinity sense—the creative imagination. There's no limit to it."

Starn hardly heard him, because the world that had opened when he was eight years old had finally, irretrievably closed. He was no unique step toward the Ultimate Novo. He was, in fact, little more than what he looked like—an Olsapern with a silly imagination!

His failure to make Higgins see the value of the Novo senses was another blow. Because he had been wrong about one thing—himself—he had given Higgins the only excuse the man needed to conclude, quite comfortably, that he was wrong about everything else as well.

Why, if Higgins thought his mind was so uniquely gifted, was he so eager to discard its products?

Because, Starn realized. Higgins had a mind every bit as tightly closed as that of Starn's own father, back in Foser Compound preaching the gospel of the Sacred Gene and belaboring the sins of the Olsaperns! Higgins could give all the lip service he wished to "objectivity" and willing receptiveness of new data and theories, but on the subject of Novo senses his views were more firmly fixed than the stars in the sky. Reasoning and debating the question would never sway him, nor in all probability the majority of Olsaperns, by an inch!

And with that thought, Starn suddenly saw what he had to do. The infinity sense? That's what Higgins had called it, although creative imagination was not really a "sense" in a strict interpretation of the word. But if that was what Starn had, he might as well put it to work!

Higgins was talking: " . . . So why don't you dress and I'll send in your wife and son? Too bad we can't continue this discussion for hours, and clear up some of your faulty assumptions. But other duties are calling me."

"O.K.," said Starn distractedly, and began dressing as Higgins left.

His reunion with Cytherni and his introduction to his son was a moment of joy that briefly dispelled his doubts and gloom. But the decision he had reached a few moments earlier was going to affect the futures of his wife and child as well as himself. He had to talk it over with her, and hardly knew how to begin.

For a while Cytherni did not give him a chance. He had never seen her in such a talkative mood.

"And you should see the lovely house and things they've given us," she chattered rapidly, "with a garden and lots of forest and a sciencey kitchen you just wouldn't believe and a whole room full of books and a flier I've already learned to operate and I've taken up paint-sculpturing which is an art-form and a lot of people like my work and say it's imaginative and . . ."

She saw that Starn was staring at her strangely, and came to an uneasy silence. She looked embarrassed.

"You have liked it here?" he asked.

"Oh yes!"

Starn sighed. That eased him of part of his burden, at least.

"Cythie," he began, "it's been so long since we've talked that I'm afraid I'll sound like a stranger to you. I've thought about things we never thought about before. The Olsaperns aren't wrong about everything, Cythie. They've got a part of the truth. Their science has a reality. But in the Packs we have another part, and it is real and true, too, in its way.

"But . . . but the two parts have to be put together, Cythie! And nobody wants to! The Packs want nothing to do with Olsaperns and their science, and the Olsaperns refuse to study the Novo senses of the Packs. But if we ever hope to know the whole truth—and maybe if we ever expect to reach Ultimate Novo—they have to come together!

"The Olsaperns say I have an unusually strong creative imagination, Cythie . . . "

"Oh, you *have,* Starn," she replied earnestly.

"Well, it looks like that's about the only thing unusual I do have," he said, "so I'm going to use it. I'm going to stay here and try to become a scientist, Cythie! I'll never convince the Packs and Olsaperns that they have to get together by arguing with them. I'll have to show them! I'll have to prove the value of studying the Novo senses by doing it myself, and then producing results!

"So I can't go home, Cythie! There's too much to learn here that I can't learn in the Compound. And I already know things the Olsaperns couldn't let me take home in my head, so they would have to put me through hypnotic erasure to remove that knowledge, and I'd have to start from scratch when I came back.

"I'll have to spend my whole life with the Olsaperns, Cythie, because . . . well, because this is what I have to do. I hope you will stay too. This must sound strange and outlandish to you, but one thing about me hasn't changed. I still love you. Very much."

Suddenly she was in his arms sobbing happily. "Oh, Starn, you big oaf! I was so afraid you would insist on going back! And I don't think I could have, not with little William, or Billy, or Huill, or whatever you decide to call him! Did you think for a second that I could allow our son to suffer through the same kind of childhood we had, with those awful telepaths telling him what he could and couldn't think? I couldn't bear it!"

"You mean you would want to stay here, even if I didn't?" Starn asked, astonished.

"Yes. And don't worry about our people wondering what became of us. When the Olsaperns picked me up at Pile-Up Mountain, they took me to Foser Compound, and the telepaths read me. They know I killed Nornt and they think you're dead, because that's what I thought then. I had ... gone crazy ... so the people let the Olsaperns take me to cure me. That's all Higgins says the Pack people ought to ever know. We don't have to go back."

Starn held her close. Cytherni, the very best part of his old world now closed forever, was going to be with him in whatever new world was opening. And ahead was work to be done—a challenge of sweeping import that would have been incomprehensible to him in his earlier life.

The realization came abruptly that he had gained far more than he had lost.

The Mind-Changer

When the opportunity finally came, Starn didn't like it.

The worst aspect of it was that he would have to use his wife Cytherni, without her knowledge or agreement. This would be far less forgivable than the use Higgins had made of *him*, to get rid of the telehypnotic megalomaniac Nagister Nornt. Although Starn had required a little coaxing along the way, he had been a willing weapon in the hands of the Olsapern Minister of Domestic Defense. Nornt had abducted Cytherni, and that gave Starn ample reason of his own for wanting the man killed.

Nevertheless, while he liked Higgins well enough, Starn could not quite forget that the man had used him. This was a source of antagonism that lingered after five years of frequent association between the two men. Higgins had done his duty effectively by using Starn, and had to be respected for that. But Starn couldn't *admire* him for it.

How, then, could he ever hope for Cytherni to forgive her own husband if he pulled the scheme he had in mind?

The idea hit him late one afternoon when, feeling frustrated by the slowness of his research work, he had left his workshop and strolled through the house to visit Cytherni's studio. She was working on a large abstract piece of paint-sculpture, so he perched on a stool to chat with her while he watched.

Paint-sculpting was a highly sophisticated and effective art form, and the process of creating in this field was a fascinating one to observe. The "canvas" was a three-dimensional matrix of menergy—stuff related to the solid force fields which formed the Hard Line defensive barrier along the Olsapern border—into which paint was injected and precisely located through slender needles of unwettable insulation. The elements of the menergy matrix were flexible enough to allow limited motion, which was powered like the matrix itself by a small nuclear source that usually wound up well concealed in the finished work of art.

The injected paint did not dry; it remained liquid and mobile, but confined by the matrix elements to its proper place in the composition. It could gleam with the wetness of life, of glowing lips or bedewed leaves. And depending on the motions of matrix elements, lips could smile, leaves could quake, sunlit waters could ripple.

The art form was one which Cytherni had mastered quickly after coming to Olsapern country. Because of her Pack upbringing, her works had an appeal for the Olsaperns that was both primitive and exotic, and were in much demand.

In a way this bothered Starn. In the austere society of the Packs, a husband who did not provide for his family was a worthless creature, deserving of little respect. Conditions were, of course, different among the Olsaperns. The necessity of "earning a living" was a concept that didn't apply where advanced technologies supplied an abundance of the necessities and luxuries of life. A person's worth was judged by criteria other than his earning power.

Yet, even from the Olsapern viewpoint, the fact was that Cytherni was providing something society found worthwhile, and Starn was not. She was the valuable member of the family. And Starn, who chose to devote himself to investigation of the Novo senses, was doing something the Olsaperns not only failed to appreciate, but refused to recognize as even having potential value.

Starn was as philosophical as he could be about this, but couldn't help feeling like a squaw-man sometimes. His self-esteem had to suffer terrific punishment, and would have suffered still more if he hadn't been thoroughly convinced of the importance of his researches.

But all in all, he was not an unhappy man. He could appreciate his work though nobody else could—except, of course, his young son Billy and to some extent Cytherni. And he had his wife and boy.

For a man who was grimly determined to rip up the fabric of human society, Starn was about as content as any man could possibly be.

"What do you think you're grinning at?" Cytherni mock-scolded. Starn chuckled. "Same thing as usual. Those busts of Billy." He motioned toward the two life-size replicas of their son's head and shoulders sitting side by side on a nearby table. "Maybe they're not great art to the Olsaperns, but I think they're the most delightful work you've done!"

"You're as bad as Billy!" she complained, although she was obviously pleased. "It's not enough for him to stand giggling at them for ten minutes at a time. After lunch today he brought three of his playmates in to join him."

"Did they see the humor?"

"Yes indeed. The little Carsen boy nearly split his sides. They're not *that* funny!"

"I'm not so sure," said Starn, walking over to take another close look at the heads.

Unlike her usual work, these were strictly representational. Each of them looked enough like Billy to be a color triphoto. And at first glance, there was no difference at all between the pair. Only after looking at them for a few moments would someone who knew the boy's parents realize that one of the pieces grasped that which was his mother in the son while the other portrayed him as a reincarnation of his father. To a large degree, these separate resemblances were brought out not by form but by subtle differences in motion of the head, eyes, eyebrows, lips and chin. The movements were all slight, but they succeeded in capturing the special little individual mannerisms of each parent.

The wonder of it to Starn was that Cytherni had been able to portray *herself* with such amused objectivity.

Why had she done the pair of portraits? His guess was that they had a religious significance to her, that they were an apologetic memorial to a god she no longer worshiped: the Sacred Gene, deity of the Packs.

"I know who would like to have them, and wouldn't find them funny at all," she remarked.

"Who?"

"The grandparents. The one with you in it for your folks, and the one I'm in for mine."

Starn nodded thoughtfully. Yes, his own parents would cherish that lifelike representation of Billy, especially so since they had never been permitted to learn that Starn himself had survived the conflict with Nagister Nornt. So would Cytherni's people in Pack Diston. Continuity of genetic inheritance was all-important to Pack people. A concrete reminder of Billy's existence would mean much to his grandparents.

"Do you suppose we can send them the portraits?" asked Cytherni.

"We can ask Higgins about it tonight," said Starn. "It will be up to him to say if it's all right."

"You'll ask him?" Cytherni persisted.

"Yes, after supper when he's full of venison steak."

She nodded her satisfaction.

But Starn had little doubt that Higgins' answer would be negative. Because . . . well, he could imagine a number of reasons the Defense Minister might consider important.

That was when the idea struck him. He fought against it for a while, dismayed by the personal unhappiness it could bring to his wife—and also to himself and to Billy.

But he had a strong conviction his scheme would work, while nothing else would.

So, if Higgins did turn down their request, and if Cytherni's desire to get the portraits to the grandparents was as determined as Starn suspected, then . . .

"Why so silent, lover?" Cytherni asked.

"Oh . . . thinking about my work," said Starn, "trying to figure out how to make some progress with it." Which was true enough.

Cytherni smiled encouragingly. "Give yourself time, Starn. You'll do it."

"Maybe." He stood up. "I'll give it a little more effort before supper."

He walked back toward his workshop, but detoured into the flier port on the way. If he tried his scheme, there were preparations to be made, precautions to be taken, things to be checked.

He spent several minutes going over the flier, and examining the emergency supplies and equipment in its luggage compartment. He added a few more items from his workshop and the kitchen shelves. Then he stood in the port, gazing at the craft in momentary uncertainty.

There would be at least one tracking device on the flier, probably several. Without question, he and Cytherni were kept under close surveillance by Higgins' department. Nothing less than that would make sense. While he and Cytherni had been welcomed into Olsapern society and given all the freedom of other Olsapern citizens, the fact remained that they were enemy aliens by birth and upbringing. The Minister of Domestic

Defense would have had to be stupid indeed not to keep close tabs on their behavior.

So the ship contained trackers—and for that matter so doubtless did his own body, and Cytherni's, perhaps Billy's as well. And a tracker could do double duty as an auditory pickup, a bug. On his forays against Nagister Nornt, Starn's fortunes had been followed from a distance, through such devices in his body, by Olsapern observers and mop-up men.

The trackers in the flier, he decided, would have to be left undisturbed. But not those in himself, his wife, and son. They had to be put out of action when the proper time came.

And he wasn't at all sure he could knock out the trackers by the method he had in mind! If he failed, his scheme was doomed from the beginning—and the Olsaperns certainly would not allow him sufficient freedom afterward to try again.

A man had to be pretty desperate, he suddenly realized, to forge ahead with so risky an enterprise. But if he passed up the opportunity Cytherni had unwittingly provided, when, if ever, would he get another?

He couldn't back down.

After Higgins and Starn were settled down to the enjoyment of a couple of pre-supper drinks, the conversation was inconsequential for a while. Then Higgins asked in a slighting tone, "Well, lad, I suppose you're still trying to make sense out of the Novo senses?"

Starn nodded. He had hoped Higgins would bring the subject up during this visit. "Yes, I'm still at it. In fact,

I think I'm making some progress. There's something I'd like you to look at while you're here."

Higgins grimaced. "No thanks. Such things are out of my line. If you think you've discovered something worth consideration by others, take it up with some expert in the field."

"Such as who?" demanded Starn with a humorless grin. "You have no experts on the Novo senses—only experts in saying the field isn't worth studying."

Higgins shrugged. "Well, they ought to know! I wish, Starn, that you would get this pointless obsession out of your system, and devote yourself to *valuable* work. It's a shame for a creative talent such as yours to go to waste. I mean that! You've got one of the best minds on Earth, and one that has become well-educated since you left the Packs. Why can't you put it to work on one of the major unsolved mysteries of science, for instance?"

"Aside from the fact that I think what I'm doing is more important," Starn answered slowly, "there's also the point that I haven't lived with my Olsapern education long enough to use it with the ease a creative researcher needs. My memory's full of new information, but somehow that information is not wholly available to my thinking processes. For example, I've learned a great deal about microlek circuitry, but I don't think I'll ever be able to use that learning to discover a useful new circuit. In the work I'm doing now, when I need to devise a circuit, I seem to fall back on what I've known about basic electricity ever since I was a boy."

He shook his head and added, "Even if my mind is all you say it is, I can't compete with Olsapern scientists who grew up knowing things I've just learned for the first time. I wish I could. If I could really bring Olsapern science to bear on the problem of the Novo senses, well, I imagine the results would startle all of us! That's what gripes me, Higgins. You have people with the background and ability to break open a vast area of knowledge—knowledge about man himself!—but these people's minds are completely closed. Your so-called experts won't give the Novo senses the briefest attention!"

Higgins chuckled. "We've been over all this before, Starn. I've explained the limitations of Novo senses that make them a dead end. The human nervous system has to function within its structural boundaries. Your best telepaths, for instance, have a range of little more than half a mile. But through the use of his vocal chords, aided by languages and electronic devices conceived by his fertile imagination, the ordinary man can communicate over distances of millions of miles.

"So, when you start trying to develop Novo senses, you can't go very far before you come to an impassable barrier, erected by the limited size and power of the human brain. That stops you cold! Whereas, if you would forget these Novo senses, and put your bet on the unlimited ability of the imagination to devise means of extending and strengthening our natural abilities —means such as languages, telescopes, power tools, powered vehicles, and so on—no stopping place is ever reached!"

"But what you refuse to see," complained Starn, "is that the Novo senses *are* natural abilities, just waiting to be extended and strengthened! You're concentrating on aiding only a few of our senses while neglecting a vast unexplored range!"

Higgins frowned. Starn had never expressed his views in just that way before, and it gave the Defense Minister a thought to pause over. "In a way, that's true, Starn. But by its very nature, science has to be universally applicable. The results of an experiment must be verifiable by another experimenter, working under strictly specified and controlled conditions. And the products of science, therefore, must be useful to everyone. Even if telepathy were likely to survive as a human sense—which it is not, of course—the scientist could not afford to waste much of his energies trying to produce a . . . a *pathoscope* . . . to permit telepaths to read minds over great distances. Not unless telepathy became universal. At this time not even a majority of Pack men have it."

"We don't *know* that," objected Starn. "We only know that a minority of people have enough telepathy for it to be useful. Maybe everybody has a touch of it, waiting to be amplified and extended. That's one of the possibilities we ought to be investigating."

"However," grinned Higgins, "none of the regular senses are subliminal. We have enough sight, hearing, smell, taste and touch to use very well the way we're born with them. I can't take this idea of 'hidden senses' very seriously."

"What you say reminds me of what the common-sense folk said when inventors were working on the first aircraft," Starn remarked. " 'If God meant for man to fly, He would have given us wings.' "

Higgins laughed. "Trying to win an argument with you, Starn, is a task I hope my life never depends upon!

You always have a comeback! Unfortunately, though, scientific discoveries aren't made by winning debates. Discoveries require demonstrable proof, not argument."

"And you or nobody else is about to look at what demonstrable proof I have," Starn finished sadly. "Oh, well. How's your own work going, Higgins?"

"Fine."

"The defense system's working like a well-oiled machine, huh?"

Higgins puckered his lips. "I wish you wouldn't bring up the word 'oil,' " he complained wryly. "That's one of my biggest headaches."

"Oil is?" asked Starn as if he didn't know.

"Yes."

"Isn't oil easy to produce?"

"Well, that depends on the oil. Some kinds are very difficult to synthesize out of vegetable products. We must still depend on natural petroleum deposits for those. The trouble is that the deposits were badly drained during the Science Age, to use as fuel, of all things!" He sipped his drink and added, "Of course we've located new deposits, but they're subject to strict conservation restrictions, which allow us to tap only twenty percent of known reserves at any time. As of right now, we've used sixteen percent, and no new oil has been discovered lately. I'd hate to see us forced by necessity to ease our conservation policy, and start plundering the planet the way our ancestors did."

Starn nodded. "Cut down on your need for the oils you can't synthesize," he suggested.

"Oh, we've done that. But for certain types of heavy defense equipment—"

"That's what I mean. Cut down on your need for defense equipment. Make peace with the Packs."

Higgins laughed. "Not only does it take two to make a fight, lad; it takes two to make peace once the fight has started. When I say 'defense' equipment I'm not employing a euphemism. You know as well as I that it is the Packs who really have the tradition of combat. You yourself were a warrior by profession! If we want to keep our land orderly, we have to keep Pack raiders out, and keep their conflicts among themselves down to a reasonable level. No, we need the defenses we have in operable condition, Starn."

"I suppose so," the younger man replied. "Tell me, Higgins, can you get the oil out of deep shale deposits?"

"Shale underground? Yes, a special sweating process was developed years ago for that. Why do you ask?"

"Because I know where such a deposit is," Starn replied casually, although this was the disclosure he had been building toward. "It's about thirty miles southwest of Norhog Mountain. The oil shale is seventy feet thick, lies about twenty-six hundred feet below the surface, and has an area of a little more than nine square miles."

Higgins put his drink down so hard that some sloshed onto the table. "What . . . how . . . ?"

Starn got up and pulled a map from his desk. "This shows its outline, marked in red," he said, handing the map over.

Higgins clutched the paper and stared at the marked area. Finally he looked up. "Are you sure about this? Deep shale deposits aren't easy to detect, the oil experts tell me. Whose equipment did you use, and how did you happen to go looking for oil? I thought you were all wrapped up in this Novo sense business."

"This *is* Novo sense business," said Starn. "The equipment I used was some I made myself, based on the ancient dowsing rod. Only I didn't use the equipment myself. Billy was the operator. He seems to have a stronger perception sense. We hit upon that shale oil deposit by accident during a short camping trip I took him on in late spring. I made a game out of it for the boy. We crisscrossed the area in the flier for an hour or so while he mapped the deposit's boundaries."

Higgins threw the map down with a grunt of disgust. "I should've guessed it would be something like that, coming from you!" he huffed. He finished the remains of his drink and stared angrily at the wall while Starn refilled his glass.

"I thought of drilling an exploratory well, to prove the oil is there," said Starn, "but decided to leave that up to you. If you need oil so badly, you can't afford not to send somebody out there to take a look."

"Nonsense! There's no oil there!"

"There might be, for all you know," Starn replied. "If you need an excuse, you can always say you were looking through some old geological studies and found previously ignored indications that the area might yield oil."

"Forget it, Starn! I'm not wasting anybody's time by sending them on a wild-goose chase!"

Starn shrugged and changed the subject. But he noticed that Higgins glanced sideways at the map several times before Cytherni called them to supper.

The venison steak quickly brought Higgins out of the grumpy mood Starn had gotten him into. "I'll leave it to others to gush over your paint-sculptures, Cytherni," he said when he finally pushed away from the table. "What you do in the kitchen is art enough for me!"

"Thank you," she murmured modestly.

"Cythie's done a couple of pieces since you were here before," Starn said, "that you might like. Come take a look at them, won't you?"

Higgins regarded him with friendly suspicion. "Nothing Novo-sensey about them, is there?"

"No," Starn laughed. "No more of that tonight."

"All right."

Cytherni led the way into her studio where Higgins admired the busts of Billy with genuine approval. At length Starn said, "We were thinking the boy's grandparents would enjoy these more than anybody else. Could you arrange to have one delivered at Foser Compound and the other at Diston Compound?"

Higgins thought about it for a moment, then shook his head regretfully. "I'm afraid not. It would be unwise to remind your families of yourselves, and especially of your son. Those portraits would be a constant source of agitation, I'm afraid. The Packs recognized you as a remarkable man, Starn, with an ability that was unheard of—your trick of acting swiftly, without an instant of forethought that a telepath could detect. If they were reminded by these portraits that you had a son who is in our hands, there's no telling what ridiculous lengths they would go to, trying to get him away from us. It's best for everybody, Starn, for them not to know for sure that Cytherni ever recovered from her trauma sufficiently to give birth to her child, or to have even the slightest suspicion—which one of these portraits might arouse—that you are alive."

He looked at them and saw the deep disappointment in Cytherni's face. "I'm really sorry," he said sincerely. "I know the grandparents would love to have these, but . . . well, I'm sorry."

"That's O.K.," said Starn. "We know how it is."

But Cytherni said nothing, and had a stubborn glint in her eyes, Starn noticed.

As soon as Higgins' flier lifted away into the dark night Cytherni erupted. "Starn, I'm *not* going to just forget—"

He put his hand over his mouth and looked meaningfully at her. She fell silent.

"Let's go inside," he said. "Did you see the drawings Billy brought home from school this morning?" he asked. "They're over here. Maybe he's an artist, too. Come take a look."

"He didn't say anything to me—" Cytherni began in a puzzled tone, following Starn to the desk.

He picked up a note pad and wrote on it: *"Don't answer out loud. How badly do you want the portraits delivered?"*

She took the pad and scrawled in large angry letters: *"VERY!"*

Starn wrote: "O.K., *we'll deliver them ourselves.*"

Cytherni: *"How and when?"*

Starn: *"By flier. We leave before dawn."*

For a moment Cytherni seemed about to reject the idea. She wrote: *"We can't leave Billy by himself."*

Starn: *"We'll take him along."*

Cytherni: *"Higgins will throw a fit!"*

Starn: *"Let him."* He was glad he was writing instead of saying all this. A frog of guilt was clogging his throat.

Cytherni: *"I'll go alone. You stay with Billy."*

Starn: *"We share everything including trouble. We all go, or nobody goes."*

Cytherni's eyes moistened, and suddenly she kissed him. *"All right,"* she wrote, *"what do we have to do?"*

Starn: *"Leave that to me. Let's get to bed."* Aloud he said, "Well, what do you think of Billy's art?"

"Perhaps he takes more after you than me," she said.

Starn chuckled.

2

At four a.m. Starn woke. He rose quietly and went into his workshop where he paused uncertainly, asking himself if, in the near-dawn of a new day, he really wanted to go through with this.

His determination overrode his misgivings. He sat down at the bench on which the small dowser machine was perched and picked up the sensor unit. Slowly, he explored his arms and legs with the device, moving it along his skin with only a fraction of an inch keeping it from touching him. He needed to practice that, because when he was through with himself he would have to search Cytherni and Billy the same way, but without waking them.

As he had expected, the machine told his perception of no device in arms or legs. Limbs can be lost in accidents, making them poor locations for tracker bugs. He was relieved when an examination of his head failed to wiggle the rod needles. He went on to explore his body.

The device was buried inside his rib cage, near the front and to the right. When he found it, he took readings on it from several directions, to pinpoint its location as finely as his not-too-precise machine would permit.

Then came the crucial job: the destruction of the bug. With access to the proper Olsapern surgical equipment, the device could have simply been removed, painlessly and without leaving a scar. But Starn had no such equipment. He had to take the far less certain course of attempting to knock out the bug and leave its wreckage in place.

One of the difficulties was that he had no sample bug with which to experiment. He had to assume the device was similar in construction to other small microlek gadgets, and could be disrupted by a focused ultrasonic beam, which was the only tool at Starn's disposal that seemed remotely likely to do the job.

He had to use the beam cautiously. If the focus fell outside the bug rather than inside it, the ultrasonics could produce potentially dangerous internal injuries. He positioned the beamer with care, and triggered a three-second burst. He felt a tingle but no real pain, so the focus probably had been on target.

At any rate he had to assume that. Somewhere miles away, in some Domestic Defense installation, a point of light on a map had suddenly gone dark, he guessed. And perhaps, too, an alarm had gone off. He would have to move fast from now on.

He took his equipment into the bedroom where Cytherni was still sleeping soundly. Luckily for his purpose, she was lying on her back, and he quickly learned that her tracker bug was located similarly to his own. When he hit it with the ultrasonics she did not flinch, but stirred slightly. He quickly shoved his equipment under the bed and out of sight.

Cytherni opened her eyes and started to speak. He laid his fingers on her lips for an instant. She nodded, and he gestured the message that she should go prepare breakfast.

When she was in the kitchen Starn took his equipment to Billy's bedside. The boy didn't wake when Starn triggered the ultrasonics, which was all to the good. The longer he slept, the longer telltale conversation could be delayed.

Twenty minutes later, after a silent, hurried breakfast with Cytherni, Starn helped her place the portraits in cushioned cartons and load them into the flier. Then he carried the still-sleeping Billy aboard and bedded him comfortably on the long passenger seat. With Cytherni beside him, he sat down at the controls, turned on the engines, and lifted the craft out of its housing and into a steep, southward climb.

He didn't really expect immediate pursuit. What he was doing was far from an everyday occurrence. Whatever Olsapern defensemen were keeping vigil at this hour of the morning should, for a little while, be more puzzled than alarmed by whatever their instruments were telling them. By the time they swung into action, he hoped, he would be far to the south of the Hard Line. Then they could pursue him, but not intercept him.

As it turned out no pursuit at all materialized. Not once did another flier come within craft-radar range as

Starn streaked south, high over the Hard Line and into Pack territory.

"Hey! Are we going camping?" Billy piped suddenly, waking up and staring around.

Starn turned in his seat and grinned at the boy. "Good morning, sleepy-head. We're delivering some presents."

"Oh. What happened to breakfast?"

"We brought yours along," said his mother, rising. "Come sit up front with Daddy and I'll get it."

The boy took her place and stared out curiously. The sun was rising and he remarked knowingly, "We're going south!"

"That's right," said Starn. "We're taking presents to my mommy and daddy, and to Mommy's mommy and daddy."

Billy thought this over while Cytherni snapped his tray into the seat-rack. "Will we get to see them?" he asked.

"No. We'll drop their presents by chute."

Billy nodded thoughtfully and began eating.

"I'll put the chutes on now," said Cytherni.

"Better put one on yourself, for safety," said Starn carefully. "Unless you want to pilot while I toss them out."

"No, I'll do it." Cytherni strapped on a chute and busied herself with the packages.

"At this altitude we'd better put on helmets, too, before I open the hatch," said Starn.

"I will when I finish eating," said Billy.

Several minutes passed. "Coming up on Diston Compound in thirty seconds," Starn announced, mashing the hatch-control button.

Billy snorted as the air thinned and put on his helmet. "Where?" he asked, craning his neck. "I want to see."

"There," Starn pointed.

Billy busied himself with the magniviewer, with which he was quite proficient, and studied the close-up appearance of his mother's home village with intense curiosity. Starn, meanwhile, was timing the drop and keeping an eye on Cytherni in the rearview mirror.

"About time now," he warned. "Be careful around that open hatch."

"O.K. Say when," Cytherni's voice sounded in his helmet phones over the roar of wind past the open hatch in front of her.

"Five seconds," replied Starn. "Two, one, *now!*"

Cytherni pushed a carton out, and leaned forward to watch it fall, one hand grasping the edge of the opening while she needlessly shielded her goggle-protected eyes from the wind with the other.

"Chute's working fine," she reported,

"Good. We're about two minutes from Foser Compound. Get the other one in position."

"Can I help?" asked Billy, stirring in his seat.

"No," said Starn tightly. "Stay where you are so you can see the Compound."

"In fact," said Starn, "I'd better strap you in to make sure you do." He leaned over and snapped the safety belt in place over the boy's middle.

"Good idea," approved Cytherni. "It's too windy back here for you, Billy."

"There's Foser Compound now, son," Starn pointed. The boy's attention was again glued on the magniviewer. "See the river? I swam there when I was your age."

"How's the time?" demanded Cytherni.

"Eighteen seconds yet. No hurry," said Starn, hoping he did not sound as tight as he felt. "Five . . . Two, one, *now!*"

The second carton went through the hatch and again Cytherni leaned after it with her precarious one-handed grip.

Starn's teeth clenched as he gave the control wheel a sudden jerk. The flier rolled to the left and swerved to the right . . . and Cytherni was jerked through the hatch.

"*Starn! I fell out!*" Her voice yelped in his earphones.

"Your chute!" he snapped.

"It's working. I'm all right. We must have hit an air pocket! I was holding on, Starn!" she apologized. "Really I was!"

"Don't worry about it," said Starn. "I'll bring the flier down after you, and pick you up."

"*No!* Not here, with Billy aboard!" she objected.

"I'll try to make it quick," argued Starn.

"Absolutely no!" Cytherni ruled. "I won't permit our son to have contact with these telepaths! You know how I feel about that!"

Indeed Starn did. He felt the same way himself, to some extent. As children, he and his wife had been obliged to try to channel their very thoughts into lines approved by Pack society, and enforced by Pack telepaths. Cytherni had never adjusted to these mental restrictions, and had not been truly happy until happenstance left her among the Olsaperns, who were not only nontelepathic but detested all the Novo senses.

In Starn's judgment, a brief encounter with the disapproval of Pack telepaths might be unpleasant for Billy, but would be a challenge that might actually do the boy more good than harm. After all, Billy was over six years old, and already had a self-confidence that was not easily shaken. But Cytherni could not take that rational view—in fact, Starn had counted on her reacting in just this manner.

"Besides," she was saying, "you should stay up beyond telepathic range. It's bad enough for them to learn what I know! Oh, Starn, why did I get us into this awful mess?"

"Easy, dearest!" he soothed. "It's not as awful as all that! Despite what the Olsaperns think, I don't believe a knowledge of the strength of Olsapern civilization will turn the Packs into jungle animals! A lot of Olsapern ideas about genetic history are pure rot, used to justify the Olsaperns' belief in their own superiority. The Packs aren't on the edge of a genetic collapse!"

"I hope you're right," responded Cytherni uncertainly. "But just the same, you and Billy stay up there!"

"All right," agreed Starn. "It's too late to hope to keep this little jaunt a secret from Higgins, anyway. I'll circle till you're down safely. The Olsapern defensemen can come later to pick you up. Is that O.K.?"

"Yes."

"One thing, Cythie," Starn said hesitantly. "Whatever happens, remember that I love you . . . very much."

"I do, too, Mommy!" put in Billy, who had been sitting still, in shocked dismay, ever since his mother tumbled from the flier.

"Bless you both!" she sobbed.

When she was safely on the ground Starn returned the flier to a straight course.

"Mommy will be all right, won't she?" asked Billy.

"Yes, the Fosers will be nice to her," Starn assured him.

That satisfied the boy, and he again turned his attention to their flight. "We're still going south," he remarked.

"Southwest," said Starn.

"Not going home?" Billy asked.

"No . . . since your mommy's not there."

This made sense to Billy. He nodded. "Camping, then?"

"Yes, we're going camping."

"Will you let me shoot this time?"

Starn nodded. "Yes, I'll show you how to shoot."

"Oh boy!" exclaimed Billy in delight.

Starn put the controls on automatic, with the flight computer programmed to keep the southwest heading for eight hours and then bring the flier down for a landing. That would put the craft far south of the equator, and over the ocean. With the hatch left open, the flier would sink when it landed.

He left his seat and went into the back of the flier where he had stored the equipment and supplies. He bundled the stuff stoutly into two chute packs and placed them by the hatch. He strapped the one remaining chute to himself.

"Where are we going to camp?" asked Billy.

"That'll be a surprise. Somewhere you haven't been before." By now, Starn was certain, Olsapern ears were straining for every word of conversation detected by the flier's bugs. He wanted to say nothing that would tell more of his destination than the Olsaperns could learn from the path of the flier. In fact, he hoped to make them uncertain of the exact time he chuted out.

He went forward to stand by Billy's chair, and gazed down at the landscape for a moment. They were already well into the modest heights of the northern end of the mountain range. Packs were scattered through these hills, but not farther south, where the peaks soared high and discouragingly steep. In old times, Starn knew, even the tallest mountains felt the tread of man's boots, and the blades of his dozers. But now the heart of the range stood wrapped in lonely grandeur, unwanted by men too engrossed in other pursuits to expend their energies exploring territory that was, after all, thoroughly mapped by their ancestors. The dense cover of fir and pine now sheltered only such creatures as were there before men came, and after men left.

The taller peaks were coming into view as Starn watched. He unsnapped the breakfast tray from Billy's chair and helped the boy to his feet.

"Now," he said, "no more talking. I have a special reason. O.K.?"

Billy looked up at him with wide eyes, and nodded.

Starn patted him approvingly on the head and led him back through the cabin. From some extra cargo straps he rigged a body-harness for the boy, and tied a strap-end tightly around his own belt. He intended to chute out carrying the boy in his arms, but if the wind tore them apart the harness would enable him to pull the boy back.

As an afterthought he removed both their helmets, which were probably as trackable as bugs to the Olsap-erns. And for the hundredth time since the trip started, he wondered if he had really succeeded in disrupting their body bugs. He shrugged. He would know in an hour or two. If the Olsapern defensemen came swarming down around them, the bugs would still be doing their job.

He leaned out the hatch from time to time to study the land below. The sun was now high enough for him to judge the roughness of terrain by the size, shape, and depth of shadows, without which the rugged hills would have appeared paper-flat from the flier's altitude.

At last he decided the mountains were as high and desolate as they were going to get. He motioned Billy to him, cradled the boy tightly against his chest, kicked the chute packs out the hatch, and jumped after them.

The flier was already out of sight when he thought to look for it. Billy was hammering his arm with a little fist. "What is it, son?" he said.

"Can I talk now?" Billy asked.

3

Cytherni was, by nature, a blabber-brain. It was this trait that had made her childhood and adolescence in Pack Diston so miserable. Her mind simply refused self-censorship, and the very act of attempting to direct it into the channels prescribed by Pack mores was all too likely to trigger the forbidden thought-train she was trying hardest to avoid. Throughout her early years she had felt a cloud of disapproval hovering about her wherever she went.

Her marriage to Starn, and entry into Pack Foser, had partially dispersed this cloud, not due to any conscious effort on her part but simply because being Starn's wife preoccupied her mind with thoughts that were quite normal for a young married woman and, therefore, thoroughly acceptable.

But not until she had lived among the Olsaperns for a while did she come to appreciate that the untamable quality of her mind could be anything but a disastrous handicap, that it was indeed the kind of mind that creates most of the world's great art. A mind that accepts the discipline of form, but that insists on having its way about content.

Not surprisingly, after basking in Olsapern approval for several years, her mind was now less controllable than ever.

Thus, the people of Pack Foser had learned, within an hour after she chuted down in a nearby cabbage field, more about Olsapern civilization and Olsapern world views than any followers of the Sacred Gene had ever known before. The knowledge was greeted with shock, surprise, dismay, and some disbelief, but mostly with disdain.

And the news of it began to spread, in the usual erratic way, through telepathic farmers who lived within range of both the Compound and more distant telepaths. Also, a messenger on horseback was sent to carry the word of Cytherni's return to Diston Compound some thirty-five miles away.

"Please don't read me!" she had begged when the men had come running from Foser Compound to the spot where she landed. *"It might hurt you!"*

Of course her plea had no effect. They read, and talked, and read.

Her first encounter with Starn's old crony Rob, after she was brought into the Compound, was more or less typical. It began with surprise at the emblem of Raid Leader that adorned Rob's belt, and at hearing him addressed as "Foser." Later she learned that the old Foser had died quite recently, and Rob had been elevated to the Pack chieftainship but was retaining his old post until a new Raid Leader could be competitively selected.

She was surprised because she remembered Rob as a pleasant fellow for a telepath, but nevertheless a coward. Could *he* be a Raid Leader of Pack Foser, she wondered, after a man like Starn? But, she recalled, Rob *had* done one brave, almost foolhardy, thing: he had volunteered to go with some Olsapern defensemen on a mission across the Hard Line, to monitor and validate to Starn a lecture on genetic history by the Olsapern scientist Richhold. Starn had related the details of that meeting to her, and she recalled them well, including the fact that Rob's memory of the affair was erased before he was returned home.

"So *that's* what happened!" remarked Rob with a cold smile. "I've often wondered. And Starn says this Richhold had me halfway convinced, huh?"

Cytherni nodded. Richhold's lecture had been an eye-opener for both of the young Pack men, who knew of the infidel theories of the Olsaperns but had not previously been exposed to the evidence on which the theories were based. It was much later before Starn arrived at some theories of his own that accounted for the evidence at least as well as did the beliefs of the Olsaperns.

Starn had been "present" at the lecture through an artificial body, and Rob had been unable to read him
because his brain was far away, in the hospital, directing
the growth of a new normal body to replace the one
damaged beyond repair when Starn and Huill made their
first attack on Nagister Nornt . . .

"An artificial body I couldn't read?" Rob demanded
in astonishment.

Yes. She recalled the one time she had seen that body,
apparently bleeding from a dozen wounds but actually
oozing red oil while it made its terrifying final assault on
Nornt in his cavern hideaway. She had been pregnant
with Billy then—Billy William Huill—and she had cowered until Nornt was frightened completely out of his
mind and then she had shot him herself and what she
thought was Starn was lying dead on the floor and . . .

"Stop!" grunted Rob. "You named your son after
Huill?"

"We call him Billy. Huill was such a good friend—for
a telepath—and so brave . . . the way he died. He was a
real chum, he and Starn at ease together, but Rob here
always uncomfortable . . . wanting to be a chum but . . .
That's why he went to Richhold with the defensemen
that time! Huill had been killed, which left him a live
coward with his brave friends gone. So he was trying
to—make up for it! Maybe he still is!"

"O.K.!" Rob rasped, his thin face showing red behind
his beard. "So I know what fear is! I also have learned
how to fight it, because a man does what he has to!"

"I'm sorry," murmured Cytherni.

"Never mind," Rob said in disgust. "You've turned
Olsapern, that's for sure! I shouldn't expect anything better from the likes of you! What a man like Starn ever

saw—" He strode angrily about the room in which he was interviewing her, trying to regain his composure.

"Did he admire Starn so much?" Cytherni wondered in surprise. She had never suspected it. But that would help explain . . .

"Look!" Rob yelped. "What about these theories of Starn's, and what's he up to?"

How was she supposed to answer that? She understood Starn's work about as well as he did her art—which wasn't much. Did Starn view her work with the same kind of fond but uninterested indulgence with which she viewed his? Let's see . . . His main idea was that the Packs and the Olsaperns each had a segment of the truth, but to get anywhere they would have to put these segments together. But since they would not, he was working alone, trying to apply what he had learned of Olsapern science to understanding and extending the Novo senses. He was making some progress, especially when he worked with Billy's perception sense. They had discovered a large oil deposit and he tried last night to interest Higgins in it . . . Starn took disappointment awfully well. He took Higgins' rejection so good-naturedly last night, even though she knew how determined he was to get his work accepted.

"Are you sure you have the right understanding of what Starn's trying to do?" Rob demanded in disbelief.

Cytherni frowned. Well, she *thought* she understood it fairly well. A combining of science and the Novo senses . . .

"*Sacrilege!*" muttered Rob. Cytherni blinked. She had never thought of it that way, but it was true. In the view of the Packs, the gifts of the Sacred Gene would be

profaned by contact with the cursed evils of the Science
Age. And for that matter, she realized, the Olsaperns'
objections amounted to the same thing, except that they
saw the positions of good and evil reversed.

Thank heavens she hadn't let Starn land the flier here
to pick her up! Not that his old friends in Pack Foser
would have . . . have *harmed* him, but they would have
made their condemnation plain. And luckily it was she,
not he, who had fallen from the flier.

"Starn's changed in more ways than one," Rob commented sadly. "The man who was our Raid Leader would
never have let his wife do the more dangerous of two
tasks."

What did Rob mean by that? Oh, yes. Starn piloting
the flier while she pushed the packs out the hatch. Well,
she was on her feet, having got up to bring Billy his
breakfast, and Starn was the better pilot, and she wanted
to make sure the right pack was dropped at the right
Compound, and . . .

Bob was shaking his head. "You don't think he's
changed," he said, "but that still doesn't sound like Starn
to me."

On second thought, it didn't sound like Starn to her,
either. But . . . well, people are complicated. They don't
stay in what we think is their character all the time. So
this morning Starn's chivalry had slipped a little. Perhaps
he was quietly annoyed with her for getting them
involved in such a silly adventure

"Then this trip was your idea?" asked Rob.

Yes . . . or . . . well . . . Starn had put the idea into
actual words first, but he was just going along with her
desire to get the portraits of Billy to the grandparents.

"You *think* he was just going along with your wishes," Rob corrected her. "You don't *know* that."

You crummy, prying telepaths do the knowing.

"And knowing's not the supreme pleasure you think it is," Rob commented sourly. He paused, either to think or to communicate with someone outside, then said, "If you don't understand Starn's work, you probably don't understand Olsapern science. You know some of the things it can do, but not how."

Yes. Starn understands it better, but he complains about how little he really comprehends. But Billy, starting as a child, will learn it all.

All I know is the products—menergy, artificial bodies and new bodies, fliers, power sources the size of peas that last for years, beautiful houses and clothing and . . . *What am I doing to you!*

Rob grunted. "What we're learning isn't hurting us! Don't be afraid of that! Knowledge of Olsapern science won't shock us into primitivism like they claim. How is it the Olsaperns I've seen—the trading-post men, the flier pilots and defensemen—don't know about all this?"

Because they're not the bright ones. They don't care to learn, so they're not taught much. They're the only ones allowed in reading distance of Pack men. What they know won't hurt you.

Rob chuckled caustically. "Or won't let us learn anything that could hurt the Olsaperns! What a pack of idiots!" He prowled restlessly about the room for a moment, then added, "But perhaps more dangerous, and less idiotic, than their dull-witted front men led us to believe. Unwittingly, Cytherni, you've done the Packs a great service today. We've been underestimating the power of the evil forces in the world. We know those forces better now, and can deal with them accordingly." He hesitated for several seconds before saying, "If the other Packs share the views of the men of Foser, there will be no more trading with—or raiding of—the Olsapern trading posts, for one thing. No further association at all."

"But the Olsaperns want friendship eventually," Cytherni protested aloud. "They want the peoples to come together!"

"Not while Pack men have their Novo senses, they don't," Rob contradicted.

This, Cytherni had to admit, was true. Obviously, her unplanned visit to Foser Compound had done more damage to Pack-Olsapern relations than could be repaired in a dozen generations. Every thought that passed through her head only seemed to make matters worse. She had to get out of Pack country!

"A flier landed several minutes ago, to dicker for your release," Rob informed her. "But I don't know if we'll let them have you. It's true you're more Olsapern than Pack woman now, but perhaps you're not beyond rehabilitation. Perhaps you can still be reclaimed for some worthy purpose of the Sacred Gene. Why haven't you and Starn had any children since Billy? Were you Treated?"

No. We could have children but . . . but—

"You're not sure of the answer," said Rob. "Maybe it was Starn's doing."

No. Why? Birth control is so simple there that . . . No, that's not it. I used to *want* children, but then I didn't.

Yes, I did, too, but I didn't want Starn to feel confined by a large family

"Starn wanted children, too," said Rob. He studied her intently, attempting to ferret out thoughts that had never been fully conscious with her. At last he asked, "Did you feel, perhaps, that Starn was not ready to settle down to family life, that his work or something would require him, sooner or later, to take action that would be made more difficult for him by a large family?"

That sounded almost right. "I felt that he wasn't quite . . . domesticated," she said slowly.

Rob frowned and grunted. "I think maybe you were right. I'm having those Olsapern defensemen invited in. They won't know much, but maybe I can learn something from just what they don't know."

Let me go home with them. Please. I belong with Starn and Billy.

Rob shrugged impatiently and said nothing.

When the two defensemen were brought in a few minutes later, one was carrying an audiovisual transceiver equipped with droplegs. On its screen was the face of Higgins. Cytherni was relieved to see this trusted friend taking a personal hand in obtaining her release.

Rob ignored the transceiver, and snapped a question at the defensemen. "Where's the flier she fell from?"

The Olsaperns looked startled and remained silent.

"I suggest you direct your questions at me, Foser," Higgins' cross voice came from the speaker. "I'm—"

"I know who you are, Higgins," said Rob coldly. "I'll talk to you, but let it be understood that I take your failure to come dicker in person as an admission of your inferiority. We have Cytherni's knowledge now, so your old alibi of shielding us from damaging information no longer holds up. From now on you'll have to admit to yourselves that you're avoiding contact with us out of fear."

"Think what you please, Foser," retorted Higgins. "I'm not parleying with you to argue that matter, but to obtain the return of Cytherni. I assume you know my offer—two special shipments of tropical fruits per winter to Foser Compound for a period of fifteen years, with the . . ."

"Your offer is rejected," said Rob. "The Pack's conditions for the release of Cytherni is that she will be exchanged for her son Huill—Billy to you—when and if you capture Starn and the boy."

"Capture?" demanded Higgins innocently.

"Don't play games, Higgins!" Rob growled. "Don't try to pretend that Starn came dashing back to you for help after Cytherni fell out of the flier! That's what Starn led her to believe he'd do, but I don't buy it! Now, my deal is this: You catch Starn and the boy, turn the boy over to the Pack, with which he belongs, and Cytherni can either go or stay as she wishes. The boy is only six, and has the Novo sense of a Pack man. Even if his parents have turned Olsapern it's not too late to save him. That's the deal, Higgins. The only deal I'm offering."

Higgins' face stared threateningly for a moment before he grated, "Cytherni's misadventure has lifted the lid in more ways than one, Foser! We can recover her, whether you like it or not. We can flood Foser Compound with a sleep gas, for instance, that will knock all of you out. Our men could then safely remove Cytherni and, as an object lesson, sterilize every man, woman and child in the Pack!"

Rob laughed at him. "I imagine you could do that, Higgins, but I don't imagine you will. Not while Starn is on the loose you won't! You want Cytherni back, but that's not your primary objective. What damage she could do you was done during the first half hour after she landed. Except as bait for Starn, she's no longer important enough to warrant drastic action. And since Starn dumped her here, you can't really be sure she's attractive bait!"

"I wasn't dumped!" cried Cytherni, dismayed by the implications of the word, and by Rob's stubbornness. "I fell!"

Rob turned to her and said in a more gentle tone than he had used before, "You were dumped, Cytherni. I'm sorry, but that's the way it was. Starn's flier didn't just happen to hit an air pocket, in the middle of a smooth flight, at the precise instant when you were hanging out the hatch. And it didn't just happen that you were unloading the chute packs instead of him. Or that he proposed starting the trip at an hour when Billy would have to be taken along. Or that Higgins isn't disputing my statement that Starn hasn't returned." He glanced at Higgins and said, "Cytherni believes this whole trip was her doing, not Starn's. There were some portraits of the boy she wanted delivered to the grandparents, you know. If you had agreed to deliver them last night, you would have wrecked Starn's scheme."

Higgins cursed angrily. "Why didn't *you* ask me to do it, Cytherni?" he demanded. "I'd have found a way. But

Starn had me annoyed over one of his ridiculous arguments, and . . . well, when *he* asked me, I turned him down."

"Maybe he had that figured, too," said Rob.

Higgins glared at him. "There's a clever brain in that throw-back skull of yours, Foser. Maybe you can figure out what Starn's purpose is in all this, since you're so smart."

Rob shrugged. "Isn't that obvious to you, Higgins? He's continuing his work in isolation, where neither you, nor I, nor Cytherni can stop him! One thing I can agree with you about, Higgins, is that Starn is engaged in an evil pursuit. He's a bigger threat to the safety of the world than Nagister Nornt could've ever become!"

His voice grew wrathful as he continued, "But you, Higgins, are the guilty party in all this! Starn was a fine man, one who would have been long honored in the legends of Pack Foser, until you subverted him! You made him the madman he is today, a man with a freakish mind that is neither Pack nor Olsapern! That's what comes from an unnatural mingling between Pack men and Olsaperns! And that's why we will have no future associations with you, once this matter is ended. You may as well close down your stupid trading posts, Higgins. We won't even bother to raid them hereafter!"

After a frigid silence, Higgins said formally, "Your proposal to exchange Cytherni for the boy Billy will be discussed in our council, Foser. You will be advised of our decision. Let's go, men!"

The defensemen took the transceiver and marched out of the room.

"But . . . " murmured Cytherni, "if Starn did that, why didn't he take me along?"

Rob did not seem to hear her for a moment, but sat with a distracted look. At last he roused himself and looked at her. "Because your attitudes are pretty typically Olsapern. You disapprove of his work, although you try not to. In fact, you're jealous of his work, which has kept him from being the kind of man you want for a father of the children you haven't had."

"Oh," gulped Cytherni in a small voice. Then she turned and ran from the room, in search of some spot where her grief could be suffered in a semblance of privacy—though she knew there was no privacy to be had in Foser Compound.

Four days passed before an Olsapern flier again landed near the Compound. Once more the transceiver was brought into Rob's quarters, and Cytherni was invited to attend the parley.

Rob gave the image of Higgins a hard look and demanded, "Well?"

"The council has considered your proposal," Higgins said, "and while we don't like it we are willing to accept your terms."

"All right. Bring us the boy."

"The problem is," Higgins continued uncomfortably, "that we haven't yet located Starn and Billy. We know, in general, where they are, but that is a mountainous area of sizable extent, a strip two hundred and fifty miles long and we would estimate twenty miles wide."

"The offer," said Rob, "was for you to turn the boy over after he and his father were captured. If you haven't caught them yet, what are we talking about?"

"As you remarked yourself at our last meeting," said Higgins, "Starn is a grave threat to the safety of the world—to your people as well as our own. I agree with that, and as for my own role in making him the danger he is, well, let me assure you that this strengthens my resolve to compensate for past errors. However, the crucial fact is that we have not found him, and he *must* be found! Under the circumstances, we think a cooperative effort, a joint search, is justified."

Rob lifted an eyebrow. "Do I detect a more worried tone in your voice, Higgins? Perhaps you've checked that oil deposit Starn and Billy mapped. Was oil there?"

Higgins' mouth tightened. "The map was accurate," he admitted.

"Anything else to shake you up?" asked Rob.

"Well . . . yes. We have means of locating lost persons, small tracking devices implanted in the body. In some manner, Starn found where these implants were in himself and his wife and son. Minutes before leaving, he put them out of action, probably with a focused ultrasonic beam. Those implants are small, and made intentionally hard to locate. Starn once returned to Foser Compound with such implants in him. Did any of your people know they were there?"

"No. I remember the time of which you speak," said Rob. "With these tracker devices not working, then, you have no way of locating Starn and Billy?"

"That's correct. The devices on his flier were not disturbed, however, and we have a plot of its course from the time it took off until it came down and sank in the ocean some nine hours later."

"Oh!" moaned Cytherni.

"But Starn and Billy chuted out long before then. Unfortunately, we cannot pinpoint the time they did so much closer than ten minutes, which leaves us with a considerable stretch of the flier's course to search. And we assume that Starn would not hike, with the boy, more than ten miles east or west, probably not that much.

"Anyway, he's already had four days for whatever it is he's doing. And I'll admit, Foser, that I'm now more convinced that he is . . . on the track of something that could be most unsettling to us all. If you're really convinced of your own statement that he is a serious threat, you must help us find him."

"That sort of entanglement with you," glowered Rob, "is exactly what we are determined to avoid."

"The feeling is mutual," flared Higgins, "but this is a task that has to be done!"

Rob said slowly, "I don't know just how we could help you, anyway. What did you have in mind?"

"We comb the territory with fliers, as we've been doing, but this time with one or more of your telepaths aboard each craft to detect Starn's mind when a flier comes in range."

Rob shook his head. "I guessed it was something like that. It won't work. The rub would be to come in range. And stay there long enough for a telepath to pick up and even start to identify Starn's thoughts. Keep in mind that maximum telepathic range is half a mile, and in the High Mountains, which I presume are the ones you're talking about, there are valleys over a quarter of a mile below the ridges. You couldn't cover the area so thoroughly as to be sure a flier would pass directly over Starn; each telepath would have to scan a strip of, say, a quarter of a mile on each side of the flier. The air can be rough over mountains, can't it? So your fliers would have to stay a couple of hundred feet above the ridgetops if they move with any speed at all.

"Maybe you've taken all that into account, all except the time it takes a telepath to detect a mind. It isn't instantaneous, Higgins. And it isn't certain. The detected mind has to be thinking thoughts the telepath can readily distinguish from his own. If Starn and the boy were down in a valley, they would be within extreme telepathic range of a flier passing low above the ridges for a very few seconds, unless the flier was moving extremely slow. So, unless you've got enough fliers, and we can round up enough telepaths, to creep through those mountains at treetop level, following the terrain up and down, we would have to be plain lucky to find Starn by that method. You could probably do as well with your infrared detectors as with our telepaths."

"You're sure of that?" asked Higgins.

"Yes." Rob frowned and added, "I've given some thought to a joint search myself since we last talked, because I guessed you wouldn't find Starn."

"Well, if my plan won't work, what will?" Higgins demanded.

"I'm not sure. We've got to remember that Starn's too much of a hunter not to know all the tricks of the hunted." Rob's eyes studied Cytherni. "There's one possibility I can think of, but that involves the active assistance of Starn's wife, and she isn't in a helpful frame of mind."

"Oh? How are you, Cytherni?" asked Higgins.

"Very well, thank you," she said.

"Why won't you help us bring Starn back to you, dear?" asked Higgins.

Rob laughed dryly. "Sweet talk will get you nowhere," he said. "Cytherni's torn up by all this, and blames herself for what she thinks was a disloyal attitude toward her husband's work. Anyhow, she's determined to be on his side from now on."

"And she could help us, if she would?" Higgins asked.

"Yes. It's . . . it's rather complicated to explain to somebody who doesn't understand the Novo senses. But there is an emotional tie between parent and child, Higgins, that stays intact even when they're miles apart. It's something quite different from telepathy, and only serves as a line of communication in moments of great stress. But there are some of us who can help others use this linkage. That's the way we locate lost children who have wandered or have been carried out of telepathic range.

"But for it to work, the parent must actively desire the recovery of the child. In our case, Cytherni refuses to cooperate. She is willing to leave the boy with Starn."

"Well, I'm glad you're a reasonable enough man, Foser, to consider cooperation, even if Cytherni is not. Perhaps we can think of some other approach, if your people share your viewpoint."

"They do."

"Good. I'll leave these men and their flier near your Compound, if that meets your approval, while all of us give this matter more thought. I suggest that you try to convince Cytherni to help us, Foser, since she offers the only prospect we know of right now."

"That won't be easy," grumbled Rob.

The next day Rob sent for Cytherni.

"I'm not going to try to talk you into anything," he said, "but I want you to know of a thought that has come to me. You asked the other day why Starn left you here, and I said because you oppose him. That wasn't a very satisfactory, or true, answer, I realize now. You have your doubts about his work, but you are his wife, and in a pinch you would stand with him. You've been proving that. What's more, I think Starn would have known it all along.

"Then why did he leave you here? A number of us have been thinking about that, Cytherni, people who knew Starn well in the old days, and understand the kind of person he is, and how grim he can be when he's determined to do something.

"We've thought about it at length," he said, watching her face, "and the conclusion we've reached is more disturbing than anything else in this whole affair. He dumped you here, Cytherni, *because his plans involve something you couldn't possibly approve.* Something you would have to fight to prevent, even against your own husband.

"As to what that could be—well, Billy is the subject in Starn's experiments, the only subject with a strong Novo sense available to him. Now I'm sure Starn wouldn't do anything which he was convinced would be harmful to the boy, but he must have had something in mind that would be risky, at least. He's working in unexplored fields, where nobody knows what is and is not dangerous. So—"

"*Stop it!*" cried Cytherni, a wild look in her eyes. Rob's mouth twisted in an unhappy little smile of victory. He

rose and led her across the Compound to the hut of
Virnce, Starn's father, where the Pack's finder, an old
man named Harnk, joined them very quickly. "She's
ready?" Harnk asked.

Rob nodded. "She's ready." Harnk pointed to the
paint-sculptured portrait of Billy. "Look at that," he told
Cytherni. "You want to find your son? Yes . . . yes
. . . indeed you do." He was silent for a moment, then
looked up at Rob. "I need pen and paper."

Virnce produced the writing equipment and Harnk
began sketching. "This is the aspect of a mountainside
which catches the morning light. The boy can see it
across a narrow valley. See how the rocks tilt in this
double row of cliffs. The trees cover everything else. He
sees a crestline that humps here and here, and dips here.
He is sitting—or will be sitting when you find him—on
a rock by a tent of Olsapern stuff, tall trees all around.
The tent must be straight across the valley from this
point on the mountain."

"Excellent, Harnk!" Rob applauded, looking over the
old man's shoulder at the scrawly sketch. "Good work!
Now, where's the mountain?"

Harnk shook his head. "I get no other impressions,"
he said.

Rob grunted in disappointment. "It's somewhere in
the High Mountains, but you have no idea where?"

"No."

"Then how are we supposed to find the boy?"

Harnk lifted his shoulders. "Find the mountain, and
the boy will be there."

"Yeah, find the mountain," parroted Rob in annoyance. "But who knows where a mountain that looks like
that is located?"

Cytherni moved forward hesitantly and looked at the sketch. She did not recognize the mountain, of course, but its shape interested her as an artist. She recalled the massive triphoto geographical survey albums the Olsaperns had developed over the years, and which she had examined as part of her preparation to do landscapes. Probably the very mountainside Harnk had sketched was included in those albums.

Rob sighed. "I'd hoped we could handle this without the Olsaperns," he said, "but we'll need flier transportation, anyway. Somebody go tell the defensemen to bring the Higgins box in again."

4

"When are we going hunting, Daddy?" asked Billy.

"This afternoon," Starn replied. It was the day after they had chuted from the flier. Starn was relaxing in a folding chair while the boy played around the camp. He grinned at his son. "For someone who put in a hard day yesterday, you're awfully eager to start chasing coons."

"Oh, you did most of the work," Billy replied. "Are you tired today?"

"No, I'm just thinking."

"Oh. What about?"

"How to make your perception work better."

"It works good now, Daddy, with the needle rods. Can I take them along when we go hunting? I think I can find a coon with them. What does a coon look like?"

Starn described the raccoon's appearance, and asked, "Does knowing what a coon looks like help you percept it?"

The boy thought about this before shaking his head. "I don't think so. But that'll let me know what I've found when I've found one." Starn chuckled, and the boy said, "While you're thinking, let me take the needle rods and practice. Maybe there's a coon close by."

"O.K., but don't go far." Starn had misgivings about letting Billy out of sight in such wild country, but memories of himself running loose at the boy's age kept him from being too restrictive during outings such as this.

He settled back into his chair, and his brow creased in a concentrated effort to think the problem out.

The trouble was that his unconscious just wasn't producing. Despite his reading of everything in Olsapern literature that pertained even slightly to the Novo senses, and his own numerous experiments with Billy and himself, his unconscious still seemed to lack the clues necessary to produce that sudden burst of insight. This meant that he was missing some basic point, he guessed, some key concept that had to be fed to his unconscious before the problem would be solvable. What was it?

About an hour later Billy returned, a little winded from climbing about the steep mountainside. "I didn't find a coon," he reported, "but I found two chipmunks. The needle rod works good for animals, even when I stand still and don't move it."

Starn nodded. Perception worked only in the presence of motion. The object could be moving, or the perceptor, or the percepting device in the perceptor's hands. The more motion the better. Probably that was why dowsing rods had traditionally been used more often to find underground water than for any other purpose. The water was moving, the dowser was walking more often than not, and when water was detected the rods moved.

But this was a line of thought Starn had pursued often before, to no new conclusion. Motion might be basic to perception, but it didn't seem to be—at least not in any gross form—to the other Novo senses. That made it unlikely to offer the opening he seemed to need.

Billy got a drink of water, puttered about the camp for a few minutes, and sat down at last by Starn's chair.

"Can I help think, Daddy?" he asked.

"Maybe so, son," Starn smiled. "I could certainly use some help."

Billy nodded gravely, and wrinkled his brow in imitation of his father. But in short order he looked up to complain, "I have to know how percepting works before I can think about it."

"If I knew how it worked—" Starn began. He stopped and began trying to explain. "Perception is a sense, Billy, like seeing, hearing, tasting, smelling, and feeling. But not everybody has perception. That's the main reason it's called a Novo sense. There are others like it, such as being able to know what somebody else is thinking, called telepathy, or to know things that haven't happened yet, which is premonating.

"Now, people have all sorts of contrivances to extend their ability to see and hear—telescopes, microscopes, sound amplifiers, radios, infrared viewers, and so on. They have done less with smell, taste, and touch. They have made mechanical feelers that can tell a lot more about the feel of something than you could with your fingers, but these machines report their findings to our eyes and ears, so they're extensions of our sense of touch only indirectly. As for smell and taste, what they do with those is mostly to control what we smell and taste, to give us the ones we like and get rid of the ones we don't like.

"What I want to do is find ways to extend the Novo senses, the way telescopes and radios extend seeing and hearing. That's what the dowsing machine with the needle rods does for perception, but it doesn't do it very well. I want something much better than that."

Billy was silent for a while after Starn finished. Then he asked, "How do the regular senses work, Daddy?"

Hiding a touch of impatience, Starn said, "Well, there are thousands of tiny nerve ends at the back of our eyeballs, and in our ears, and in our skin. When we open our eyes, light reflected from the things around us goes in and excites our eye nerves in different ways, and this pattern of excitements go to our brain which interprets them as an image of whatever we're looking at. Or a sound we hear is a vibration of the air in our ears, which makes little membranes and bones vibrate, too, and the ear nerves take the message of those vibrations to the brain. Or when we press a finger against something, like this piece of bark, for example, the nerves in our skin are excited, and the pattern of excitements tells the brain if we're feeling something smooth or rough, hard or soft, or cold or hot."

"That makes perception a lot like feeling and hearing," said Billy, "but not much like seeing, don't it?"

Starn blinked. "How is that?"

"Well, you got to move to touch something, or the air's got to move for you to hear something. But nothing has to move for you to see something."

"That's right," Starn grinned with amusement. "But seeing requires light, which is moving, although much too rapidly for you to be aware of it as motion. Light, like air vibrations, is energy, and all the senses, even smell and taste, need energy to make them work."

"Yeah, you need to breathe in the air to smell," agreed Billy wisely, "or put something in your mouth to taste it."

"I wasn't thinking of that, exactly," said Starn. "The food in your mouth and the smelly molecules in your nose have to undergo a chemical reaction with the liquid on your tongue or your nasal passage. They give up chemical energy to work your senses. In fact—"

Starn hesitated. It was not a new thought, exactly, that stopped him. It was an old one that had never come through to him quite so vividly before. "In fact," he repeated slowly, "it is energy, and not substance, that *all* our senses detect."

His mind was a whirl of activity. No wonder perception required motion, which was itself an aspect of energy. But what about telepathy? Brainwaves? Energy in the electromagnetic spectrum? That was hardly likely, or the Olsaperns would have devised a means of telepathic jamming long ago. Even a flash of lightning would create telepathic static if that were the case, and lightning did no such thing.

Also, gross motion could not be the only energy involved in perception. The motion had to set up an energy *field* of some sort; otherwise the motion could not be perceived at a distance. Whether or not this field was the same kind of energy that powered telepathy he couldn't guess. It could be the same, or it could be as different as a light photon is from a sound vibration.

And what about the energy that premonating would require—an energy that went backward through time? Well, weren't some subatomic particles time-reversible? He seemed to recall reading that they were, but that was an area of science that he knew little about.

The trouble was, he thought with frustration, there was precious little he understood about any science at all. Take the medium Cytherni used for her paint-sculptures, for instance: menergy. He understood what it was only in a very general, and, therefore, highly uninformative, way. Matrices of "solid" energy, or self-containing energy.

And that, he had a hunch, was something he definitely should understand, because as he had finally realized, the key to the secret of the Novo senses was hidden in the concept of energy, which made that a subject he couldn't know too much about!

Billy had to repeat his question before Starn heard him.

"Where are the perception nerve ends, Daddy?"

"Huh?"

"The seeing nerve ends are in the eyeballs, and the feeling nerve ends are in the skin. Where are the perception nerve ends?"

"Oh. I don't know. Perhaps all through us. Or perhaps those nerves end inside the brain, with no external sense organs. Maybe that's the difference between Novo and regular senses."

In which case Novo energy would have to be of a kind that passed readily through flesh and bone, like a ghostly type of X-ray.

Starn got up and went into the tent, where he rummaged around in the bottom of the chutepacks for several minutes before he found what he thought would be there somewhere. A pack of collapsed menergy matrices, of the small size used by Cytherni for quick outdoor sketches. He took one out and activated it, watching and feeling the way it expanded in his hand from a tiny gray wafer to a clearly transparent, slightly shimmering cube with eight-inch sides. Inside, near the center, he could see the pea-sized black sphere that powered the matrix.

An eight-inch cube of energy . . . but what *kind* of energy? Starn's comprehension stopped far short of the answer to that. "Pure energy," one of the Olsaperns had told him, but what did "pure" mean when applied to energy? Wasn't light pure? Or relative motion? Obviously "pure" in this context had a specialized meaning that was a mystery to him.

Still carrying the menergy matrix, he went back to his chair. "Did you get an idea, Daddy?" Billy asked.

"Maybe the start of one. Let's let it rest a while and see. Right now, how about some lunch, then I'll show you how to handle a gun, and we'll do a little hunting."

"Oh, boy!" Billy exclaimed.

The next day Starn had enough tentative ideas to try some experiments. They were failures. Working from the analogy between ancient crystal-radio receivers versus powered electron-tube receivers—which had the advantage of being understandable to him—he tried to apply power to his dowsing machine circuit. The hope was to amplify the output, thus extending the device's range.

Not that he hadn't tried that before, but previously he had tried to energize the circuit with electricity. This time, working on the assumption that there might be something truly fundamental about the "pure" energy of a menergy matrix, he used a matrix as his power source. He tried every circuit arrangement he could imagine. Using techniques he had learned from watching his wife work, he even built a needle rod device completely inside a matrix, hoping to saturate it with the energy present there. It worked no better or worse than before.

He had to conclude that he was going about his job the wrong way. His device was *not* a detector like a radio receiver; the detector system was within the human perceptor. That, he realized with annoyance, should have been clear to him all along. The needle rod device was . . . well, an auxiliary device, an extension of the human "antenna" perhaps, plus a visual read-out unit. Or maybe it was analogous to a tuning coil. Or perhaps a tuned antenna.

There was a thought! If it were a tuning device, perhaps something very like it could be used to "tune" energy, not for itself but for the central perception circuitry in the human brain!

Billy's restlessness and his own uncertainty of how to proceed caused him to put off further tests until the next day, and to go exploring with the boy. This was something he had to do, anyway, to familiarize himself quite thoroughly with the neighboring terrain. If, by some chance, the Olsaperns and/or the Pack men located him sooner than his scheme called for, he would have to know every possible route of escape from his camp area.

That night as he and Billy ate supper, the boy asked, "How long are we going to camp, Daddy?"

"I'm not sure," said Starn. Realizing that this was an insufficient answer he added, "You see, Billy, we're playing a game like hide-and-seek with Higgins, and with my old friends in Pack Foser. So we have to stay hidden until some of them find us. I don't know how long that will take."

"Oh," said Billy, obviously pleased to be playing a game with grown-ups, and as his father's teammate. "Do you guess they're hunting us right now?"

Starn smiled. "I'm quite sure they are, son," he said, "quite sure, indeed."

But, he wondered silently, are they hunting together or separately?

When he woke the following morning the solution was waiting for him. It unfolded in his conscious, rough-hewn to be sure, but complete. And as one often does when a simple answer finally dawns, he wondered why he had missed it before.

As soon as breakfast was over and Billy was off in pursuit of whatever mountain fauna he could scare up, Starn got to work again. Energy *could* be tuned to supplement that normally available to the perceptive circuitry in the human nervous system! The needle rod device could do it. His trouble before was that he had been trying to go in the wrong direction. The device was essentially a . . . not a filter, exactly, but something like that. The Olsaperns would have a proper descriptive word for it, but Starn was less interested in words than results. A filter took out what was not wanted, but his device catalyzed what was not wanted into what was.

What he had to do was surround an energy source with this pseudo-filtering effect. The job was a tricky one for his amateur hands. It involved reshaping a cubical, leak-proof menergy matrix into one that was spherical and, therefore, thoroughly leaky, and enclosing the sphere with his pseudofilter. Actually, the effective circuitry surrounded not the sphere but the small central power source, and that made the fabrication process much simpler.

An hour of painstaking effort produced a carefully trimmed wafer of unactivated menergy with a knot of microlek components at its center, with two raw-ended wires trailing away from the knot. Starn took a deep breath, stood back, and touched the wire ends together.

The sphere expanded to a nine-inch diameter, glittering with escaping energy, then over a period of seconds dimmed and shrunk to the size of a tennis ball. As it did so a soundless "noise" poured into Starn's brain, a noise that made him whirl and crouch reflexively, alert for whatever monstrous danger was creeping up behind him.

In his alarm, he dropped the wires and their ends fell apart. The tennis ball collapsed into a wafer, the noise vanished, and with it the monstrous danger.

A bearlike bellow of protest came dimly to his ears from some distance away. Closer at hand he heard Billy's alarmed screech, *"Daddy!"*

Starn galloped down the mountain slope in the boy's direction, filled with puzzled concern. If his experiment had harmed the boy he . . . !

Billy came in sight legging it hard toward the camp. He slowed when he saw his father and his fright diminished. "There was an awful loud noise, Daddy!" he exclaimed, wide-eyed. "Do you know what made it?"

"I made it, son, with a gadget I was working on. Did it hurt you?"

"No, I guess it didn't," said Billy. "It just scared me. A little bit. It was such a funny kind of noise."

Starn took the boy's hand and walked back toward the camp. "You mean it wasn't a noise you heard, but one you percepted?"

"That's right!" said the boy. "It was like . . . like perception-stuff was packed tight all around me, and making an awful racket! Gosh, you made a gadget that really works, this time, Daddy!"

Starn nodded slowly. "Looks like I did at that, son. But it doesn't work the way I meant it to."

"What was it supposed to do?"

"It was supposed to be a . . . a kind of light for perception, to let your perception see better. But instead of lighting up things, it shined in your eyes instead, and blinded you."

"You don't *see* when you percept, you *hear,* kind of," the boy objected. "But it did make a kind of light, too. But the light wasn't as much as the noise."

Noise *and* light? Starn considered this. Telepaths always spoke of "reading" thoughts, as if the process were related to seeing. And for Billy, with perhaps an unusably weak telepathic sense, the gadget had made a light that was, to him, minor compared to the noise. Probably a telepath would have experienced a blinding flash of "light" accompanied by a slight noise.

But it was not strange for an energy source to produce signals that reached more than one sense. A dynamite explosion, for instance, was quite evident to ears and eyes—and if close enough it could also be smelled, tasted and felt! Quite possibly, then, the gadget was an undiscriminating transmitter of Novo energy. Just how it could be used, and what effect it would have on the Novo senses . . .

Careful to hide his sudden worry, Starn said, "What can you find with your needle rods here, Billy?"

The boy got the sensor unit out of his pocket and held it in front of him as they trudged up the mountainside. He watched it a moment, then slapped it against the palm of his other hand. "It's stopped working, Daddy. It don't show anything at all."

"What can you percept without it?"

After a moment of concentration, Billy replied in consternation: "Nothing. Nothing at all!"

Starn nodded grimly. "I'm afraid that noise deafened your perception, Billy," he said.

The boy's face puckered. "Forever?" he asked after a moment.

"We can hope not. We'll have to wait and see."

Lunch was a sober affair for both of them. Afterward Starn sat in his chair, glumly puzzling over what had happened to Billy, and why. The boy stretched out on the dead leaves where a spot of sunlight came through the trees and was soon napping.

An hour and a half later he sat up suddenly. "Daddy, I can percept again! Just as good as ever!"

Starn heaved a mighty sigh of relief and grinned.

"That's fine, son, just fine!"

The boy went to the water jug and drank thirstily. "What are you going to try now?" he asked.

"Nothing," said Starn. "That gadget proved that this is too risky to fool with."

"Aw," said Billy. "It wasn't that bad! It was like looking at a bright light, and then looking at something else and not being able to see it right off. But it went away in a little while!"

"Yes," said Starn, "but if a person looks directly at the sun too often, or too long, he can blind himself permanently."

Billy thought this over. "Could you make the noise dimmer, so it wouldn't hurt? Or maybe aim it so it would hit what I was trying to percept instead of hitting me?"

"I've been trying to think of a way to shield it in specific directions," replied Starn, "but I don't believe it can be shielded. Once this energy is generated, there's no stopping it."

"But do you have to generate it every which way?" asked Billy insistently.

"I don't know," replied Starn, eyeing the boy curiously. "You seem awfully eager about this," he remarked.

"Gosh, yes!" exclaimed Billy. "If you could make something that would percept for miles and miles, through mountains and everything, that'd be the best thing you've *ever* made for me! It would be a lot of fun!"

A *toy!* That's what it would be to Billy. What would it be to others? *If* others unbent from their prejudices sufficiently to accept it? To Higgins, a way to find needed oil and other resources, or a means of spying on the Pack men. To the Pack men, a weapon to be used in their feuds with each other, and perhaps against Olsaperns.

Certainly as a weapon against anyone employing a Novo sense. In fact, the transmitter Starn had already made was that. Whatever else he did, he decided he would produce a supply of such transmitters before nightfall, and keep them handy just in case.

But a Novo energy transmitter that could be aimed at the thing to be sensed, without overloading the mind's sensors with a flood of energy . . . The only way was to create a directional radiation of the energy at the beginning, instead of attempting to provide directional shielding after it was created. And the amount of energy should be far less than the transmitter had produced. The spherical menergy matrix leaked entirely too much . . .

And there was the answer, of course, neatly packaged for him by Olsapern technology, which was as it should be. The cubical matrix leaked no energy at all. So all he had to do, really, was make another transmitter like the first, but housed in a matrix flat on five faces and bulging only the slightest amount on the sixth. Only as the energy leaked away from the matrix was it converted into the medium that impinged on the Novo senses, and it would leak away in one direction only, from the one, bulged face of the cube.

"All right, Billy," said Starn, "I'll have another go at it."

The boy wandered off to a nearby spring while Starn worked. The beam was finished before he returned. Starn aimed it straight up as he activated the matrix, which in appearance at least was little different from those into which Cytherni injected paint. The curvature of the bulged side was too slight to be visible, and the energy escapage was too minor to gray it noticeably. It differed from the other sides only in appearing to be covered with a light film.

Holding his breath, Starn aimed the Novo beam at himself. A sound? Yes, perhaps, it could be called that. It was barely noticeable. The sense was definitely there, though, that something was creeping up behind him. It was less powerful than the real thing. Perhaps with the beam generator at an appreciable distance, the effect would not come through at all.

He pointed the beam in front of him and slowly turned around. It was as if he had been blind all his life and someone had suddenly supplied him with eyes. There was Billy down by the spring. Does he know the beam is on him? Apparently not. *Hey, Billy, what are you doing?* That made him jump! He's looking up here and grinning. Now he's coming this way.

Starn continued to turn. There's a family of bears, over on the next mountain. One roared this morning. Minerals? Yes, but I don't know how to identify them from what I sense.

"Let me try it, Daddy," pleaded Billy, dashing up panting.

Starn handed it over with the admonition, "You will probably be able to reach farther than I can with it, son. If you reach any people, don't call to them, or you'll give our presence here away, and we're still in that hide-and-seek game."

"All right, Daddy." The boy seized the beam and began avidly studying his surroundings, exclaiming excitedly over the results. Starn stood watching, feeling that supreme exaltation that comes only in a moment of high discovery.

"Hey, there's Mommy!" yelled Billy.

"What? Where?"

"She's at Foser Compound. That's hundreds of miles away! But it's her all right."

"What is she doing?" asked Starn, feeling a pang of guilt.

"Nothing much. Just sitting around. I think she's mad at somebody, but I can't tell why." He held the beam steady for several seconds before moving on around. Starn, momentarily distraught by his regrets concerning Cytherni, was not aware of Billy swinging the beam toward him until his danger sense alerted him. He jumped.

Billy had lowered the beam and was staring at him in hurt surprise. "Gosh, Daddy! If you flipped her out of the flier, no wonder she's mad!"

After a stunned moment, Starn asked, "Did you see that in my mind?"

"I guess so," said Billy. "It was there when I pointed the beam at you."

"Don't point it at me again while we're here, son," said Starn. "Did you see that I didn't really want to do that to your mother?"

"Yes. You didn't want to but you had to, but you didn't think why."

"Good. I don't want you to know why just yet, Billy. If you know I regret that I—"

"It's all right, Daddy. I'm not mad or anything. And maybe Mommy's mad about something else. She's so far away that all I could tell was that she was mad."

Starn nodded, greatly relieved at the way Billy was taking his discovery. "What do you say we quit working and go exploring?" he asked.

"Hot dog!" Billy shouted, and thoughts of his angry mother were forgotten.

But every few hours after that, Billy would reactivate the beam and aim it northeast for a few minutes, to see what his mother was doing. Starn was glad he did, because Billy reported on what he saw and, in a way, kept Starn in touch with his wife.

It was two days later before Billy reported anything unusual. "She's awful worried and scared," he said half tearfully. "She's running somewhere with some- body—Now she's looking at me! No, not at *me*, at one of her paint things of me! Gosh, I thought for a second there that I'd showed her—Now somebody else *is* look- ing at me, Daddy! He's an old man, kind of scrawny, and he's looking at Mommy and seeing me! He sees that mountain over there, and our tent, and me sitting on that big rock, but I'm not on the rock! How come he sees me like that?"

It took Starn a moment to figure out what was happen- ing. "Old Harnk, the finder," he muttered. "I'd forgotten about him. We'll have to—" He stopped. What should he do now? This was an unexpected development that would destroy his scheme before it had a chance to bear fruit.

Obviously, he had to get away from the camp immediately—and leave Billy behind. With old Harnk in the picture, the boy would be found anywhere he went, and if he stayed with his father, then Starn could be found, too. That is, if—

"Are the Olsaperns going to help them come and get you?" he asked.

"I guess so. They're talking about it."

"Then they'll be here soon, Billy. Our game is half over. They've found you, but not me. You'll have to stay here and wait for them, and I'll go hide somewhere else." He began putting together a light pack, taking nothing but what he had to have, or didn't dare leave behind. "Did you watch me close enough, Billy, to see how I made the energy transmitter, or the beam?"

"No, I don't guess so. But, if you'll show me how, I'll remember it, all right."

Starn smiled. "No. It'll be more fun to make the Pack men and Olsaperns hunt me without knowing how to make such gadgets, and if you knew, the telepaths could find out from you."

Starn was careful to gather up all the needle rods, transmitters, and beam projectors he had made in his experiments and stuff them into his pack. "Sorry our camping trip has to end so quickly, son," he said to the glum-faced boy. "But they'll be here to get you in an hour or two, and then they'll take you to Mother. You'll like being with her again, won't you?"

The boy nodded.

Starn strapped on the pack, then knelt and gave the boy a squeeze. "Give her my love, won't you?"

"O.K., Daddy."

Rising hurriedly, Starn strode away from the camp and Billy sat down on the big rock to wait.

5

The two fliers were manned by a mixture of Olsapern defensemen and Foser raiders. Men from both sides were lowered into the camp from the craft that hovered over the trees, while the other began circling in search of Starn's telepathic scent.

He had not been able to go far over such difficult terrain in so short a time. Soon they had him located. Both fliers hovered near the spot and the Pack men swarmed down the droplines.

Peering upward, Starn guessed that the Olsapern defensemen were, very wisely, being held in reserve. This kind of action was not their meat. He had to guard his thoughts carefully with so many telepaths within range . . . think only of the immediate problem of escape and nothing else.

He fitted an arrow to which a—*No! Don't think it!*—was tied into his bow and shot it high into the trunk of a large oak. When the arrow struck a glowing ball lit up, dangling from it. The ball dimmed, and a confusion of shouts arose from the Pack men.

Every one of the Foser raiders would doubtless be strongly Novo-sensed, he assumed. The transmitter would do more than blind their special senses; the flood of "static" would drive them half out of their wits. He took the opportunity to change his position and pass between his would-be captors.

The difficulty was that on board the fliers were instruments such as infrared detectors that would not be confused by the Novo transmitter. As long as he stayed near Foser raiders, who were now stumbling about aimlessly and almost drunkenly, the Olsapern instruments would probably be unable to single him out. But if he began moving away, the action would identify him. Not that the defensemen could expect to come down the drop-lines and capture him where the Pack men had failed, but they could kill him very easily, if they wished, without leaving the fliers.

He crouched out of sight in a bush-covered crevice for several minutes, listening to the raiders call to each other and thrash about, trying to get themselves orga-nized. If it were only dark, he thought with annoyance, he could mingle freely with the Pack men, even join their search for him, and if they dispersed to scout the surrounding mountains he could get out of range of Olsapern instruments. But darkness was hours away. Long before that someone would succeed in silencing his transmitter. Novo senses would remain blinded for a while, but with the static stopped the raiders would be less confused and—

Another sound joined the voices of the Pack men. It was distant but coming closer: the growls of bears, sound-ing extremely annoyed over something. The big animals had made themselves scarce in the vicinity of his camp, their old and well-learned distrust of man augmented by the barkings of his and Billy's rifles when they went hunt-ing. Only once during their stay had Starn even heard a bear, and that one in the distance just after he had briefly activated his first Novo energy transmitter.

And that had been a roar of protest!

Whether or not bears were Novo-sensed was a ques-tion for later investigation. But obviously there was some-thing about the radiations from a Novo transmitter that bothered them, and bothered them bad! Right now they were heading toward the scene of the search from several directions, with the evident intent of laying heavy paws on the source of those irksome energies.

"Bears!" a Foser man bellowed. More yells followed, then rifle shots, and roars of pain from wounded animals. Starn eased out of hiding in time to see a large female bear, dripping blood from a flesh wound in her flank, retreating in his direction. He stepped aside and behind a tree to let her lumber past.

What annoyance the transmitter caused the animals was not enough to make them brave a barrage of rifle fire. They were leaving the scene, and scattering.

Starn joined them.

Relationships were strained at Foser Compound.

The Olsaperns were angry and suspicious over Starn's escape from the party of raiders. The Pack had Billy, under the agreement between Rob and Higgins, but the Olsaperns did not have Starn, who was to have been theirs. Therefore, they argued, the agreement was invalid, and Cytherni and the boy should be turned over to them.

And there was the embarrassing and somewhat dismaying fact that Starn's Novo "flare" had not only rendered the Foser raiders practically helpless; it had had similar if less drastic effects on a few of the Olsapern defensemen who had been in the fliers. Though the Olsaperns owned no usable Novo senses, it seemed hard to deny that some of them had the inherent ability for such senses.

Also, recriminations were harsh the next day, when it was realized that Starn's "flare" device should have been brought back for study, and a second visit to the mountain site discovered the flare was gone. There were claw marks on the tree in which it had been lodged, and the ground was covered with bear tracks. But except for a broken arrow, a few strands of wire, and the shredded remains of a de-energized menergy wafer, nothing was there to be found.

The strain was not eased by the Packs' failure to inform the Olsaperns of what they learned from Billy about the Novo energy beam device until after Higgins had figured out—from the fact that Starn had known to desert the camp and leave Billy behind—that the fugitive had devised some means of learning that the camp had been located.

"There is such a thing as good faith," his image glowered at Rob. "At least there is among civilized men. You have shown little evidence of good faith in this whole affair, Foser."

"Don't talk to me about honor, Olsapern!" the Pack chief snapped back. "You can't regard us as animals and still expect us to give you the respect due to equals! Certainly we're not fools enough to tell you anything about a weapon you would delight in using against us!"

"We have no intention of using any weapon against you!" stormed Higgins. "We never have! All we've ever done has been protect ourselves against your childish attacks—attacks that were aimed more often than not at posts we established solely to assist you!"

Rob replied coldly, "We've learned from Cytherni that Starn had a more likely explanation for your trading posts."

"You're citing Starn as an authority?" sneered Higgins. "But never mind answering that. We're getting away from the basic point I'm trying to make, that we've never fought an aggressive battle with Pack men. On the record, you don't have the slightest excuse for withholding information about weapons developed by a man who is a danger to us all!"

"But on the other hand," retorted Rob, "I notice you are deadly afraid of letting any knowledge of Olsapern weapons fall in Pack hands. Not once has an engineer or a scientist come south of the Hard Line."

"Aren't we justified in that?" Higgins demanded. "Haven't we been given every reason to expect that better weapons would make the Packs bigger and bloodier nuisances?"

"Not if you would drop that silly attitude of superiority!" blared Rob. "Close down those insulting trading posts! Ask our permission when you want to dig a mine in Pack country! And when you have to deal with us at all, stop sending your village idiots as envoys! It's no skin off our noses if you don't follow the Sacred Gene; neither do the animals of the forest! We don't fight you because of religion, but because you're so despicable!"

Higgins looked startled. "That's a surprising revelation, if true."

Rob was silent for a moment, then said, "The members of Pack Foser, as well as the travelers from other Packs who are here at the moment, agree that it is true. Although we have perhaps thought otherwise in the past."

"Very well," said Higgins. "If it's your price for cooperation in the present emergency, we'll be glad to withdraw our trading posts and have no more dealings with the Packs than are absolutely essential in the future. You can starve when a drought ruins your primitive agriculture, or die in an epidemic for lack of decent medicine. To use your own phrase, that's no skin off our noses."

Rob frowned but did not speak.

Higgins continued: "As for quelling the danger that Starn poses, my scientists and engineers can do the job if you'll give us what you've learned about those devices of his. Unfortunately, he left nothing at his home to give us a clue to his approach. So, if you will tell us what you've learned from Cytherni and Billy about the construction of his inventions, we'll get busy."

Rob shrugged. "They don't know. Cytherni wasn't interested enough to learn, and Starn sidetracked Billy when the boy became curious about the structural details of the gadgets. About all we know is that he used that menergy stuff in the things he made in the mountains. Billy has some vague ideas about other details, but I can't make enough sense out of them to describe them." He stared thoughtfully at Higgins' image. "If you want to make some headway on Starn," he said, "you'd better send a team of scientists down here. Maybe they'll know what kind of questions to ask Billy, to bring out what he does know.

"And besides, Higgins, the Packs will be able to see cooperating with you much easier if the work is done here, where we can be sure we know what's being accomplished, and that you're not preparing any unpleasant surprises for us. You'll have close access to Billy, and to other persons with well-developed Novo senses. It's not going to help you to build extensors for those senses unless you have the senses to apply them when they're complete."

Higgins fidgeted unhappily. "Sending scientists down there is out of the question," he said with a lack of conviction, "and it has been demonstrated that we normals often have touches of these senses."

"Touches is about all," said Rob.

"Damn!" cursed Higgins. "I wouldn't listen to such a nonsensical proposal for a minute if these new devices of Starn's didn't have such a disturbing potential!"

"Nor would I have suggested it," came Rob's tart reply. "We have no stomach for the close association with Olsaperns this emergency is forcing on us. But the point is that if we put our differences aside temporarily, and solve this problem quickly, the association can be kept brief. The way things are going, it could drag on for months—even years if Starn comes up with something new! Let's take the bitter pill quick, Higgins, and quit agonizing over it!"

Finally Higgins nodded grudgingly. "I'll take it up with our council and let you know," he agreed.

6

At first Starn traveled by night and slept by day, staying in deep valleys as much as possible. His reason for this was to elude telepathic detection if Pack-Olsapern teams were continuing the search for him.

Most of the searching, he assumed, would be done during daylight hours, and a sleeping mind is harder to detect, and still harder to identify, than one that is awake.

He tried to push himself severely enough during each night's trek to be dog-tired by dawn, so that he would sleep soundly until nightfall.

The pace began to tell on him in less than a week, and he eased off a bit. By then he was far from the spot where Billy had been taken, and could feel reasonably safe from anything except chance discovery or a massive search . . . or, of course, a search conducted with strongly extended Novo senses.

By now, he guessed, the Packs and the Olsaperns would be working hard—and together—on sense extensions, if they were ever going to work together at all. He had tried to leave nothing behind that would be too helpful to them; he had even risked returning to the scene of his escape from the Foser raiders, after he saw the fliers lifting away, to retrieve the Novo energy transmitter from the oak tree, but found that the bears had returned ahead of him and had left little to worry about.

He kept moving southward at a leisurely, cautious rate. Movement itself brought some risk of discovery, but summer was drawing to a close and he had no real idea how long he could remain untaken. Months, perhaps, in which case he wanted to seek winter quarters in a warm southern clime.

But the mountains were petering out, and at last he was forced to halt by the near certainty that Packs were living in the foothills ahead. In fact, he retreated northward a long march, to get out of range of winter hunting parties. There, in a cove that was both secluded and sheltered, he threw up a tight lean-to and settled down to wait.

It was with some wonder that he realized that matters which had been of vital concern to him only a few weeks ago now seemed distant, and of little pressing interest. This, he mused, was probably what happened when people went "back to nature." The draining demands of extracting food, shelter, and other bodily comforts from a primitive environment left little energy for other pursuits.

Thus, he thought a little about improving upon his menergy-powered devices, but no ideas came, so he did nothing more than think. His creative unconscious was not presented with an urgent need to produce new ideas, so it failed to produce.

Also, in his imagination he could see joint teams of Olsapern scientists and strong-sensed Pack men hard at work, exploring avenues that he—neither scientific nor strongly-sensed—could not even be aware of. What was the point of trying to compete with something like that?

More often his thoughts were of Cytherni. Of course she had learned from Billy, if she hadn't guessed before, that what had happened was not the result of an accidental fall from the flier. What would she be thinking of her loving husband now? Even a full explanation of the reasons for his actions, Starn fretted, might sound awfully empty to her. The point would still remain, as he had known it would from the beginning, that he had used her, not with her knowing compliance, but as an unwitting tool. How could any explanation make that right?

The weeks dragged by and summer faded. The mountain forest flamed with autumn reds and yellows. Starn eyed the empty sky with growing impatience. With every passing day the guessed-at activities of Pack men and Olsaperns seemed less important, and the need to see Cytherni and settle things with her one way or the other grew more insistent.

When the shadow of a hovering flier passed over him at last he almost yelled and waved, like a stranded castaway at the first sight of a rescuer. Before he recovered from this reaction he realized he had given his true feelings away to such an extent that it would be silly to make a pretense of trying to escape again, or to do battle with his captors. Indeed, it was also too late to activate a Novo transmitter to blind any telepaths aboard to his thoughts.

His game was over. He waited quietly.

A dropline snaked from the flier and one man came down. Starn walked forward. When he saw who it was, he said, "Hello, Rob."

Rob's feet touched the ground and he stood glaring angrily at Starn. Without trying to control his thoughts, Starn waited patiently while the telepath learned what he wanted to know.

"I'm usually called Foser now," Rob said rather stiffly. Then: "So you were never a threat, after all."

"How could I be?" shrugged Starn. "If I were both a gifted Novo and a knowledgeable scientist, maybe I could have hid out somewhere and developed the means of producing a revolution. But I was neither of those things. All I could do, with Billy's help, was make a start. That was enough, I hope, to get you and the Olsaperns into action, to produce the revolution I couldn't."

He grinned at the glowing Pack chief. "Looks like I succeeded. You've found me, at any rate. And what's that strange-looking helmet you're wearing?"

"A defense against your energy transmitter. A shield, but one I can read through."

"Sounds impressive," approved Starn. "Do you have much more stuff like that?"

"Too much more!" snapped Rob. "If you have anything to pack, pack it! If not, let's be on our way."

The dozen or so Pack men and Olsaperns on the flier watched Starn with various shades of silent disapproval as he climbed in and took a seat. Rob settled down near him as the flier headed north.

"Where are we going?" Starn asked.

"To the Compound," was Rob's short reply. In a moment he relented slightly and added, "The Olsaperns take you from there, according to our agreement. I don't know where. Don't care either."

"Are Cytherni and Billy at the Compound?"

Rob nodded. "They'll be staying there . . . or . . . well, the Olsaperns can have them, too, as far as I'm concerned! I'm fed up with the lot of you!"

The discovery of the manner in which he had been had by Starn was plainly annoying to Rob, despite the fact that the Olsaperns had been had just as thoroughly. Starn's antics had forced both peoples to spend months in unwilling—and to them unnatural—association and cooperation, and to learn now that he had been developing no monstrous weapons must come as a blow. They had been collaborating against a nonexistent danger.

"I'm sorry, Rob," Starn said softly. "It had to be done, and there was no other way I could do it."

"It *didn't* have to be done!" snarled Rob. "Things were going fine the way they were! Now you've got everyone confused and upset—and I might add you've caused your old father more heartbreak than any father deserves, much less a fine, gentle man like Virnce! You've undermined the faith of the Packs disastrously!"

The reference to his father stung Starn. He had known it would grieve Virnce, the Speaker at the Tenthday Services, to learn his own son had turned iconoclast. But it was a grief that had to be borne.

"If the faith of the Packs can be undermined by a few new facts," he said slowly, "it isn't much of a faith. Just as the science of the Olsaperns has already proved it isn't much of a science," he went on with a glance at the defensemen, "by rejecting new facts until they were shoved down its throat.

"The point is that, separately, the Packs and the Olsaperns were both wrong. Together they might be right—or at least closer to right. Both sides claim to love the truth. All right. Think of all the truth you've learned while working together! That helmet you're wearing. Whatever kind of gadget you used to locate me. Probably a lot of other things I don't know about. You understand your Novo senses better, and can use them more effectively. And Olsapern science has been broadened immeasurably. These are the fruits—"

"Bitter, unhealthy fruits!" hissed Rob.

"You don't know that," said Starn. "I'm not sure you even think it. You've merely been thrown off-balance because the world is changing after all these centuries, and you're not used to change. Nobody is."

"The world has always been changing," Rob argued. "We've been progressing steadily toward the Ultimate Novo."

"At a snail's pace, maybe we have. The Packs don't have to lose that goal of the ideal, fully-sensed man. But with the help of Olsapern science, which you've ignored up to now, don't you think you might reach your goal much quicker?"

"Ugh!" Rob grunted in disgust, and turned away.

Talk, Starn realized, would not make much impact on Rob's feelings—or, for that matter, on the course of events his actions had set in motion. What had been accomplished had been accomplished, and that was irretrievably that. His scheme had worked, and would open human horizons to undreamed-of breadth.

Also, it was a source of annoyance to a lot of people, including Rob, and of genuine personal grief to some, such as Starn's father, and to Cytherni—and thus in all likelihood to Starn himself.

The successful revolutionist sat in silence, lost in glum thoughts, for the remainder of the flight.

A large prefabricated building had risen in Smirth's meadow not far from the Compound, to house the joint research projects of Pack men and Olsapern scientists. It was surrounded by smaller sheds and numerous tents. The flier landed in a cleared area near the main building's entrance.

"Follow me," Rob ordered, and led Starn inside.

There a heated discussion was in progress among a sizable group of people from both sides of the Hard Line. Rob entered right into it, but Starn, not being telepathic, spent several minutes trying to figure out what was being debated. Meanwhile he was largely ignored by everyone present, including the image of Higgins which, after a passing angry glare at him, returned its attention to the argument.

These people, thought Starn, with a left-out feeling, *are all experts—some for what they know and some for what they are—and I'm a mere layman. A troublesome layman, at that.*

They used terms he couldn't guess the meaning of, but he kept trying to follow the argument until he finally caught on.

Word of his capture, and of his harmless recent activities, had of course been radioed ahead of the flier. So the people in the research center were discussing ways and means of concluding their joint project, now that the reason for it had been removed.

Starn laughed rather loudly, a derisive bark that brought all eyes on him.

"Nonsense!" snapped Rob, and several other telepaths grumbled.

"What's he thinking?" a scientist demanded.

"I'm thinking you'll never make it," Starn replied. "Now that you've started researching together, neither of you will dare break off the relationship. The Pack men have learned too much science to be trusted to work alone by the Olsaperns, and the Olsaperns could do too much with their own Novo senses to be trusted by the Packs!

"All you have to do to end your collaboration is learn to trust each other completely," he finished with a grin. "But if you could do that you wouldn't object to working together in the first place!"

Higgins' voice rumbled from a speaker: "I suppose you counted on this, too, didn't you?"

Starn shook his head slowly. "No. I never thought it through quite to this point. Other things could have happened. For one thing, you might have learned before now to like each other, because basically you're all pretty good folk.

"All I tried to do," he continued, "was to enable both sides to change their minds just enough to start working together, and to take the potentials of extended Novo senses seriously. You could have avoided all this, Higgins, if you hadn't refused to see plain facts when they were laid before you. Before any of you would look at the facts, the facts had to become a threat. That's what I made them. I don't believe either of you was afraid of what I, personally, would do with whatever I discovered, but you were afraid of what either of you would do to the other if just one of you got your hands on my gadgets.

"Something slightly like this happened back in the Science Age, you know. Everybody who was supposed to have good sense thought space travel was absurd, until a madman named Hitler started using giant rockets to carry weapons. Hitler was beaten too quickly for his enemies to team up and outdo him at building space rockets. After the war they started competing rocket programs, and explored separately because they were afraid to let any one nation take full control of space.

"If Hitler had lasted longer, and his enemies had gotten started in space on a cooperative basis, probably they wouldn't have dared to split up when the war ended. That's why I couldn't let you catch me too soon, and why I had to have something new and frightening to show

· you when you came after Billy. You had seen the threat by then, and that was enough of a mind-changer to start you working separately, just as the old nations did on space travel. I had to keep the threat going long enough after that to make you change your minds about working together as well. And now that you've—"

"Oh, shut up and get out of here!" roared Higgins. "We're going to work out a sensible plan to discontinue this project, young man, and we don't intend to be disrupted by your defeatist propagandizing! Get him out of there, won't you, Foser?"

"Scram, Starn!" snapped Rob. "We'll have no more troublemaking from you!"

Starn shrugged and wandered out of the building, feeling thoroughly deflated. He was no sooner outside than a small boy, belted with an assortment of unlikely gadgets and festooned with dangling wires, streaked up to him.

"Daddy!" the boy howled *joyfully*.

"Billy!" exclaimed Starn, hugging the boy close. "How's—"

"She'll be here in a minute. I run faster than she does. She don't want me to say anything about her."

"Oh." The boy was obviously rigged for telepathy and . . . probably Cytherni was right in not wanting the boy to try to act as a telepathic peacemaker. What was between her and Starn was best dealt with in their own modes of communication. "Why all the gadgets?" he asked to change the subject.

"So I can play with the Pack kids," said Billy. "Of course, I can do a lot of things they can't, with all this stuff of mine, and their folks won't let them use gadgets—most of 'em, anyway. And they can't sneak and do it, because their folks know everything they do! I'm sure glad we don't live here all the time!"

Before Starn could frame a reply to that, Cytherni came in sight. He put Billy down and walked toward her. The boy watched them for a moment, and then dashed away.

When they reached each other, Starn said, "I love you, Cythie. I hope you can still believe that."

"I've never doubted it, Starn," she replied softly. "And I love you."

"But I *used* you!" he said. "That's not something to forgive!"

"Not for you to forgive yourself for, but . . . you're forgiven by me." She looked curiously into his pained eyes and said, "If you can't use someone you love, and who loves you, when you have to, then who *can* you use?".

Starn puzzled over this line of reasoning, and shook his head. But things were going to be all right between them, and that was the important thing.

"I suppose I should visit my parents," he said after a moment, "if I will be welcome in my father's hut."

"You won't be welcome," she said, "but you must go, anyway. They will be more injured if you don't come. Then we can go home, the three of us. Everybody here will be glad to see us leave, Billy tells me."

"And I'll be glad to go," Starn said fervently.

But after two months of cozy, anticlimactic inactivity Starn grew dissatisfied with himself. There were compensations, certainly, such as Cytherni's announcement that she was pregnant, but Starn was a man whose goal had been attained, and he was left without a new aim, a motive for purposeful activity.

Cytherni had attacked her art with a strong burst of renewed inspiration, and Billy was busy with schooling, and the boy had also taken over the workshop Starn no longer cared to use. The boy apparently was brilliant, and his weeks of getting underfoot at the joint research center had left him, Starn thought at times, knowing as much as all the scientists and Pack men together.

But Starn was at loose ends, and getting miserable.

Finally he risked a call to Higgins, and was pleased to find that the Defense Minister's anger with him had faded.

"Sure, I can find a job for you!" Higgins responded to his request. "There are plenty of administrative problems in our relations with the Packs—things you ought to know how to deal with. But don't expect any key positions, boy, not for a long time! You've made too many people too mad for that! But this is an expanding field, what with all the research and increased trade and what not. Come by tomorrow afternoon and we'll talk."

Starn thanked him and hung up in better spirits than he had been for days. If he, a revolutionary, could be of some value to the new world he had opened . . . well, so far as most historical precedents were concerned that would be a unique contribution in itself!

Billy came into his study, having detected, Starn guessed, his improved mood.

"Daddy, I know how to think things in a way that telepaths can't read, without using a shield or anything," the boy announced.

Starn considered this thoughtfully, and without much surprise. At last he said, "But aren't you giving the trick away in telling me about it? If others find out from me that you can have secret thoughts they'll know at least not to trust the thoughts they *think* are all you are having."

"I know that, Daddy," the boy said gravely. "So I want to show you how to think secret, too, so you can hide this."

"It would be a good ability to have in this job I was talking to Higgins about," Starn mused. "O.K."

He followed the boy into the workshop, and half an hour later he had learned the trick—plus a lot about the working of the human mind that he had never suspected.

"How did you get onto this?" he asked.

"By turning the gadgets on myself, instead of the environment," the boy replied. "Mommy thinks I have a Narcissus complex, and I guess I have a little. Anyway, I wanted to look at me, and when I did, one of the things I learned was how to think secret."

Starn chuckled and regarded the boy proudly. "Anything else important in you?" he asked.

Billy nodded. "I guess I can tell you, now that you can hide it: That theory about a communication line between the unconscious and the genes is right, only the line don't work very well, or very often. I found how to make it work good, in me or in anybody."

"You mean," asked Starn through a suddenly dry throat, "that you can order genetic changes of any kind you wish?"

"Uh-huh," the boy nodded.

"Billy," Starn began tightly, "you haven't meddled—"

"Oh, no. You and Mommy wouldn't like that! My baby sister will be pretty much like me, I guess. But my own children—"

Starn's knees felt weak, so he sank into a chair, staring at his seven-year-old son.

At least the boy wasn't going off half-cocked, testing his new-found ability of genetic manipulation. Maybe by the time he was old enough to have children of his own he also would have the wisdom.

Or would he? Did *anybody* ever get *that* wise? Wise enough and knowledgeable enough to make *balanced and desirable* genetic changes? Capable of deciding that which generations beyond count had puzzled over with total lack of success—*what, precisely, should be the nature of the man who followed man?*

Could any human, with his finite knowledge, ever answer a question that posed such infinite possibilities and complexities? Why have a god, such as the Great Gene, if you did not mean to leave such matters in his hands?

Billy was looking at him with a slight smile. "Gosh, Daddy, you're an awful alarmist!" he said soothingly and with a touch of amusement. "It won't be that hard to do."

Starn, a revolutionary who had ripped the status quo asunder and filled countless complacent lives with the uncertain gales of change, continued to stare at his son, shocked to the core of his being by the realization that his own grandchildren would be Ultimate Novo!

Or . . . *something!*

Afterword

Baen Books has now reissued the complete writings of Howard L. Myers in two volumes. Below, for those readers interested, we append the complete bibliography of the author. All of Myers' stories were short fiction except for his one novel, *Cloud Chamber*—although if both parts are combined, as we did in this volume, *The Ultimo Novo* constitutes a second novel.

Eric Flint and Guy Gordon

Title of story	Pen-name	Date	First publication	Volume
The Reluctant Weapon		Dec 1952	*Galaxy*	1
Lost Calling	Verge Foray	Sept 1967	*Analog*	1
Practice!	Verge Foray	Mar 1968	*Analog*	1
His Master's Vice	Verge Foray	May 1968	*Analog*	2
The Creatures of Man	Verge Foray	May 1968	*IF*	1
Partner (aka "Duplex")	Verge Foray	June 1968	*Analog*	1
The Infinity Sense	Verge Foray	Nov. 1968	*Analog*	2
The Mind-Changer	Verge Foray	July 1969	*Analog*	2
Ten Percent of Glory		Oct 1969	*Fantastic*	2
Questor		Jan. 1970	*Amazing*	1
The Pyrophylic Saurian		Jan. 1970	*Analog*	2
Psychovore		June 1970	*Fantastic*	1
Heavy Thinker		Aug 1970	*Analog*	1
Forever Enemy		Dec. 1970	*Analog*	1
Soul Affrighted		Jan 1971	*Amazing*	2
Polywater Doodle		Feb 1971	*Analog*	2
Bowerbird	Verge Foray	Feb 1971	*Fantastic*	2
Fit For a Dog		Sept 1971	*Magazine of F&SF*	1
The Other Way Around		1971	Infinity 2	1
All Around the Universe		Jan 1972	*Magazine of F&SF*	1
War in Our Time		Mar 1972	*Analog*	1
Misinformation		April 1972	*Analog*	1
Out, Wit!		June 1972	*Analog*	1
Man Off a White Horse		July 1972	*Analog*	2
Health Hazard		Jan 1973	*Analog*	1
The Earth of Nenkunal		Jan. 1974	*Fantastic*	1
Little Game	Verge Foray	June 1974	*Galaxy*	1
The Frontliners	Verge Foray	July 1974	*Galaxy*	1
Cloud Chamber		1977	Popular Library	2

Note: "Volume" refers to the Baen Books volume in
which the story appears. The title of Volume 1 is *The
Creatures of Man*, that of Volume 2, *A Sense of Infinity*.

The Following is an excerpt from:

TIME SPIKE

ERIC FLINT
MARILYN KOSMATKA

Available from Baen Books
January 2010

Chapter 1

"Sorry about the rotation list, Andy." Lieutenant Joseph Schuler shrugged and shot the captain a look halfway between pity and resignation. "We're just too short of people to staff any shift the way we should. As for midnights . . . You know how it is."

Captain Andrew Blacklock knew how it was. The same way it had been since the day he started working at the state of Illinois' maximum-security prison just across the road from the Mississippi River. But tonight's numbers were worse than usual. The coverage was nowhere nearly adequate. He looked at the men and women ready to punch out and squelched the thought of asking them to work over. They had worked short. They were beat. He

579

knew over half of them had worked a double shift. Probably the third one this week, the sixth this pay-period.

Andy forced a wry grin. *Some things never change. Pay everyone overtime, but keep the other costs low. Don't hire anyone new. The state can't afford the bennies. Health, dental, vision. Nope, overtime's cheaper.*

"We'll make it, Joe," he said. "We always do." Andy looked away from the man he was relieving and toward the metal detectors. Three guards were lined up in front of the machines at the prison entrance waiting to process the oncoming shift. Andy wasn't worried. Just irritated.

He hated taking shortcuts, and that's exactly what had to be done when working a skeleton crew. One set of rounds for every two that should be done. Everyone locked down come morning. Day-shift was going to start out behind, and he knew they could no more afford it than he could afford to send the prisoners to the cafeteria for breakfast. Or to the infirmary for their meds. He stifled a curse. The nurses were always ticked when they had to hand-deliver the morning meds to the cellblocks. They were even more short-staffed than he was.

There was no department within the prison system with enough people. Not even at the top end, the administrative level. It was lean times for the state and cuts had been made. More cuts than could be safely tolerated. The prisons of today were different from those of the past. Prisoners could not be locked down for months at a time. They had to be given exercise periods. They were allowed to talk. Imprisonment was no longer forced labor coupled with solitude. And more had changed than just the rules.

The prisoners of today were as different as the rules that regulated their incarceration. At least at this particular prison. X-house—death row—was filled to capacity. Two thirds of the men awaiting execution were drug addicts who had fried their brains before exiting their teens. Schizophrenia was rampant; delusions of grandeur were almost the norm. And remorse was something few actually felt. Most could find an excuse for what they did. Those who couldn't, didn't seem to care.

The last man to be given a hot shot—the series of three lethal injections deemed acceptable to the state—was one of those men without a conscience. He had raped, mutilated, and killed little girls. Grade-schoolers, the oldest of whom was nine.

Without a struggle, he had walked out of the small room where he had spent his last day on Earth. Meekly, he had lain on the gurney and allowed the guards to strap him down and roll him to the viewing area. He was sad-eyed, gentle talking, sincere. Claiming to be a born-again Christian. Even at the last minute he was working the system, hoping for a stay of execution. It hadn't come. An I.V. had been inserted, and a saline solution began its journey from the dangling plastic bag to his vein. Then from behind a wall—so none of the witnesses could see who administered the deadly doses—an anesthetic, sodium thiopental, was injected into the tubing by a physician. This was followed by an equally lethal dose of pancuronium bromide, a chemical that paralyzed the diaphragm and lungs. Then came the potassium chloride. It didn't take long for this newest addition to his bloodstream to interrupt the electrical signaling of his heart and cause cardiac arrest. The only tears shed that day had been those of the girls' parents. The monster's mother had been dry-eyed. His father had not come to say good-bye.

Andy suppressed a shudder.

Lieutenant Schuler frowned. "Next week, and the week after, are going to be rough. The staffing situation is going to get worse before it gets any better. Keith Woeltje is going out on medical. He has to have knee surgery. And Kathleen Hanrahan will be starting her maternity leave."

Andy rolled his eyes, since Joe wasn't looking at him. Schuler was a good manager, but he was close to burning out. He needed to take a little time off. Not that that would happen any time soon, even though the man had the time coming. He hadn't taken a sick day or personal day in years. He hadn't taken a vacation for the last two. They were too short-handed.

Joe was flipping through the stack of papers he carried. He was new to the afternoon shift and was still trying to get a handle on his crew and the new routine. He was also trying to come to grips with a divorce and his children living two hours away. Andy knew all the gossip. Maria Schuler had gotten tired of the long hours her man put in and found herself one who would be home every night by five-thirty. The fact that the guy made two dollars for every one Joe earned hadn't hurt the situation any.

Marriages didn't usually fare well for those who worked the prison.

Andy's own marriage had gone by the wayside three years back. For different reasons, but the end result was the same. His wife had been the personnel director of a good-sized manufacturing firm. The company grew. The promotions and raises came. And she found it harder and harder to introduce her husband to the people she worked with. His job at the prison, fine the day they married, was no longer something she wanted. She reminded him daily of his lack of ambition, of his dead end situation. When the split finally came, he had been relieved. And grateful. Connie hadn't wanted children. Not yet. She felt twenty-eight was too young to be saddled with kids. Deep down, he suspected she would never want any. Kids were too messy, too noisy, and too expensive for her to enjoy.

Andy gave the man next to him a long look. Schuler was a big boy, over six-four, and weighing in at a little over two hundred fifty pounds. All bone and muscle. A member of the E-team, he was on the fast track to making captain.

"Relax, Joe," he said. "Just go home. There's nothing you can do about it. We'll be okay. We always are."

Schuler nodded. "Sometimes, I think that's the problem. We always manage."

He handed Andy the papers he had been going over and took off the radio hanging on his belt. He passed it to his relief with a shrug. "You'll need this before the night's out. There's only about a dozen of them working anywhere close to right. Man, what a mess. Makes me want to play the lottery."

Andy laughed. "Sure. And after you won, what would you do with all that time on your hands? You would miss us. Besides, men like you and me, we're not here for the money. Don't you watch the talk shows? It's the uniform. The ego trip. Get home and catch some shut-eye."

Joe's forehead lost a few of its creases but not all of them.

Always worried. Andy clapped the man on the back. "Joe, don't take this place home with you. If you do, you won't make fifty. Do what you can, then leave it here." He smiled, but this time it didn't touch his eyes. He was thinking of another officer who, the year before, died of a heart attack at the age of thirty-eight. The man hadn't left anyone behind because he gave everything he had to the job. There was nothing left for him to build a life with outside the walls. "Stop off for a beer on your way home. One won't do you any harm, and it could do a lot of good."

Joe shook his head. He didn't drink, except very occasionally. Didn't gamble. Didn't smoke. He ate right. Tried to get at least six hours sleep out of every twenty-four, and when he could he got in eight. He was one of the new breed of guards who took their physical health seriously. It was men like him that changed the title of "Prison Guard" to that of "CO, Correctional Officer." They took their health seriously, and they took their jobs seriously. Sometimes, too much so.

Schuler was checking out the state employees lining up to enter the prison. Andy knew he was counting them. One assistant superintendent, three zone lieutenants, seven zone sergeants, twenty-nine guards and two nurses: that was who he would be running the prison with. A thirty-percent shortage of bodies. They weren't all here yet. Most of them would show up in the last five minutes.

Andy watched Joe watching the midnight shift arrive. *Good man, but he's going to worry himself into an early grave.*

He glanced around the twenty-five by forty-five foot entry area and saw Lieutenant Rodney Hulbert, the afternoon shift's second in command.

Rod seemed as small as Joe did large. Just a hair over five-six and with no extra meat on him anywhere, he looked like a strong breeze could blow him away. Andy knew the appearance of frailty was about as far from the truth as you could get. The man was a survival hobbyist and hard as nails. He was also the best marksman the prison had, by the proverbial country mile. Every year for the past three, he'd been a serious competitor in the National Rifle Matches held at Camp Perry.

"No full moon, but the crazies are wired tonight," Rod said, when he came up. He stuck his hand out and shook Andy's. "I'll be glad to go home."

"That bad, huh?"

"Yeah. Two attempted suicides, a half dozen shoving matches, and I don't know how many solitary temper tantrums. It's been hell. We've had to use the extraction team three times and the first responders were called out on two medicals."

Andy shot Joe a quizzical look and the man shrugged. "I was waiting till the charge nurse called in. It seems quite a few inmates have refused their meds. With most of them it doesn't amount to much. But some of them, well . . . the psych meds . . . " He glanced back toward the bars separating the entrance area from the prison. "Even some of the diabetics and epileptics turned down tonight's med pass."

And he was working short! Andy would swear he could feel his blood pressure climbing, even though he knew that was impossible. Not the climbing—he was damn sure that was happening—but being able to feel it.

"Hey, I told you it was going to be a bad night. But who knows, maybe they'll settle down. It's been crazy for over five hours."

"Yeah, maybe." Andy thought for a moment. "Any chance of getting one of the afternoon nurses to stay over? Or maybe a day nurse to come in early?"

Joe shook his head. "Can't. We worked with only two, and they were both held over from days. I've already told Sterling she has to be here by four in the morning. She said she would. She'll even try to get here a little earlier to help with the set up for the first med pass."

Rod nodded his head in agreement. "They're even shorter than we are. You have to remember, the state doesn't pay squat compared to the public sector. We're lucky we've got any nurses."

Andy almost gritted his teeth. He remembered the last meeting. The nurses and the guards were paid the same. The one took a minimum of two years education plus state licensing; the other was anyone with a GED and up. The workload was the same. The danger was the same. The guards were to *be nice* to the nurses. The state couldn't afford to lose any more.

"Okay, let's get report over with. I have a lot to do." He led them to one of the three six-foot conference tables situated close to the glass double doors separating the entry area and the prison grounds. The wind was blowing in from the northwest, causing the doors to rattle with each new gust. He knew that at forty-three degrees—the temperature the bank's sign flashed as he drove past it a half hour earlier—the wind would feel below freezing. Stacks of insurance forms and in-service announcements lying on the counter that ran the length of the east wall fluttered each time the door opened and a guard entered. Andy hoped like hell the nurses showed.

*** End Excerpt ***